THE
CINDERELLA
REFLEX

THE
CINDERELLA
REFLEX

JOAN BRADY

POOLBEG

Published 2017
by Poolbeg Press Ltd
123 Grange Hill, Baldoyle
Dublin 13, Ireland
E-mail: poolbeg@poolbeg.com
www.poolbeg.com

Copyright for editing, typesetting, layout, design, ebook
© Poolbeg Press Ltd

1

A catalogue record for this book is available from the British Library.

ISBN 978-1-78199-8793

Typeset by Poolbeg Press Ltd

Printed and bound by CPI Group (UK) Ltd, Croydon, CR0 4YY

www.poolbeg.com

About the author

Joan Brady is a journalist and freelance writer. She started her career as a features writer and newspaper columnist for the *Irish Independent* and *Evening Herald*. She's also worked as a researcher and producer with RTÉ radio on programmes like *The Gay Byrne Show*, *Today with Pat Kenny*, *Liveline*, *Drivetime* and *The Late Debate*.

In between, she's found employment as a waitress, a secretary, an agony aunt and a bartender.

The Cinderella Reflex is her first novel.

Joan lives in Portmarnock, Dublin.

Acknowledgements

I would like to say a big thank-you to:

My three writing buddies, Tara Sparling, Bernadette Kearns and Carolann Copland – between us all, we got Cinderella to the ball.

My agent Tracy Brennan of the Trace Literary Agency for all her enthusiasm and hard work.

All at the Focal literary festival in Wexford for re-igniting my creativity, especially editor Mary McCauley, who told me about the Date With An Agent event, and author Carmel Harrington for all her encouragement.

Gaye Shortland for helping to make the story better and Paula Campbell for loving Cinderella as much as I do.

Pat Costello and Kate Shanahan for reading the manuscript and all their good advice.

Noreen McDougall for not allowing me to forget that I'd always said I'd write a book one day.

And a special shout-out to Jane and Dave who've been with me on my writing journey from the beginning, back in the day when I was wrestling with a certain character called Johnny One. I told you both it would all come to something one day.

For Vera,
who inspired me to write in the first place with these words
of wisdom:
"All you have to do to get good marks in English is to make
things up."

CHAPTER ONE

There were days when Tess Morgan wished she was back in Bali. Like today. Her boss, Helene Harper, was standing behind her, hands on hips, the pointy toe of one red shoe tapping impatiently on the floor. In front of her, Ollie Andrews, presenter of *This Morning with Ollie Andrews*, Atlantic 1FM's prime-time radio programme glowered out at her from behind the soundproofed glass window of his studio.

"Are you asleep or what?" Helene's voice cracked through the room. "Ollie has just got his facts wrong!"

Tess peered in at Ollie. His popularity – such as it was, considering his plummeting listenership – was a bit of a mystery to her. He had dark bushy eyebrows dominating a pale, almost waxen complexion, a mouth curved downwards in perpetual disappointment and thin hair dyed black in a ludicrous attempt to hold back the years. He managed to look somewhere between forty and forty-five but Tess happened to know he was actually nearer to fifty. She had googled him one day when he had been particularly vile to her and discovered from an old gossip column that he customarily shaved years off his age. She could understand why he was trying to look young though. '*Youth Audience*' seemed to be the mantra for the media industry. And while

Atlantic 1FM had once been tipped to get a national licence and put everyone working there on the map, today it held only the faint whiff of desperation as people sensed their careers sliding silently down the drain.

Tess leaned forward, trying to catch up with the conversation between Ollie and his telephone guest. They were perfectly audible but with all the other things she had to do in studio – making sure she had another guest lined up, checking the ad breaks were ready to go, and always having to keep an eye on the clock to make sure the programme fit into the time allotted – it was easy to forget you were supposed to be listening to them as well.

In fact, when Helene had burst in behind her a few minutes before, Tess had been in a pleasant daydream of how different her life had been this time last year. Beach in Bali. Blissed out and suntanned. No responsibility.

She dragged herself back to the present. They seemed to be trying to unravel the complex labyrinth of the banking crisis and the fact that the country was now up to its neck in hock for generations to come. At least that's what Tess thought they were doing.

"Eh, Ollie, go easy there, will you? We wouldn't want to libel anyone!"

Ollie Andrews flicked a switch on his mike so the listeners couldn't hear him.

"I can't get any more out of this numbskull!"

Tess sighed. She had tried to put Ollie off this particular item but he had insisted that the banking crisis was still hot among the trendy young business-heads. Tess wasn't sure she followed his logic. As far as she knew, the banks were now a complete bore to everyone. But she was still relatively new to the job and had assumed he must know something she didn't.

But now it seemed that even Ollie was getting bored. Tess clenched her fists as she watched the telltale signs. He was sighing and pushing his hands through his hair and muttering. But if he finished this item too early it was going to leave her with a gaping big hole to fill. In a show that was going out live. Not to too many people, if the programme's figures were anything to go by. But still. Dead air was the cardinal sin of the radio producer.

And Tess couldn't afford any more mistakes. She needed this job. She flipped the talkback button.

"Ask him …" She looked down at her notes, trying to frame a question which would enable Ollie to prolong the interview. But she was too late. Of course she was! Ollie Andrews was on-air again.

"So thank you so much for that insightful if controversial analysis of the situation. Of course we could talk about this subject all day, but time, I'm afraid, has run away with us again. So let's take a break!"

As the ad-break jingle filled the room, Tess heard Helene Harper sighing dramatically. Tess's eyes flicked to the wall clock. Her next item up was about a gangland killing in Dublin. But the eyewitness Tess had talked to earlier was nervous and she couldn't rely on Ollie to draw him out – not when he was throwing her dagger looks through the glass.

"Sara!" Tess turned to her assistant who was busy examining her nails – long oval talons, varnished carefully in thin red and black stripes. "Ring Mandy Foley – she's a councillor in that neighbourhood. Maybe she can add something to prolong the discussion."

Tess jumped as Helene gave one more theatrical sigh and barged back out of the studio, slamming the door behind her.

Sara raised a perfectly plucked eyebrow. "We tried Mandy earlier. She's not available this morning. Like, have you forgotten?"

Tess stifled a sigh. She had forgotten. She was thirty years old, and the fresh-out-of-college, super-confident Sara could make her feel ancient. And incompetent. And not too well groomed either. She put the eyewitness through to Ollie, consulting her dog-eared address book at the same time. Tess didn't trust electronic gadgets, not since her computer had caught a virus two weeks before and wiped out all her contacts.

"Try Adam Ellington then." Tess scribbled a telephone number on a scrap of paper and pushed it across the desk. She jiggled her foot, mentally urging Sara to hurry as she leisurely pressed out the number with one perfectly painted finger.

Ollie's interview about the gangland killing was a disaster. The man was giving monosyllabic answers and Ollie was doing nothing to save the item. If he finished up this one early too …

"Hi, Atlantic 1FM here," said Sara. "Mr Adam Ellington, please? Oh hello, Mr Ellington!"

Tess felt herself relaxing slightly as she realised Sara had got her man. Ellington was a well-known human rights lawyer who liked nothing better than the sound of his own voice, preferably on the airways. He'd definitely take a call.

"Streptococcal throat? Right … yeah … we understand. You need to go to bed and get yourself a hot drink and an aspirin … right …"

Tess resisted the urge to reach over and slam down the phone. 'Like', could Sara read the clock?

"Sara!" Her voice rose semi-hysterically and Sara replaced the receiver with a dramatic sigh.

She followed Tess's glance at the studio clock. "I'll try Simon Prenderville." She was already punching out his number before Tess could protest.

Tess's shoulders slumped. Ollie would hate it! Prenderville was a local politician who was on the warpath about making pooper scoopers mandatory for dog-walkers. It would sound ridiculous coming after the gangland killing, but she was up against the clock and she didn't have an alternative. She listened tensely as Sara went through the drill.

"Hi, Mr Prenderville, you will be on-air in just a minute, okay? No, we won't be covering any other topics. Only pooper scoopers, yeah."

Tess took a deep breath and pulled back the talkback button.

"Ollie? Er … Simon Prenderville is on the line for you. He wants to talk about his plan for more pooper scoopers for Killty."

"What?" Ollie's features flushed scarlet. "We had him on only last week!"

Actually it was two weeks ago, Tess thought. But luckily she didn't have to reply. The red light was shining and they were back on-air. She leaned back slightly while Ollie and Simon Prenderville talked about pooper scoopers. Ollie would make her pay for this of course. But the main thing now was that the item would bring them to the end of today's programme. And tomorrow, in the immortal words of Scarlett O'Hara, was Another Day.

And finally, there it was. The sweet sound of Ollie wrapping up the programme.

"So okay, Councillor Prenderville, thank you for that scoop, *ha ha ha*! And that's all we have for you today, listeners. Until tomorrow then, when you can tune in to

This Morning again and hear more of the stories you *really* want to hear ... Bye-bye now!"

As the music faded away the smile drained from Ollie's face. Sometimes, Tess mused, he seemed so angry she thought his head might do a 360-degree-turn rotation like a scene out of *The Exorcist*. She stood up, swooping up her pile of manila work files and clutching them to her chest like a shield. She had to get out of here before Ollie stumbled out of his little glass box.

She nodded at Sara. "Er ... I have stuff I need to do. Can you tell Ollie I'll talk to him later?"

Sara gave her a disapproving look. "He'll want to talk to you about the show," she reminded her.

Tess shrugged. She'd have to listen to him soon enough about the bloody show. This afternoon to be precise. At the post-mortem meeting where everyone would put in his or her tuppence-worth about what had worked and what hadn't worked.

But, for now, she needed a break.

Ten minutes later Tess was staring at her reflection in the cracked mirror above the sink in the cramped Ladies' room. Her skin was flushed red and two stains of damp showed darkly under the arms of her white shirt. She pushed her hair out of her eyes, blowing out a sigh. Maybe she'd train for something else. She was good at sketching. And she'd always enjoyed taking photographs. But that only made her thoughts turn to her sister, the super-successful designer in London. While Verity had been busy turning the dream she'd had since she was eleven into a reality, Tess had been drifting from one temporary job to another and from one country to another until finally she'd ended up back in Ireland again.

And now she was in a job that made her feel like a square peg in a round hole. Or a fish out of water. Or some other metaphor that she couldn't think of right now. She winced. She could hear her parents already. "You have to settle at something, Tess. You're *thirty*. Look at Verity, and how well she's doing. That's because she stuck at something."

Tess's mobile bleeped and she pulled it out of her bag, her stomach twisting in case it was Ollie or Helene summoning her.

U free for lunch? Zelda's in ten? A.

Tess brightened. Andrea McAdams, her friend from college, was the reason she was working at Atlantic 1FM in the first place. She had been at home living with her parents for exactly three weeks when Andrea had emailed her about this job. Three weeks in which she had felt as if she'd never left home. So, when Andrea had told her there was an opening at the radio station where she was working as a reporter, Tess had grasped at the offer like a starving person, convinced she could make a success of it. She had a journalism degree and a few freelance bits and pieces on her CV – stuff she'd done in between the beach-bar jobs and the office jobs and the looking-after-children jobs that had paid for her travels around the world. How hard could the gig be?

Only a living nightmare, she had to concede now.

She was supposed to be Ollie's boss but, unfortunately, Ollie thought he was the boss of everyone. And Tess couldn't help wondering if Ollie sensed how scared she was of displeasing him.

Travelling like an itinerant had given her amazing experiences she'd remember forever but had also left her with an alarming financial situation, an overwhelming impulse to 'catch up' with her peers, and a major crisis of confidence when things went against her. Which they seemed to do on an almost daily basis since she'd arrived here six months ago.

Already she'd overheard Ollie complaining about her to Helene.

"She doesn't have what it takes, Helene. Face it!" he'd barked, his face taking on that puce hue that appeared whenever he was even angrier than normal.

"You'll just have to suffer on, Ollie," Helene said flatly. "I don't have time to find someone else right now. Besides, Andrea recommended her – and she does have a journalism degree."

"Journalism degree? She doesn't have a clue!" Ollie exclaimed.

"Well, she's bound to get better. She just needs more experience."

"She's thirty! She should have experience. Can't you get me someone better?"

"I've told you. I don't have time. Give her another three months and I'll reconsider then."

After that, Tess seemed to make one mistake after another. Now with the post-mortem meeting looming she knew lunch was a luxury she couldn't afford. Regretfully, she tapped out her reply.

Working through. Too much of a backlog. See you this afternoon.

She hit send and went off to unpack her plastic box of sandwiches and fruit and settle down to figure out how she was going to defend herself this afternoon.

As soon as she pushed open the door to Helene Harper's office Tess knew that lunch had done nothing to improve

Ollie's temper. Several chairs were clustered around the battered brown table that Helene persisted in calling a conference table. Helene hadn't arrived yet but Ollie was sprawled on the chair just inside the door.

"Afternoon," he muttered, barely looking up from his newspaper.

Tess gave him a cursory nod and picked a chair at the opposite end of the table. She flicked her notebook open and started doodling, trying to ignore Ollie ignoring her.

The door opened and Helene arrived. She flung her purple pashmina on the back of a chair and dumped a mountain of newspaper cuttings and press releases onto the table. "Are we the only ones here?" She pursed her lips and glanced at the wall clock just as Andrea arrived.

"Sorry I'm late." Andrea sat down beside Tess. She looked flustered. Her normally perfect auburn bob was dishevelled and her trademark red lipstick smudged, as if she had attempted to touch it up and then realised it was just too late to bother. "Unforeseen circumstances," she added breathlessly to Helene.

Helene sighed. "More domestic drama, I presume? Well, you're here now at least. So, Ollie, what did you think of this morning's programme?"

Ollie glanced down to where Tess was trying to make herself invisible. "It was not our finest hour, Helene."

"No. It wasn't. But this afternoon I'd like us to talk about improvement. Improving our listenership, improving our programmes, improving *ourselves*." Helene looked around the table. "You all know from the latest figures that we need to – we *must* – come up with better ideas. Tess, you'll be glad to know I intend to put this morning's programme behind us. So – going forward – what are your thoughts?"

Tess swallowed. She had spent the entire lunch hour thinking up ways to justify this morning and now Helene was springing something completely different on her. She looked down at her file. She had spent a large part of Sunday swotting over a pile of newspapers the size of a small country, trying to come up with ideas. But every time she'd notice a story she thought might be worth following up she would remember Ollie and what he'd said about her to Helene and start to question her own judgement. Now she had very little to choose from but she had to try, at least.

She slid a cutting out of the yellow folder in front of her. "I was thinking about doing a slot on how important pets are to people," she said. "This Sunday supplement feature is all about how some people feel just as bereaved by the loss of a pet as they do with a family member and how they can have them buried in a pet cemetery and …"

Ollie and Helene stared at her in stony silence.

"It would be very popular," she continued uncertainly. "I mean, pets are very in. All the celebrities have dogs they can fit in their handbags …"

"I wonder if they have pooper scoopers, too?" Ollie asked.

Tess ignored him. "I just think people's pets are important to them – I mean my auntie says her dog is half-human and –"

Andrea kicked her under the table. They both knew that once Ollie or Helene didn't like your idea, it was toast. And, sure enough, Helene was raising her hand imperiously – an unmistakeable signal for Tess to stop.

"I don't think pet bereavement is really us. But I have a great idea myself as it happens. It's a slot on how to look ten years younger!"

10

"Now *that* is a great idea!" Ollie Andrews banged his thigh with satisfaction.

"It is, isn't it?" Helene beamed at him. "I mean, I know *Ten Years Younger* isn't exactly a new or novel idea, what with every TV programme doing it for years now. But it hasn't been done on radio!"

And that would be because no one will be able to see the makeover on radio, Tess thought.

"It would," Helene continued, "be extreme makeover meets positive thinking meets brand-new future!" She looked expectantly around the table for reaction. "Andrea? What do you think?"

"Em … I suppose …" Andrea was momentarily lost for words.

"What do you think?" Helene repeated impatiently. "About extreme makeovers?"

"I suppose it depends on just how extreme you were thinking," Andrea said cautiously. "I mean, I wouldn't be prepared to go under the knife or anything like that. Maybe Botox."

"And who said you would be going under anything?" Helene interrupted her.

"Oh! I thought you meant I should do a personal-experience report."

"Why?" Helene's voice was brusque.

"W-w-well, I am the reporter for *This Morning*." Andrea stammered a bit, uncharacteristically unsure of herself in the face of Helene's hostility.

"*W-w-well*, we need new voices," Helene mimicked her. "Your reports haven't exactly been setting the world on fire lately, if I may say so. No, I thought I could do the *Ten Years Younger* slot myself actually."

Tess and Andrea exchanged sceptical looks. New voices,

my arse. It was obvious Helene had just had some big freebie offered to her in return for a big plug on Atlantic 1FM. But Helene was a disaster on-air.

Tess had seen cases where people walked into the studio appearing to be really coy and shy, and then, as soon as the red light came on, they suddenly became charged with adrenaline and performed to perfection. Helene was the opposite of those people. On the few occasions she insisted on doing a broadcast her face had glowed as red as the on-air light, with a nervous rash spreading all over her face and neck. She'd stumbled through her scripts, her normal acerbic fluency deserting her as she *ummed* and *ahhed* and rambled down all sorts of blind alleys without ever really getting her point across. Nobody ever told her this, of course. Everyone simply tried to discourage her from ideas that would involve her going on-air.

But today, she was fired up with enthusiasm and would not be deterred. She was rummaging through the enormous pile of papers she had dumped on the table, her voice getting higher as she spoke.

"Let me explain. The Spa Fantastic is keen to get more publicity and they've offered us a weekend of *Ten Years Younger* treatments! Now where did I leave their brochure? Ah yes, here it is!" Helene pulled a pink brochure from the pile in front of her and began to read: "*The Spa Fantastic Experience can make you feel ten years younger. In this oasis of Me Time you can take a break from the stress of day-to-day living. Take the time to be pampered with our fully trained therapists. Have a four-handed hot stone massage . . .*'"

Four hands? What the hell does that mean, thought Tess.

Helene glanced on down the page, "*Blah blah blah . . .* well, we get the idea anyway." She looked around the room for reaction.

"How is it going to work on radio?" Tess ventured. "I mean, nobody will be able to see the result of the makeover."

No one answered, so Tess tossed out an idea.

"Maybe we could run a competition? We could ask the listeners to email us as to why they feel they need to look ten years younger in the first place? We could get a very interesting debate going about why our society is so obsessed with youth. It would be great material for us and the contestants would feel rewarded for listening to *This Morning*."

"Excuse me?" Ollie sat up straighter in his seat. "Since when did listeners need a reward to listen to me?" he asked icily.

"I meant a bonus," Tess amended hastily.

"I'm sure you did!" Ollie turned to Helene. "I think it would be best if I did the *Ten Years Younger* slot myself, Helene."

"And how would that work?" Helene raised an eyebrow. "You interviewing yourself about your experience at the spa? I think not, Ollie."

"It's me the listeners are interested in!" Ollie persisted. "Maybe we could go together, Helene?"

Helene threw the Spa Fantastic Experience brochure down on the table with considerable force. "I am going to do it, Ollie. By myself. That's the end of the discussion. Tess! Can you get on the case and set it all up for me? The weekend at the Spa Fantastic will be just the start. For instance, Botox. Does anyone know if it hurts much?" She looked directly at Ollie's suspiciously smooth forehead.

Ollie narrowed his eyes, but didn't respond.

Helene shrugged. "Tess, find out if Botox is painful!"

Andrea wrote '*Get Sara to do it*,' on her notepad and

leaned in towards Tess so she could read it. Tess hid a smile. Sara, who still hadn't shown up, would have the beauty industry thinking their product name was being heard by hundreds of thousands of listeners instead of simply hundreds, purely by virtue of her snooty attitude.

At that moment, the door opened and Sara burst in. Helene went through the same routine she had with Andrea, looking at the wall clock with a pained expression. But Sara just put on her most stuck-up impression.

"Bloody traffic. I simply couldn't get parking. You'd want to be driving, like, a Smart car to get parking in this town. And Daddy wouldn't put up with that at all – he says it would make him the laughing stock of the golf club if he bought me one of those!" She slipped into one of the seats and looked expectantly around the room. Her pale-blonde hair fell in an expensive cut around her exquisite, heart-shaped face, and her outfit, Tess calculated, probably cost the equivalent of six months' wages.

Helene muttered something under her breath, but she seemed almost embarrassed to be chastising Sara. Yet she'd practically bitten the head off Andrea earlier. Tess sighed. No matter what treatments they drummed up for Helene, none of them were going to make her ten times nicer. When was someone going to come up with a serum for that, she wondered.

Helene turned to Sara. "We're thinking of doing an item on *Ten Years Younger*. Do you have any ideas about that, Sara?"

"Me?" A bewildered look passed over Sara's beautiful face. "Why would I want to know anything about looking ten years younger? I mean, if I looked ten years younger, I'd only look about twelve. I already have trouble getting served drink unless I have ID with me. Of course," she looked around the room thoughtfully, "it's probably a good idea for the rest of you." Then she asked kindly, "Would you like me to do some research on it, Helene?"

"You can give Tess a hand," Helene muttered. "Now. Can we have your ideas for the week please, Andrea?"

Andrea looked panicked. "I don't have anything nailed down at the moment. But," she added hurriedly as Helene's features darkened, "I do have a few ideas floating around in the ether ..."

"The ether?" Ollie cut in. "That's the place to have them all right!"

"There's no need to be sarcastic, Ollie!" Helene admonished him. "We must all be positive together now! We are losing listeners but we can turn it around! Can't we, people?" She looked challengingly from face to face.

Nobody said a word.

Then Ollie spoke. Or rather shouted. "*How* can we turn it around? *How?*" His face was flushed and his brown eyes were bulging. "Will we get more listeners with Andrea's ideas – out in the ether? Or with Tess's stories about pooper scoopers? As for your idea, Helene! How to look ten years younger! That is just a ruse to get a freeloading weekend and I am so stressed right now I could do with one of those myself. But how is it going to improve my figures?"

"Your figures are not my only problem, Ollie," Helene said coolly.

"You can say that again, lady!" Ollie jumped to his feet. "And trying to look ten years younger won't help your problems either! Try ten decades. Ten decades of the Rosary, that is!" And with that Ollie stormed out, nearly taking the door off its hinges as he slammed it behind him.

Inside the room there was complete silence. All Tess could hear was the ticking of the wall clock. She focussed hard on her notebook, pretending to be reading over her notes.

Finally Helene broke the silence. "So!" she beamed around the room. "That was a frank exchange of ideas! Lots of creative tension – that's good! That's what we need to turn this station around, folks. And now I have another meeting to attend. You can all go now."

As Tess stood up to leave she could hear Helene clicking and unclicking the top of her biro compulsively – the only outward sign that Ollie's tantrum had rattled her in any way whatsoever.

CHAPTER TWO

Helene strode out of the office and into the street, stumbling slightly as her stiletto caught in a ridge on the pavement. She blinked in the sunshine, not quite sure where to go. After Ollie Andrews had belittled her in front of her staff like that, she'd had to invent a bogus meeting just to get out of the office. Damn Ollie, she seethed. She had brought him into Atlantic 1FM and now she found herself in the peculiar position of having to defend someone she had come to despise.

It had all been so different when she'd poached him from a rival local radio station, luring him over with the promise of a glittering career. But that was five years ago, when she, like everyone else, had thought the station was going national. Now it was becoming clear that that wasn't going to happen and Ollie was holding her responsible. Helene had told him to his face that he was as much to blame himself. More, in fact. He was meant to be the shock jock, courting controversy and building publicity and listeners in equal measures. Well, he was shocking all right, she thought darkly. Shockingly awful.

He annoyed Helene on an almost daily basis, alienated the rest of the staff and – this bit was the most important – aggravated the hell out of the listeners. Ollie insisted on

mixing heavy current affairs with a mad mix of music –
from country to middle-of-the-road, light opera, and on the
days when he was feeling particularly bad-tempered, a blast
of heavy metal could be heard thumping out of the studio.

This Morning was the flagship programme for Atlantic
1FM and as each set of figures showed that his show was
collapsing Ollie had become more needy, more panicky
and, perversely, more arrogant. He had taken to phoning
Helene at all hours of the day and night with demands and
complaints and whinges.

A gust of wind whipped Helene's long dark hair across her
face as she started to walk towards the coast road. Killty was
a seaside town on the commuter belt for Dublin and was
populated with young couples starting their families and
wealthy retirees who frequented the health-food stores and
alternative-treatment centres that were scattered along the
main street. The town was big enough to be anonymous if
that's what you really wanted – and Helene did – but she
liked how the people still seemed to be interested in each
other and she often found herself eavesdropping on the
friendly banter in the shops and cafés.

She reached the seashore and stood for a few minutes
watching the waves breaking in white frothy patterns on
the sand. It was early spring and people were emerging
from their winter hibernation. An elderly couple sat on a
bench on a patch of grass above the sand, their cocker
spaniel wheeling around in wide circles on the strand in
front of them.

A couple of joggers passed her by, earphones in their ears
and their eyes firmly ahead.

Helene turned and started along the tarmac path which
hugged the coastline, walking as fast as her heels would
allow her, trying to work off her temper. According to the

tiny tourist office the town offered stunning walks along the sea cliffs, and abundant wildlife, but Helene had never ventured into those straggling bits of it.

A few minutes later she stopped and looked around her curiously. This area of the town had once been earmarked for "gentrification" as the *Killty Times* had put it. Old, run-down buildings had been bulldozed for new blocks of identical, red-bricked apartments. There was to be a crèche for the children of the working couples destined for the apartments, and a shopping centre, and a gym. But then the financial crash had taken a wrecking-ball to Ireland's economy and all building had stopped. Now Helene was surprised to see there were small signs of regeneration here again. Some of the identikit apartment blocks looked inhabited now and there was a bulldozer starting up on a patch of green down the road. A hoarding with colourful murals had been built around the vacant shopping centre and she could see several planning signs seeking permission to renovate in the gardens of old buildings that had survived the first ill-fated development of the area.

There was a slightly grubby-looking café across the street. Helene crossed over to reach it with a sense of relief. It was nice there was a new place to go to get a break from work. And a strong coffee would psych her up for going back to the office.

She pushed at the blue door of the café gingerly, the hinges groaning as it creaked open. She stood for a few seconds while her brain made the transition from the sunny afternoon outside to the dim interior of the café. There was a strong smell of fresh paint and, when her sight finally adjusted, she realised the café was in the process of being renovated. Damn. She'd been looking forward to a breather.

She spotted a sandy-haired man standing at the counter, his shoulders hunched over a sheaf of papers he was studying. He looked up absentmindedly, rubbing his hand on a blue-and-white check teacloth.

"Hi, can I help you?"

He was mid-thirties, Helene guessed, clean-cut and fit looking. He was dressed casually in black cotton trousers and a blue striped shirt.

"Are you open?" she asked.

He raised an eyebrow, looking around the ramshackle room. A paint-splattered wooden ladder leaned against one wall; tall stacks of books were piled up beside it.

"Er ... do we look open?" His smile softened the question.

"I just wanted a coffee." Helene gestured at the bubbling coffee machine beside him.

"Oh, that ..." His eyes flickered to the machine. "I was just about to have one myself, so I suppose I can let you have one too. You can be my guinea pig if you like."

"Fine," Helene agreed. As he busied himself with the machine she sank into an ancient armchair by the window. "Cappuccino," she specified to the owner.

She looked around the room critically. It really was run-down – even the cacti on the scuffed yellow-pine table in front of her looked ancient.

He poured out the coffee and ambled down to her. "You're my first customer, so it's on the house – I'm Matt, by the way." He beamed as he placed an old-fashioned, floral-patterned cup and saucer in front of her.

Helene looked at him suspiciously. What did he have to be so cheerful about, trying to run this dump? "Thanks." She turned away, staring out the window. All the buildings seemed to be either empty or in the process of being renovated and she wondered absently where Matt thought he was going to get his customers from.

He coughed slightly.

"So?" he asked expectantly. "You're my guinea pig, remember? What do you think of the coffee?"

"Oh!" Helene glanced down at the cup of cappuccino, and noticed how there was a heart-shape of chocolate traced onto the white froth. "That's a nice touch," she acknowledged. She sipped the coffee. "It's good. So when are you opening?"

Matt scratched his head, looked around helplessly. "It was supposed to be last week, but it's all got a bit overwhelming to be honest. It's a lot harder than I thought it was going to be." He placed his own cup of coffee on the table next to hers and sat down.

Helene looked at him in alarm. She hoped he wasn't going to start talking about his problems. She needed to think about how to handle Ollie Andrews and … oh, a million and one other things. She looked at him pointedly.

"I'm a bit busy."

"I've given you free coffee because chatting to a potential customer is a perfect guilt-free break for me," he countered.

"Sorry, but I have things I need to work out." Helene pulled a notebook and pen out of her bag to make her point. She needed a break herself – and preferably in a five-star hotel, not in this run-down café. But she had to work out her strategy for reviving Atlantic 1FM's dwindling audience.

She stared into the froth of the cappuccino, one part of her brain automatically calculating its calorie content, the rest of it wrestling with what to do about Ollie.

Richard, her boss, was breathing down her neck about

him day and night lately. He seemed to have decided that the entire future of the station depended on the success, or otherwise, of the *This Morning* show and that it was up to Helene to make it work. That's why he had promoted her to executive editor, he'd reminded her a few days ago – on the strength of her self-professed talent for good ideas. He had said it half-jokingly, but Helene didn't miss the ill-concealed barb. She frowned at the memory. She had claimed to be a good ideas person, not a bloody miracle-worker. How could anyone have predicted that Ollie Andrews would turn out to be so volatile? He had been super-charming when they'd first met to talk about his new role at Atlantic 1FM – but that was probably because she had just agreed to double his salary if he came on board, she acknowledged bleakly.

"Maybe I can help?"

She looked over at Matt who was still sitting at the next table, looking at her quizzically.

"I doubt it." Helene flicked open her spiral notebook and stared at the blank page, biting on the end of her biro. "I'm looking for ideas for a radio show. *This Morning with Ollie Andrews* – do you know it?" She looked around the café, realising the radio wasn't on. By rights, Matt should have Atlantic 1FM on, keeping him company.

"I think I've heard it once or twice," he said vaguely. "To be honest, I have too many problems to attend to in this place to be distracted by the radio."

Helene looked down at her notebook and began to write. Now he'd have to take the hint and leave her alone. She scribbled down '*Ideas*' and underlined the word twice. Underneath she added '*Ten Years Younger/Me*'. She smiled and relaxed a little. Seeing her ideas down in black and white always cheered her up. And the *Ten Years Younger* project was a win-win situation for her. She'd get a break at that top spa and look a lot younger – or better anyway – at the end of it. But what else? She thought of what Matt had just said: 'I have too many problems to attend to in this place to be distracted by the radio.' That was it! The radio version of a problem page! People were always fascinated with other people's problems.

She looked over at Matt and smiled. "Actually you've just given me an idea!"

"Really?" Matt was astonished. "What is it?"

"It's a problem slot. For radio."

"Okay." Matt looked mystified.

"Your mention of having problems, you know?"

"Oh. Well, happy to oblige." He stood up. "Right, I'd better get back to getting this place up and running. It has to open next week!"

Helene turned her attention back to her notebook and scribbled down the line '*Agony Aunt of the Airwaves*'. She looked at the words, her pulse quickening. It was bound to be a success. She alone had enough problems to fill that slot for months! As her thoughts drifted to her personal life she turned on to a new page and jotted some of her problems down, partly as a way of working out how the agony-aunt slot might work, and partly because she thought it would be good to get them off her chest for five minutes.

One: Milestone birthdays.

Helene rested her chin on her hand, eyes fixed on the middle distance. Her big Four-O was coming up. The birthday that had been hovering on the horizon for ages and now was nearly here. Was that why she'd been so unsettled lately, she wondered? Feeling as if she was at a particularly precarious crossroads in her life and that one false move could spell disaster.

She would wake up with a start at night, a feeling of impending doom settling like a swamp in her stomach. The clock on her bedside locker always flashed roughly the same time – thirty minutes either side of four o'clock – the figures displayed in mocking red neon. And then she'd start to panic because her alarm was due to go off at six and the panic woke her up even more.

She had spent a lot of time trying to figure out what the feeling was about exactly. It wasn't just connected to her job. There was also the vexed question of Richard to consider. Reluctantly she scribbled down: *Two: Richard*.

She sighed, trying to figure out when Richard had become a problem. She had met him five years before, when he'd interviewed her for the job in Atlantic IFM, which he was just setting up at the time. He was ten years older than her and, definitely, she had thought at the time, not her type. She had been seeing someone else back then – Derek, a nice-looking dentist who had wanted to settle down with her. And yet, within weeks, she and Richard had become lovers. She had never really worked out how it had happened. He was certainly wealthy and generous but then so was Derek. But Richard had listened attentively when Helene talked about her hopes and her dreams and, in hindsight, if she was honest with herself, she had thought he might be a conduit to making those hopes and dreams come true for her. Richard had a knack of making life seem easy and, for Helene, who was used to fighting tooth and nail for everything, it was a powerful attraction.

She rose effortlessly from her original position as administration clerk to her current job as an executive editor. But as her salary and status had increased so had her responsibility and stress levels, and now her life didn't begin to resemble what it had been like at the beginning.

Back then, work had seemed like one long, glorious holiday. Richard invited her to attend glamorous work dinners and product launch parties and Helene had been enthralled by it all – by the feigned but fawning adoration of the glamorous PR people who pressed goody bags of beauty and fashion items on her and invited her on weekends to promote whatever product they were plugging at the time. And always there was Richard in the background, flattering her, telling her she was fantastic, telling her that one day she would have her own show. Of course, that hadn't worked out either. She was too busy working on other people's shows to get a moment to herself, never mind figuring out how she could get herself on-air.

Back then everything had seemed so easy. Richard regularly told his wife he was working late so they could get together, and because Helene lived alone and didn't have the sort of friends who called unannounced, they had both the time and the opportunity to be together. Of course, she had known he was married from the beginning. She had noticed the photograph on his desk at their very first meeting, the day he'd interviewed her for the job. There was Richard, looking younger and more hopeful somehow than he did today, with his arm draped around a dark-haired voluptuous beauty – who, Helene later learned, was his wife Louisa – his eyes resting fondly on the two gawky teenagers who turned out to be his children.

Why hadn't she paid more attention to that photograph, she asked herself ruefully now, stirring a spoon aimlessly around in her coffee. If she'd taken heed of how besotted Richard looked in it she might have been forewarned about just what she was taking on when she'd agreed to go out with him. Because Richard's offspring had turned out to be the most demanding teenagers in the history of adolescence. A collage of memories flooded through Helene's mind.

There had been the driving lessons Richard had to personally provide himself, because "Anna wants her daddy to teach her", even though it must have taken a hundred lessons before his idiot daughter was finally able to put away her L-plate. There were the teenage discos Anna and David had to be escorted to and collected from every Saturday night for years. There had even been David's "little drug problem" which had only involved the youngster smoking a bit of hash but which had been blown into a full-scale crisis by Louisa and ended up with the entire family strong-armed into co-dependency counselling. Oh, and what about the hysterics when Anna didn't get enough points in her exams to study psychology? And the drama when David was caught driving over the limit?

On and on it had gone – was still going on, actually – taking up Richard's valuable time, *time* he was supposed to be spending with *her*, the only time they had together until the time was finally right for him to leave Louisa. So far Helene's goal of becoming the new Mrs Armstrong – which Richard had agreed was a logical, if long-range one – had been continuously postponed because the time never seemed right for Richard to leave the "children".

The fact that the children were now of an age when most people were out busy building their own lives seemed to be lost on Richard, who was as endlessly besotted with Anna and David as ever. What surprised Helene most was that she had allowed all this to happen.

She doodled idly now on her notebook, trying to figure it out. She liked to think of herself as possessing a sharp and analytical mind. She would not have survived the cutthroat nature of the business she was in otherwise. She thrived on competition and, frankly, the contest between herself and Louisa should have been over ages ago. And would have been, she reminded herself, if it hadn't been for Anna and David.

Through the years, whenever she'd had a horrible day – like today for instance when Ollie Andrews was being his usual despicable self, Andrea McAdams was preoccupied with one of her interminable domestic crises, and Tess Morgan was at her most irritating – Helene had always soothed herself with the thought that it wasn't going to be forever. Richard would eventually make good on his promise, leave Louisa and marry her.

There had been a few scary moments along the way, mind you, when Helene had been forced to question her beliefs. Like the time Louisa had gone in for a boob job, for instance. What had all that been about? Helene had lain awake at night at the time, worrying about it. But Louisa's boobs, Richard had been quick to convince her, were irrelevant in a relationship that had been on the rocks for years.

"She's feeling her age because the kids are growing up and away," he had explained fondly, as if he really liked his wife. "Louisa doesn't have a career like you and she doesn't know what to do with herself. She says the surgery makes her feel better about herself but I think it's a distraction because she's dreading the time when David and Anna leave home and she will be left facing an empty nest."

Like that was going to happen any time soon, Helene thought crossly. And Louisa could have *her* career, if she wanted one so badly. See how she felt about it after a week in charge of Ollie Andrews.

Helene would quite like to be able to pick and choose whether she worked or not. She'd like to ramble along to a quiet gym at eleven in the morning instead of having to squeeze into the overcrowded, sweaty after-work classes. She'd like to indulge in leisurely lunches that didn't involve endless brainstorming for ideas and ... and ... Helene searched her mind for what else she would like to do as a lady of leisure. She would go to art galleries or those lunchtime plays she was always seeing being advertised – something like that, anyway.

But when was that ever going to happen? Normally she ignored this small voice inside her. But today it was more persistent, grabbing at the sides of her mind, forcing her to pay attention to her own intuition. And the fact was that she had begun to have a distinctly bad feeling where Richard was concerned. For one thing, he had started to hint recently about the possibility of being taken to the cleaners if he left Louisa. *If* he left Louisa!

Now he fucking tells me! she'd thought in a rage when he'd come out with that one night at her apartment after an evening "working late" together. Now, when the crow's feet are crawling all over my face, and I'm worn to a thread between work and sweating it out at the gym three times a week, trying to keep my figure. And do *I* have the money for new boobs, if I needed them? No!

But Helene had forced all those feelings to the back of her mind, and lay down and invited Richard to inspect her new Brazilian wax. Afterwards she'd convinced herself they were back on track again. Richard was feeling edgy, that was all. But sooner or later, he was going to leave Louisa for her.

He had better, Helene thought now, a feeling of fury sweeping over her suddenly. She banged her coffee cup down on the saucer with such force it should have broken. She stared at the overturned cup, vaguely alarmed at both the force of her feelings and the way the coffee splattered all over everything: the table, her handbag, her shoes, the flagstones on the floor. It was the thought that somehow, after everything, she might actually have to continue to make her living in this job for the next two and a half decades that made her want to break something. Or else curl up and cry with exhaustion.

"Are you okay?"

Helene looked up to see the café owner hovering over her, concern in his eyes. She came back to the present with some difficulty. What had he said his name was again? Matt … yes, that was it.

"I'm fine …" Helene's hands fluttered vaguely in the direction of the china cup she'd just overturned.

"Your coffee – you've spilt most of it." Matt wiped a cloth over the table, mopping up the liquid. "Here, let me get you a refill." He reached over to take the cup.

"No. No more coffee. I have to be going anyway," Helene protested, but Matt had crossed the room and was back in no time with a fresh cappuccino and a pile of white napkins for her to dry off her bag and shoes. Helene was surprised to see her hand was shaking slightly as she shoved her notebook and biro back into her bag. "Thanks," she said and meant it. She felt slightly guilty now for snubbing him earlier. She looked around the café. "It looks as if you have a lot of work to do here still?"

"I have … but it will be worth it." Matt's face lit up as he started to tell her about his ambitions for the café. "I'm going to call it the Travel Café and I'm hoping backpackers and gap-year people – travellers of all sorts, really – will use this place when they are planning or living their big adventure. They can have breakfast or lunch, drink coffee, use the internet, buy their maps and guidebooks and travel journals all under one roof. I've just come back from travelling myself and so I can offer first-hand advice." His enthusiasm was catching, and Helene found herself looking around the dusty, run-down room through Matt's eyes.

She saw now that he had pinned an enormous map of the world onto one wall, with yellow pins stuck on various locations from South America to Africa to Australia. He followed her gaze.

"They're all the places I've been," he said a bit wistfully.

"Really?" Helene was impressed. She'd only ever been abroad on holidays and never further than Europe. "So what on earth brought you to Killty?"

If she'd gone to the bother of travelling to the four corners of the earth it would be an anti-climax of quite stunning dimensions to end up in Killty.

"Ah, you can't keep moving forever. And my folks live around here," he said easily.

Helene stared at the map, trying to picture Matt arriving at all those places, and then, just like that, leaving them again in a few weeks or months or whenever the fancy took him. And just for a moment, sitting there in the dilapidated café, she felt her own world expand. To somewhere beyond Atlantic 1FM and the constant worry about Ollie Andrews and his flop radio show and Richard and his complicated family set-up and his two children with the Peter Pan Syndrome. The small yellow pins seemed to be shining at her, offering her a way out, whispering that her life might hold possibilities she had never thought of before.

And then her eyes strayed past the map towards the clock on the wall and she gave a gasp of disbelief. She hadn't realised how long she'd been out of the office. Scrambling to her feet, she grabbed her bag and made for the door. It was all very nice and dandy fantasising about travelling the world but the journey she needed to be making right now was the one back to work. Pronto.

"Best of luck with your new venture!" she called from the door.

"Thanks." Matt was already back at his paperwork. "Don't forget to tell all your friends about the café!"

Helene smiled ruefully. Matt would never have guessed it, but her cast of friends would barely fill one table in this café. She needed to add that to her list of problems as soon as she was back at her desk. It would be something else for Tess Morgan to work on when Helene made her Agony Aunt of the Airwaves.

CHAPTER THREE

Tess sat at her desk, twirling a strand of hair around her finger. She was working her way diligently through the stack of magazines on her desk, desperate for new ideas. But by the time she finished the last magazine, she still hadn't come up with any new angles. She logged on to her computer, hoping an email might throw up something she could use. She flicked her eyes down the list of mail, ignoring the predictable clutch of correspondence from PR people. If she could just find something a little bit offbeat … and then her eyes widened as she saw a name from her past.

Her heart beat a little faster. Chris Conroy. Now why would *he* be getting in touch with her, after all this time? Their relationship had ended badly ten years ago. By text, actually. Chris Conroy was a big part of the reason she had left Ireland in the first place. They had been together for less than a year and she hadn't seen the break-up coming at all. At the time she'd been busy studying for her finals, so maybe she'd missed the signs but she had never really been able to figure it out. All she knew was she could still remember the gut-wrenching devastation she'd felt in the months after they'd split up.

She hadn't heard from him since. But she had sure heard

a lot about him. Firstly, because she had kept tabs on him through social media and, secondly, because since she'd come home it was hard to avoid him, with his picture byline peering out at her every other day from the pages of national newspapers and even international magazines. He was always turning up on television and radio talk shows too, commentating on the affairs of the day. Politics, business, wars – there appeared to be no end to what Chris Conroy could talk about.

Tess felt faintly depressed as she compared his glittering career to her decidedly non-glittering one. While he was now a household name, she was just starting out in local radio. She clicked open the email and scanned his message. As her eyes darted down the screen, her mood darkened even further. Despite the fact that he'd typed "**Something you'll be interested in**" in the subject line the email was actually a round robin, addressed to some of her old college year, including Andrea, and it was about a reunion he was organising.

"**Hi. I can't believe how the years have flown since we were all at college together. I seem to have lost touch with everybody! I've travelled a lot – US elections, embedded in Iraq, covered Afghanistan. I felt privileged to be there. It made all the hard work at college worthwhile. But I'm back for the foreseeable future and I thought it would be a good opportunity to meet up ten years on, to see how we're all doing.**"

How we're all doing indeed, Tess thought, as she scrolled down to where Chris suggested they all link up via a special reunion Facebook page. The difference between how she was doing and how Chris Conroy was doing was extreme. They had both travelled the world – separately, of course – but Chris had come back with an amazing CV while Tess was going to have to explain to every prospective employer forever why her one-year career break had morphed into almost a decade-long one. The first year had turned into two and then, when she had come home, she couldn't settle. So after a few temping jobs she was off on her travels again. It was only when she had started receiving news of her friends getting bling rings and having gigantic weddings and babies, for God's sake, that she'd panicked and come home.

She hit the reply button now and began to compose a note of regret, then paused – she'd better discuss it with Andrea first.

"Anything interesting?"

It was Helene, hovering again.

Tess swiftly minimised her email. "Er … I was making a few notes for the show."

"Great!" Helene sat on the edge of the desk. "We'll all have to do better, Tess. That's what I've come to talk to you about, actually."

"You have?" Tess asked cautiously.

"Yes, I've been thinking. I think it's time you went on-air."

"*What?*" Tess swung around to face her boss, astonished.

"It would only be part-time," Helene warned, "and it would be on top of your work producing *This Morning* of course. But it's a good opportunity for you and –"

"What would I be doing?" Tess was acutely aware that Andrea was at the next desk, pretending to be concentrating on something on her computer but listening closely to the conversation. She didn't want Andrea to feel threatened, particularly as she was the one who'd got her the job here in the first place.

"You're our new Agony Aunt!" Helene beamed. She shoved her notebook in front of Tess. "See? I'm going to call you 'Agony Aunt of the Airwaves'. It has a good ring to it, hasn't it?"

"*What?*" Tess stared at Helene, mystified.

"What?" Andrea's head whipped away from the computer screen.

"Will you all stop saying 'what'?" Helene said testily. "I am telling you *what* right now. *What* I want is an agony-aunt slot, Tess, once a week. And I want you to make it really hot and sexy."

"You want me to be a *sex* agony aunt?" Tess felt a flicker of anger. That would be just perfect, if she did ever bump into Chris Conroy again, explaining how she had ended up as a sex advisor.

"Not talking about actual sex," Helene said impatiently. "Well, not necessarily. But just make the slot sexy. You know ... career women climbing the corporate ladder who are too busy to meet Mr Right. Or," she glanced sideways towards Andrea, "women who are trying to juggle work and family and finding it all too much of a struggle. Or," Helene tapped her biro on Tess's desk, "women who are in relationships with commitment-phobic men. There's a lot of that about I can tell you. Or men whose bitter ex-wives won't let them see their kids. That sort of thing."

"But I wouldn't know how to do that!" Tess blurted out.

"What's there to know?" Helene demanded.

"How will I find suitable people to call in with their problems? And, more to the point, where will I find the answers?"

"How the hell do I know?" Helene snapped. "Put out a call for people to contact us and, in the meantime, make up the problems. And the answers while you're at it. Make 'em short, make 'em snappy, and make 'em up! That can be your motto." She smiled as if she'd solved Tess's problem.

"It doesn't sound very ethical," Tess pointed out, "and even if it was … well, I don't think being an agony aunt is exactly my forte, Helene."

"Really?" Helene asked coolly. "And what do you think your forte is, exactly? Yesterday you finished your programme with an item about pooper scoopers, which Ollie is still wrecking my head over. So maybe you should start thinking about what exactly your forte is before you go dissing my ideas!"

Tess bit her lip. "Of course I'll think about it. When were you thinking of starting it – the agony-aunt slot?"

"Immediately would be good." Helene was already moving away from the desk, her heels clicking on the wooden floor.

"When is immediately?" Tess called after her in alarm.

Helene stifled a sigh. "What does 'immediately' usually mean, Tess? How does tomorrow sound?"

"Tomorrow? Are you mad?" Fear made Tess sound a lot more forceful than she felt. "I've never been on-air before. And I don't have anything prepared! There's no way I can do this tomorrow!"

"Well, as I was saying earlier, how hard can it be?" Helene turned back to face her. "Make up a few problems to get yourself started. I'm fed up with talking about how things have to change around here. But have you ever noticed how everything somehow remains exactly the same?"

Tess *had* noticed, as a matter of fact. But she didn't see how making a show of herself on-air was going to improve that.

"Helene," she said reasonably, "I really don't have a

handle on how this slot is going to work. It's all very well
to say to make up a few problems to start us off. But what
then? What if it doesn't work? What if we don't have
enough people phoning in with their problems?"

Listeners to talk-shows thought there was an endless
supply of people just dying to get on-air, but Tess knew it
took a lot of behind-the-scenes work to get the right type of
caller, one that wasn't going to dry up on air, someone who
would sound as interesting as a professional broadcaster
but who was actually just an average citizen. It was a tall
order, and one that bigger radio stations employed entire
teams to work on. She would have to do everything herself,
and she was already overloaded with work.

"Run out of problems?" Helene looked at Tess
incredulously. "I have just given you a list of problems. And
there's more where they came from. Women whose love
affairs have gone pear-shaped. Whose careers are facing
meltdown. Who might be joining the ranks of the
unemployed pretty soon!" Her voice rose slightly. "Because
in case you haven't noticed, Tess, we could all be out of
here on our ear if this station closes down! And, believe me,
that is a possibility. So if you would just give it some
thought, you might find plenty of problems *from your own
life* to be getting on with." She snapped her fingers.
"Because just as soon as you think you have your life
sorted, it ups and throws a curveball at you just for the hell
of it! Don't you find that, Tess?"

Tess swallowed. She thought life might have just thrown
her a curveball right now. She could hardly solve her own
problems – dead-end career, non-existent love life – never
mind anyone else's.

"I won't be ready to start it tomorrow, Helene," Tess
said firmly. "Or the day after. I ... er ... need to brainstorm

around the concept a bit."

Helene shrugged. "Okay. Brainstorm all you want. For a week. That's all I'm prepared to give you. After that? Just *do* it, Tess!"

Tess raised her eyebrows as she watched Helene stride out of the office.

Andrea had inserted headphones in her ears and had turned back to her computer screen and the report she was working on. Tess felt it wasn't a good time to ask her friend for much-needed advice.

Chewing her bottom lip, she typed **"agony aunts"** into her search engine. She had to start somewhere and tomorrow's show was pretty well organised, albeit with mundane stories that Ollie Andrews was going to scream blue murder about – pretty much as he had about this morning's programme. But that was tomorrow. She jiggled her foot, impatient for the results to load.

"*O! My! God!*" Sara exclaimed suddenly.

Tess looked across at her.

Sara's mouth formed a perfect O of astonishment. She had her silver mobile pressed to her ear.

"What is it now?" Tess asked easily. Sara's 'O My Gods' occurred several times a day, sometimes simply because her favourite make-up was out of stock or because she'd broken one of those nails she spent hours painting designs on.

"I've just heard something big. I need to check that it's accurate!" Her face was alight with excitement.

Tess could hear only her side of the conversation.

"And you're absolutely certain?" There was a note of incredulity in her voice. "You are? *O! My! God!*"

Sara closed down her phone and hurried over to Tess's desk.

"Did you hear any of that?"

"I heard 'Oh My God'," Tess replied. "Several times. So what's happened? Your favourite nail bar fallen victim to the recession?"

"It's Atlantic 1FM!" Sara's blue eyes were dancing. "It's about to be taken over!"

"*What?*" Tess dropped her pen on the desk, a dozen questions forming in her mind.

"Andrea!" Sara crossed the room to Andrea's desk. "Have you heard?"

"Heard what?" Andrea pulled her earphones off when she saw the look on Sara's face.

"The rumour that we're about to be taken over! Daddy just told me – he thinks it's pretty accurate." Then she added importantly, "He heard it from one of his business associates."

"Taken over?" Andrea looked at her, bewildered. "But why? Did he say who was supposed to be taking it over?"

Tess flew across the room and perched on a corner of Andrea's desk.

Sara shrugged. "Some whizz kid apparently. And wait for the best part. Apparently, he plans to finally take the station national!"

"Are you sure?" A frown creased Andrea's forehead.

"Yes, I'm sure. His name ... is ..." Sara frowned and she went back to her own desk where she peered at a scrap of paper. "I wrote it down ... Jack. That's it. Jack McCabe." She looked up expectantly. "Have either of you ever heard of him?"

"Jack McCabe?" Tess said. "No, never."

But Andrea had already tapped the name into Google. Tess waited tensely, Sara standing behind her now, both of them jiggling impatiently. Seconds later Andrea was reading aloud: "'*Jack McCabe made most of his money courtesy of the property boom and crucially got out before the crash. Gifted with the Midas touch, McCabe is known for turning ailing businesses around even where others have failed. His business instincts have been described as uncanny and he is famed for not shying away from hard decisions when it comes to profit margins.*'"

"Oh my God!" Sara butted in. "That fits in exactly with what Daddy said! He says Jack McCabe will go for a really youth-orientated vibe. He's heard he's going to axe the entire staff and only employ people who are under thirty!"

"Is that not illegal?" Tess asked faintly.

"Of course it's illegal!" Andrea snapped, eyes squinting as she read on silently. "Besides, this is all only gossip and rumour. There's no evidence whatsoever that Atlantic is going to be taken over at all! Where exactly did your dad hear it anyway, Sara?"

"Golf club." Sara shrugged insouciantly as she walked away. "And he says this could be my big chance because I *am* young!"

Tess and Andrea exchanged glances.

"Coffee?" Andrea mouthed, making a coffee-cup gesture with her hand.

Tess nodded. They needed to analyse and parse this, to try and figure out what, if it were true, it might mean for them. But she had only taken her jacket off the back of her chair when the phone buzzed. She reluctantly picked up the handset.

"Yes, Helene? In five minutes? Okay, I'll tell the others." She replaced the receiver and looked over at Andrea. "Looks like Sara and her dad aren't the only ones who've heard the rumours. Helene wants us all in her office in five minutes."

Minutes later, they were all crowded into Helene's office and it was clear the news about the takeover was more than a rumour. The room was thick with tension. Tess slipped into the chair opposite Ollie, who was cracking his knuckles restlessly. Two lines formed a deep frown between his eyebrows, and his complexion had a grey pallor about it, as if he hadn't slept in days.

He's evidently heard Atlantic might soon be a wrinkly-free zone, Tess thought. Serves him right. It might teach him a bit of humility.

Helene was sitting at the top of the table, two spots of scarlet staining her cheeks. "Right, that's everyone here," she said as Sara pushed closed the door. "I've called you here because ... because in the next few days you may hear some, er, rumours about this station."

"We already have," Sara cut in.

Helene raised her eyebrows and Sara fell silent.

"And if you do," Helene continued, "I want you all to remember that any information about Atlantic 1FM is commercially sensitive and therefore you are not – repeat, *not* – at liberty to discuss it."

"So is it rumour or is it true?" Andrea asked directly.

Helene flung her hair over her shoulder. "To be honest, I don't have very much information at present. But, as soon as I know, you'll know." She looked closely at Sara. "So what have you heard, Sara?"

"I thought you just said we can't discuss it?" Sara pouted.

"Outside here we can't discuss it. Inside, we can! Now tell me what you know." Helene folded her arms on the desk.

Sara began, delighted to have centre stage. "Well, from what I hear, this Jack McCabe is taking us over. He's reputed to have the Midas touch and is not shy of making the hard decisions."

Ollie breathed a long, exasperated sigh. "You've just read that on the internet, Sara! Is there anything you know that isn't common knowledge, by any chance?"

"Actually, there is!" Sara bristled. "I've heard that Jack McCabe likes to have something good to look at when he comes in!" She pushed out her boobs and curled a tendril of hair around one stripy-nailed finger. Ollie's eyes went out on stalks. Sara glared at him and let her hair go. "And," she snapped, "I've heard he wants a youth vibe going on and that staff over thirty aren't going to be very popular once he arrives!"

"We'll see about that, missy." Ollie pulled a book out of his briefcase and jabbed his finger at the title, *Seven Habits of Effective People*. "It takes more than flashing your eyes at someone to make it in this business!"

"Really?" Sara was ready for a row but Helene silenced her.

"Can you both just shut up?" She had her head in her hands.

Everyone fell silent. Helene looked up slowly, picked up a pencil and starting tapping it on the table.

Tess realised she was holding her breath.

"Look, there's not much we can do about any of this – apart from working our arses off, that is," Helene said flatly. "If this Jack McCabe does decide to take over or buy Atlantic or whatever it is he is considering, then he must not find us wanting. When he arrives, we must give the impression of being dynamic and ambitious ..."

"And young," Sara added helpfully.

"... and working to improve our listenership," Helene finished icily.

After that there was an outbreak of questions, none of which Helene appeared to have the answers to. When the meeting finally broke up, the atmosphere was subdued and heavy.

Tess walked slowly back to her desk, a feeling of dread settling over her. She had known the station was struggling but she had simply not seen this coming. None of them had.

"What about that coffee?" she called over to Andrea.

But Andrea was already packing up her stuff. "Sorry, I'm going to go home, try and get my head round this stuff. I honestly thought Sara was just repeating ill-founded gossip earlier, but after that," she jerked her head towards Helene's office, "it doesn't look like it."

As Andrea hurried out, Tess looked forlornly around her desk. Everything was changing in her life again. So much for thinking that this job was going to provide some stability for her at last. And who was this Jack McCabe anyhow?

She logged back on to her computer, intent on finding out more about him. The results for the agony aunts' search she had entered into Google earlier were displayed and Tess glanced at them without much enthusiasm. What was the point, when she might be out of a job altogether soon? It was all very well for Helene to lecture them about working their arses off. Tess was already working harder than she'd ever believed possible and the thought that Helene was now going to up the ante was not a pleasant prospect. But, since the recession, everyone was intent on keeping their heads down, their mouths shut and their salaries coming into their accounts every month.

One of the results of her agony-aunt search made her smile though:

Are you suffering from the agony of unrequited love?

Are you uncertain of what the future holds?

Let Grandma Rosa read your fortune.

Tea leaves (cup of tea free!), Cards and Crystal.

Seventh Daughter of a Seventh Daughter!

Tess read on, her interest piqued. The address was quite near to where she lived. She'd never had her fortune told, but she was definitely uncertain about the future. If Grandma Rosa could foresee anything on the horizon that wasn't doom and gloom, Tess would love to hear it. In fact, the woman might even give her a few tips about answering people's problems. It could be a research trip!

She could ask her about the station getting taken over. And tell her about how worried she was about being forced to become Agony Aunt of the Airwaves. She was sick of the tension in this office. She needed distraction. She needed gossip. She needed Grandma Rosa.

She turned over her spiral jotter, filled with the doodles and sketches she'd made of people she'd spotted around Killty, picked up the phone and dialled the number.

CHAPTER FOUR

Helene hunched over her desk, frowning at the piles of paper in front of her. She was having a very bad day. It had been a series of bad days really, ever since the announcement that the station might be taken over. She stretched and yawned, her eyes straying to the clock. She had let herself into an empty building, clutching her skinny latte and determined to make headway with the mountain of tasks ahead of her. Now, two hours later, it was still only nine o'clock.

She felt wrecked and hadn't made any real progress. Ever since Richard had heard about the possible takeover he had changed into one hell of a taskmaster. Overnight, it seemed, she had gone from being a big fish, albeit in a very small pond, to a minnow, darting this way and that as she tried to respond to Richard's ever-escalating demands. This latest thing she was working on was "a full appraisal of the Ollie Andrews show" – who were the anchors, who were the contributors, who were the advertisers, *blah blah blah*.

"Don't you know all that already?" she'd asked crossly when Richard had given her the assignment. But apparently it was all for the benefit of the mysterious Jack McCabe.

Helene had been furious that Sara, the most junior staff member, had found out about him at precisely the same time as she had.

"Do you know how that made me feel?" she had railed at Richard that evening when he'd dropped by her apartment.

"Truthfully? No." He took off his tortoiseshell glasses and polished them with a cloth he took from his pocket. "But I know how we'll both feel if this takeover doesn't happen."

A nerve was twitching in his right temple and Helene noticed the deep lines etching his forehead, the vague look in his eyes. He seemed unusually stressed, and she couldn't help feeling he knew more than he was telling her.

"But are you still in charge?" she cajoled.

He gave her a half-smile. "I am at the moment – Helene, I've told you all I'm prepared to tell you for now. All of this is deeply confidential. You need to make sure the staff keep these rumours to themselves."

She laughed out loud. "They're *journalists*, Richard! There's no way this will be kept secret. Just tell me this – is my job safe?"

But Richard had refused to talk about the takeover any more and she'd had to leave it at that. They had opened a bottle of wine, and watched a DVD, but Richard had left early, saying he needed an early night.

The phone on her desk jangled loudly, interrupting her thoughts. She sighed. She knew who it would be even before she lifted the receiver.

"Yes, Paulina, what is it this time?"

"Ah ... Helene, there are a few more things I need to know ..."

There would be, Helene thought wearily, pressing the save and close buttons on her computer. This was the third time Paulina had phoned that morning and Helene was finding it increasingly difficult to be nice to her. But

Richard had warned her that this woman was Jack McCabe's Representative on Earth and Helene was at all times to furnish her with whatever she needed to know. Which was an apparently endless supply of information about the radio station and all who worked in it.

Yet for all Paulina wanted to know about them, Helene suddenly realised she knew very little about her. Apart from the fact that she was a PR supremo, whatever that meant. But if she was so important, maybe she should be making an effort to get to know her a bit better?

"Paulina, why don't we meet up and we can go over this stuff in person?" she asked suddenly. "I'm almost finished that appraisal you wanted."

"Sure. When?" Paulina sounded as perky as she had on her first call at eight.

"How about later this morning?" Helene asked hopefully. The walls of her office were starting to close in on her.

"I'd have to reschedule my other appointments." Paulina seemed doubtful. "But it's a good idea to meet up. Let me just check with my PA ... Anita!"

Helene heard her calling her assistant and made a face into the phone. That's what she should have said! 'Let me check with my assistant. Maybe she can find a window for you ...'

"Helene?" Paulina was back. "I can make eleven if that suits you? Shall I come around to the office?"

"God no!" Helene blurted out. That was the last thing she wanted.

She could – and probably should – meet Paulina in the local hotel they used for work meetings but it was a soulless building and Helene badly needed to be somewhere she could relax, even a little. The headache that had been threatening was in danger of developing into a real humdinger – the result of too much caffeine and fretting about work, Richard and life in general.

She thought of the new coffee shop, which was near enough to the office. She had gone back there on Saturday, curious about the sense of expanding horizons she'd felt when she was looking at the big wall map of the world. And she'd found herself wondering how Matt, the owner, was getting on with his target of having the café up and running in a week.

When she got there, she'd been amazed to find the little café had been transformed in just a few days. The words 'Travel Café' were painted boldly in blue and white above the door, and the windows were framed with blue-and-white gingham curtains. When she pushed open the door, it no longer creaked and inside all the clutter had been replaced with polished pine tables, cosy-looking old yellow lamps, more world maps hanging in glass-fronted frames on the walls and shelves stuffed full of travel books.

For a few seconds Helene had just stood there, breathing in the atmosphere. Matt had managed to magically conjure up a sense of time being plentiful here – something to be enjoyed rather than endured. For Helene, whose life was tormented with to-do lists – things to do for work, or before she was forty, or even before she *died* – it was intoxicating.

"Repeat business! We must be doing something right!" Matt smiled broadly when he saw her. "It's good to see you here again. I didn't catch your name last time?"

"It's Helene. Helene Harper." She looked around at the transformed café. "This place looks fantastic. You've worked miracles to get it finished."

"I know." Matt looked around the café as if he couldn't

believe it either. "I had to pull a few all-nighters, but I did it. We're open!"

But Helene had still been his only customer and she reckoned now he could do with a boost. On impulse she suggested to Paulina they meet there. It was pretty near the office, and the atmosphere was exactly what she needed.

"It's a new, trendy little café," she began.

"The address?"

Helene told her and began to give directions, but Paulina cut her off.

"I'll find it," she said and hung up.

Helene put the phone down and sat back in her chair, her hand unconsciously rubbing the nape of her neck. Insomnia was wrecking her life, she thought wearily. Last night she'd fallen into an exhausted sleep only to wake as usual at four, her mind racing over the implications of this new situation at work.

Where would she fit into the hierarchy if Atlantic 1FM was sold? That was her main concern, really, and Richard had been of no help to her whatsoever. She'd hardly seen him since that night in her apartment in fact, because he was up to his eyes in whatever machinations were going on behind the scenes.

Helene pulled a mirror out of her desk drawer and scrutinised her features. At least the stress wasn't showing in her face. Her strict pampering regime was standing her in good stead, she consoled herself. Her skin looked dewy, as it should after all the serum and primer and sunscreen she'd lavished on it. The tired bags under her eyes were camouflaged under layers of concealer, foundation, blusher and bronzer and her hair was still gleaming after her expensive salon appointment yesterday.

Satisfied, Helene put away the mirror, swallowed two

51

painkillers with the cold dregs of her coffee and settled down to finish her appraisal of the *This Morning* programme. Ninety minutes later she was putting the finishing touches to the report. Pleased with her work, she reached under her desk for her high heels, slipped on her charcoal jacket like a suit of armour, squared her shoulders and left the building.

A frisson of excitement shot through her as she realised she would soon be meeting Jack McCabe's Representative on Earth. Tottering along the pavement, she plotted how she wanted the meeting to go. Mostly she needed to know more about Jack McCabe. What were his plans for the station? How long had Paulina known him? What were his likes and dislikes? She needed to fish out all this information, without appearing to be too nosy.

She reached the café early and was surprised to see that it was almost full. She took a table beside the window. She glanced up as the door swung open but it was Matt, carrying a pile of cardboard boxes.

He smiled broadly when he saw her. "Are you being looked after?"

"Not yet. But it's fine. I'm waiting for someone. Business meeting."

He raised his eyebrows. "I didn't think we'd attract the business type. But it's great. Hope it goes well for you."

Helene watched as he loped off, stopping at nearly every table for a word with the customers as he brought his stock through to the back. There was a sense of cheerfulness about him that she found fascinating. It was probably all the travelling that had him chilled out, she decided.

Maybe it was something she should do. Her and Richard. The thought came out of nowhere and Helene's pulse quickened at the prospect. If they went away, they would be free of all the strain of a covert affair. They would finally be free to go public with their relationship. Richard had always been adamant that their romance stayed a secret, but only, he said, because they worked together and he was her boss. But while that had been thrilling in the beginning, as time went on it just made their relationship seem less than what it was.

She gave herself a mental shake. What was she thinking of? Richard was an alpha male – that's what had attracted her to him in the first place. He wasn't the type to just bum around the world, with no goals to reach and no achievements to celebrate. And neither was she. She was Helene Harper. Executive Editor at Atlantic 1FM. Atlantic 1FM that might soon be bankrolled by a tycoon with the Midas touch. A tycoon whose Representative on Earth she was about to meet! Helene sat up straighter in her seat. It was time to change this challenge into an opportunity.

As if on cue the door swung open again and a tall, blonde woman stepped into the café. Helene knew straight away that it had to be Paulina. Everyone else in the café was lounging around in scruffy jeans, their feet on their backpacks. This woman was clutching an expensive briefcase and was dressed in designer gear – a caramel-coloured suit, navy silk shirt and, like Helene, wore killer heels. Her ash-blonde hair was poker-straight, and a gold chain glistened against her throat. She looked mid-thirties, Helene reckoned. Forty if she was having Botox.

"Paulina?" Helene stood up.

The other woman crossed the room in a flurry. "And you must be Helene!" She air-kissed Helene on both cheeks. "It's so good to meet you at last. It's so difficult to get to know someone without seeing them face to face." She sat down in the chair opposite. "Sorry I'm late – and also for being a bit of a pain these last few days. But Jack has given me such a tight schedule I have no option but to work from six each morning!" She placed her phone on the table between them. "It will bleep when it's time for my next appointment." She threw her eyes heavenwards at the sheer busyness of her life.

So your time is precious, Helene interpreted the business-speak rapidly. She'd better get cracking if she was to find out all she needed to know.

A pleasant-faced waitress took their order – carrot cake and a latte for Paulina, black coffee for Helene. They chitchatted about what was in the news headlines for a bit and then Helene decided to go for it.

"So, Paulina. Have you ever worked with a radio station before?"

"No! But it's *so* exciting. Neither has Jack, actually, so it's a bit of a learning curve for both of us."

Great, Helene thought. They didn't have a clue what they were letting themselves in for. Maybe she could make herself indispensable.

"If I knew exactly what your end goal is I might be able to help," she offered. She couldn't help wondering why someone like Jack McCabe would be interested in a tiny, local station in the first place, but she knew enough not to ask outright. Better to try and tease things out as diplomatically as she could with Paulina.

"Well, my focus on the project will be to help relaunch Atlantic 1FM as a major player in the media market – rebrand it totally. That's if Jack finally decides to buy in, of course. Which I think will depend on whether he gets the licence to take it national. But if he does decide to go ahead, it will be a case of hitting the ground running. I know from working with him on other projects that once he makes up his mind Jack doesn't waste much time."

The waitress returned with their order and Helene was momentarily distracted from her mission as she watched Paulina fork a huge piece of carrot cake into her mouth. Clearly the concept of Size Zero was not something that kept this woman awake at night.

"So how did you meet Jack?" she asked finally. She sat back, preparing to extract any useful information from the vague, non-committal answers Paulina was bound to give her. But to her astonishment, Paulina happily launched into the story of her life so far.

She explained how she had started out as a young gofer in a large PR organisation, but had decided pretty early on that the only way for an ambitious woman to avoid the glass ceiling was to set up on her own. After that she had been lucky, she said, and had been in the right place at the right time.

Right, Helene thought, keeping a fixed smile on her face. That was the mantra of every successful business person she had ever interviewed. She hadn't believed any of them. The only way to get on, Helene believed, was to be ruthless yourself and to protect yourself from other ruthless people. It was that simple.

Still, she listened attentively as Paulina continued her story. Jack had been an early client of hers and, as his star had risen, he had brought Paulina along with him, using her for his own projects and also helpfully passing on her name to his many and varied contacts.

At this stage of her life, Paulina revealed, she was as successful as she wanted to be, really. She had enough money in the bank and enough smart investments (made, naturally, on the shrewd advice of Jack) that she could walk away from the business now if she wanted to. She had lost some money during the crash, everyone had. But she still had enough to be a lady of leisure.

"But why would I want that?" she asked, finishing her cake with relish. "I mean, I'd do this work for nothing if I had to!"

Helene smiled understandingly and slid a mushroom-coloured paper file across the table. "You wanted a profile of Ollie Andrews' show. I haven't finished it but you'll get the gist of what it's all about from this."

She watched as Paulina opened the file and scanned through her report rapidly, her eyebrows rising quizzically as she read.

"He doesn't seem to be doing so well, does he?" she murmured.

"Well, we're taking steps to improve that," Helene said quickly. "We've had a new producer working with Ollie but I am now going to be much more hands-on in overhauling the whole programme. We have a new agony-aunt slot coming up which I think will be a massive success. And ..." she paused – time to mark herself down as something more than just a back-room person, "I myself am doing a *Ten Years Younger* feature. Reporting on all the new scientific methods women and men are using to keep themselves looking younger. Both those slots should attract advertising."

"Right," Paulina said absentmindedly, still scanning the report. "Well, there's no harm in going ahead with all that for now. But I have to say that if Jack does buy in he will be looking towards a complete shake-up. He will be looking for someone to take the station on to the national stage. Someone with the X-factor, y'know? And, so far, I am not sure if Ollie Andrews is that person. Are you?"

"Well, we're working on Ollie," Helene said quickly. If

Ollie were to get the boot, then she would suffer the fallout as well because she had been the one who had brought him into Atlantic 1FM in the first place. "So – what exactly do you mean by the X-factor?" She hoped she didn't sound sarcastic. But seriously? *The X-factor*?

"I'm not sure," Paulina said vaguely. "It's more I know what I *don't* want."

"Male, female, young, old, serious, zany?" Helene prompted, trying to catch Paulina's eye for clues.

But Paulina simply shrugged. "I really can't say. But I'd know if I saw it – or in this case *heard* it. Let's call it instinct."

Helene tried to keep her face expressionless as Paulina ate the last crumbs of her cake. She couldn't help feeling annoyed that Paulina could sit there and be so bloody casual about it all. There were people's livelihoods at stake here.

"Anyway, it doesn't really matter what I think," Paulina said, "because it's Jack who will have the final say."

"And does he make his decisions in the same way – on instinct?" Helene was finding it more and more difficult to sound neutral. To her mind, it was beyond bizarre that Jack and Paulina would make such important decisions on the basis of their own, very vague feelings. Where was their business plan, their strategy, their *lists*, for heaven's sake?

"Well, Jack will own the place so I suppose he's entitled to make his decisions in whatever way he chooses," Paulina pointed out cheerily.

Helene flushed but pushed on. "There's something I need to ask you about. I'm sure this is all just rumour, but we have heard that he may want new staff ... who are ... er ... younger?"

"I'm not sure about *young*," Paulina said pensively. "But

57

if Jack feels that someone's face doesn't fit he wouldn't be long in telling them. Although, he'd be pretty generous with severance payments," she added reassuringly.

She glanced down at her phone just before it bleeped.

"That's my next meeting, I'm afraid." She raised her eyebrows in mock panic. "It's all go these days. But it's been good to meet you, Helene. And thanks for this." She waved Helene's report in the air.

"It's been good to meet you too," Helene said automatically. She watched while Paulina gathered her things and got up to leave, and she kept her composure intact until the blonde head had finally disappeared from sight.

Then she slumped in her chair, a feeling of foreboding flooding through her. '*If someone's face doesn't fit, Jack wouldn't be long in telling them.*' That's what Paulina had said. Suddenly Helene was gripped by panic that it would be her face that didn't fit into Jack McCabe's vision for Atlantic 1 FM. What if she ended up unemployed? And alone, after Richard dumped her because she was a visible *failure*? And homeless because she wouldn't be able to afford the mortgage? What if she ended up on the streets with all her stuff on a supermarket trolley, like a bag lady? What if ...

Stop! A small, saner part of her mind intervened. She tried hard to obey it. She took deep slow breaths, trying to stop her thoughts from careering out of control. She would be okay. Of course she would. But she couldn't stop herself from comparing her circumstances to Paulina's. While the other woman had appeared to be sure of herself, and contented – fulfilled at work, financially secure, and able to eat huge chunks of cake without giving one thought to its calorie count – she, Helene, was looking at life through a much different lens. Up until now, she had always thought of herself as an independent career woman. She earned her own money. She had bought her own apartment. She even had staff working for her! But now, in the cold light of possible redundancy, she realised that in actual fact she only had enough money in the bank to maintain her present lifestyle for a few months at most. Paulina had said that Jack would be generous with severance payments but what good was that to her? Whatever he paid, it was hardly going to last the rest of her life. And what about her identity? If she wasn't Helene Harper, Executive Editor of Atlantic 1FM, who was she? She was an almost-forty-year-old woman, that was who, in a complicated relationship with her married boss and with very little energy or inclination for starting over.

Helene looked around her, as if for inspiration, and her gaze rested on the bookshelves lining the walls of the Travel Café. Out of the blue she remembered a book she had read many years ago: *The Cinderella Complex*, by an author called Colette Dowling. It was all about how perfectly intelligent women failed to secure their own futures because they were still subconsciously waiting for a man to come and rescue them.

Helene had read it for work and she'd thought it was pretty interesting at the time. But not interesting enough, she thought ruefully, for her to have picked up on any of its tips or suggestions. But of course at that stage she hadn't felt it held any special resonance for *her*.

It was only now, with the twenty-twenty vision of hindsight, that she realised that of course it had. Because here she was, a dozen years later, without the savings plan, the pension, the investments that Paulina had so casually listed earlier on.

In fact, Helene thought, panic rising up in her again, all she had to show for years of effort was a wall-to-wall wardrobe bulging with clothes and shoes and products. Anti-ageing serums, primers, hair stuff. They all promised miracles and delivered absolutely nothing apart from a short feel-good factor and lots of shiny boxes.

In truth, Helene had always thought Richard was going to be her pension. But was he? Or was she now that walking cliché: a woman having an affair with a married man who was having cold feet about leaving his wife?

The ringing of her phone interrupted her thoughts. She grabbed it out of her pocket, glad of the distraction, and checked caller ID: Richard. No doubt with another few tasks for her to-do list. She watched for several seconds as the phone flashed his name at her, wondering if he had been taking her for a fool all this time.

She pressed the reject button and shoved the phone into the bottom of her handbag. Then she ordered another coffee and settled back down to her brooding.

CHAPTER FIVE

Tess sat on the sofa in the bay window of her living room, looking pensively out at the waves breaking on the seashore and wondering what this latest bombshell was going to mean for her. Her laptop was open at a jobs site but it had taken her only a few minutes to see there was nothing suitable on it. And then she had become distracted by the view from the window. One of the silver linings of the recession was that she could afford to rent this apartment at a fraction of what it would have cost in the boom times and it was nicer than anywhere she had lived over the past decade. But now it looked like she might be moving on again sooner rather than later.

Apart from work, there was nothing for her in Killty. She and Andrea had been friends in college but now Andrea was married with two children and a husband who'd recently been made redundant. Socialising with Tess wasn't high on her list of priorities, but Tess had been so focussed on getting to grips with the new job that it hadn't bothered her too much. Weekdays flew by in a blur and at night she was too tired to care that she had nothing in her life except work. Her weekends were filled with trying to catch up with the chores she didn't have time for during the week,

Joan Brady

and trying to prepare for the coming week.

The prospect of changes at Atlantic was forcing her to reassess her life once more. She could move somewhere else, she supposed. She was used to travelling on a shoestring. But where? Now that she was thirty, a big part of her felt it was time to settle down. To something.

She glanced at her laptop. Maybe she should go to this reunion after all. At the very least it would be a social outlet, and who knew – maybe she'd get a job lead there? Of course, it would mean meeting Chris Conroy again. She bit her lip. She had stopped thinking about Chris as the One Who Got Away long ago but that didn't mean she wanted to see him any time soon. She glanced at the clock and saw it was time to go and see Grandma Rosa, the fortune teller. Resolving to look at Chris's email again later on, she grabbed her coat and bag and set off.

By the time she reached Rose Cottage Tess had cheered up immensely. The walk from her apartment had taken her along by the shore and up a cliff road she had never been on before. It afforded her a ridiculously beautiful view over the sea and the climb made her legs ache and her heart beat faster. With each lungful of air her thoughts cleared a little more and by the time she stood outside the cottage she had begun to put her work problems in perspective. She was young, she was healthy, and she had friends around the world. How had she allowed herself to get so wrapped up in Helene Harper and Ollie Andrews and their stupid mind games over the last six months?

The house itself was postcard pretty – whitewashed walls, an untidy thatched roof, a crooked wooden fence and the words '*Rose Cottage*' painted onto a wooden sign in the middle of the garden. Underneath were the words:

Seventh Daughter of a Seventh Daughter!
Let Grandma Rosa foretell your future!
Tea leaves (cup of tea free!), Cards and Crystals.

Tess lifted the heavy brass doorknocker and hopped from one foot to the other until she heard a tinny voice over an intercom.

"Push the door and wait in the kitchen, dear! I'm just finishing a reading."

Tess stepped tentatively into a small dark hallway. She could hear the rise and fall of voices coming from a room on the right-hand side – presumably that was where the readings went on. She walked to the end of the hall, pushed open the door there and stepped into a room flooded with sunlight.

A shabby floral sofa was angled to get a perfect view of the back garden, through white French windows, where fat red tulips sprang upwards in joyous clumps among the fading daffodils. Tess stared at it for a moment, overcome with nostalgia. The garden reminded her of her parents' house in the country with its big rambling back garden.

She sat gingerly on the edge of the sofa, shoving her satchel under the scratched oak coffee table. Something soft brushed against her leg and she looked down into the green eyes of a very black, very fat cat. Tess was delighted to have something to distract her and she felt herself relaxing slightly as she moved her fingers through the black fur.

She wondered what its owner would be like. Her own maternal grandmother had died before she was born, but she remembered her paternal grandmother, Nan Sheila, well. She had worn her steel-grey hair in a bun pinned back with silver clips and was never seen without her apron with the pots-and-pans pattern on it. She had baked bread and scones and cooked a dinner for her large family every day

63

of her life. She would have laughed out loud if she'd known Tess was visiting a fortune teller. Tess could almost hear her now – '*A fool and her money are easily parted*' – but she would have been smiling when she said it.

She smiled at the memory of her departed grandmother. Of course, she was right. Tess didn't believe in fortune tellers – this visit was light relief from all her problems at work. She had spent the last few nights studying the agony-aunt columns of newspapers and magazines and as far as she could see the problems all boiled down to three basic dilemmas: dysfunctional families, unrequited love, and meeting and finding The One. But how could she turn that into a radio slot?

"That's odd. Millie likes you – she never likes strangers."

Tess turned in the direction of the voice and started at the sight of the woman strolling into the kitchen. Grandma Rosa looked to be in her seventies but any similarity between her and Nan Sheila ended there. Her hair was a strange shade of plum, with huge chunks of grey peeking through a very badly done home-dye. She was wearing denim jeans, a white frilly blouse – and were they Ugg boots? The only thing that looked remotely like Tess's notions of what a fortune teller might wear was the enormous pair of silver rings dangling out of her ears.

Rosa caught her staring and looked down at her boots, one of which she tapped with the folded magazine she was carrying.

"What do you think?" she demanded. "Do the boots work?"

"Er ... work for what?" Tess asked uncertainly.

"I'm aiming for a funkier, younger image. This is what young people wear, isn't it? Uggs?"

Dear God, did the whole world want to look younger?

Tess wondered wildly, thinking of Helene and her *Ten Years Younger* project.

"Young people wear Uggs, yes," Tess said, nodding. "But er ... why do you want a new image?"

"It's to do with my career. I'm trying to diversify and *this* is part of it." Rosa pointed vaguely towards her hair. "You're a young person. What do you think?"

"You look ... fine. But isn't a fortune teller meant to look ... well, old ... and wise?"

"That was the old way all right, but at the psychic club night all they ever talk about are the new 'in' things. Aura readings. Angel-card therapy. Coffee-cup readings." Her mouth curled in derision. "Coffee readings? Seriously? And that last client who was in with me? That was Mrs O'Brien. She's been coming to me for over twenty years for readings. I was the one who told her that Alfie, her late husband, would never come out of the hospital and that she should find a new direction for herself for when he'd gone. I told her that her son would go off to Australia and meet an Aussie girl and settle down there. All came true. But now! Now Mrs O'Brien thinks traditional fortune telling is over. Passé. And it's all because of this!" She placed the magazine she was carrying on the table and indicated an article underscored with red biro.

Tess scanned it curiously. It was a New Age story about Cosmic Ordering – how you simply placed your order and waited for it to be delivered. There was a story about it in some magazine or book every other week as far as Tess could tell. She glanced up.

"So what does Cosmic Ordering have to do with Mrs O'Brien getting her fortune told?" she asked.

"Well, why does she need to pay me to find out what the future holds if she can just ask the cosmos for anything she wants? Make up her own future?" Rosa threw her eyes heavenwards. "No wonder my business is going down the tubes."

"So this Mrs O'Brien – does she think Cosmic Ordering really works?"

"She says she *knows* it does. She doesn't see how gullible that makes her. She can't see it's just another fad. As I said to her, 'Mrs O'Brien, if Cosmic Ordering worked why would the vast majority of people spend their days beating their way through gridlocked traffic to spend ten hours a day at work when they could be asking the Universe for a new life somewhere warm and interesting?' But she wouldn't listen. Said she asked the Universe for a surprise and she won a hundred euro on a scratch card."

"One hundred euro?" Tess protested.

"Well, that was just for her to test the theory, she says!"

Tess thought of what she'd ask for. For Ollie to disappear, for Helene to stop being a bully, for Jack McCabe not to take over the radio station and throw her out of her job. To be back in Bali. Or to have a different job altogether, a fantastic high-profile career so she could swan into the reunion Chris Conroy was organising with her head held high.

"But the point is," Grandma Rosa rolled her big brown eyes dramatically again, "this is going to affect my living. That's why I hired a webmaster to get me on the Net. Is that how you heard of me?"

"Er … yes, actually," Tess replied.

"Well, it must be working then." Rosa looked satisfied. "He's going to set me up on Facebook and Twitter next. So," she sank down into the sofa beside Tess and looked at her sharply, "what can I do for you now? Tarot, the crystal ball, tea leaves?"

"Well ..." Tess began but stopped at the sound of the front door knocker banging again.

"Just give me a minute." Grandma Rosa sprang off the sofa and marched out to answer the door. Moments later she returned with a man in tow.

"I have another client," she announced cheerily. "That Net is a miracle. Now if you can both wait here while I go and clear the parlour of Mrs O'Brien's aura, I'll be back in a jiffy."

Tess smiled uncertainly at the newcomer. He was tall and rangy-looking with very dark hair curling over his collar and a natural tan he hadn't acquired in Ireland – not at this time of the year, anyway. He was dressed in faded blue denim jeans and a light cotton shirt. No jewellery. No wedding ring. Gay?

He raised his eyebrows and Tess flushed as she realised he knew she was checking him out.

"So – is she any good?" He jerked his head in the direction of the kitchen door.

"Haven't a clue – I've never been here before. It's your first time too then?"

"Yeah." He gave a wry smile. "My sister says it's cheaper than therapy. And more fun."

Tess frowned. "I don't think fortune telling is suitable for serious problems that require therapy."

"Don't look so worried – my problem isn't that serious. I just need some advice about something I can't make up my mind about. So, in the interests of being open to new experiences – here I am."

He flopped down into an armchair. Tess thought it weird that a guy would go to a fortune teller. Still, if he had a problem ...

Her eyes widened a fraction as her brain caught up with

what he'd just said. Here was someone sitting in front of her who had a problem and was looking for advice about it. Exactly what she was looking for! She took a deep breath.

"So what sort of problem do you have then?"

He let out a sigh. "It's a very boring sort of problem, I'm afraid. It's not a big love triangle or anything as interesting."

"So." Tess looked at him speculatively. "Let me guess then. Is it to do with a dysfunctional family?"

"Sort of." He sounded impressed. "Hey, how did you know that?"

Hah, she thought triumphantly. All that swotting up on the agony columns had paid off already.

"I happen to have a particular interest in people with problems, that's all," she said, shrugging nonchalantly.

"Really? Why?" He steepled his fingers in front of him and watched her closely.

"Well, it's just at the moment. I mean ..." she hesitated – she hoped she wouldn't sound slightly insane, "I'm actually looking for people with problems. So I can solve them."

"Really?" He gave her a disbelieving look.

"Yes, really. It's part of my job. Well," she amended, "what will be my job – if I can make it work." She took another deep breath. "*My* problem, you see, is that I don't actually have any people to tell me what their problems are."

"What sort of a job is that?" He looked baffled.

"It's in a radio station. I'm a producer there at the moment. But I'm about to become ... er ... an agony aunt."

He sat up straighter. "A radio agony aunt? So who do you work for?"

"Oh, it's nowhere important," she said dismissively. "The local radio station here – Atlantic 1FM. Do you listen to it?"

"I don't live in Killty – I'm just in town on business." He raised an eyebrow. "But how can I help you?"

"Well, I've never done anything like this before and I haven't a clue how to kick it all off. It's not that easy to get the right sort of callers – people who are fluent and who won't dry up under the pressure of being on the radio. They don't just ring in out of the blue. You have to go out and find them. My boss thinks I should make some stuff up to start it off, but I'm not sure if that's exactly ethical." Her voice trailed off. When she said it out loud like that, it sounded pretty precious. Maybe Helene was right. Maybe she should just make the stuff up and stop stressing so much about it?

"But you think it would be ethical for me to ring you?" He pushed long legs out in front of him and gave her a quizzical look.

"Well, of course it would be. You're a real person with a real problem. You've just said so yourself. So it would be authentic and our listeners would get that straight away. It would be perfect to get me started off."

He smiled. "So tell me a bit more about it then. Are you excited about this chance to go on-air?"

"Excited? No. Terrified more like. I've told Helene it's probably going to flop. Helene's my boss."

"So how do you know it's going to be a flop?"

Tess shrugged. She was beginning to regret starting up this conversation. She thought he'd just agree to do what she asked, or not. But he was giving her the third degree. "I suppose I don't know for sure. But ..."

"Look, I'd *like* to help," he said. "But it does seem

weird, if you don't mind me saying so. I'd have to broadcast my problem on-air and have everyone hear it?"

"Well, you don't have to worry about anybody recognising you, if you don't live around here. It's not as if Atlantic has a huge audience. Helene, my boss, says we're haemorrhaging listeners! As a matter of fact, I wouldn't be surprised if the only people who get to hear your problem are myself and Ollie, the presenter. And Helene and a few of the rest of the staff of course. And my parents – they always listen in on the internet. And my sister Verity – she lives in London."

"So what else can you tell me about the station?"

"It's tiny. But maybe for not much longer."

"Why?"

Now he really was curious! Hah – she was reeling him in! But just in time she remembered Helene's dire warnings about not spreading rumours and she pursed her lips.

"I can't really say any more. Sorry."

"Okay. So what if I want to help you out? How do we do it?"

Tess felt a wave of elation. He was interested! She sat back and breathed a long sigh of relief. "That would be fantastic! This is my plan. You tell me what your problem is, I go away and research all I can about it – see what a real professional might have to say about it. And then when you ring me on-air on Monday," she added rapidly before he could change his mind, "I'll have the answer all ready for you. The listeners will think you've just phoned in off the cuff and I'm just very clever at answering problems." She made a face. "Sorry if I'm destroying the magic of radio for you."

He leaned back in his chair, contemplating his scuffed, tan cowboy boots. "No, it's all very interesting. But here's something I don't understand. You have a new slot on a tiny flop of a station with hardly any listeners – if nobody rings in, what's the big deal? If there's so few people listening in, who will even know?"

"I'll know. And Ollie Andrews – the presenter – will know and will smirk into my face about it. And Helene Harper will know and use it to get on my case even more afterwards. But if people hear you it will encourage them. That often happens – when people hear other people talking about something on radio, they ring in too." She stopped, catching his expression. "You think only crazy people with nothing else to do ring in to radio stations, don't you? Maybe you're right." Her earlier elation had started to evaporate now.

"Maybe." He shrugged and shoved a hand into his jeans pocket and pulled out a biro. "What telephone number do I ring?"

"You're going to do it? Oh thank you, thank you, thank you! So – the show is called *This Morning with* –"

"*This Morning with Ollie Andrews*? Cos that's the presenter's name?"

"Right." Tess reeled off the telephone number and watched as he scribbled it down on a used brown envelope he had pulled out of his other pocket. He seemed pleased with himself.

"I'm getting the hang of this," he said.

"You are. But you need to listen to the programme for a while first so it sounds natural when you get put on-air," Tess explained.

"And is the show recorded or does it go out live?"

"It's live. So – tell me what your problem is?" She pulled out her own pen and notebook so she could take his details. She hoped it wouldn't be too difficult to work out how to answer it. But she could worry about that later. At least it was a real problem! This was the break she'd been praying for.

"Well … I have a little condition to my participation in the programme."

"What condition?" Tess asked carefully. It was starting to go wrong again.

"I don't want to tell you what the problem is in advance of the show."

"But that's the whole point!" Tess burst out. Then she stopped. Maybe this wasn't such a good idea after all. She didn't know the first thing about this guy. And she had thought it was weird from the start: a bloke coming to a fortune teller on his own. She wiped a damp hand on her skirt.

"I think it would be better if you were to ad-lib the answer," he said. "That's what people want to hear – what your take is on the problem, not some second-hand regurgitation of what a professional might say. Your own opinion would make for much better radio."

"And you know this – how exactly?" Disappointment made Tess sound more belligerent than she intended. But people were always thinking they knew what made better radio when in reality they didn't have a clue. They thought it involved just getting behind a mike and talking. But there was a lot more to it – not enough people realised that.

"It's just a feeling," he said mildly. "There's no need to get so disturbed about it."

That was exactly the word for her, Tess thought. *Disturbed*. She'd come to a fortune teller and ended up giving her advice on her new, 'funky' image! And then she'd asked this perfect stranger to ring her on-air when for all she knew he could be a psycho-stalker from hell. She was taking the whole thing far too seriously. She stuffed her pen and notebook back into her satchel.

"Listen," she said, "I've changed my mind about you ringing. It was a mistake. So let's just pretend this conversation never happened. Okay?"

"But what about all that stuff you said about being afraid of making a show of yourself in front of the presenter? And your boss getting on your case?" He looked baffled again.

"Well, that's for me to worry about," Tess said shortly. "I told you from the start I would need to know what your problem was because I don't have any experience in answering problems. That was the whole *point* of the conversation!"

"Look, if it's that important to you, I'll do it. Take your pen back out. I'll tell you what my problem is."

Tess looked at him, flustered. She didn't know what to do now.

Then the kitchen door opened and Rosa appeared in the hallway, beckoning for Tess to follow her into the parlour.

Tess stood up. "It's too late now. Let's just forget it."

"Really?" He scratched his five o'clock shadow and had the nerve to look disappointed. "Well, good luck with it anyway."

Tess rolled her eyes to heaven and turned to follow Grandma Rosa into the tiny front room. She could hardly remember what she had come here for now. She perched on the edge of another ancient sofa, across a coffee table from Rosa. She shrugged her shoulders, trying to dissipate the tension.

"You seem nervous," Rosa said. She had a deck of tarot cards in her hands. She shuffled them and held them out to Tess. "Here, pick nine cards."

Tess picked the cards absentmindedly and waited while Rosa arranged them into a cross shape on the coffee table. She was still thinking of the guy in the waiting room.

"Sorry for keeping you waiting." Rosa was studying the cards. "Well, the first thing the cards are telling us today is that there are big changes on the horizon for you."

"Yes, I know that! That's why I'm here. The reason I came was because the radio station I work for is about to be taken over and –"

Rosa's eyes widened. "You work in a radio station?"

"Yes, but I don't know for how much longer. I'm not sure if the new owner will want to keep the same staff and –"

"Do you think you could get me on the radio? Doing fortunes? Maybe even Cosmic Ordering? Listeners would love it! And if I had a media profile I'd never be out of work. What's the radio station called?"

"Atlantic 1FM – you must know it – it's the local station here in Killty. It's tiny. You'd be better trying somewhere bigger," Tess said apologetically.

"No – local would be good, especially for drumming up new business. And, yes, I know Atlantic 1FM – I listen to that show in the morning. What's it called again?"

"*This Morning with Ollie Andrews*. That's the one I produce."

"You're the producer!" Grandma Rosa was impressed. "So you could get me a slot then?"

"It's not that easy!" Tess sighed. "There might be a new station owner and he is supposed to only want young people! And I know you've had your makeover and everything, but I mean *really* young. In fact, even I might be too old to work there myself soon."

"What?" Rosa blanched. "Sure you're only a child!"

"I'm not! I'm thirty! And Sara, that's the girl I work

74

with, she says the new boss might only want *under*-thirty-year-olds. She heard it from her father who knows all these business types. But even apart from the station being taken over, my job is terrible at the moment." Tess's thoughts came out in a jumble. "My boss keeps hounding me to come up with better ideas and get more listeners. And now? Now she wants me to be an agony aunt!"

Rosa looked down at the cards, her head leaning to one side. "That's something I'd be very good at, if you don't mind me saying – an agony aunt! But you're right – I couldn't pass for under thirty. It was a makeover I had, not a miracle. But the point is, I'd *love* to do it. So why is it a problem for you then?"

"Because I'd feel sorry for someone if I'm their only port of call when they have a problem. I can't even sort out my own problems. And it seems exploitative. And unethical." There was that word again. Tess was beginning to get on her own nerves saying it.

"So maybe it's time you moved on if you find yourself compelled to do things that are unethical and exploitative," Rosa said calmly.

"It's not that easy ..." Tess began.

"You keep saying that," Rosa pointed out.

"Do I?" Tess hadn't noticed.

"Look. Worthwhile things are rarely easy. And staying in a job you hate and doing things you find unethical – well, that can't be easy either." Rosa overturned another of Tess's card choices and peered at it. "What about love and romance? Tell me, have you someone new in your life?"

Tess shook her head dumbly. There wasn't a single man in the whole of Killty as far as she could tell and with her debut slot as Agony Aunt of the Airwaves starting on Monday, romance was the last thing on her mind.

"Are you sure?" Creases appeared in Grandma Rosa's forehead as she concentrated on her cards. "There's a big romance showing here. Have you got your eye on someone maybe?"

Rosa sounded so convinced that, despite herself, Tess peered at the cards.

"How can you tell?"

"It's my skill." Rosa looked at her. "So do you know who it might be?"

"Haven't a clue. I've been concentrating on my career lately."

"What sort of a life is that? Especially with the problematic career you have?" Rosa was openly incredulous.

"But that's why I'm here. Because I want help to sort it all out."

"Well then, you'll think about what I said. About moving on."

"Look," Tess said forcefully, "the media industry is not an easy place to be job-hopping in at the moment. Lots of people would do what I do for nothing, just to get a foot in the door."

Rosa flipped over another card and her eyes widened. "You'll be getting a proposition shortly – I'm not sure what sort. When I was young a proposition would have meant an engagement ring. But these days that could just mean a sleepover. Or," she raised her hand in anticipation of Tess's further protest, "a career move."

Tess smiled. She didn't mean to be uncharitable, but it was no wonder business was going down the tubes for Grandma Rosa if this was the best she could come up with. A new romance, big changes on the horizon. So far, so predictable.

Still, she'd come this far so she'd give her a chance. For

the next thirty minutes she listened carefully as Rosa turned one card over and then another. In fairness, some things struck a chord for Tess. Like she was missing someone special from her life. That would be Verity, her sister, who had moved to London with her husband. So London wasn't Australia and they kept in close contact still, but it wasn't only the geographical distance that was the problem. It was the fact that when Verity got married Tess felt she'd moved on to an altogether more grown-up phase of her life, creating a gap between them.

Rosa also pointed out that Tess needed to listen to her heart instead of her head more often, something she agreed with readily. She knew she was being very analytic about her life lately, but that was because she trying to be strategic about getting a career for herself.

But, by the end of the session, Tess just felt like she'd enjoyed a harmless distraction from life, that was all. There was no big reveal, no inspirational guidance to take home with her.

So much for being the seventh daughter of a seventh daughter, she smiled to herself as she handed over her money and Rosa deposited it into an old, red tea caddy.

She let herself out, resisting the temptation to look back towards the kitchen.

CHAPTER SIX

Tess looked up as the café door swung open and Andrea swept in. She had been here half an hour already and was enjoying the ambience of the Travel Café, remembering all the good times of her own globetrotting days. Andrea had mentioned that a new café had opened recently and they had arranged to meet to discuss Tess's new role as agony aunt.

Tess had got here deliberately early and spent some time browsing through the brochures and books. Andrea, on the other hand, arrived after a five-kilometre run. Her auburn hair was plastered into her head and she was out of breath but she looked pink-cheeked and exhilarated. Sunday mornings were what she called her 'sanity time' and Tess was grateful she was taking the time out to give her some advice.

She sat down opposite Tess and ordered herself a herbal tea. "So! How is the *Agony Aunt of the Airwaves* slot coming along?"

Tess rolled her eyes. "Not very well, actually. The harder I try to relax, the more wound up I get about it. I keep picturing Ollie's sneering face on the other side of the table. I feel like a square peg in a round hole in this job, Andrea."

"You need to ignore Ollie and concentrate on yourself," Andrea advised.

"But he hates me. And so does Helene," Tess sighed.

"Helene has it in for us all." Andrea shrugged. "She considers me a liability because I have children and I can't be at her beck and call twenty-four hours a day. I'm already getting that anxious Monday feeling because I have zero ideas for tomorrow. I need to find time to look through the newspapers this afternoon but then Paul will be like a demon because he says Sundays are supposed to be family time. Sometimes I feel like I'm being pulled in two."

"How's he getting on with being a house husband then?" Tess asked speculatively. She'd noticed that since Paul had lost his job her friend had become much more distracted at work.

Andrea raised her eyes heavenwards. "Hmm. Mondays he coaches school football, Wednesdays he's involved in computer classes for the elderly, Thursdays it's a support group for men made redundant. Not a lot of housework going on. And now he needs – get this – Me Time!"

Tess stifled a snigger. "I thought that only existed inside the pages of women's magazines?" But she felt bad about making fun of him. Andrea was the reporter across all of the weekday programmes on Atlantic, which meant a lot of unsociable and unpredictable hours. It couldn't be easy for him, adjusting to a life at home and having to deal with all of that too.

"Well, Paul says Me Time is hugely important when you're a stay-at-home dad. Otherwise your creativity gets stifled, apparently." She shrugged. "Anyhow, have you brought your script for tomorrow?"

"I was just going through it when you arrived." Tess shoved a sheet of paper across the table.

Andrea glanced through it and slid it back. "It's absolutely fine to start you off. Next week, when the problems start rolling in, we can sit down and work out a detailed plan. Just get it kicked off tomorrow."

"Thanks." Tess shoved the paper into her bag. She had planned to rehearse it with Andrea, but it was clear her friend had more than enough on her plate.

As it turned out, she hadn't even got around to telling her that she'd been to see the fortune teller when Andrea's mobile bleeped. She squinted at the screen, sighed, and pushed her half-full cup of tea to one side. "Time's up, I'm afraid. See you tomorrow so. And stop worrying, Tess. You'll be absolutely fine."

And she was gone, streaking past the window in a fast jog.

Tess left soon after and ambled along the seafront until she found a bench. She pulled out her journal and jotted down random thoughts as they occurred to her. It was a habit she'd got into when she'd first set off on her travels. She had so many memories recorded now that she didn't want to give it up, even while she was here in Killty where most of her journal entries consisted of whinges about what Ollie or Helene had done to torture her on a particular day.

She spent the rest of the day trying to relax but she still slept badly that night. By the time her alarm went off next morning, she felt as if she'd had no sleep at all.

She got to work early and settled down with a coffee in the bit of scrubland that passed for a garden at the back of the radio-station building. The sun was warm on her back but she was too keyed up to appreciate it.

"'*So if you would like to write or email me in with your problem I promise I'll do my best to help,*'" she read out loud.

She wiped her clammy hands in her jeans. Why was she finding this so difficult? It wasn't as if she had to worry about live callers. After the fiasco with the strange man she'd run into at Rose Cottage she had given up trying to find a guinea-pig caller. She had decided that this morning would be just about announcing the agony-aunt slot and inviting listeners to contact her. Helene wouldn't be pleased of course. But – Tess stiffened her spine – it was the best she could do on short notice so she'd have no choice but to go along with it, at least until after the programme. When she would probably have her guts for garters, but she could worry about that when the time came.

"So this is where you've got to!"

She looked up to see Sara barging through the door into the garden.

"You're on in fifteen minutes and Helene wants to speak to you about it first."

"Yeah, I need to talk to her too – make sure she's okay with this script. I was looking for her earlier." She got up and began to gather her things together.

"She's only just arrived and I have to warn you – she's like a demon today. And she's producing the show herself, after promising she'd give me a shot at it!" Sara looked mutinous. "Daddy doesn't understand why I want to work here at all. I'm never going to get a break."

"I'm sorry," Tess said and meant it. Sara had been due to act as producer for the day to allow Tess to concentrate on being on-air. Now the thought of Helene scrutinising her every mistake from the control room made Tess feel more nervous than ever.

She followed Sara back into the building.

"It's not even certain Jack McCabe is going to buy in at all," Sara continued. "Daddy says Jack may have the Midas touch, but even he can't work miracles." She looked back at Tess. "So should I just go ahead with setting up the *Ten*

Years Younger item then? It might help Helene to calm down. But then, what if Jack drops it? It's all very confusing here lately."

"We continue as normal," Tess said, absently repeating the current mantra of everyone at Atlantic 1FM.

They had reached the studio and she'd barely have enough time to talk to Helene before it was time for her to go on-air.

But as soon as she swung open the door she could see something was wrong. Helene was sitting ramrod straight, her whole body rigid with tension, her left leg jigging up and down under the desk. She looked at Tess and gestured angrily at the clock overhead.

"You've left it late enough. I wanted to discuss the slot with you before you went on, but a call has fallen through now so you'll have to go on early. As in *now*, Tess!"

"Oh, okay ..." Tess hurried through to sit down opposite Ollie, her fragile confidence faltering with this unexpected change to the schedule. She glanced out at Helene, looking for reassurance, but she was deep in conversation with Sara.

Tess placed her hands on the desk, saw they were shaking and shoved them into her lap. Ollie glanced down at her knowingly and she ducked her head down towards her script so she wouldn't have to look at him.

And then, there it was. The familiar signature tune for *This Morning with Ollie Andrews* was jingling through the room. The same tune she had heard over and over again for the last six months. She had imagined that hearing it would settle her down, make her feel professional. Instead she felt the start of panic beginning to lick around her insides.

She closed her eyes briefly and focussed on her breathing. Andrea had instructed her to take a deep, slow breath at the beginning of each sentence, which would stop her making the beginner broadcaster's mistake of having to take huge, audible gulps of air at inappropriate places.

But Tess's breath was coming in short little gasps and she felt nauseous. She tried again. Breathe in to the count of four, out to the count of six. But it wasn't working. *It wasn't working.* She was going to be sick – but there was no time to be sick because she saw the red light come on and she could hear Ollie's voice, sounding tinny and as if it were coming from a great distance. There it was. They were on-air.

"Good morning, folks! This is Ollie Andrews and this is the *This Morning* show! Well, we've lots of stuff lined up for you today as usual, and one special treat to start with. In studio with me this morning is Tess Morgan. That name might be familiar to some of you and that's because Tess is the producer of this programme. But today she's swapping her behind-the-scenes role to become your very own … agony aunt." Ollie's voice dipped in a sneer. "Tess Morgan – Agony Aunt of the Airwaves! But first – let's have some music …"

A blast of heavy metal music filled the studio and Tess blinked in astonishment. Why was he playing this? It must be to unsettle her. She could feel the deep *boom boom* of the beat juddering through the room. She looked out for Helene's reaction but she was still busy talking to Sara.

Tess hunched over her script and tried to block out the noise. She had prepared a composite of typical problems to give listeners a flavour of the issues she intended to deal with. She would then invite them to email or write in with their own dilemmas and that was it really for today. If she could just stop panicking …

From the corner of her eye she noticed Helene gesticulating to get her attention, stabbing her finger downwards in a vigorous motion. Tess squinted through the soundproofed glass window, trying to figure out what she meant.

"Put on your headphones!" Ollie barked.

"Oh, right." Flustered, Tess clamped them onto her head, her ears still ringing from the raucous music that was thankfully fading away now. What did she need the headphones for, Tess wondered vaguely, trying to stop her papers from rustling.

She understood why too late.

"Tess!" Helene was hissing into her ear. "You have a caller!"

"What?" Tess jerked her head up and saw Ollie glaring at her, warning her that she was now on-air and that listeners would hear whatever she said.

"Ask her what her name and her problem is!" Helene instructed.

Tess opened her mouth but no sound came out. She swallowed. Her mouth was parched. Shakily, she took a sip of water. Why hadn't Helene warned her about this? She heard the voice of a young woman.

"Hello? Hello, Tess?" She sounded shy and a bit hesitant.

"Tess Morgan," she confirmed. "How … how can I help you?"

"Well, my name is Cindy and I have a problem."

Her air of vulnerability made Tess begin to forget her own fears.

"Right. And you … er … you want to tell us about that, do you?" Tess stammered. She tried to ignore Ollie who was rolling his eyes and shaking his head in disbelief that his show had come to this.

"Yes, I do. My problem is this." The woman's tone of voice changed suddenly. "My boyfriend is a bastard!"

"Right." Tess lifted her script in front of her face, trying to block out the sight of Ollie who was now openly sniggering. "So ... er ... what makes you say that?"

"Well, I didn't always think it. Obviously when we met I thought he was quite different. I thought it was serious between us. I thought he was serious!" She sighed heavily. "And he was. Seriously married!"

"Married? How did you find that out?" Tess was interested despite herself.

"His wife rang me," Cindy's voice got stronger. "She said I should leave her husband alone. She said if I didn't, she would come and find me and cut me!"

"Cut you?" Tess was appalled. The woman should be visiting the police, not ringing a radio station. She looked out at Helene for direction but her boss looked as bewildered as she did.

"So what did *you* say?" Tess decided to play for time, giving Helene an opportunity to decide how to cut the woman off. Maybe she could get Ollie to cue a break or something ...

"I didn't get a chance to say anything!" Cindy continued. "She kept going on at me! Said I wasn't the first girlfriend he'd had and that I wouldn't be the last. She said," Cindy dipped her voice as if she were in the movies, "'Remember this, *bitch* – he always comes back to me. Always!'" She sniffed. "She became very emotional.'"

"Well, she would do," Tess said reasonably. "In the circumstances."

"Whatever," Cindy said offhandedly. "The point is – what should I do?"

"What should you do?" Tess cast around in her mind for an answer.

Ollie was leaning back in his chair, his mouth curved in a wide smile, hugely enjoying her discomfort.

"Well, if you ask me it all sounds very clichéd," Tess said finally.

"*If* I ask you?" Cindy sounded mystified. "Of course I'm asking you. Isn't that why I rang up the show? And what do you mean by it all sounds very clichéd? Are you saying I'm making it up?" Her voice rose. "Or that I'm some sort of fantasist?"

"Well, it's an old story, isn't it?" Tess pointed out patiently. "The married man. The girl who thinks he's going to marry her. The wife who finds out. I've read about lots of similar situations in magazines." Especially the magazines she'd been swotting up on all last week.

"Would you read in a magazine that the wife said she'd come and cut me?" Cindy challenged.

"Well, maybe not that part," Tess admitted.

"Well, anyway." Cindy took a deep breath. "It's even more complicated than that."

Jesus, Tess thought. She looked out at Helene again, making a throat-cutting gesture to indicate she should cut the caller off. Now!

"Em … so how is it more complicated?" she asked.

"Well, I gave up my job for him, for one thing."

"What did you do that for?" Tess couldn't keep the astonishment out of her voice.

"We worked in the same firm and he said it would look bad if it got out about us. Anyway, being a trophy girlfriend was a job in itself, I can tell you," Cindy said with feeling. "All those manicures and pedicures and waxes and shopping. He said that me looking good made *him* look good. Hah! We'll see how good he looks when his wife gets around to him. I wonder will she threaten to cut *him*?" Her voice rose hopefully.

This was insane. Tess was going to have to end it. "How old are you, Cindy?" she asked briskly.

"Twenty-five."

"And your boyfriend is?"

"Forty-five. Ish."

"And before his wife rang you to say she'd cut you if you didn't leave him alone, did you never suspect that he might be married already? At forty-five years of age?"

"He said he was separated," Cindy said sulkily.

"So what did you work at before you became a … er … trophy girlfriend?"

"I was a secretary. His secretary. He's a partner in a law firm."

"And how much did you earn?"

Ollie leaned forward on his desk again, interested now despite himself.

"Thirty thousand euro."

"And so was he going to pay you thirty thousand euro a year for being his girlfriend?"

"*No!*" Cindy was horrified. "What do you think I am? A prostitute?"

"I just wondered how you thought you could afford to give up your job, that's all," Tess said mildly.

"I didn't think of it like that. We were having fun. We went to restaurants, weekends away …" Cindy sounded wistful now.

"But now you're left with no job and no boyfriend and a wife threatening you."

"You're not very sympathetic!" Cindy burst out. "You're supposed to be an agony aunt. Aren't you supposed to be giving me advice?"

"Yes, well … I'm getting to that," Tess countered. "I think you should dump him."

"That's it?" Cindy was incredulous. "That's your advice?"

"Yes, it is. You're involved in a situation that is making you unhappy. And unsafe. Who wants to be in a situation where someone is threatening to come around and cut them? So, yes, Cindy – I say dump him. Go out with your friends. Research new career options. Read a good book. Get a life!" Oh dear. She hadn't meant to sound so harsh. Still, she *had* asked. "So anyway, that's my advice," she said in a softer tone. "And er ... thank you for calling." Her whole body was now bathed in a film of sweat and she badly needed to get some air. And maybe a vodka and tonic.

"And now ..." She took a deep breath and looked down to finally read her script.

"Tess! You have another caller!" Helene sounded surprised herself this time. "Er ... the same drill as before, I suppose. Ask her for her name and her problem."

Tess had to swallow hard before she could speak. "Okay so ... and I believe we have another caller. Hello, caller, may I ask your name? Caller?" I'm babbling, Tess thought wildly, I need to stop babbling.

"Certainly, dearie. My name is Rosa. But most people call me Grandma Rosa."

Tess felt the blood drain from her face. The *fortune teller* was calling her?

"So you have a problem, Grandma Rosa?" she asked in a strained voice.

"Yes!" Rosa's voice was filled with suppressed excitement. "I was listening in and I heard you're called the Agony Aunt of the Airwaves. So I thought, well, I have plenty of agony going on in my life at the moment. Do you think you can help me?"

"Well, that depends on what the problem is." Tess's words felt like cotton wool in her mouth.

"In a nutshell? That's easy – my business is going down the drain."

Tess opened her mouth to reply but, again, no sound came out. She could hear the silence roaring in her ears. But what was she supposed to say here? She wasn't a business guru! And she knew by now there was no point in looking to Helene or Ollie for help.

"So aren't you going to ask me what my business is, dearie?" Rosa said.

"Right. Good idea." Even to her own ears, Tess sounded slightly dazed. "So what is your business, Grandma Rosa?"

"I'm a fortune teller. But," Rosa's voice dipped to a confidential tone, "things have been pretty slow of late. I think one of the reasons is because I had a little heart scare? Maybe my clients think I'm out of action, but I am most certainly not. I'm fully recovered and if I could just give out my number …"

"Oh, we're not a free advertising service!" Tess cut in quickly.

"Oh!" Rosa sounded disappointed.

"The problems we're interested in hearing about are the kind that other listeners might identify with. Maybe more of an emotional nature? For a business venture, perhaps you might be better off contacting your local enterprise board?"

"Well, I'm sure I'm not the only listener with business problems," Rosa replied. "Not in this day and age. I mean, if Michael O'Leary or Richard Branson, for instance, rang to say they were having a slump in their business, would you tell them to contact their local enterprise board?"

Tess massaged a vein pulsing in her temple. If Michael O'Leary or Richard Branson were to ring an agony aunt on a flop local radio station looking for business advice, proverbial pigs would be flying around the studio.

"I don't think that scenario is very likely, do you?" she managed to mutter.

"Hmmm ... I suppose it isn't, now that you say it," Rosa agreed. "Look, I'll be honest with you. What I really want to know is how can I get on to the radio like you? Telling fortunes? People would be very interested, I think. And it would give my business a nice little boost."

Tess put her head in her hands and, at the same time, Helene finally came back to life.

"I'm cutting off this old bat!" she hissed in Tess's ear. "Just say goodbye to her and that you hope she has better 'fortune' coming to her. Geddit?" She laughed mirthlessly at her own joke before adding ominously, "And Tess? You have another caller!"

Tess looked out at her in alarm. Where were they all coming from? Tess had no sooner said goodbye to Rosa than Helene had plugged the next caller through.

"Hello, caller, can I ask you your name and problem?" Tess asked tonelessly.

"Yes. Like your last caller, my problem is a business-orientated one."

It was a male voice.

"Well, you must have also heard me say that we're just dealing with emotional problems this morning," Tess said flatly.

"But there's an emotional side to it as well," the caller cut in quickly.

Tess thought she caught a funny, familiar lilt to his voice.

"So? Are you going to tell me what it is? The problem?" she asked impatiently. She was aware of Helene giving her dagger looks through the glass screen but all Tess cared about at this stage was getting rid of this caller and getting herself out of the studio.

"Well," he said slowly, "I'm considering investing in a business. But it's mainly because someone very close to me has asked me to. And I'm not convinced it's a good idea."

"And?"

"So should I heed what my head is telling me to do and give the business a wide berth – which is what any self-respecting businessman would do? Or should I indulge the person who wants me to invest and, for once in my life, do something that isn't motivated by the bottom line?"

His voice rose on the last word and Tess realised why he sounded familiar. He was the guy she'd met at the fortune teller's house! She drew her brows together, perplexed. How strange he would call directly after Rosa. But she had no time to figure it out. They were still live and she needed to perform.

"You're asking if you should indulge the person who wants you to invest. But isn't the standard advice for business folk that you don't let your heart rule your head?"

"Yes, it is. But isn't there more to life than business?" the caller countered.

Ollie chose that moment – finally – to speak.

"I think you seem to be going around in circles here, Tess!" he sniggered.

"Yes, I think we are," Tess quickly agreed. She had told everyone this was going to be a disaster, but it gave her no pleasure to be proven right. She leaned into the mike. "In fact, I don't think I'm the best person to consult on this problem. So from Tess Morgan on the *This Morning* show … it's goodbye." Tess heard her voice shake on the last word.

"No. Wait!"

The caller was still on the line, but Tess threw her headphones onto the desk. She stood up to leave. She could vaguely hear Ollie talking to the caller in soothing tones, apologising on her behalf.

"I'm so sorry about this, caller. But it seems that's all for today, folks, from our new Agony Aunt of the Airwaves, Tess Morgan. Not exactly what I was expecting, mind you, and probably not what you were expecting at home either. But these things take time to settle and no doubt Tess will be back soon to 'solve' another batch of your problems. Can't wait. Meanwhile, it's time for another disc."

And the sound of another heavy-metal number blasted over the airwaves.

CHAPTER SEVEN

Tess's face was flushed scarlet as she stumbled out of the studio. She was dimly aware of Helene waving her arms at her, exclaiming how she had just abandoned a caller on air, and Sara saying she hadn't given any details for where listeners should send their problems.

Tess rushed past them, close to tears. She hurried to her desk, intent on grabbing her bag and getting out of the building. She glanced at Andrea, who was staring at the radio with a bewildered expression. She jumped up when she saw Tess, her eyebrows almost disappearing under her fringe.

"*What* just happened?"

Not trusting herself to speak, Tess gestured for Andrea to follow her. Outside on the main street, while she waited for Andrea to catch up, she gulped in deep breaths of fresh, cold air. Passers-by were going about their business, shopping and sipping coffee in Zelda's café across the street, unaware and uncaring that Tess had just made a monumental fool of herself. That thought calmed Tess down somehow and, by the time Andrea exited the building, she was already beginning to rationalise everything.

The sky hadn't fallen in, she told herself, as Andrea linked her arm and steered her across the road. People were continuing with their lives, oblivious to Tess Morgan's woes. They by-passed Zelda's, the smell of greasy fish and chips making Tess feel nauseous, and headed automatically for Ryan's bar. The dark cool interior of the pub felt safe after the experience in the studio. Tess picked a seat at the back while Andrea went to get the drinks.

"Bit early for vodka, but in the circumstances," Andrea said wryly a few minutes later, plonking two glasses of vodka and miniature bottles of tonic water on the table between them. She poured, then took a sip of her own drink, looked at Tess gravely and deadpanned, "Well, the slot didn't go too badly in the end, did it?"

Despite herself, Tess felt her mouth twitching. "It's launched my new career in style, that's for sure," she joked, but her hand still shook a little as she took up her glass. "Cheers!"

"Did you know the fortune teller was going to ring?" Andrea was perplexed.

"Of course I didn't know! I thought I would be doing a straightforward read-through of the script, like you and I prepared." Tess closed her eyes against the memory.

"And that Cindy! And the guy saying he wanted to know if he should allow his head to rule his heart. I was dying to hear more from him."

"I met that guy when I went to the fortune teller's. I'm almost sure of it. I recognised his voice. It is so weird that they both rang in today! I wonder if they planned it?"

Andrea shrugged. "Maybe he'll call back next week and you can find out."

"Or *you* can find out. Helene will be hunting for a new Agony Aunt of the Airways so you'd better start preparing now."

"She's not going to drop you the first time out. Look,

Tess, today was a baptism of fire, but you'll know what to expect next time. You'll be better prepared *and* you'll soon learn to think on your feet."

Tess shuddered. "No. Even if Helene doesn't axe me, I'm done. In fact, if you see me going near a microphone again you have permission to cut my head off." She shook her head ruefully. "Remind me again why I thought Ollie's job was easy?"

"It looks easier than it actually is. Maybe that's why Ollie is always bad-tempered. He's probably full of stress with his figures spiralling downwards."

"I'm full of stress and I don't bite people's heads off on a daily basis," Tess said sharply. "Although maybe I did today."

"Anyway," Andrea swirled her drink around her glass, "we'd better think up a defence for the post-mortem this afternoon."

"*Yes, and it had better be a bloody good one!*" came an assertive voice.

Tess whipped around to see Sara approaching their table, a reproachful look on her face.

"How did you find us?" Tess asked. She needed to be left alone until she and Andrea could work out how to minimise the damage she'd done.

Hand on hip, Sara looked at her pityingly. "Zelda's? Ryan's? It wasn't difficult to check both venues." She pulled up a chair and plonked herself down, looking at Tess with saucer eyes. "What happened to you in there?"

"I didn't know anyone was going to ring in and so I didn't have any answers prepared," Tess said. "I don't have Ollie's gift for ad-libbing."

"But you were doing so well – giving Cindy all that advice. Telling her to get a life – that was priceless!"

"Really?" Tess was astonished at what sounded like praise.

"It was great," Andrea agreed. "Radio gold."

"Except you ruined everything by walking off mid-conversation," Sara reminded her. "What came over you?"

"I think I may just have had my first panic attack. I guess I'm not cut out to be on-air, which serves me right for all the times I sniggered at Helene for her efforts. Is she furious because I walked out?" She interlinked her fingers to stop herself from fidgeting and steeled herself to hear all about the fallout from her disastrous debut.

"Furious is an understatement." Sara looked up as the barman approached and ordered herself fizzy water.

"Helene is always furious about something," Andrea pointed out. "She'll get over it."

"But this is different. Because something happened after you left. Something big!" Sara looked from Tess to Andrea with suppressed excitement. "Guess what it was?"

Tess shook her head and Andrea shrugged.

"Guess who the guy was who called in?"

"An escaped prisoner?" Tess offered mildly.

"Hah!" Sara laughed mirthlessly. "Can you guess, Andrea?"

Andrea shook her head. "Tess met him at the fortune teller's house – but she didn't know either of them was going to ring in to the show. Come on, tell us who it was, Sara! Tess has had a very bad morning – and she still has to face Helene and Ollie this afternoon. We don't really have time for guessing games."

Sara tutted. "Call yourselves journalists!" She sat up straighter. "That caller," she took a deep breath and put on her most important voice, "was Jack. As in Jack 'Midas-touch' McCabe!"

"*What?*" Tess shot upright, spilling her drink in the process.

"Don't be ridiculous," Andrea nabbed a wedge of napkins from the tray of a passing barman and dabbed vigorously at the liquid pooling in the middle of their table.

"It's true!" Sara's voice rose an octave. "Richard Armstrong recognised his voice straight away. He came storming into the studio just after you left, Tess. He really laid into Helene for letting Jack McCabe on without telling him about it first. Said negotiations are at a very sensitive stage. Helene asked him how she was supposed to know it was Jack McCabe when he didn't give his name and Richard hadn't told her *anything*. And then she started quizzing him about that caller Cindy who was having the affair with the married man. She said to him, '*Did it remind you of anyone, Richard? Like us, perhaps?*'." Sara stopped to take a breath. "Did you two know Helene and Richard were having an affair?"

"No!" Tess was shocked.

But Andrea was silent, still swirling the dregs of her drink around the bottom of her glass.

"You knew, Andrea?" Sara was openly astonished.

"I had a suspicion, that's all." Andrea changed the subject. "So, what's the strategy for the post-mortem?"

"I don't know." Tess was still trying to get her head around the fact that she had just left the future owner of the station dangling in the middle of an on-air call. "That can't be right, can it, though? A top businessman looking for advice from an agony aunt? And going to a fortune teller? What sort of man would do that?"

"I know." Andrea shook her head. "You couldn't make it up!"

"I suppose I did ask him to ring ..." Tess said vaguely.

"You what?" Andrea looked bewildered.

"When I met him at Rose Cottage – that's where the fortune teller lives – I asked him to call in to the programme with a problem to start the slot off, but then he wouldn't tell me what his problem was so I told him not to bother."

"But he was Jack McCabe, so he did, " Sara butted in. "Of course he did! He was probably doing his research."

"Into what?" Andrea raised her eyebrows.

"Into the station. How we get our stories, that sort of thing."

"But he never said who he was – even after I said I worked for Atlantic," Tess said.

"Well, he wouldn't. It was probably a test," Sara declared.

"And, er … did you ask the fortune teller to call in too?" Andrea asked.

"No! I wasn't expecting either of them! Or Cindy, whoever she is. But look, hands up. I should have been able to handle the situation no matter what was thrown at me. As I keep saying, being on air is just not me."

"You're being way too hard on yourself!" Andrea protested. "Everybody makes mistakes the first time they try something. It's just that yours was very visible, and that makes it harder. But, if we're to believe Helene about our falling listenership, not that many people will have heard it anyway."

"But the people who mattered heard it. Helene. Richard Armstrong. Jack McCabe. But on the bright side," Sara said, "there was a very good reaction to Grandma Rosa – loads of people were ringing in for her number."

"Really?" Tess brightened. Maybe things wouldn't be so bad once she'd faced the wrath of Ollie and Helene.

But, back at the station, as the time came and went for the programme meeting there was no sign of either Helene or

Ollie. Tess's dark thoughts returned. They were probably having a summit meeting about this morning's fiasco. She tried to concentrate on her work but the time crawled by. She was delighted when Andrea swung by on her way home.

"I have an hour before my train leaves if you want to talk about it some more?"

"Great!" Tess gathered her things. "Where?"

"The pub?" Andrea flashed her a sympathetic look.

But Tess's hopes of a quiet drink were dashed almost as soon as she walked back into Ryan's bar. She was carrying drinks down to their table when she caught a glimpse of Helene, partially hidden by a marble pillar, and perched on a bar stool.

Tess tiptoed by and had just reached her table, congratulating herself on passing by unseen, when Helen's voice cracked after her like a whip.

"Tess Morgan!"

She turned to see Helene lurching unsteadily towards their table.

"Here comes trouble," Andrea muttered as Tess hastily sat down.

Tess frowned as Helene came closer. Two patches of bright red flushed her cheeks and her eyes were glazed as if she was having trouble focussing. She seemed drunk. But Helene was far too much of a control freak for that to happen at this stage of the early evening.

Seconds later, as Helene banged her glass of wine so hard onto the table that it spilt over the top, Tess had to hastily revise her opinion. She grabbed some tissues out of her bag and mopped at the blood-red wine.

"Helene, why don't you sit down and join us?" Andrea said coolly.

Helene slumped into a seat and peered at Tess over the

rim of her glass. "So this is where you've got to. You storm out of the studio leaving me to deal with your mess. And here you are – drinking!"

Tess raised her eyebrows. Kettles calling pots black came to her mind, but she thought she should at least make it clear that she had spent the afternoon at the station. She opened her mouth to speak but Helene raised an imperious hand.

"Save it, Tess. I've given you every opportunity to better yourself. I gave you your own *on-air slot* for God's sake. But you not only made a mess of it, you walked out on your mistakes as well. And that," she grabbed her glass and took a big gulp, "is a heinous crime in my book."

Tess stifled a giggle. A heinous crime indeed. What would Helene call a mass murder?

Helene surveyed her suspiciously. "Do you think it's funny?"

"No." Tess bit her lip.

"Did you know that caller was actually Jack McCabe?"

"No! How could I have known that?" Tess was indignant. "Sara told us at lunchtime. Before that I didn't have a clue."

"Did you know?" Helene turned to Andrea.

Andrea shook her head.

Helene looked at Tess malevolently. "He was probably putting us through some sort of test. One that we've obviously failed. Thanks to you!"

"But why would he do something like that?" Tess asked a bit desperately. She thought of what Sara had said earlier. "Was it some sort of market research, do you think?"

"How the hell do I know?" Helene snapped. "The point is you should have been prepared to talk off the cuff to callers. You were billed as an Agony Aunt of the Airwaves for God's sake!"

"I didn't think *any* callers were ringing in today," Tess pointed out. "I thought I was simply reading a script."

"And she didn't know he was Jack McCabe when she asked him to ring in!" Andrea said in support.

Helene swivelled around and glared at Tess. "You *asked* Jack McCabe to ring in? And you didn't tell me?" Her voice rose incredulously. "Didn't you just say you didn't know who he was?"

"I asked a random stranger to ring in – I didn't know who he was at the time. And in the end I told him not to bother!" Tess desperately tried to explain. "If I'd known he was Jack McCabe I wouldn't even have spoken to him."

"Where did you meet him?" Helene asked suspiciously.

"At that fortune teller's. Grandma Rosa's."

"Grandma Rosa? So you invited that old bat to ring in today too! The one looking for her own slot?"

"No!" Tess said quickly. "I had no idea she was going to ring. Or Cindy either!"

"Well, at least I knew about Cindy." Helene lifted her glass and drank deeply.

"You knew about Cindy?" Andrea raised her eyebrows.

"Well, I didn't know what she was going to say. Richard said he'd set someone up to help Tess out – and to give the slot a kick-start. Not that it matters now." She stared moodily into her drink.

"It's clear I'm not cut out for being on-air," Tess offered. She swung her satchel onto her shoulder, preparing for an early exit.

"You can say that again," Helene responded bitterly. "What you did," she narrowed her eyes across the table at Tess, "is a sackable offence!"

"Excuse me?" Tess was dumbfounded. First it was a 'heinous crime' and now this? Helene was obviously even drunker than she looked.

"Not being properly prepared for your work. Walking out of studio." Helene stared at the drink in front of Tess. "Drinking!"

Tess looked at Helene's wineglass pointedly. "It's five thirty, Helene. We're entitled to have a drink if we want to."

"Maybe we've all had a bit too much to drink," said Andrea.

"Yes," Tess agreed. "We can talk about it tomorrow."

"Why did you tell Cindy to dump her lover?" Helene asked abruptly.

"I just said the first thing that came into my head!" Tess stopped short, remembering what Sara had said about Helene having an affair with Richard. Did she think Tess had known about the affair and was making fun of her? "Helene, I would never assume to know what other people should do with their lives," she said hesitantly. "That's why I was so worried about taking up the agony-aunt slot in the first place."

"You can cut the Little Miss Innocent act," Helene snapped. "I know what you must think about me and Richard. What everyone thinks. But that's not the point. The real issue here is that you walked out of studio. I just don't know if I can trust you again, Tess."

"I didn't know anything about you and Richard," Tess began but felt a sharp jab as Andrea's elbow made contact with her ribs. She bit her lip to stop herself from saying any more. But suddenly she was sick of it all. Of being scapegoated by Ollie when things went wrong, of being hounded by Helene to produce better results, of trying in vain to get validation for her efforts from either of them. But none of it had worked.

"It's true. I *can't* trust you any more, Tess." Helene obviously hadn't finished with her yet.

Tess slumped back down in her seat, defeated. She'd just have to wait for the onslaught to pass.

"Which is why," Helene knocked back the rest of her wine in one gulp, "I'm going to have to let you go. I'll have to find someone else to do the slot."

"Oh, hang on a minute!" Andrea intervened.

But Tess felt a wave of relief sweep over her. She was dismayed at how much of a flop she had been but at least now she wouldn't have to go through it all again next week. She could concentrate on the job she had and hope she kept it when the takeover happened.

"No argument," Helene said. "I'm letting you go. And from being producer on *This Morning* too. I am going to give Sara the opportunity, see what she makes of it. You can have her job if you like. But that means Sara will be your boss so I'll understand if you want to consider your options."

"You can't be serious?" Tess couldn't keep the dismay out of her voice.

"You can't just demote someone in a pub!" Andrea gave Helene a warning look. "Especially after you've had a bit to drink."

Helene twisted her head to look at Andrea, and Tess realised she was about to turn on her too.

"Leave it, Andrea." Tess turned to face Helene. "Do you think it's pleasant working for you, Helene? Someone whose moods change like the weather? Someone who likes to dish out the blame but can't face up to their own part in things?" Her voice rose, a well of suppressed feelings suddenly exploding inside her. "And do you think I studied my arse off in college to sit listening to people phoning me

Joan Brady

in with problems I do not have *any* idea how to solve?"

"If that's how you feel, you're clearly in the wrong job, because that is exactly what I needed you to do," Helene retorted. "So if you don't want to work under Sara, consider yourself sacked."

"That's constructive dismissal," Andrea said quickly. "It's – er – illegal."

"I'm glad you can find something constructive about today." Helene gave them both the benefit of a glassy smile.

Tess stood up shakily.

"Tess!" Andrea put her hand on Tess's arm. "Sit down," she commanded. "We can work this out. Helene! Please!"

But Helene had a stubborn set to her mouth and didn't look in the mood to change her mind.

Tess brushed off Andrea's hand and made for the exit, half expecting Helene to call her back, to tell her that the whole thing had got out of hand and they would talk about it again tomorrow.

But she reached the door and Helene had still made no move to stop her. She pushed it open and blinked into the early evening. A fine drizzle of rain had started. She stepped out onto the pavement, bending her head against the misty droplets. She could hardly believe what had just happened. She was out of Atlantic 1FM.

CHAPTER EIGHT

Helene stretched out on a day bed at Spa Fantastic, propped up on a giant cushion. With all the drama at work she had almost forgotten about her *Ten Years Younger* project. Sara had texted her late last night to remind her she was booked into the hotel today and she was glad to get away for a couple of days. But now that she was actually here, it all felt a bit spooky.

She had read up on all the latest treatments available and, frankly, they sounded terrifying – ranging from needles being stuck in your face to chemical peels that would leave your complexion raw and red for days before the new, younger skin would allegedly put in an appearance. So, she'd opted for all the pain-free treatments instead.

She looked around the room, at the dimmed lights and flickering candles. Multi-coloured tropical fish were swimming aimlessly from one end of a huge aquarium to the other and weird whale music spilled from the speakers on the wall. The other six loungers, resplendent with huge white cushions and fluffy comfort blankets, were empty.

Helene's nerves were still frayed over the Agony Aunt of the Airwaves debacle, and the fact that she had somehow managed to sack Tess. She didn't want to think about it but the silence at the spa was unnerving. She pulled out her mobile to see if she had any messages. She half expected to see a text from Tess, asking for her job back. That would have allowed her to agree magnanimously and everything could be back to normal before anyone realised anything about it. But there were no new messages.

She felt someone standing behind her and looked up to see the manager, shaking his head reprovingly at her phone.

"What?" she snapped. "Are you afraid it will disturb the fish?" She shoved the phone into the pocket of her fluffy robe, pressed her head back into the cushion, and ordered herself to relax. This was her chance to get de-stressed, detoxed and distracted from the toxic atmosphere at work and she wasn't going to waste it.

So far she'd had a Reiki session, a Hopi ear candle treatment and was now waiting to get something called a Sole to Soul holistic experience, which involved a foot massage and some weird chanting. Sara had organised it, but how it was supposed to make her look ten years younger was anyone's guess. And the real irony, Helene reflected ruefully, was that she now felt about a hundred instead of forty.

She felt so wound-up that when she closed her eyes, instead of visualising a perfect white Caribbean beach, as the therapist had instructed her to do earlier, all she could see was the agony-aunt slot playing across her mind like an unwanted film.

How had it all happened, Helene wondered, giving her shoulders a little shake. How had she, Helene Harper, self-confessed control freak, let it all happen? She cast her mind back over the sequence of events. First up, there had been the call from Cindy. Helene had been expecting her to call, was waiting to plug her through to Tess. But when she had heard her 'problem'– which mirrored her own life so neatly – she had been dumbstruck.

It had been Richard's idea to use Cindy in the first place. Helene's eyes narrowed as she tried to piece it all together.

The night before the agony-aunt slot was due to air she and Richard had finally got some time together. It was the first uninterrupted evening they had spent together since all the changes had taken place at work and Helene had been determined to make the most of it. Richard had dropped in to her apartment unexpectedly around seven and, naturally, they had gone straight to bed. Richard had been ebullient, she remembered, giddily optimistic about the future. Afterwards, he had been all over Helene, even insisting on cooking for her. He had whisked up his speciality dish of linguine pasta with asparagus sauce, which Helene had interpreted as a very encouraging gesture indeed.

As they shared a bottle of wine, she confided that she was worried about the agony-aunt slot.

"That's your trouble, Helene," Richard teased, kissing her on the forehead. "You worry too much."

"But I want it to go well," she fretted. "Maybe I should have arranged for someone to ring in?" She looked at the clock. "I wonder is it too late to get someone now?"

"It's never too late, Helene," Richard said jovially, pouring himself another glass of wine.

She looked at the half-empty bottle. She had barely started on her wine. She sipped some while she watched him punching some numbers into his phone.

He looked at her. "Relax. I'll deal with it."

Helene heard a female voice on the other end as Richard took the phone out to the hall. When he returned, he told her everything was sorted. A woman named Cindy, who he described as an out-of-work actress, would call in to the show the next day and she'd have a problem. Simple.

Relieved, Helene had finally allowed herself to relax. They had gone back to bed and he'd stayed much longer than normal. At one stage she even thought he was going to stay the night but at the last minute he insisted he had to go home. But everything had seemed absolutely fine. Better than fine.

And then, the very next morning, all hell had broken loose. Helene had been so preoccupied with Cindy's 'problem', and why the hell it had been about a love triangle involving a married boss, and whether Richard was making some sort of passive-aggressive point, that she hadn't paid any attention to the caller who had turned out to be Jack McCabe.

She had thought he was a random caller and put him through as absentmindedly as she would anybody. Next thing she knew Tess Morgan was barging out of studio, leaving the caller hanging on in mid-sentence. And then, just as she was trying to find out from Sara what the hell had happened, Richard had come storming into the studio, asking why had Helene allowed Jack McCabe to go on air without informing him.

"He hasn't signed on the dotted line yet, Helene! Didn't you think it *important* enough to tell me he was about to go on air?"

She had never seen him like that before. Looking at him, in a full-on temper tantrum, with his complexion all red and his eyes sort of bulging, she'd been afraid he might have a heart attack there in front of her. She'd been that concerned for him.

But then he'd hissed at her, "I cannot stress how important it is that Jack McCabe buys in, Helene. I just hope you haven't blown it!"

"Actually, I was listening to Cindy, and her interesting

problem about having an affair with a married man," she'd snapped. "Did it remind you of anyone, Richard? Like us, perhaps? Did you tell Cindy what to say?"

Richard had looked at her as if she'd lost her mind. "Of course I didn't. She's an *actress*. She made it up."

"Well, I think it's a great big coincidence that Cindy would just happen to phone in with that particular problem," she'd said stubbornly.

"Helene!" Richard had thrown a warning look at Sara, who was all ears, her head swivelling from Richard to Helene and back again, openly staring at them as it dawned on her that her boss and her boss's boss were having an affair. "Great! Bloody great!"

Richard turned on his heel and left, slamming the studio door behind him.

Helene had settled back shakily into her chair. She was acutely conscious of Sara stealing sidelong glances at her and knew it was only a matter of time before it was all over Facebook, Twitter and whatever other hideous social-networking site had been invented in the ten minutes since Helene had last looked ... unless she could come up with a way of silencing her assistant. That's when she'd had the idea of offering her the producer job she'd wanted for so long. Tess Morgan's job. It had only been a fleeting thought. She would never have gone through with it if she hadn't gone to Ryan's. She had left a message on Richard's phone, asking him to meet her there but he hadn't shown up. And she had become so stressed that she drank the whole bottle of wine she had ordered for them to share. She had then spotted Tess Morgan acting as if nothing at all had happened and something in her had snapped.

Now, of course, she realised she had acted way over her pay grade. She didn't actually have the right to fire anyone.

She was surprised Tess hadn't figured that out by now. She was probably going to sue her for wrongful dismissal! Helene wiped her forehead with one of the white towels piled up beside her and picked up a leaflet from the table – anything to distract herself from the torture of her own thoughts. *The Spa Fantastic is where top people come to relax and be pampered*, she read. *A sumptuous oasis of Me Time, a place to renew and revitalise.*

It was exactly what Helene had thought she needed. But when she turned her gaze towards the floor-to-ceiling windows of the spa, all she could see was rain driving through the fields. She could hear the wind howling like a banshee through a small vent in the windows.

"You ready for your Sole to Soul experience?" A girl with an Australian accent appeared beside Helene's day bed. She had a name badge with *Annie* printed on it pinned to her white therapist jacket.

Annie looked unnervingly healthy – a tall and tanned young woman with athletic limbs, big white teeth and an absurdly cheerful countenance.

"I think so," Helene said with some trepidation.

She followed Annie down a dim corridor and into one of the treatment rooms, her spa slippers sinking into the thick pile carpet.

"Just relax," Annie soothed.

She started by pouring oil on Helene's feet and as the scent of roses filled the room Helene could feel the muscles in her body relaxing. But then Annie got her to remove her robe and began to hum and wave her hands in a weird formation over Helene's body, stopping at certain parts as if she was listening to something.

Helene's shoulders shot up around her ears, all the tension back again.

"Relax. I'm trying to unblock your chakras," Annie explained cheerfully.

"My whats?" Helene frowned.

"Your energy points, according to Eastern philosophy. Your throat chakra in particular feels blocked. That means you have a lot to say for yourself but you've never really been able to express it. Does that make sense to you?"

"Yes, it does!" Helene was amazed. That's exactly how she felt when she was talking to Richard lately. Unheard. She felt a surge of excitement. "Can you unblock it for me? The chakra whatsit?"

"Not in one session, mate," Annie replied, thumping her on the shoulders. "And not by me. It's something I picked up on in India but I'm only a beginner."

"You've been to India?" Helene thought of Matt and all the places he'd been to, and the way he'd marked them out with tiny yellow pins on the map on the wall of the café.

"Yeah. It was part of my world trip. This is too."

Annie asked Helene to turn on to her stomach and began to knead the knotted-up muscles in her neck and shoulders.

It must be the travelling that made Annie and Matt so relaxed, Helene decided.

The thought of her and Richard travelling together came back to her and she drifted into a very pleasant daydream where she was backpacking with Richard in India. She had given away all her designer clothes and she didn't need any products at all, just a bit of soap and a toothbrush and an old comb because her hair was cut really short.

But then Annie spoilt it by giving her a slap across the small of her back.

"That's it," she said. "You're all done."

She led Helene to yet another relaxation area, where a tray of mint tea and a single strawberry was set out on a small table beside another heated lounger. Helene settled into it, sipping the tea and flicking through the pages of one of the glossy magazines piled up on the table beside her. After only a few minutes she dropped the magazine listlessly. Jesus, she hadn't realised spas were so *boring*.

She fished out her mobile again and felt her heart rate quicken. Four missed calls! She'd switched her phone to silent while she'd been having the Sole to Soul treatment. She stared at the screen. They were all from the same number: Richard's. She hadn't heard from him since he'd stormed off in his huff, even though she had texted him several times. Well, she wasn't going to be available as soon as he decided he was ready to talk to her.

She stuffed the mobile unanswered into the pocket of her robe and picked up a silver vanity mirror from the side-table. She pulled her chestnut-brown hair away from her face and scrutinised her features carefully. Her eyebrows were artfully plucked, her hair carefully coloured, her high, disdainful cheekbones a distinct genetic advantage. She looked at her long, pale throat, picturing it blocked because she couldn't express herself.

She spotted Annie carrying a bale of white towels to another treatment room.

"Hey! Can you tell me how I can find out more about this chakra stuff?" she called after her. She felt excited at the idea of being able to express herself properly.

"Sorry, I have another client at the moment," Annie called back.

"Well, can you get me a radio then?" Helene had promised herself a media-free few days, but the whale music echoing eerily through the room was seriously freaking her out.

"I'll get the manager to look after you," Annie promised,

disappearing into a therapy room.

Five minutes later the manager arrived at Helene's lounger, proffering a personal radio with earphones.

"Is everything to your satisfaction, madam?"

Helene nodded and clamped the earphones over her ears, already fiddling with the dials on the radio, trying to tune in to Atlantic 1FM. All she could find was a local station playing country songs. As she listened to some love-gone-wrong song, her eyelids grew heavy and she dozed off into a dream where Richard told her that he and Louisa had mended their relationship, and were going to travel the world together, and she was pleading with them to take her along too, that three wasn't really a crowd, and Richard was telling her to answer the phone ... answer the phone ...

Helene awoke with a start, conscious of something vibrating against her thigh. Bleary-eyed, she groped around until her hand closed over her mobile. She pulled it out in a panic and squinted at the screen. Richard. Deeply upset by her nightmare, she hit reply straightaway.

"Hello ..." she began. She saw the manager lurking behind a palm-tree plant and hissed, "I'm in a *spa*, Richard. Supposed to be chilling. Why didn't you call me before now?"

But even as she spoke Richard said something in an urgent tone. She only caught the words "get back".

"I need to get back? Why?" She looked at her phone. Maybe she had misheard.

"No. Get *her* back!"

"Who back?" Helene frowned as she tried to focus. She was still feeling quite drowsy.

"Tess Morgan! Andrea told me you *sacked* her?"

"Um ... it was a breakdown in communication, actually." She chewed on her lip.

115

"Jack McCabe *likes* her, Helene!"

"Likes her?" Helene was mystified. "What was there to like? She was on-air for ten minutes and caused absolute chaos in that time!"

"Be that as it may," he replied, "Jack has been on to me raving about her. I think he's definitely going to buy, Helene." He couldn't keep the excitement out of his voice. "So it's up to you to get Tess back – to keep Jack on side."

Helene thought of her last meeting with Tess and swallowed.

"It might not be that easy," she said cautiously.

"Offer her more money. Or her own programme. Whatever it takes," he instructed as if she hadn't spoken.

"Her own programme?" Helene was outraged. "The whole reason the agony-aunt slot went so wrong in the first place is because Tess is not cut out to be on-air."

Jesus. Didn't Richard ever listen to a word she said?

"Well, persuade her, Helene," he said flatly. And then, "Look, as soon as Jack signs on the dotted line, it won't affect us whether Tess Morgan creates chaos or not."

Helene's heart skittered. He had said "us".

"Because we'll be leaving Atlantic?" She held her breath.

"It will be all to play for," he confirmed. "But nothing can go wrong at this juncture, Helene. So I want you to leave whatever it is you're doing there and go and find Tess Morgan."

"Right this minute?" She thought of the paraffin pedicure she had lined up next.

"Yes." A touch of impatience entered Richard's voice. "There'll be plenty of time for spas later."

"It's *work*," she reminded him acidly. "Research for my *Ten Years Younger* series. Why can't you just phone her yourself, anyway? Say it was all a mistake and that you're going over my head."

"Tried already, I'm afraid. Her mobile is switched off."

Helene wrinkled her forehead. He'd already tried to go over her head without even informing her? That wasn't good. But then everything was all mixed up since the takeover bid. As soon as Atlantic was sold, she and Richard could get back to normal. Hopefully.

"Andrea will know where she lives," she said. Maybe *you* could call around?"

"Andrea is off work today. Apparently one of her kids is sick."

Helene snorted. "Welcome to my world. Now you know what I have to deal with every day."

"Look, Helene," he confided, "I shouldn't really be telling anyone this yet, but Jack is about to make his announcement about buying the station shortly."

Helene recalled her conversation with Paulina, Jack's right-hand woman. "Really? And have you heard anything about a search for a new star? One with the ... er ... X-factor?"

"How do you know about that?" Richard asked sharply.

"Oh, there are lots of things you don't know about me, Richard Armstrong," she said flirtatiously.

But Richard wasn't in the mood. "Can you get Tess Morgan back?" he asked sharply.

"Fine," she snapped, deflated. "I'll do it! But, Richard?"

"Yes?"

"*Afterwards*," she let the word hang meaningfully in the air, "you had better make this up to me!"

The phone went dead and Helene tossed it into her bag. She looked at the tropical fish in their aquarium and envied them their simple life. Then she belted up her robe, shoved her feet into her slippers and went up to her bedroom to pack. She'd had only one night here but she checked out with little regret. Spas were not really her thing, she realised, as she threw her weekend case into the boot of her car. She was far too dynamic for all that sitting around.

By the time she arrived home, however, Helene was feeling far from dynamic. Her stomach felt sick and her right ear was itching like mad – probably from that Hopi ear candle therapy she'd had earlier. She threw her bags on the floor in the hall, went into her bedroom and lay down, pulling her patchwork quilt around her shoulders. Far from being revitalised, as the spa had promised, she felt utterly exhausted.

A wave of nausea overcame her and she got up reluctantly, padding into the kitchen searching for something to eat. The hotel's meals had been sparse, tiny portions of health food all designed, allegedly, to help the body to detox. Maybe that's why she felt so ill now?

But she didn't have time to detox, she thought, as she picked up the phone and dialled in an order to the local Chinese takeaway. She still had to figure out how to get Tess back to work. She didn't want to go kow-towing to her, like Richard had suggested. She would just get too big for her boots. No, she would prefer if Tess made the request herself. She just had to figure out how to make that happen.

When the food arrived, the sight of the rice and chicken in their silver aluminium boxes lined up on her kitchen table brought on a fresh wave of nausea and she had to rush for the bathroom. As she dry-retched into the sink, she felt irked all over again that Richard had summoned her back from the spa. Getting Tess back could have waited.

In fact, she thought, with a flash of defiance, it could still wait. She would go and find Tess when she was good and ready. Not a moment before. She dumped the food into the bin, made herself a pot of tea, put on her favourite box set and, for once, forgot about work completely.

CHAPTER NINE

It was the day Jack McCabe was due to make his big announcement about taking over Atlantic 1FM. Rachel Joy, a reporter with the *Killty Times*, was standing at the entrance to the hotel conference room. She was accompanied by a photographer. Helene shifted in her chair and watched them closely. She knew Rachel's unabashed ambition was to work for *The Sun* and with her instinct for trouble there was no reason why she wouldn't achieve it.

Today it was obvious that Rachel had her sights firmly trained on Ollie Andrews. And there was no question but that he was already heavily under the influence. Helene had spoken to him when she had arrived. He was mad as hell at the rumour that Jack McCabe was to announce a competition for a new star today and that he intended to do it in public, so it would be a fait accompli and there wouldn't be anything Ollie could do about it. He hadn't even bothered to suck a mint to camouflage the smell of whiskey on his breath. Glancing back at him now, slumped on a chair in the row behind her, Helene reflected that Jack had yet to realise that Ollie was a law onto himself, and didn't operate by the same social dogma as the rest of the world. After all, Richard wasn't going to tell him how unstable Ollie was, not when he was so desperate for Jack to buy the station.

Richard was sitting at the top table, facing the audience. He was fidgeting, tapping his biro on the white tablecloth and throwing anxious glances at the two empty chairs on either side of him. Helene was delighted to see him so evidently uncomfortable. He had called unexpectedly into her office earlier, asking whether she'd managed to persuade Tess to come back to work yet. She had tried to explain how nauseous and lightheaded she'd been feeling over the last few days – how she hadn't been able to concentrate on anything else – but Richard hadn't even been listening to her.

"Anyhow, what's with Jack McCabe's sudden obsession with Tess Morgan?" she had asked finally. "It doesn't make any sense!"

"I don't know and I don't care," Richard had snapped and banged out of the office.

A movement nearby caught Helene's attention and she turned to see that Jack had finally arrived. Her stomach lurched unexpectedly and she folded her arms protectively around her stomach. Everyone was nervous here today. It was only natural, with so much uncertainty about.

Jack cut an arresting figure as he strode towards the podium to join Richard. He was dressed in a well-cut black suit, white shirt and scarlet tie. Paulina followed him. Her pale blonde hair was caught back in a chignon and her make-up was impeccable. She wore a cherry-red dress and jacket and managed to look both sexy and business-like.

Helene looked around the room to see how other people were reacting to the first sighting of Jack McCabe. Andrea was sitting a few seats down from her, pale-faced and white-knuckled, her hands gripping the arms of her chair. Sara was craning her neck, trying to get a better look at Jack. She was wearing a new outfit, a black fitted short skirt and matching jacket, which, she'd announced earlier, she'd bought especially for today.

"Jack McCabe is, like, a gazillionaire," she'd pointed out seriously, "and still unattached as far as I can make out."

Up on the podium, Jack and Richard exchanged brief nods. Paulina nodded down at Helene and, thrilled with the public recognition, Helene gave her a little wave. She and Paulina had been in touch several times since they'd met at Matt's café. She had been surprised to find Paulina had been every bit as helpful as she was at that first meeting – open about her success and generous with tips on how Helene could take her career forward to the next level. And, if Paulina liked her, surely that was a sign that she would survive the changes that were coming?

Jack got to his feet and tapped the microphone in front of him. A hush came over the crowd.

"Hello there!" He smiled into the audience, commanding the attention of the room instantly. "Firstly, I must apologise for being late. As I'm sure Richard has already explained to you, I was unavoidably delayed with other business, but I appreciate that you're all still here. And, since you've all waited long enough already, I think we should just get on with things, shall we?"

A murmur of assent swept through the room and Jack consulted his notes.

"Secondly, I want to officially confirm that I have bought Atlantic 1FM ..."

Helene let out an audible sigh of relief. Richard was free! She could hardly believe it. After that, she only half listened to the rest of the speech – how Jack was confident he could transform the station into a dynamic new entity, *blah blah blah*.

"The wheels are in motion for us to get a national broadcasting licence . . ."

Then Helene was jolted out of her reverie by Ollie shouting, "*Yeah!*" very loudly and drumming his heels on the ground in a little victory dance.

"Yes, Ollie – it is good news," Jack looked directly at the presenter. "But as I think we've all guessed by now, it will mean changes. And change always brings challenges."

Here it comes, Helene thought, folding her arms tighter. This is where Jack was going to declare he wanted to bring in his own people – young people. People under thirty, with the X-factor. She twisted around to see Ollie's reaction.

"Change is good," Ollie asserted, nodding his head agreeably. His eyes were bloodshot and Helene noticed a warning vein pulsing at his temple.

"So yes, we will be expanding," Jack continued. "And yes, we will be improving. But it's going to take an awful lot of effort from everyone. The station needs to build up its listenership dramatically and we'll need lots of innovative ideas to do that. We also need to re-brand and re-position ourselves in the market, and while I intend to be very hands-on in this project, I have to confess that marketing is not my forte so I am going to hand you over now to Paulina Fox."

A polite round of applause broke out as Paulina got to her feet.

"Thank you." Paulina fingered the pile of papers in front of her and gave a dazzling smile before she began her speech. "As Jack has just said, we have challenging times ahead of us. But sometimes change brings opportunity as well. And for one person – maybe even someone who is here with us today – this could be a very special opportunity to play a very big part in the new, improved Atlantic 1FM!"

Helene leaned forward in her chair.

Paulina cleared her throat and consulted her notes before continuing. "I have been working on the new brand over the past few weeks and Jack and I have agreed that we need to create a new personality to be the face of the revamped station."

Helene glanced back at Ollie. A deathly pallor had replaced his usual high colour and she could see a sheen of sweat glistening on his forehead.

"What do you think that will mean for you, Ollie?" Sara whispered, her eyes wide with alarm.

"What do I think? What do I think? Who the hell cares what I think?" Colour flooded back into Ollie's pale cheeks as his rage rose.

Immediately the press photographer turned his camera away from the podium and trained it on the fuming presenter. Then he twisted it back to Paulina, who was looking at Ollie with open fascination, as if he were an exhibit from a zoo.

"Yes, well, there will be plenty of time to hear what people think later," Paulina said tightly. "But we're here today to launch a competition for the new face of Atlantic 1FM. The person we are looking for must have the X-factor and –"

"The X-factor – hell, that's original!" Ollie Andrews snorted.

He was staring at Paulina with open hatred now and Rachel Joy edged closer, delighted she was getting something juicier than a run-of-the-mill business story.

"The winner," Paulina continued bravely, but her voice was shaking a bit now, "will get his or her own show. In fact, the competition is called '*It's My Show*' and contestants will have to convince us – through a pilot programme, a written paper and perhaps a portfolio of relevant work – that he or she is the person we are looking for."

"I am the voice of Atlantic 1FM," Ollie interrupted, "so why do we need a new *face*?"

Jack stood up and smartly stepped into the breach.

"Let's not get side-tracked here. As Paulina said, we are looking for a *new* person to front the newly revamped station." He held Ollie's gaze until Ollie looked away, before continuing, "That person could be in this room. *It's My Show* is a nationwide competition, but everyone here has the experience to be a serious contender. And, remember, even if you're not the winner, the contest will be a fantastic shop window for your ideas. Ideas are the lifeblood of every organisation and I'm sure I don't have to remind you," he glanced at Ollie again, "it is in *all* our interests to make Atlantic 1FM viable." He sat down, nodding at Paulina to continue.

She smiled gratefully and cleared her throat. "Thank you, Jack. So, what else is there to say?" She glanced at her notes again. "We want to encourage everyone here to put themselves forward for this contest as soon as possible. We are planning a major relaunch party where we will announce the winner. We should have more news about Atlantic 1FM getting a national licence by then too, so we are expecting a strong national media presence there." She glanced around the room, "Any questions?"

"Do I take it I have to apply for my own job?" Ollie asked belligerently.

"As I said, the contest is open to everyone in the room."

"What's in it for the winner?" Rachel Joy pushed a lock of lank fair hair behind her ear and kept her eyes trained on Ollie.

"The winner will have their own weekday show which will run for two hours – he or she will be the face of Atlantic 1FM, an ambassador for the revamped station," Paulina replied smoothly.

"And, as I think someone has already brought up, what will that mean for *This Morning with Ollie Andrews*? Will that show then be axed?" Rachel persisted.

"We will be looking at all our programming in the coming weeks but no decisions have been taken yet." Paulina scanned the room again, looking for someone else to speak.

But it was Rachel who spoke again. "Excuse me? Paulina, isn't it? Is it true there have been problems behind the scenes on *This Morning*? I'm referring to the recent incident where your Tess Morgan walked out of studio in the middle of the broadcast. Is your Agony Aunt of the Airwaves having some work-related problems of her own, perhaps?"

A low titter rose from the crowd.

Paulina coughed. "The Agony Aunt was a pilot slot and, as I said, we will be looking at all our programming."

"Sources suggest there was a personality clash between Ollie Andrews and Tess Morgan," Rachel persisted.

"I'm not aware of that," Paulina replied.

"So why has Tess Morgan left the station then?" Rachel asked.

"Well, I'll have to ask Tess's boss that question." Paulina looked at Helene.

"Um … Tess has other projects on at the moment so it's unclear what her commitment to Atlantic 1FM is." Helene hoped she'd get away with that. It was the safest answer in the circumstances – at least until she got a chance to talk to Tess.

"Thank you, Helene. So ..." Paulina glanced at her notes. "The contestants will have access to whatever expertise they need – a stylist, make-up artist, nutritionist, voice coach maybe. And Jack and I will be on hand to give tips to anyone who wants them. It's really up to the individual to convince us that he or she has what we're looking for. We will be promoting the station on cross media – television advertisements and guest slots as well as blogs and social networking sites – so we want the winner to feel supported. Any more questions?"

"Yes!" Sara's hand shot up. "You mentioned television just there. Is it true the cameras add on ten pounds?"

Everyone laughed except Ollie, who nervously ran his hand over his stomach.

"Yes, they do," Paulina replied. "But we don't want anybody going on a crash diet. We're looking for someone with talent, brains and ambition, not a stick insect."

"So what're the criteria to win?" Andrea asked.

"As I said earlier, it's up to you to convince us with your submissions."

Jack leaned over to whisper something to Paulina. She looked surprised but nodded.

"Jack thinks that some people might like to put forward their names for the contest right now?" She looked at Rachel Joy. "And perhaps the media might talk to those people later about their ambitions?"

Helene threw her eyes heavenwards. Surely she didn't think that was going to distract Rachel Joy from reporting on Ollie's tired and emotional outbursts? She glanced over at Andrea who was opening a file with '*Ideas*' marked on it in blue felt pen. The sight of it reminded Helene of all the ideas she'd had throughout the years, and how hard she'd worked to execute them. All the time and energy she had spent trying to make Ollie Andrew's show successful and to get Richard to want to marry her. Where had it all got her? Nowhere, that was where. Maybe if she'd put all that energy into her own career she could have been as successful as Paulina was now.

Paulina had told her that she'd decided a long time ago to make herself the number-one priority in her own life. And looking at her there on the podium, talking discreetly to Jack about their plans, Helene felt a flash of envy mixed with admiration. Maybe it's not too late, a little voice inside her suggested. Maybe this was an opportunity to reinvent herself? Richard had always promised Helene she would have her own show one day, but it had never happened. How could she be sure that he would ever leave Louisa either? It was the fear that made up her mind. Her hand shot up. If she declared herself as a contestant now she wouldn't be able to talk herself out of it later.

"Yes, Helene?" Paulina smiled encouragingly.

"Hello, Paulina." Helene stood up. "And ... Mr McCabe."

"It's Jack," he said with a smile.

"Well, Jack, my name is Helene Harper and I am currently an executive editor at Atlantic 1FM. I'd like to be considered for the new um ... the new face of the station."

"Traitor!" Helene heard Ollie hissing at her but she ignored him.

The photographer was angling his camera to get a close-up of Helene and she beamed at him encouragingly. She was in the limelight already! Out of the corner of her eye she could see Richard looking at her in bafflement but she ignored him as well, anxious that the photographer should get a good shot of her.

"Great, Helene. Well done!" Paulina looked pleased. She

waved a pen in the air. "Anyone else?"

Sara sprang off her chair. "Count me in!"

"You? Up until recently you were only an assistant!" Ollie exploded.

"Why not? I'm young and I'm hot!" Sara whipped around to face Ollie.

The photographer abandoned Helene instantly and made a beeline for Sara, where he was rewarded with a sexy pout.

Ollie had had enough. He scraped back his chair and stood up.

"This contest is a charade," he announced. "A cheap publicity stunt. I am currently the voice *and* the face of Atlantic 1FM. And I intend to stay that way. I have a loyal audience who will not be impressed if I am replaced by some ... some ... whippersnapper! And," he turned to face Rachel Joy, "you can quote me on that!"

"Oh, I will." Rachel was scribbling again, a beatific smile on her face.

"Yes, well, let's wrap it up for today then, shall we?" Paulina said quickly. She sat down and shuffled her papers, looking drained. Jack put a comforting hand on her shoulder.

Helene looked around the room, mentally checking out the competition so far, giving each of her potential rivals a score out of ten.

Andrea would only get a four – she was bound to put herself forward later on, but she had too many domestic commitments to be truly single-minded about the contest. Ollie was now clearly yesterday's man so she was giving him a big fat zero. Sara was bright and energetic and certainly had potential but she lacked the killer instinct – too spoilt by Daddy's money, Helene reckoned – and wouldn't be prepared to put in anything like the work required. She would give her a six.

That left her as the leader by a long shot. Of course, there would be external candidates, but Helene liked a challenge. Isn't that why she'd stuck with Richard for so long? As if on cue, she noticed Richard walking towards her, not bothering to hide his discomfort.

Helene hesitated. She had just made a very public pitch for a very public role when their plan had always been for both of them to make their new life far away from the limelight. Up to today, she would have been more than happy with that. She had seen her hopes of her own show fading over the years and she had come to accept that it wasn't going to happen for her.

But now everything had changed. Richard's intentions were unclear to say the least and now this career opportunity had opened up right in front of her.

"I need to talk to you," Richard hissed.

He grabbed her by the arm and manhandled her towards a corner of the room, away from any eavesdroppers.

"What did you go and enter the competition for?" he asked.

"Because I want my own show! Why do you think?" She shrugged off Richard's grip.

"I don't want you in the limelight, Helene. You know that."

"You know I always wanted my own show!" she retorted. They had never discussed how it had never happened for her. Whenever she had tried to bring it up in the past, Richard had changed the subject.

"I think Jack knows I'm having an affair!" Richard's eyes were bulging slightly.

"With me?" Her pulse quickened.

"I don't think he knows it's with you. Yet. But if you're

competing for *It's My Show* you're hardly going to blend into the background, now are you?"

Helene raised her eyebrows. "Tell me what I'm missing here, Richard? You are leaving Atlantic. So our having an affair is Jack's business because ...?"

Richard averted his eyes. "Look, I haven't been exactly straight with you about something. But now ... well, I ... I need to tell you that ..."

"What?" Helene felt a stab of fear.

"Jack McCabe is Louisa's brother."

Helene stifled a laugh. "Richard, that is so spectacularly unfunny!"

"It's not a joke," he said flatly.

"Jack McCabe is your brother-in-law?" Helene was frankly incredulous.

"I'm afraid so. It's the only reason he's buying into the station in the first place."

"And you're only telling me this now?" She was genuinely mystified.

"I didn't think you needed to know," he said.

"Oh, so you're like the CIA now – supplying information on a need-to-know basis?" she snapped.

"I've only just found out that Jack suspects I'm having an affair," he pleaded. "It was something he said when he arrived today ..." He threw a worried look back at the podium. "But I'm pretty sure he doesn't realise it's with you. So act professional."

Helene followed his gaze and saw Jack's eyes trained on them. It's actually true, she thought, sick to the pit of her stomach. He did suspect something. Then another thought struck her.

"So this means that Anna and David are – Jack's niece and nephew?"

Richard nodded. Helene clutched her stomach. Jack McCabe was going to hate her. Not only would she not get the *It's My Show* gig, she would probably be booted out of her job altogether.

"Are you sure he doesn't know that I'm the other woman?"

Richard shook his head. "I've just said. I'm pretty sure he doesn't."

"I'll withdraw from the contest. I'll resign from Atlantic 1FM altogether. We can go away, me and you. We can go travelling!" She grasped his arm. "I've been to this amazing new café at the end of the village. It's called the Travel Café and you can find out anything you want to know about trips abroad. I know the guy who runs it and he'll help me. I'll do all the research, plan our itinerary ... Richard, maybe this is all for the best. Now we're forced to be up front with people, we can finally be together. And it won't be as difficult as it would be if we were still living and working around here."

She stopped, conscious that she was babbling.

"Are you mad?" It was his turn to shrug her off. "I can't leave my children to go off gallivanting with you. And I'll have to build up a new business. Look, we just need to lie low for a while, that's all. You pull out of the contest – take the attention away from yourself. And obviously we won't be able to see each other for a while ..."

Helene shivered. Her hunch had been right. All that talk about him leaving Louisa was just that – talk.

"If we're not seeing each other it won't matter whether or not I'm in the contest."

"I'd still prefer if you weren't." Richard was adamant. "And it would be better if you left the station because I'm going to have to work here for a few more months, during the handover period."

She took a deep steadying breath. Did Richard actually think she was that much of an eejit that she was going to give up her job after what he'd just told her? She looked at him as if he were a stranger. And it was in that moment that the scales finally fell from her eyes. Richard only had one agenda going on here and that was his own best interest. Was that how it had always been? Helene still didn't know. But she was sure of one thing. All the energy she had poured into him and into the Ollie Andrews's programme would now be going in one direction only. Towards Helene Harper Inc. She was surprised at the frisson of excitement that shot through her at the thought of it. In fact, as soon as she'd stood up to declare her interest in *It's My Show*, she'd felt an energy, a high, she hadn't experienced in years.

Out of the corner of her eye, she noticed Rachel Joy standing close by, throwing curious glances their way. On impulse she stepped towards her.

"Hi, Rachel. Can I tell you about my plans for the contest? It's Helene Harper. Helene, spelled with an 'e'."

As Rachel opened her notebook on a new page, Helene watched Richard going back up to the podium, looking murderous, and she knew she had crossed a line. But if Jack McCabe was looking for the next big thing, who deserved it more than she did, after working so hard for the last five years? He need never find out that *she* was the one Richard was having the affair with.

For the next while, Helene concentrated on her interview with Rachel Joy. Then she gathered up her belongings and swept out of the room, barely giving Richard a glance as she passed him by. She was in the contest now and, after the conversation they had just had this evening, she was definitely in it to win it.

CHAPTER TEN

Tess opened her eyes and lay very still, aware of something nudging at the edge of her consciousness, something vaguely worrying. Still half asleep, she automatically ran through her to-do list for the week.

There was that weekend home she'd been promising herself. There was the mountain of laundry piling up in her closet. And she wanted to finish reading a new self-help book about dealing with difficult people. Its basic message was that there was no such thing as difficult people, only people with difficulties, and Tess had made up her mind to adopt this strategy in future when she was dealing with Ollie.

And then she remembered. She wouldn't have to deal with Ollie Andrews today. Or tomorrow. Or ever again. She had been sacked from Atlantic 1FM.

Ever since that night in Ryan's bar, Tess had retreated into a self-protective state of shock, refusing to face reality. This was how she coped when bad things happened – she convinced herself that if she didn't acknowledge it then it couldn't be so.

Andrea had been texting every day begging her to get in touch with Helene Harper and sort it out, until finally Tess had replied that she didn't want to talk about it. In truth she had been half expecting Helene to call, realising she'd overreacted and asking her to come back to work. But it hadn't happened and finally Tess had switched off her mobile just to stop herself checking it every five minutes.

She shoved her feet into her slippers and pulled on her ancient pink dressing gown. It was the comfort garment she had taken with her when she left home, the one she wore whenever she had a bad day. She had worn it for a month after Chris Conroy dumped her. She had worn it when her sister Verity had gone to live in London. And she had worn it every day since she had been sacked.

She pulled the belt tightly around her now and wandered into the kitchen. It was time to face reality. Okay, so she had never been sacked before but she had been unemployed many times in the last decade and something had always turned up. Of course the whole reason she had worked so hard at Atlantic was because she had thought it was her chance to get a foot on the ladder of a real career. But it hadn't worked out and it was time to move on.

She filled the kettle and rooted around in the cupboards, making a face at the couple of slices of stale bread lurking there. She used to buy a coffee and croissant on her way to work and eat breakfast at her desk. She'd have lunch out with Andrea and pick at something in the evening. Clearly the first thing she had to do in her new life was to stock up on food. Now that she was unemployed she could seize the opportunity to sort out her life completely, tackle all the stuff she'd put off because she'd been too busy or stressed or preoccupied.

The kettle hissed to boiling point. She threw a teabag into a mug, added water and a drop of milk and wandered into the living room. She sank onto the sofa and leaned back, racking her brain as to what she should do next.

She felt too bruised to start over quite yet. She couldn't trust Helene to give her a good reference either. She opened her laptop to check the online version of the *Killty Times* with the forlorn hope that she might find something in the jobs ads that might suit her for a few weeks while she was wondering what to do next. Her eyes widened when she saw their lead story.

STORMS BREWING AS ATLANTIC 1FM SOLD TO DUBLIN TYCOON

Tensions were evident at local radio station Atlantic 1FM this week when entrepreneur Jack McCabe finally confirmed his plans to buy the ailing station. But the business sound bites of the day were drowned out by the sound of a storm brewing at the station.

Flamboyant presenter Ollie Andrews, well known for his eccentric on-air outbursts, slammed future plans for the station, which include a nationwide contest for a new star. He called *It's My Show* a shameless publicity stunt, and insisted he was the real star of Atlantic 1FM. Former producer Tess Morgan walked out of studio recently in the middle of her debut stint as an agony aunt on Andrews' show and hasn't been heard of since. Insiders say the real reason for Morgan's untimely departure from the station was a massive personality clash with Ollie. Yesterday, Helene Harper, Morgan's former boss, said Morgan was pursuing other projects and it was unclear if she'd be back on-air soon.

Meanwhile ... who's the busy executive enjoying a radio romance with someone they shouldn't be? Watch this space . . . Rachel Joy.

Tess blinked. Insiders? What insiders? She read the

report again. Clearly the mention of romance related to Helene and Richard but who was giving Rachel Joy her information? She squinted at the accompanying photograph. Jack was barely recognisable from the guy she'd met at Rose Cottage. In the picture he was every inch the business tycoon. The five o'clock shadow had been replaced by a close shave and he was wearing a sharp black suit, white shirt and a scarlet tie. He was flanked by a beautiful blonde woman described as his PR guru.

The sound of the doorbell pealed through the apartment and Tess looked towards the hall door, puzzled. Nobody called here in the middle of the morning. Most of her neighbours left at the crack of dawn, dropping children off at crèches before going on to work. She reckoned it must be a door-to-door salesman or someone doing a survey. She considered not answering at all, but she had done enough of those sorts of jobs herself to be nice to other people doing them. She opened the door – steeling herself to be diplomatic with whoever was on the other side – and took a step backwards in surprise.

Jack McCabe – the phantom phone-in caller, the newly announced owner of Atlantic 1FM, the man who would have been her new boss if she still had a job – was standing on her doorstep.

"What do you want?" Tess asked belligerently.

After all, this was the man who was at least partially responsible for the fiasco that had led to her losing her job. If he hadn't phoned into the show when he did, she would have limped to the end of her slot without disaster striking. She would be at work now, part of all the buzz for the soon-to-be-revamped Atlantic 1FM, instead of at home, still in her dressing gown, trying to think of yet another new direction.

"I'm glad I caught you in," Jack said.

He was dressed the same as he had been in the newspaper photo – all designer-looking. Tess looked in alarm at the black crocodile briefcase he was carrying. Maybe he was going to sue her for breach of contract because she'd walked off *This Morning*? She thought of having to use her meagre savings to pay legal fees to defend herself against the media mogul standing in front of her. She'd be stuck in Killty forever at this rate.

"Look, I'm a bit busy." She took a deep breath as Jack started fiddling with his briefcase.

He looked at her quizzically. "Are you okay?"

"No comment." Tess half-closed the door in his face, determined not to incriminate herself.

"Er ... right." He flashed her his disarming smile. "It's just that you've gone a bit pale. Look, I ..."

One of the locks on the briefcase snapped open and Tess took a step backwards. Maybe she should just slam the door in his face before he could serve her with a summons paper or whatever it was you did when you were suing someone? Then, thankfully, she heard her landline phone ringing.

"Er ... I have to get that." She moved to close the door fully but Jack stepped smartly into the hall first.

"I can wait – it's no bother."

Tess snatched up the phone, acutely conscious of him standing behind her.

"Hello?"

She gestured for Jack to go into the living room. The hall was much too tiny for both of them. She could smell his aftershave, a citrusy scent that would have been pleasant if she hadn't been way too tense to care about such things.

"Hi," she whispered into the receiver.

"Tess!" It was Andrea. "Why aren't you answering your mobile? I've left a ton of messages!"

"I had it switched off."

"Why are you whispering?"

"I can't talk at the moment."

"Why, who's there?"

Tess sneaked a look in through the open door to her living room and saw Jack throw his jacket over the side of the sofa and loosen the knot in his tie as he sat down.

"You wouldn't believe me if I told you," she breathed.

"Oh! Well, ring me as soon as you can," Andrea ordered. "Have you heard the news? About Jack McCabe confirming he's bought Atlantic?"

"I've just read about it online. But I can't talk about it right now. Look, I'll call you back, okay?" She replaced the receiver without waiting for a reply and walked warily into the living room.

Jack had the briefcase on the sofa beside him. He opened his mouth to speak but Tess got there first.

"I'm a bit busy, actually. Late breakfast." She took the dozen steps to reach her tiny kitchenette and turned on the kettle switch.

"I'd love a cup of tea if there's one going. And maybe a bit of toast? I haven't eaten all day and I've been up since five."

"Five? What are you – an insomniac?" Tess cut blue bits of mould off the last two slices of bread and stuck them into the toaster.

"Only when I'm excited about something." Jack appeared in the doorway of her kitchenette, dwarfing the tiny space. "And I'm excited now, about buying into Atlantic. It's funny, now that I've made up my mind, I can see it was always the right decision." He parked himself on one of the two breakfast stools. "But beforehand? I just didn't know." He shook his head ruefully. "Normally when it comes to business, I'm the decisive type. Yes. No. Buy or let go. But this was more difficult for me because it really was a dilemma about whether I should let my heart rule my head for a change."

Tess remembered him saying that on the radio.

"So what made you change your mind?" She pushed a mug of tea towards him and poured milk into her own. "Clearly it wasn't my advice," she added pointedly.

"Well, it was in a way," Jack said slowly. "It was my sister Louisa who really wanted me to buy into the station. But I didn't agree with her reasons." He gave her a speculative look. "You know Louisa is married to Richard Armstrong?"

Tess spluttered as a mouthful of tea went down the wrong way. Richard Armstrong, who was having an affair with Helene Harper?

"Er ... no, I didn't know that," she mumbled, looking at him over the rim of her mug.

"Yeah, well, she is." Jack's face darkened. "More fool her, if you ask me. Slippery Dicky is hardly what you'd call catch of the day in the husband stakes. But Louisa has always adored him, and keeps making excuses for him, even now when he has finally run his business into the ground. And," his mouth tightened, "she suspects he's seeing someone else now as well."

"Right." Tess bit her lip. This was way too much information.

"Anyhow," Jack continued, "Louisa thinks that me buying the station will take the pressure off the business, which in turn will take the pressure off their marriage. Which, of course, it won't, because Richard will still be a

141

prick." His jaw tightened. "It was Louisa who got me to go to Grandma Rosa. She's been going to her since she and Richard moved to Killty. Said she'd helped her with lots of stuff. I thought it was all old guff to be honest. I only went to humour her because she's been so miserable. But then I met you there," he smiled, "and when I heard you worked at Atlantic – well, even I thought it might be fate. So when you asked me to phone in with a problem I saw it as an opportunity to get a feel for the business."

"Well, I'm glad it worked out for you." Tess's tone was clipped. "Grandma Rosa didn't prove to be as lucky for me, unfortunately."

"That's why I'm here." Jack was eager to explain. "I don't understand what happened that day. What made you walk out like that during the show?"

"It's a long story." Tess pulled her dressing-gown cord tighter around her. She felt at a distinct disadvantage beside Jack in his sharp business suit. And she couldn't stop thinking of the briefcase. He was probably taping this meeting so he'd have it on the record when she incriminated herself. She wished she were recording the meeting herself actually, in case she needed it in court.

"I have time," Jack said easily.

"I wasn't expecting any phone calls so I wasn't prepared," she said simply. She threw him an accusing look. "I *told* you not to call."

"But I thought you were just panicking. It was a good idea, getting someone like me to ring in to kick the agony-aunt slot off. I just thought it would make better radio if you ad-libbed rather than use a rehearsed answer."

Tess folded her arms. "So after a couple of days of thinking about whether you should buy the station, you're now an expert in what makes good radio? Believe me, it's not that easy. I've been there months and I still don't have a clue."

"I tried to find out what happened to you. After you ran off like that. Richard said he'd sort it, but then I came up against a stone wall with him. So I thought I'd find out for myself."

So he didn't know that Helene had sacked her, Tess realised. But what good would it do if she told him now? He would never take her side over a manager. Bosses never did. She shrugged.

"I've just told you. I panicked on-air, that's all." Let him sue her if he had to.

"But that's no reason to *leave*," he countered. "Someone did contact you to ask you to change your mind, I hope?"

Tess looked at him blankly.

"Richard said he'd get Helene Harper to come and talk to you about it. I thought the agony-aunt slot was great – except the part where you walked out, of course. It's *exactly* the sort of thing I have in mind for when I revamp the station."

Tess opened her mouth to speak and closed it again. He had no idea what had really been going on. Helene had wanted to get rid of her, she thought dully. She'd agreed with Ollie that she just didn't have what it takes. They'd probably cooked up the agony-aunt slot for her, knowing she'd make a complete mess of it and give Helene the perfect excuse to fire her. And she had walked straight into their trap.

"So?" Jack was still waiting for an answer. "Helene said yesterday you were looking at other options?"

Tess thought quickly. She didn't want to look like a complete loser.

"Actually, I've decided to concentrate on other things. I'm er … writing a book and I need to devote a lot more time to it if I'm ever going to get it finished." As soon as the sentence left her mouth, she wished she could take it back.

"Really?" Jack's eyes widened in admiration. "So that's why you're still in your dressing gown?" He looked her up and down. "I was wondering about that."

"Yes, that's it. I don't feel I can write a word unless I have my lucky dressing gown on." Tess gave a slightly hysterical laugh.

"So what's it about – the book?" he asked.

What was it with all the questions? This guy should have been a journalist himself.

"It's … it's a self-help book … how to deal with difficult people."

"Oh!" Jack looked distinctly underwhelmed. "Who's publishing it?"

"I don't have a publisher yet. But," she had a flash of inspiration, "I have a meeting set up with an old college friend of mine. Chris Conroy?" She waited for name recognition to dawn on Jack. He looked at her blankly and she continued encouragingly, "Chris Conroy? Former foreign correspondent. Commentator on TV shows?"

"No, I can't say I've heard of him. Not that that would mean anything, because I generally only watch movies or business programmes. Looks like I have a lot to learn about the media business," he said cheerfully.

"Well, he's, like, famous. And he's promised to help me find a publisher or, like, an agent or something."

"That's great – if it's what you want to do. But I'm disappointed you won't be coming back to us." He got off the stool and moved towards the living room. "Still, I'd like to thank you for helping me with my dilemma, and apologise for any trouble I caused. It wasn't intended." He reached into his briefcase and held out a parcel. "Peace offering?"

"Oh!" Tess slipped off the brown-paper wrapping to reveal a framed black-and-white caricature of her sitting in studio with headphones on and an *Agony Aunt of the Airwaves* banner behind her.

"I got it done because I thought you'd be staying on at Atlantic 1FM," Jack said apologetically. "But I can see now it should have been a writer starving in a garret." He looked around Tess's tiny apartment. "Not much money in self-help books then?"

"Nor in local radio," she reminded him. She tapped the glass frame. "Thank you for this. You really didn't have to."

"I wanted to. I'm just sorry we weren't able to persuade you to come back."

Tess opened her mouth to speak. This was the time to tell him the truth, that there was no book and no big meeting with Chris Conroy. She could have her job back there and then. But then she remembered Helene in Ryan's bar, the way she had sacked her without mercy. And Ollie and the way he'd made her life so difficult over the last few months. And Grandma Rosa suggesting that maybe it was time to move on if she was finding her situation so difficult. Maybe it *was* time to do something else – go somewhere she didn't feel like a square peg in a round hole?

Jack closed the briefcase and hoisted its strap over one shoulder. He gave her a lopsided smile and Tess felt a powerful, magnetic pull towards him. For a second she felt as if she'd met him before somewhere, in another life even.

"Good luck with everything," he said as he left.

"Yeah, thanks," she said shyly.

She walked over to her bay window and watched him drive away. Funny, he hadn't seemed like the psycho-stalker she'd thought he was, after all. He had been perfectly pleasant today. Funny even. She found herself wishing she could get to know him better. But he was bound to have a partner already, probably a go-getter like himself. He'd hardly be interested in a hippy drifter like her.

She switched on her mobile and rang Andrea who was all agog with the news that Jack had bought the station.

"You should have been there when the woman – Paulina her name is – I think she and Jack might be an item actually – anyway, when she said they were launching the contest to find a new star Ollie went mental! I think he might have been drunk. Now, it seems Atlantic will definitely go national later this year. Tess, you have to ring Helene and get back in here before you leave it too late!"

Tess glanced at the framed caricature of herself. She already felt ridiculous for spinning such a web of lies to Jack.

"I think I already have, Andrea."

CHAPTER ELEVEN

"So what are you going to do now?" Andrea asked anxiously.

"Get another job?" Tess shrugged. They were chatting over a coffee and Tess had filled Andrea in on Jack's astonishing visit.

"Where, though?" Andrea persisted.

"I don't know. *Somewhere.* Atlantic 1FM isn't the only employer in the world, you know. Look at Chris Conroy and how well he's doing for himself."

"Chris?" Andrea couldn't hide her surprise. "You're hoping you'll get a job like *his*?"

"Hey, I got *better* results than he did in college!" Tess said defensively.

"And then you went rambling around the world," Andrea reminded her, "while he devoted himself to his career!"

"Thanks for the vote of confidence." Tess didn't need reminding of the ten-year gap on her CV just now.

"I'm just saying that maybe you should have more realistic expectations. What about that reunion he emailed us about – it's next week, in Dublin? I can't make it, but you should go. It would be a good place to start networking."

"I'm a bit reluctant though because, well, you remember what happened between myself and Chris."

"You and Chris broke up years ago," Andrea reminded her.

"I know. But I wasn't planning on meeting up with him again in this lifetime."

Andrea was well aware of how badly Tess had taken the break-up. What she didn't know though was that Tess had developed a habit of checking up on Chris afterwards. Devouring his newspaper articles online, reading his blog – and, since she'd been home, analysing his performances on radio and television in a mildly compulsive way. In fact, she had been telling herself she needed to stop when she had received his email about the reunion.

"Look, there'll be other people at the reunion besides Chris Conroy," Andrea pointed out. "People who might help you to find another job. And meeting Chris again might mean you'll finally get over him – leave you free to meet someone else."

"I am over him. So, what if everyone at the reunion has heard about the agony-aunt fiasco?"

"Come on! This is Killty we're living in. And if Helene Harper's histrionics are anything to go by, we must only have about ten listeners by now."

"That's true." Tess started to relax.

"So, that's it then." Andrea was matter of fact. "You're going to go to the reunion and network like crazy and I'm going to pitch for my own show."

"I can help with that if you like," Tess offered. "Now that I'm at a loose end."

"Would you? It would be a great help. Thanks!" Andrea smiled. "So can you tell me any more about Jack McCabe?"

"Only what you know already – he seems really keen to get started and he has big plans for Atlantic." She didn't want to talk about Jack McCabe. She didn't want to let slip that she'd felt so attracted to him. It wasn't as if anything could ever come of it, since he seemed to be with his glamorous PR woman.

A week later, Tess was standing in a dressing room in a shop off Grafton Street wearing a short red shift dress and skyscraper heels. The reunion had seemed like a good idea when she and Andrea had been talking about networking and re-inventing yourself and *yadda yadda ya*. But now that she was in Dublin, in an over-bright changing room, it felt different. Wrong somehow.

"It's perfect." The sales assistant was nodding approvingly.

The venue for the reunion was a five-star hotel and Tess simply didn't have anything suitable to wear in her wardrobe. This dress looked vaguely glamorous. She wasn't sure about it, but then she always felt awkward out of her jeans. Well, she wouldn't have to wear it after tonight. She paid with her credit card and made her way back to the hotel where she'd checked in overnight. She felt slightly paranoid that she might run into Chris if she stayed in the main shopping thoroughfare, so she spent the best part of the afternoon in the hotel's swimming pool, doing fast lengths to work off some of her nervous energy.

By the time she got back to her room she was feeling a lot calmer and more optimistic. Wrapped in the complimentary white robe she'd found in the bathroom, she sat on the bed and pulled out a photograph. It had been snapped in London, shortly before she and Chris had broken up. Tess remembered it as a golden weekend, where they had done shamelessly touristy things, getting on the London Eye and even taking a city bus tour, which seemed to mortify Chris but he'd gone along with it because Tess had been so insistent. She had given her camera to an obliging passer-by in Hyde Park. She still looked like the hippy student she had been way back then – same untamed frizzy hair, same casual wardrobe of jeans and jumpers. Chris, she knew from watching him on TV, looked even better now. He had filled out, looked more mature. Wore way better suits.

Maybe Andrea was right. Maybe she needed to get Chris out of her system once and for all so she could stop obsessing about what might have been? In her years of monitoring him, his Facebook status had changed with startling regularity – from 'Single' to 'In a relationship' to 'Still looking'. Once he'd even written In an open relationship', but Tess assumed that was a joke. Now he'd updated it again – this time to 'It's complicated'.

Since they had broken up, she'd had plenty of romances, but they had been short-lived relationships, which she ended whenever she thought they were in danger of becoming something more.

Maybe that was because Chris had hurt her all those years ago, as Andrea had been hinting. And maybe meeting him tonight might lead to closure for her after all?

She got ready in a flurry. She didn't want to spend any more time soul-searching and she headed down to the reunion early and chose a seat which gave her a vantage spot to keep an eye on the door.

She wriggled onto the bar stool, trying to get comfortable. The dress felt a little too tight and a little too short now. And if she attempted to walk far in her sky-high heels, she mused, she'd probably go flying across the floor.

Still, there was probably no need to venture far from the bar.

She ordered a vodka and tonic, and tried to stop worrying. She had lost touch with practically everyone from college and felt a bit guilty now that the only reason she was here was because she had lost her job. She spotted her reflection in the mirror running below the long row of upended spirit bottles opposite her. She'd spent yesterday afternoon at Veronica's Cuts in Killty's main street. The salon was most definitely *not* at the cutting edge of hair design. Tess's hair was still brown and still frizzy, just a little shorter. In fact, after spending so long in the swimming pool this afternoon, it was frizzier than ever. She pushed her hand through her shorn locks, trying to get it to sit straight.

"Tess Morgan! Look at you!"

Startled out of her reverie by a familiar voice, Tess swirled around.

"Katie Lawlor!" Smiling widely, she stood up to greet her old friend.

She needn't have worried that she mightn't recognise people after all. Katie looked much like she did when she'd last seen her, only a bit older. The same straw-blonde hair whipped around her freckled face, and her wide green eyes still crinkled when she smiled. She even had the same dress style. Tonight she was wearing a floral maxi and skyscraper platforms. Within minutes Tess discovered that Katie was now a divorced detective.

"A detective? How did that happen?" Tess asked amazed.

"I went on to study criminology and that became my passion." Katie shrugged.

Elaine Seymour was next to arrive – she was working as

a medical journalist. And then a whole batch of people arrived together and they were all swept up in the excitement of hearing each other's news. Jerry Healy was now a balding book publisher; Shay Murphy had put on at least two stone, worked as a news editor and had two children.

Everyone seemed well established in their careers and Tess was feeling bad about her own jobless status when Elaine suddenly said, "And you're an agony aunt, Tess." She smiled at the expression on Tess's face. "My aunt lives in Killty – and she remembered we were friends back in the day."

Tess's fingers tightened on her glass.

Katie gave her a sidelong glance. "You're an agony aunt? Remind me to tell you about a few of my problems when we get a chance." She threw back her head and laughed and Tess had to smile, despite the tension building up inside her.

She cleared her throat to explain how she didn't work in Atlantic 1FM any more but the collective attention of the group was suddenly diverted elsewhere. Tess followed their gaze and her pulse quickened. Chris Conroy had arrived. She watched as people shifted slightly as he passed, moving automatically to allow him through. He'd always had that quality, she thought. Something intangible which marked him out as different. Something people recognised and responded to.

Tess had often wondered how she'd feel when she finally saw him again in the flesh. He was certainly as good-looking as ever. His blondish hair was thinner than she remembered, with a few streaks of grey already showing around his temples, but he was tanned and fit-looking, and had a certain joie de vivre etched into his craggy features.

"Sorry I'm late, folks!" He grabbed a seat and ordered a beer. "I got called in at the last minute to do a live TV link. That's why I'm so overdressed." He looked down at his formal navy suit and sharp white shirt with self-deprecation.

"It must be great being a celebrity, Chris," Katie said slyly, but any irony was entirely lost on Chris.

Within minutes he had become the centre of attention, regaling their small group with tales of his derring-do. They sat riveted, their own achievements dwarfed by his tales of assignments in war-torn countries, the big political stories he'd broken, even a near-death experience he'd allegedly had at the hands of the Taliban. Tess felt certain he was embellishing events, but no one seemed to mind. Another effect Chris had on people.

"Tess Morgan." Finally he seemed to notice her. "Agony Aunt of the Airwaves. I tuned in to Atlantic 1FM on the internet and there was our Tess, solving the problems of the nation," He unfurled himself from the bar stool he was straddling and moved closer to Tess.

Katie, knowing their history, turned to talk to Elaine.

"So, tell me, what's this Jack McCabe really like?" Chris asked.

"I hardly know Jack McCabe," Tess said primly.

He leaned in closer, and lowered his voice, "I often wondered about you, Tess, and how life had treated you after we split up." His voice was soft. "I always harboured a vague hope that we might be friends again someday, but you seemed to go completely off the radar after college. Did you ever think of me?"

"Not that you'd notice." Tess gave a small shrug.

Chris gave a rueful smile. "I wouldn't mind but Naomi and I barely lasted five minutes after I broke up with you."

"Naomi? Her name was Claire."

"It was?" He looked perplexed. "Well, anyway. We don't want to waste time on that old story. Let's talk about you, Tess. So how did you get into radio then?"

For a moment, he looked so genuinely interested that Tess toyed with the idea of telling him the long version. About arriving home after years of travelling, desperate to put down some roots. About Andrea getting her into Atlantic 1FM but that it hadn't exactly worked out and about how she was sacked and ... but she guessed Chris would be bored with all the details.

"I've, er ... moved on from Atlantic now."

"Moved on?" Chris frowned. "But I heard you just recently."

"Yes, well, that was my last day actually."

"It was?" He was puzzled. "I thought the presenter said it was your debut slot?"

"It was. It was my first and last slot." She swallowed a large mouthful of vodka.

"Why did you leave?" Chris looked at her intently. "Did you get a better job? At a bigger radio station? What?"

Tess smiled. "None of those things. I've just told you. I've moved on from Atlantic."

"But moved on to where?" he asked patiently.

"Well, to nowhere in particular ... I haven't got another job yet. I'm examining my options."

"You've got options? In these times?" Chris raised an eyebrow.

She felt a stab of resentment. How many times had *he* switched jobs to get to where he was now, she wanted to ask him? Plenty of times, according to the stories of adventure and success he'd just been regaling them all with.

"I felt I had gone as far as I could go there, really." That sounds right, Tess thought, pleased. It was the sort of comment that an ambitious go-getter would make, not someone who had let the grass grow under her feet for the last ten years.

"Tell him about your other projects," Elaine piped up.

Tess swung around and realised that Elaine had been listening intently to their conversation.

Elaine misread her panicked expression. "Don't be modest now! My aunt lives in Killty and she read all about it in the paper. She remembered we went to college together and told me all about it." She frowned, trying to remember the details. "Wasn't there some controversy about you walking out of studio or something?"

Tess's head was starting to swim. She couldn't believe a tiny story in a tiny local paper had spread this far.

"No, that really is enough about me. Tell us about your life, Elaine."

"Well …" Elaine began, flattered to be asked.

But Chris interrupted her. "Is that true? That you walked out? I only heard the start of that item and I had to go and do an interview myself."

"Sort of …" Tess racked her brain, wondering how she could change the subject.

"But you must have heard that Atlantic might be going national?" Chris looked at her appraisingly. "Come on! And the real reason you left is?"

Tess finally broke. "Okay! I had a row with my boss over … well, it doesn't matter what it was about now. The thing is, she sacked me. But," she added quickly as there was a collective intake of breath, "then my boss's boss, Jack McCabe – the entrepreneur who is buying the station – he called to see me and said he really liked the agony-aunt slot. But by that stage I had already told him that I was … er …

writing a book. Which I am. Of course. But I do need a new job as well so if anybody knows of any openings …"

Tess looked around. She was the centre of attention now. For all the wrong reasons. She swallowed, praying for someone to break the silence. Make a joke. Anything.

Chris rested his chin on his steepled fingers. "My advice is to go back to Atlantic."

Tess stared at him. Hadn't he listened to a word she'd said? That she had been sacked and was supposed to be writing a book and exploring her options?

"Tess, they are going national and you said Jack McCabe wants you back. An opportunity like that doesn't come around every day, you know. You can't just let it slip through your fingers."

"Er … I think I already have," she reminded him.

Chris looked at her, his forehead creased in thought. "Haven't they just announced a nationwide contest – where the winner gets their own show?"

"I'm sure I'm disqualified on the grounds of being fired from there already!" she joked.

"But you just said Jack liked your agony-aunt slot. Tell him you've changed your mind, that you want to come back. That would give you a fantastic advantage over external contestants – you'll have insider information."

"I've already turned down his offer." She lifted her chin defiantly. "I'm afraid that particular ship has sailed without me, Chris."

"Persuade McCabe to take you back!" He was insistent.
"How?"

"Go and find him. Hit him with your elevator speech."

She looked at him uncomprehendingly. "My what speech?"

"Your *elevator* speech. People use them in Hollywood to

pitch ideas for a movie. They only have a short window to sell their ideas to the movers and shakers. So they encapsulate their story right down to a forty-five-second speech. The idea is if you're ever in an elevator with someone who can help you to progress your career, your pitch is powerful enough and short enough to grab their attention, while you have them as a captive audience."

"Right," Tess said slowly. "And how does that relate to me getting my job back, exactly?"

"Lots of people have adapted the idea to use in their careers," he said.

She stifled a giggle. "And do you actually have to be *in* an elevator with the very important person?" She drank more vodka, beginning to enjoy the mad twist the conversation had just taken. This was what she'd liked about being with Chris – you never knew what he was going to come out with next. She scanned his features for signs of a smile. "You are joking, aren't you?"

"I'm not. I have used my elevator speech so many times in my career. And with amazing results, if I'm allowed to blow my own trumpet for a moment."

"Right," Tess murmured. Maybe he'd gone a bit bonkers since she'd last seen him. Something to do with all those war zones he'd been caught up in.

"And I've used other psychological techniques too," Chris continued seriously. "Like ... have you heard of mirroring?"

"Erm ... no. But you're going to tell me about it, right?"

He narrowed his eyes. "This is serious stuff, Tess. It *works*. What you do is mirror people's actions back at them. So if they move their head one way you copy them. And if they cross their legs you cross yours as well." He crossed and uncrossed his long legs in demonstration.

"They get the idea that you like them – and they like you right back. It's basic but it works. It's all about body language, Tess." He reached out and grabbed her hand in his enthusiasm.

"Right." She looked down at her small hand enveloped in his large one.

"It's difficult to explain it here." He was looking at her with his intense stare again. "I'd need to show you how it all works with role-play. But I can't do it here. We'd need somewhere more private."

Tess looked around the bar. Katie and Elaine were now engaged in a giddy 'Do you remember?' game and everyone else was also deep in conversation.

"I have a room here at the hotel," she said slowly.

"Really?" Chris stroked the underside of her wrist with his thumb.

"Really," Tess said decisively.

She had wanted to lay to rest the ghost of Chris Conroy for a long time now and she was going to do it tonight. She had to admit he had a strange chat-up line nowadays. *Come up and let me role-play my weird job-seeking techniques with you.* But then he had always been a strange sort of guy. Charismatic, but strange.

She drained her glass and got to her feet, wobbling a bit on her heels. She scribbled her room number on the side of a damp beer mat.

"Follow me up in a while and don't make it obvious," she instructed.

She slipped away before anyone noticed. Once in her room, she threw off her shoes and sat on the end of the unfamiliar bed, her heart fluttering a bit too fast. Some part of her realised this probably wasn't the best idea she'd ever had.

There was Chris's 'It's complicated' Facebook status to consider. And the fact that he had dumped her before and had never tried to contact her in the intervening years. But how else was she going to do the closure thing, she asked herself, a bit drunkenly. How else was she going to quit thinking of Chris as The One Who Got Away?

The knock on the door made her jump off the bed. She padded across the room in her stocking feet and hesitated for a few seconds before twisting the doorknob and pulling it open slowly. And then it was as if ten years and a lifetime of 'What Ifs?' had disappeared and she was back to the star-struck girl she had once been.

Chris Conroy looked crazy, dirty, sexy.

"Come in," she said quietly and walked across to the window. "There are drinks in the minibar," she called over her shoulder.

Chris pulled out a bottle of beer and two miniature bottles for her – vodka and tonic, which he mixed expertly in a glass he took from her bedside locker He walked over to join her, handing her the vodka, and taking a swig of his beer straight from the bottle

Tess sipped her drink and pressed her forehead against the windowpane, taking in the cityscape below them. The reflection of the streetlights illuminated the scene outside: the lovers walking arm in arm; a tramp across the road on the corner settling in for the night with his piece of cardboard and blanket; a gang of young women, dressed in pink hen-night tack, holding each other up as they tottered along on their spindle heels, laughing uproariously.

She was aware of Chris standing behind her, so close she could feel the feather touch of his breath on the nape of her neck. She shivered and turned around to face him, lifting her face slightly to his. She had forgotten how blue his eyes were. Like cornflowers, she used to think.

"So, Tess," he said softly, "about the elevator-speech script …"

Tess snapped her head downwards. He *actually* wanted to talk about an elevator speech? She turned away, so he couldn't see the expression on her face.

"Look, Chris, I'm sure this sort of thing goes down well in Hollywood or London. Possibly even here in Dublin. But … Killty is small. And kind of … quaint. It's not an elevator-speech sort of place."

"Everywhere's an elevator speech sort of place, Tess. Besides, you won't always be stuck in Killty."

The way he said it made Tess want to jump contrarily to the town's defence. But then he put his hands on her shoulders and turned her around to face him again.

"I have a hunch about you, Tess Morgan. And my hunches are hardly ever wrong. So – trust me on this one – you need to go to Jack McCabe and pitch him the idea that you want your job back and why he should give it to you. You owe it to yourself. Promise me that you'll at least try?"

"I'll try," Tess agreed. She tilted her chin upwards again, convinced he was finally going to make his move. But he moved her to one side, placed his beer on the window-ledge and bounded across the room.

She watched, bewildered, as he hunkered down at the bedside locker and pulled out a notepad with the hotel's logo on it and a tiny pen attached with a string. He came back, brandishing the stationery like a weapon.

"We'd be better off with index cards but this will have to do for now. So, Tess … what five words would you use to describe your best qualities?"

Tess had had enough. She put her drink down beside his on the window ledge and looked at him.

"Hot. Sexy. That's two."

He looked at her, his mouth opening in surprise. She took the notepad and pen out of his hands and heard them fall with a soft thud on the thick, beige carpet.

"Adventurous." She slipped her hands into his navy jacket, inching it down his arms until it too fell to the floor.

He closed his mouth again and gave her that lazy smile she remembered.

"Spontaneous." She opened the top button of his white shirt, letting her fingers flicker over the hollow in his throat.

He arched his head back. "What else?"

"Uncomplicated."

He laughed out loud at that.

She smiled too, wondering which of the five words were the most inaccurate.

"You've changed, so." He slid one hand up her short red dress.

"It's been a long time, so that's entirely possible," she murmured.

He turned her around and pulled down the zip of her dress. He slid it down along her body, over the curve of her hips and onto the floor. She stepped out of the flimsy strip of material and turned around to face him again.

His eyes swept over her, standing there in her bra, panties, and her vertiginous, skyscraper shoes.

"Tell me some more words," he challenged.

"Powerful," she said at once. That one was true; she did feel a sense of her own power right now. She'd taken control of a situation that hadn't been going the way she wanted it to and turned it around. *Go, her!*

"Daring," she added, unfastening the second button of his shirt.

Chris bent his head to whisper in her right ear. "I think I like the new you, Tess Morgan."

She smiled. She didn't think Chris had changed, any more than she had. But right now she didn't care because she was about to have sex for the first time in so long it hurt to think about it. And with a man she'd never really given up on.

She slipped out of her skyscrapers, giving Chris an extra six inches height advantage and in response he bent down, lifted her up and carried her towards the bed.

CHAPTER TWELVE

Helene wasted no time in devising her strategy to win the contest. She'd slotted herself into *This Morning* for a series of reports on her *Ten Years Younger* efforts, determined to get her talent recognised by Jack McCabe. She decided that he couldn't know she was having an affair with Richard because he would have let her go by now.

She was finally starting to appreciate why Richard had insisted on keeping their relationship secret. Of course Rachel Joy's poisonous postscript to her report in the *Killty Times* was a cause for concern. Helene twirled a strand of hair around her finger, wondering if there was anything she could do to stop the journalist from naming her in a future edition. The phone on her desk rang and she was jolted back to reality.

"Hello, may I speak to Helene Harper?"

"Speaking …" Helene said cautiously, trying to place the voice.

"Oh! Well, look, my name is Grandma Rosa and –"

"You!" Helene remembered. It was the old bat who had phoned in to the ill-fated agony-aunt slot.

"Er … yes, it's me. I'm phoning with an idea I have for the radio? *The Psychic Granny Show*."

Despite Helene's worries, she found herself smiling. "I'm

afraid we're fighting a constant battle at Atlantic 1FM to attract younger listeners, Mrs …?"

"Grandma Rosa will do."

"Okay then, Grandma Rosa. I have to say *Psychic Granny* is a great title, but I'm afraid it's not really us."

"But it's young listeners who will like this slot the most!" Rosa persisted. "Think about it! They're the ones who are building careers, dealing with debt, looking for a partner, juggling children or else the idea of children. It's all happening for them at the same time – they *need* advice."

Tell me about it, Helene thought wryly. She had always thought her life would be sorted by forty. But here she was fighting to keep her job and having relationship difficulties all at the same time. Richard hadn't been in touch with her since the press conference and she was dismayed to find that she was missing him like crazy. She tapped her foot under the table. How was it she and Richard weren't getting along any more? She remembered Annie, the therapist at the spa, saying her throat chakra was blocked. Maybe that was it – she couldn't communicate her feelings to him properly because of the blocked chakra. Her heart quickened as a thought occurred to her. What if Grandma Rosa could unblock her chakras?

"It's young people who need *Psychic Granny* the most," Grandma Rosa was continuing with her pitch. And then, a little uncertainly, "Helloooo … are you still there?"

"Yes, I am." Helene made a fast decision. "Look, how about I come along to visit you and let me see what I think then?"

"But that's fantastic!" Grandma Rosa was delighted. "When? Can you come today? I have a free slot just after lunch. Two o'clock."

"Great." Helene scribbled down Rosa's directions. The

visit would get her out of the office, even if nothing came of it.

She put down the phone and forced herself to concentrate on her work. It was tough going lately, trying to fill the gap Tess Morgan had left, keeping up with her own job and working out how to win the contest. She worked on through her lunch, eating a yoghurt at her desk, and set off for Rose Cottage.

She parked her car in a lay-by and walked down the winding road, looking for the address. A dark-haired man, sitting on a wooden bench, was lazily rubbing the ears of a black-and-white collie panting beside him. As Helene passed him by he smiled a greeting. He looked as though he didn't have a care in the world, which reminded Helene of Matt from the Travel Café. She was going to get Matt in to do a slot soon – his enthusiasm about travelling was infectious and she was sure he would go down well with the listeners.

If only Richard was as uncomplicated and easy-going. Normally, by this stage in the day, he would have been on to her half a dozen times, either giving her work instructions or else arranging when he could get away to be with her. But since their row at the press conference he'd been keeping his distance. She hadn't realised how empty her life would feel without Richard in it.

Finally she reached Rose Cottage. She stood still for a few seconds, her hand on the rickety gate, reading the hand-painted sign in the garden.

Seventh Daughter of a Seventh Daughter!
Let Grandma Rosa foretell your future!
Tea leaves (cup of tea free!), Cards and Crystals.

The cottage had an untidy thatched roof and a crooked wooden fence. The garden was a riot of colour, with multi-coloured tulips and primulas crowded into every available space. A fat black cat was sunning himself in the window.

Helene pushed open the gate and marched purposefully up the path. She was looking for a bell when the front door opened and an elderly woman motioned for her to come in.

Helene took a step backwards. She didn't know what she'd been expecting from her Psychic Granny – but Ugg boots? Purple hair? And, perhaps most unnervingly of all, huge silver ear-hoops, not unlike Helene's own trademark earrings.

"I'm Helene Harper." She touched her right earring self-consciously. "From Atlantic 1FM."

"Of course!" Rosa opened the door wider. "I've been waiting for you. Come on in to the parlour."

Helene followed her into the hall and peered into the tiny room. It was so stuffed with clutter that Helene, whose own apartment was a monument to minimalism, felt slightly sick just looking at it. A shabby floral sofa festooned with cushions was backed up against the wall. An ancient rocking chair creaked in the corner and a low, scratched table was set with a large silver teapot and a pair of terracotta-coloured mugs. Dozens of ornamental cats jostled for space on the bookshelves. Pen-and-ink drawings of more cats crowded the walls. The smell of incense was overpowering. Something soft brushed against Helene's legs and she jumped, startled.

"Millie! How many times have I told you about frightening away my clients?" Rosa chided.

The black cat Helene had seen in the window skulked into a corner and hissed at Helene, staring at her with huge, green eyes. Helene stared back until the cat gave up and screwed itself up into a defensive black ball of fur.

"So?" Helene turned her attention to the fortune teller.

"Sit down there and make yourself comfortable." Grandma Rosa took the rocking chair and gestured for Helene to sit on the sofa.

"Would you like tea leaves, tarot cards *or*," Grandma Rosa indicated a large glass ball with a pair of white ornamental hands on top, "the crystal ball?"

"Actually," Helene sat down gingerly on the edge of the sofa, "I'd like my chakras unblocked."

"Your *whats* unblocked?" Rosa looked mystified.

"My chakras." Helene rubbed the hollow of her neck thoughtfully. She'd swear she could almost *feel* where Annie had detected the blockage. "A therapist told me my throat chakra was blocked, which means, apparently, that I find it difficult to express myself. Have you heard of chakra therapy?"

"Now that you mention it, I do remember a woman in my psychic club mentioning something about chakras – she's into the auld Reiki. They're something to do with energy, but don't ask me what. Seemed to be very complicated to me." Rosa poured out two mugs of tea. "Milk? Sugar?"

"Just milk." Helene was disappointed. "So – what *can* you do?"

"Well ... I always recommend tea leaves for first-timers." Rosa poured the milk and shoved a mug towards Helene.

"Tea leaves?" Helene raised her eyebrows. If Grandma Rosa was serious about getting a radio slot she was going to have to do better than that. She didn't want her yakking on about dark handsome men and overseas trips. She opened her mouth to say as much but Rosa interrupted her.

"To be honest this scene is changing so fast it's hard to keep up with it. Apparently, if you're not moving forward

167

you're basically dead in the business world."

Helene's mouth tightened. "Tell me about it. That's partly why I'm here."

"What other therapies have you had done?" Rosa asked.

"Oh, loads of stuff." Helene tried to remember all the therapies she'd ever had. "There was the angel workshop. Feng shui. Rescuing my inner child. Meeting my Guides. Reflexology. Iridology. Spiritual cleansing …"

"What did you do? That you needed your spirit cleansed?" Rosa asked suspiciously.

"Do? I didn't do anything. That's what the therapist was offering."

"I'd imagine you'd have to have at least murdered someone to need your spirit cleansed." Rosa pursed her lips.

"Well, I didn't murder anyone!" Helene retorted. Although, she had killed off a fair few careers in her time, she thought guiltily, an image of Tess Morgan floating in front of her. "Look, I just had stuff I needed to get off my chest with the spiritual cleansing thing."

"So why not just go to confession? Are you Catholic?"

"Eh … I don't think that's any of your business! Look, spiritual cleansing was just *in* at the time, all right?"

"I should learn about that too then. What about Cosmic Ordering? That's the latest, according to my psychic network group."

"You can do Cosmic Ordering?" Helene felt a flutter of excitement. She could order the Universe to make her the outright winner of *It's My Show*. She would become super-famous and Richard would be raging that he hadn't believed in her when he'd had the chance.

"I'm studying it," Rosa said. "What is it you want to order?"

"I want to win *It's My Show* – that's a competition Atlantic 1FM is running," Helene said without hesitation.

"Right. Well, I don't actually know how to do Cosmic Ordering yet." Rosa shuffled her tarot cards and looked at Helene shrewdly. "But I believe you can only wish for something which is for the greater good. You can't wish ill on your enemies, for instance." Her eyes brightened. "Oh yes – and you need to say what you want to happen in the present tense, as if it's already happened."

"Like '*Yes, yes, yes, I'm a millionaire-ess*'?" Helene asked tersely. "I've tried that already – it didn't work."

"Well, I think you have to really *believe* it before it can work. But, as I've explained, it's not my specialist subject." Rosa leaned towards Helene. "Look, to be honest, I *am* aiming to diversify into the new therapies but at the moment I am more comfortable with the more traditional fortune-telling techniques. Tarot and tea leaves. I think the tarot would suit your listeners best. They phone in, I concentrate on their energies over the airwaves and choose their cards on the basis of that. For example," she gave the cards one more shuffle, and fanned them out in front of Helene, "pick nine cards."

Helene chose the cards, feeling silly and nervous at the same time, and watched as Rosa arranged them in the shape of a cross and scrutinised them in silence for several seconds. Finally she spoke.

"I can see here you're going through quite a difficult time in your life right now."

Helene craned her neck to see more of the colourful cards. "That's true."

"This one," Grandma Rosa tapped firmly on one, "is telling me you're facing a big crossroads in your life. And this one," she patted another, "tells me there's someone who may be deceiving you. What they say is not necessarily what they mean."

Helene frowned. She didn't think Richard was untrustworthy, but that's what the woman seemed to be insinuating. Maybe she should find a proper New Age therapist, one who did know about Cosmic Ordering and chakras? She noticed Rosa's eyes widening slightly as they lit on another card.

"What?" Helene demanded, leaning over to try and see the card more clearly.

"It's to do with a man in your life. There's something that's not being said between you. Something you are keeping from one another. Are you torn between two lovers by any chance?"

Helene blinked. Suddenly she had an urge to spill out the whole sorry story of her and Richard to this woman with the unconventional dress sense and kind eyes. But it would be hard for even Helene's best friend – if she had a best friend – to understand the exquisite nuances of her and Richard's love affair, never mind a complete stranger who didn't know the first thing about either of them.

"Look, if I need to consider you for a slot, you'll need to tell me something I don't know already," Helene said bluntly.

Grandma Rosa looked at her levelly. "Actually, I think I can. I wasn't sure how much to reveal because it's your first time here. But if it's what you want." She waved one of the cards around in the air. "This card here, Helene. It's the Empress. It signifies fertility and motherhood. Now, that doesn't necessarily mean a baby. It could be telling you that you need to nurture your own inner self. But tell me – could you by any chance be pregnant?"

"What?" Helene spluttered out her tea and watched in

dismay as the lukewarm liquid splashed onto her yellow silk blouse, spreading an ugly tan stain over the delicate material. She grabbed a tissue from her bag and dabbed ineffectually at her blouse, her mind mentally calculating dates.

There was that time when she'd come off the pill for a little while, "to give my body a rest," as she'd explained to Richard. His reaction had been swift and involved a bulk buy of condoms, so Helene had gone back on the pill pretty quickly and had forgotten all about it. Surely it couldn't have been then?

A vein pulsed in her temple. She thought of her recent nausea and uncharacteristic tiredness, how she'd fallen asleep when she'd come home from the spa, when she was supposed to be off wooing Tess Morgan back to work. But it was too ridiculous. Helene gave herself a mental shake. Why was she even *thinking* about giving credence to this batty old woman?

"I'm definitely not pregnant," she announced confidently.

"Oh!" Rosa seemed disappointed. "Well, something else must be gestating for you. A new job, perhaps? A new direction in life? Whatever it is, the cards are telling me that you'll need to harness all your reserves of strength to deal with your new situation."

"That's *it*!" Helene laughed out loud. "It's the contest at work! A new job, and a new direction. Of course! That will require all my strength to deal with it, but I don't mind that, because I am so, so ready for it!" She clasped both hands in front of her in her enthusiasm.

"Really? So tell me more about that so." Rosa swept up the spread of cards from the table and began to shuffle them again as Helene launched into the story – Atlantic 1FM being taken over, how Jack McCabe was looking for new blood, about the relentless competition for listenership which Helene figured was now only going to intensify and, lastly, about the competition for *It's My Show*.

"Right," Rosa said, when Helene finally paused for breath. "Tell me, have you found in the past that no matter what you've achieved, you always want more?"

"Yeah – doesn't everyone?" Helene was puzzled.

"No, actually. Some people are content with what they have," Grandma Rosa said mildly. She tapped a card absentmindedly on the edge of the table. "These sorts of people take the time to savour their achievements instead of always looking towards their next goal. And, don't get me wrong, because I am all for women being ambitious, but I think it would benefit you if you started taking a more relaxed approach to life because ..." She broke off as a phone jangled in the air.

"That's me, hang on a second," Helene pulled her mobile out and breathed an audible sigh of relief. Richard! At last. "I'll have to take this." She turned her back slightly to Grandma Rosa.

A minute later she turned back and reached for her bag, her face wreathed in smiles.

"I'm afraid I'm going to have to leave. That was my boyfriend. We had a bit of a tiff but he's just told me he wants to arrange a party for my fortieth!"

"You're forty?" Rosa looked surprised. "You don't look it."

"Well, that's probably because of my *Ten Years Younger* series." Helene was gratified, but she didn't really want to think about that particular project right now. Sara had been researching more anti-ageing treatments but they still sounded gruesome in the extreme. Acid-based gels. Vein-zapping lasers. She didn't even know if she wanted to try

Botox any more. Not now that she'd read it was like injecting poison into your system. And when she realised that it hadn't done Ollie's career much good after all.

"Are you in a stable relationship with this boyfriend of yours?" Grandma Rosa asked suddenly.

Helene laughed hollowly. "Stable is the last word I'd use to describe it."

"So could he be the person who is deceiving you, then?"

Helene felt another flash of irritation. "Look, I've enjoyed our chat but I don't really believe in all of this." She picked up her handbag. "So if there isn't anything else I'll be off."

"So what about the *Psychic Granny* slot? What are your thoughts on it from what you've seen so far?"

"Oh! That." Helene banged her forehead with the palm of her hand. She had almost forgotten why she was there.

She looked at Grandma Rosa appraisingly. She was certainly chatty enough. And charismatic in an eccentric sort of way. And people did love having their fortunes told – Helene had enjoyed her visit overall, even though she didn't believe a word of it. On the other hand, Grandma Rosa was *old*. And Helene hadn't been exaggerating when she'd explained about the station's constant battle for younger listeners.

"It's not only about attracting the young," Rosa said, as if she'd read Helene's mind. "There's grey power to consider."

"Gay power?" Helene was mystified.

"*Grey* power! Seniors with money. The grey euro is the one to watch." Rosa produced a magazine with a silver-haired couple on the cover, dressed in matching grey tracksuits, sprinting along a white beach and holding hands. "Here, read about it for yourself. People are living

173

Joan Brady

longer and the over-sixties are an important consumer group."

Helene took the magazine and leafed through it. If what Grandma Rosa was saying was true, then she might be able to turn this grey power to her advantage. It could, in fact, be her unique selling point in the contest. She could suggest that Atlantic direct some of the focus away from the overcrowded youth market and make a foray into this grey-power consumer group. That could be her pitch for *It's My Show*.

"Maybe we could try *Psychic Granny* on a pilot basis," she said slowly. If she could get Rosa in on a trial basis, she could monitor what sort of listeners she was pulling in.

"That's fantastic!" Rosa reached over and pulled an A4 pad and a biro from a drawer. "So when do you want me to start?"

Helene tapped the cover of the seniors' magazine. "I'll have to do some research before I commit to anything. And it would be a short weekly slot – say about fifteen minutes – rather than a whole show. And I'll have to run it by my boss, especially the way things are at work at the moment. But, if I can swing it, I'd expect you to be ready to start straight away."

"The sooner the better!" Rosa could hardly contain her excitement.

"Fine." Helene stood up. "I'll be in touch so!"

Her mood had improved enormously. Richard had sounded like his old self on the phone and he wanted to meet her as soon as possible to talk about plans for her birthday party. Of course, there was still contentious stuff they needed to sort out. Richard had to understand that she wasn't going to pull out of competing for *It's My Show*, not now that she was so excited by the prospect of winning.

And he needed to be more – what was the word? *Present* – that was it. He needed to be more present in the relationship. But she felt confident now that she could make him understand that.

Her hand unconsciously went to the base of her throat. Funny, the Psychic Granny must have done *something*, because Helene felt as if her throat chakra was clearer already. As she turned the key in the ignition of her car, she could sense a whole new era opening up ahead of her – one where her new talent for self-expression was going to massively improve every area of her life.

CHAPTER THIRTEEN

Tess hid behind a giant palm in the lobby of a very plush hotel in the centre of Dublin city. She was waiting for Jack McCabe to arrive so she could pitch her elevator speech at him. Her script was crumpled in her sweaty hand in case she forgot what she wanted to say, even though Chris Conroy had made her go over it so many times she was more likely to forget her own name first. Now all she had to do was to find a way to waylay Jack. She wiped away a bead of perspiration from her forehead. She couldn't quite believe she was doing this. When Chris had described it he had made it sound so *normal*.

"Everyone does this sort of thing, Tess – you need to learn to fight for your career," he'd pointed out when Tess had voiced her misgivings.

But of course it wasn't normal. It was, at best, eccentric and quite possibly insane. Tess felt like a stalker and probably looked like one too, if the suspicious glances of the hotel security man were anything to go by. She looked away nervously and scanned the area. Apart from an elderly gentleman dozing on one of the armchairs and a young couple drinking cocktails, the lobby was empty.

She had arrived an hour ago, after Chris had discovered that Jack McCabe was scheduled to show up here for a meeting, apparently connected with his plans for Atlantic 1FM. Tess didn't know where Chris got his information, only that he had a lot of it.

She had been staying at his apartment in Dublin, cramming for this moment. They had made love a few more times but otherwise there had been no progress whatsoever in their personal relationship. Between getting a makeover, writing and rehearsing various scripts and learning how to visualise a positive outcome, there had been time for little else, and today was to be the culmination of all that prep work.

"You have to imagine yourself as *powerful*. Like a cinema version of yourself, you know? Cinema Tess," he'd said to her this morning, tilting her chin so he could look deep into her eyes. "At the moment, you just don't see how great you are. You keep on saying that your agony-aunt slot was a disaster. Yet Jack wanted you back. What's that telling you, Tess?"

She had opened her mouth to speak, but had closed it again as Chris answered himself.

"It's telling you that you misjudged the whole situation because of your low self-esteem, that's what. And the only way to get over that is to put yourself into situations that are outside your comfort zone. It's like when I'm going into a war zone. At first I feel terrified but then the adrenaline kicks in, and, when I've accomplished what I set out to do, I feel fantastic."

Tess looked around the luxurious lobby of the five-star hotel, with its glittering chandeliers, plush yellow sofas and piped tinkling music and felt guilty for making such a fuss about today that Chris felt obliged to compare it to being in a war zone. But, in a way, she felt as if she *was* in her own personal battlefield. The idea of waylaying Jack to ask for her job back was so way out of her comfort zone that she felt like she was about to jump off a cliff.

Dipping her head around the palm, Tess furtively scanned the lobby. Still no sign of Jack. She glanced at her watch. He was thirty minutes late.

"Are you okay there?" asked the blonde hotel receptionist.

"I ... er ... have a meeting with a Jack McCabe – could you tell me if he has a room booked?"

"All the hotel's events are posted there." The receptionist indicated a notice board beside the reception desk and peered at the tiny, gold-coloured letters. "Mr McCabe's meeting is on the fourth floor. There's someone else waiting for him in the room if you want to go on up."

"Thanks." Tess decided she needed to freshen up before she tackled Jack. She shoved her script into the pocket of her dress and slipped into the Ladies', an opulent area with huge gilt mirrors, porcelain sinks and white rolled-up hand towels stacked up in wicker baskets.

She hardly recognised her own reflection. When Chris had first suggested she needed a complete makeover to relaunch her career she thought he was joking. Again, she had been so wrong. First up had been a visit to Mr Cheung, *Hairdresser to the Stars,* according to the publicity blurb in the window of the salon. He had told Tess she was a very lucky woman to know Chris Conroy because normally there was a three-month waiting list for an appointment with Mr Cheung. As he chopped and tousled her hair this way and that, Tess wondered idly why Mr Cheung kept referring to himself in the third person. And how come Chris knew him in the first place? It wasn't as if he had enough hair left to benefit from Mr Cheung's artistry. She remembered what he'd said when he was persuading her to make the appointment. "He's expensive, but he's the best.

Look on it as an investment in your career. An investment in Tess."

And though she still felt slightly ill when she thought of his astronomical fee, Tess had to admit that Mr Cheung had turned out to be no mere mortal of a hairdresser. He had highlighted and lowlighted and blended and cut and snipped at her hair for the best part of three hours and Tess could see now that he had worked a kind of magic.

Today, her hair was a shining halo, the frizz miraculously tamed with 'a special serum'. Her fake tan was so artfully applied it looked natural. She'd had a French manicure and professionally applied make-up done early this morning. She was wearing a navy-and-white dress, which screamed 'business but classy', according to Chris. Business but classy had come with another alarming price tag that Tess didn't want to think about right now – the bills were all on her credit card and would have to be repaid eventually. But the entire procedure had transformed her from goofy hippy chick to … well, someone who looked like a stranger.

If it worked, by the end of this morning, she'd have her agony-aunt slot back again. And because she wouldn't be producing *This Morning with Ollie Andrews*, she could really concentrate on making it a success, on taking her career to the next level. That's what Chris had said, and since Chris had a stellar career and Tess had known nothing of office politics over the last ten years, she had to believe he knew what he was talking about.

She pulled the crumpled speech out again and scanned it one last time. Then, feeling as if she were about to sit an important exam that she hadn't studied properly for, she stuffed the paper into her bag.

Showtime, she thought, pushing back her shoulders as she marched back into the lobby. Just in time to see Jack

McCabe pushing his way through the revolving door of the hotel.

He was again dressed for business – dark suit, white shirt, and the crocodile briefcase. He was pulling at his tie as he strode through the hotel lobby. Tess took a few tentative steps forward. But she faltered when she realised he wasn't alone. A tall, blonde woman was trailing along behind him, carrying a pile of folders. Tess recognised her from the photograph in the *Killty Times* – the PR guru.

Her stomach seesawed in a sickening motion. In all the run-throughs with Chris, she had never considered that Jack would not arrive alone, and she felt temporarily paralysed at this unexpected turn of events. Why hadn't she anticipated this? Why hadn't Chris prepared her for such an eventuality?

She watched him pushing the button for the elevator, glancing at his watch. He was clearly in a rush to get to his meeting. He'd hardly have the time or the inclination to listen to her, and the presence of the PR woman was making it even more difficult. She considered calling the whole thing off. But the thought of another day at the Chris Conroy career boot camp galvanised her into action. She sprang forward, but she was still several paces away when the lift door slid open and Jack and his blonde companion stepped inside.

"*Wait!*" Tess shrieked as she saw the woman lean forward to press the button to close the door. She threw herself into the lift and the doors bounced off her shoulders before springing open again. "*Yeow!*" She rubbed her arm ruefully.

"Are you all right?" Jack McCabe looked at her with solemn brown eyes.

"Sure." Tess smiled nervously.

He looked at her more closely. "Hey – it's you! You look ... different. Did you get something done to your hair?"

"Just a little trim." She fingered Mr Cheung's work self-consciously.

"I almost didn't recognise you out of your dressing gown!"

The woman looked enquiringly at Tess as she pressed the button for the fourth floor.

Tess swallowed. "Eh, the fourth floor for me too."

The woman raised her eyebrows a fraction.

"Paulina," Jack turned to introduce them, "this is Tess, who did the agony-aunt slot."

"Oh?" Paulina looked Tess up and down. "So you're the woman who walked out of studio in the middle of Jack's call?"

Tess registered the unmistakeable putdown. She gave Jack what she hoped was a winning smile. "What a coincidence we should bump into each other like this!"

"Yes, it is. Are you meeting someone about getting your book published?" He turned to Paulina again. "She's writing a book about how to deal with difficult people."

"Seriously?" Paulina raised her eyebrows.

Tess flushed but a glance at the lights winking on the panel above the lift door told her she needed to get a move on with her speech.

"Jack, I've been thinking about what you said when you came to visit me. And the thing is – well, I'd like to do the *Agony Aunt of the Airwaves* slot after all. Of course I shouldn't have walked off like that when we were on air. I realise that but I also know this. It was an invaluable learning experience for me and will make me an even better agony aunt. And if you give me another chance I think you will find it will be a win-win situation for both of us and –"

The lift shuddered to a halt, and a disembodied female voice interrupted Tess in mid-flow.

"*Fourth floor. Doors open.*"

Tess blinked as the doors sprang open. She hadn't finished yet. She looked nervously at Jack, who was leaning against the wall, looking at her with a perplexed expression.

"But what about your book?" he asked, putting a finger on the button to keep the doors open.

"I can juggle the two roles!" Tess continued with her speech quickly. "In fact, they would probably complement each other. Dealing with difficult people is just dealing with people with difficulties, when you think about it." The elevator script had seemed bizarre when she had been role-playing it with Chris. Now, doing it for real, in an actual lift, in front of the blonde woman with the judgemental expression on her face, was like being in a waking nightmare.

She saw Jack exchange glances with Paulina.

Paulina stepped into the corridor. "The agony-aunt slot is on hold at the moment, as are any changes until the relaunch of Atlantic 1FM." She turned and gave Tess a malicious smile. "Sorry. You're too late."

Tess blinked. Was that it? After all the role-playing and scripting and visualising a positive outcome, she had been turned down flat. In less than three minutes? She cast around wildly for something to say. She had to think of a way to retrieve the situation. If Chris was in a war zone and his plan to get a top interview ran into a roadblock and he had travelled thousands of miles through enemy fire to get it – well, he wouldn't just walk away, would he? He would do *something*.

Just like Tess's Cinema Self would. But what? What would Cinema Tess do?

She stepped out of the lift for starters, racking her brain as to what this new heroic version of herself, who Chris said lay just under the surface of her normal personality, might do next. But nothing came. She felt as if her head were full of cotton wool. Her mouth felt parched. She had no Plan B. Why hadn't Chris given her a Plan B?

Jack was in the corridor now. He would disappear soon, into his meeting with the snooty Paulina and she couldn't think of anything to make him stay. He looked at her speculatively.

"Why don't you put in for *It's My Show*?" He pulled a sheet of paper out of his briefcase. "This is the press release. We think it's really going to pique the interest of the public."

"Jack! We're already late for our meeting," Paulina said.

At the same time Tess's phone started to ring. She pulled it out of her bag. "Just give me one more minute, can you, Jack?"

"Here, you've dropped something," he replied.

"Yes, yes, the press release. I know." Tess pressed the reject button on her phone to silence it and turned back to take the sheet of paper.

Jack was hunkered down, picking something off the floor. Something white, crumpled and very, very familiar. The elevator speech! She must have dropped it when she'd pulled the phone out of her bag. *Don't let him read it, don't let him read it, don't let him read it*, Tess begged the Universe.

But Jack had already spotted the heading on the top of the page.

"It's an elevator speech!" He stood up, looking at Tess admiringly. "I've heard about them. Hey! Are you trying to pitch your book for a film?" He looked up and down the corridor as if he were expecting a Hollywood mogul to miraculously appear. Paulina gave him a pitying look.

"No, I'm not." Tess snatched the paper before he could read any more.

"Nice to meet you, Tess." Paulina placed a firm hand on Jack's shoulder and steered him towards a nearby conference room.

He turned back and smiled, his eyes crinkling at the corners. "Don't forget. Put yourself in for the competition."

Tess followed and watched Paulina propel him into the room and bang the door in her face. She slumped against the wall. She couldn't think of one thing she could do now to retrieve the situation. Cinema Tess didn't seem to be any more resourceful than Normal Tess. The sound of her phone ringing again jolted her out of her misery. Tess glanced at the caller ID. Chris. She pressed the reply button reluctantly.

"Hello?" she whispered.

"So how did it go, babe?"

"Badly. They didn't buy it. Some woman called Paulina said the agony-aunt slot is on hold until after the relaunch. Jack said I should go in for *It's My Show* instead."

"Right. That would be a pretty big jump for you though. From, like, nothing to hosting your own show? The whole point of getting the agony-aunt gig back was so you could use it as a springboard."

"Yeah, well, I didn't," Tess reminded him.

"Right. Well, what about your old job back as Ollie's producer? Did you pitch for that?"

"No." Tess was surprised. "We didn't discuss that."

"So what was your Plan B then?"

"I was just thinking about that myself. How come you didn't give me a Plan B?"

Chris sighed heavily. "I can't do everything for you, Tess. You have to put some effort in yourself as well."

There was a silence in which Tess wondered briefly if he had hung up on her.

Then he said sharply, "Look, maybe it's not too late. Where's Jack now?"

Tess looked at the conference-room door. "He's in a meeting with that Paulina woman and I don't know who else."

"So wait around and give him another elevator speech on the way down," Chris ordered. "Take a 'you need me' angle."

"*No!*" Her response came out almost in a shout, surprising even herself. But she was done with elevator speeches for today, and possibly for the rest of her life. She retraced her footsteps back up the hotel corridor. She was going to find a decent coffee shop and buy herself a giant slice of chocolate cake.

"Okay, okay," Chris soothed. "Why don't we go for dinner tonight and we'll work on a proper Plan B then?"

"Fine," Tess said half-heartedly and hung up. She couldn't think of anything she'd like less.

She pressed the button for the lift but the sound of a commotion distracted her. The conference-room door was suddenly wrenched open and Ollie Andrews came storming through it, his face like thunder.

Tess darted backwards into an alcove beside the lift. She didn't want Ollie to see her. God forbid that he, or anyone from Atlantic 1FM, should ever, *ever* hear about her elevator speech! She waited, flattening her back against the wall until she heard Ollie step into the lift and the doors close behind him. Then she ventured cautiously out of the alcove.

Jack and Paulina were standing there, staring at the closed doors of the lift, looking nonplussed.

"Is he normally this volatile, I wonder?" Jack asked.

"Who knows?" Paulina sounded irritated. "What I do know is that the launch party is in less than a month and we don't exactly have time for celebrity histrionics! All I suggested was that maybe he should consider getting an Extreme Makeover ... I didn't think he was going to *explode* in the way –" She broke off as she noticed Tess. "Oh! You're still here."

"Tess!" Jack smiled at her. "I'm afraid Ollie didn't take what we had to say very well, at all. We obviously have a lot to learn about dealing with the artistic ego. Have you any tips on what makes him tick?"

Tess shrugged. It was clear Ollie had just treated them to one of his full-on temper tantrums. "The only predictable thing I found about Ollie was his unpredictability – he's a law onto himself, I'm afraid."

"I think we need to consider this really carefully." Paulina spoke as if Tess wasn't there. "It's a sensitive issue, taking a show away from someone like Ollie. He has a listenership who won't like it if they think we're being unfair to him. Plus he may go to the papers making all sorts of claims about us. We can't just dump people because we decide their face doesn't fit any more."

"Can't we?" Jack seemed surprised.

"Not without giving them a valid reason." Paulina massaged the bridge of her nose, deep in thought.

"Tess, how would you feel about coming back temporarily to produce Ollie again?" Jack asked. "To help us manage the transition?"

"And I can have the agony-aunt slot back?" Tess felt relief sweep through her. It was Mission Accomplished after all! Chris wouldn't be so judgemental about her lack of a Plan B now!

"I've already told you," Paulina snapped. "We can't consider that until after the relaunch. If we bring it back now it will confuse the listeners. But," she looked at Jack and shrugged, "if you want Tess to work behind the scenes, that's your decision."

Jack was looking at Tess eagerly. Tess hesitated. Chris had said this should be her Plan B. But it wasn't Chris who was going to have to work with Ollie Andrews. An Ollie who would be more difficult than ever now that he was under such intense pressure.

"It would only be temporary," Jack pleaded. "And I'll make sure you're very well rewarded financially. We," he looked at Paulina ruefully, "have never had to deal with such an ... er ... *artistic* personality before. And I can't stress how vital it is that we keep the station going as normal while we're working on the new schedule. Look," he glanced at his watch, "I have another appointment now. But how about we go for dinner later on and discuss it there?"

"Er ..." Tess remembered promising to meet Chris for dinner. But the thought of more lectures from him wasn't very tempting. And who knew? Away from Paulina's prying eyes, she might be able to persuade Jack to give her another chance at the agony-aunt slot. Chris would understand. To his mind, dinner with Jack would be like an extended version of the elevator pitch. She could hear him now: '*This will be two whole hours to convince Jack McCabe of your all-round fabulousness.*'

Besides, she was enjoying seeing Paulina looking so discomfited. Supercilious cow. She barely stopped herself from batting her eyelashes, as she'd seen Sara do so many times. Instead she put a big smile on her face and replied, "I'd love to go to dinner, Jack."

CHAPTER FOURTEEN

Tess slipped off her shoes and threw herself onto the enormous black leather sofa in Chris's living room. It was the archetypal bachelor pad: the room dominated by an enormous flat-screen television and an expensive sound system, stark white walls hung with disturbing abstract paintings. "An investment," Chris had explained when he'd shown her around. Although he needn't have bothered. Tess couldn't imagine anyone buying them for pleasure.

She thought back to the night of the reunion. Ardent as Chris had been that night in her hotel room, he had left at three o'clock, citing an early work assignment the next day. But they'd met for lunch the next day, when he'd convinced her to push herself forward more with the help of his career-coaching techniques.

And although they had made love a few times more she had to admit there was a business-like quality to the relationship that disturbed her. Chris was always yakking on about the best way to get ahead, what Jack McCabe might be looking for and how she, Tess, could give it to him. Frankly, she was exhausted by it all.

She padded through to the bedroom, trying to decide between her boring business suit or the dress she'd bought

189

for the reunion. She opted for the suit, pulling her hair back into a chignon, intent on presenting a professional front. She glanced at the clock. Still no sign of Chris. Tess tried his number but got his voicemail again. She scribbled a note, explaining that she was meeting Jack to talk about going back to Atlantic 1FM and apologising for changing their plans. She pinned it to the fridge with a magnet emblazoned with the words *You Can't Control Everything*.

Hmm, you could have fooled me, Tess thought. She opened the hall door and felt a deep sense of relief overcome her and the further she got from Chris's apartment the better she felt. Funny how she had fantasised about Chris for all these years but now that he was back in her life it felt all wrong. She wondered whether, in the intervening years, they had both changed so much that they just didn't fit together anymore? Or whether she had been wearing the proverbial rose-coloureds all those times she'd thought about him as the One Who Got Away? She didn't know the answer, and she didn't have time to figure it out now. She had her career to think of but, as she walked along the city streets, she realised her whole life didn't depend on her going back to Atlantic 1FM.

The weather was balmy and the air was alive with the promise of summer. People were sprawled on benches along the canal and sitting outside cafés sipping beer and coffee, making the most of the lengthening evenings. It occurred to Tess that she could move to Dublin, rather than start her globetrotting again. It would mean she could still get a foot on the career ladder and she had already broken the ice with her old college friends at the reunion. She had met up with Katie Lawlor for lunch during the week and got the impression that, as a new divorcee, Katie would be more than happy to have someone to hang out with. But first she'd hear what Jack had to say.

The restaurant was tucked away on a corner of a busy street, on the top floor of a handsome Georgian redbrick. A queue of people snaked down the stairs and onto the pavement outside.

Tess eyed them curiously. Everyone was suited and booted, shirts and ties for the men and formal jacket and skirts on the women. Some of them were carrying folders and one man had a briefcase. She frowned and looked down at her navy business suit. She fitted right in here.

A dark-haired woman with a pretty, open face turned to face Tess. "Can you *believe* how many people have turned up for the interviews this evening? Did you think there'd be this much competition?" She made a dramatic, eye-rolling gesture at the people just in front of her, as they shuffled self-consciously from one foot to another.

Something cold unfurled in Tess's stomach.

"Competition for what?"

"Duh – the *jobs*, of course." The woman noticed Tess's astonished expression and did the eye-rolling thing again. "I *know*. You wouldn't think a call centre would get so much interest, would you?" She waved a hand towards the queue again. "God knows how long we'll be here!"

Tess followed her gaze and saw that the people snaking down the stairs were actually queuing for a small recruitment agency's office on the first floor of the building.

The dark-haired woman was looking at her with sympathy. "So what did you do before the recession? Solicitor? No – don't tell me. You were in banking?"

"Er … I'm not here for the job. I'm going to dinner, actually." Tess apologetically gestured towards the top floor, from where the unmistakeable aroma of good Italian food was floating down to them.

"Lucky you!" The woman looked wistfully at Tess. "I used to eat in restaurants like that all the time. That was until my business went bust, of course. I owned my own florist shop – living the dream, or so I thought. But then one of the big multinationals in the town I was living in folded and trade just went through the floor. My shop's been closed almost a year now, I'm up to my eyes in debt and I've given up on being my own boss. If I don't get this, I'm going to be evicted!" She gave a small shudder.

Tess took a deep breath. If she didn't get a job before her savings ran out, she would be in much the same position. She could go home, of course. But the small village in the West of Ireland where she had grown up had even less going on in it than Killty. She felt panicky just thinking about having to live there again.

"Well, good luck anyway." She smiled awkwardly at the woman as she started to climb the stairs, her earlier optimism completely evaporated now.

She spotted Jack immediately. He was back in the casuals he'd been wearing the first day she'd met him in Rose Cottage – faded jeans and a light shirt. Tess needn't have worn her business suit after all. In fact, as she watched him smile at the waitress, a willowy young woman with a mane of dark curls framing her face, she wished she was wearing her sluttiest dress.

"Tess!" He stood up as she reached the table.

She slipped into the seat opposite him and stole a look at him from under her lashes.

He smiled, the corners of his eyes crinkling. "I'm glad you came."

The restaurant was packed and buzzing with conversation and laughter. The women in particular had dressed up, in strapless dresses and lots of bling jewellery. Tess tugged at the collar of her jacket. She could see a glimpse of a balcony through a pair of handsome French doors at the other end of the room and she had an overwhelming urge to get some fresh air.

Jack followed her gaze. "It's a bit stuffy in here, isn't it? We could take our drinks out after eating if you like?"

His hand brushed against hers, and Tess felt a flicker of electricity go through her. She looked at him, startled, trying to see if he'd felt it too, and as their eyes met she again had that odd sensation of recognition, as if she knew Jack from somewhere else, in the far distant past, almost in another life. But if he felt anything, he didn't show it and instead started talking about work.

"So. Will you come back as Ollie's producer? Hopefully it will only be temporary, just for this transition period. Tell me you're interested!"

"I'm not sure," Tess said slowly. "I mean, what happens afterwards – when the transition period is over?"

"Oh," he looked a bit nonplussed, "I haven't really thought that far ahead. Maybe you'll have won *It's My Show* by then."

Tess took a deep breath. She needed more than that. She didn't want to be thrown out on her ear when Atlantic 1FM was relaunched and Jack and Paulina no longer had any use for her. "It would help me make a decision if I knew I could resume the agony-aunt slot. I feel like a fool for the way I handled it. Making a success of it the second time around would help me get my confidence back. It's the only way I'll have a chance in the contest."

Jack gave a rueful shake of his head. "For some reason Paulina has a bee in her bonnet about that at the moment. I talked to her about it again after you left this afternoon. But she's adamant that we can't have any more chopping and changing until after the launch. And she is very good at her job and I don't have a clue about PR so I need to back her on this one. But look, once the contest is over," he looked at her winningly, "you can have it back then."

Luckily, she was saved from answering by the waitress who returned to take their order and, as she filled both their glasses with red wine, Tess began to relax at last. The food was delicious, the wine was soothing and Jack was excellent company. It turned out he was as widely travelled as Tess but, as he explained regretfully, the trips were all business-related and he'd never had time to enjoy the countries he'd visited.

"Going back to some of them is on my bucket list," he smiled.

He was fascinated with Tess's very different experience of crossing the globe on a shoestring. As she recounted some of her adventures, she remembered how wonderful they had been and, for the first time since she'd arrived home, she began to see her "decade of dithering", as her dad had once called it, in a much more positive light. There were different ways of doing things, that was all, she told herself, and, as she sat in the glow of the buzzy restaurant and Jack's company, some of the intense pressure she had been putting herself under to get on the career conveyor-belt began to melt away.

Jack's phone rang, disrupting the atmosphere. He took it out of his pocket, a frown deepening the ridges on his forehead when he glanced at the screen.

"It's Louisa – my sister. I'll have to take it." He shot her an apologetic look.

"Don't worry about it," she said lightly. "I'll get a breath of air." She still felt uncomfortable in her business suit and was glad of the chance to cool down. She took her glass of wine and walked towards the French doors, stepping out onto the small balcony.

The panorama of the city spread out before her, the old red rooftops jostling with the newer, greyer buildings. Above her, pale stars had started to spike the darkening sky. The air was heavy with the scent of the spring flowers that were stuffed into the small balcony space – extravagant arrangements of mauve and white hyacinths, late yellow daffodils and pink tulips planted in giant terracotta pots. Tess sat down at a tiny, ornate table topped with purple mosaic tiles and sipped her wine thoughtfully. Had she imagined the chemistry between Jack and her this evening?

By the time he came out to join her she was sure she had. He was rubbing one hand distractedly through his hair and looked a million miles away.

"Sorry about that. Louisa's still mixed up about that idiot Richard!" He raised his eyebrows. "I did try to tell her that her troubles wouldn't be over simply because I bought Atlantic. I couldn't make much sense of what she was saying on the phone right now to be honest. But ..." He stopped, as if wondering whether he should continue. Then he fixed solemn brown eyes on Tess. "Look, I'm just going to come out with this question. Have you heard anything about Richard having an affair with someone at work?"

"No!" The instinctive response was out before Tess could think about it. She bit her lip. That was an outright lie. But on the other hand, she wasn't one hundred per cent certain about Helene and Richard. Could Sara have taken what she'd overheard that day in the studio out of context? She was certainly prone to exaggeration. She twisted her hands together uncomfortably, as she remembered what Helene had said to her the day in the pub, just before she'd sacked her. "*I know what you must think about me and*

Richard. What everyone thinks." But that wasn't an admission of anything, was it? Tess would need cast-iron evidence of an affair before she'd say anything that would ruin a marriage.

Thankfully, Jack's phone bleeped again, this time with a text message.

"Oh, I'm so sorry. Believe me, I am not always this rude." He scanned the message and his features darkened. "It's Paulina. Something important has come up. I really am sorry but I'm afraid I'm going to have to leave."

Disappointment surged through Tess like a sudden winter shower.

"So?" Jack looked at her quizzically. "You still haven't given me your answer about coming back to produce Ollie."

She opened her mouth to reply but he held up a hand.

"Before you answer, I just want to remind you of something. When I first met you at Grandma Rosa's you told me you worked for a tiny flop radio station."

"Er ... did I say that?" Tess flushed.

"You did!" he grinned. "I remember it very well because of the misgivings I felt about it at the time. But, if you come back to work for me, you would have a chance to help change all that – to be part of something really big."

He sounded so passionate that even if she hadn't witnessed the dispiriting job queue earlier she probably would have agreed.

"Yes. I'll come back."

Jack punched the air. "Result! I promise you won't regret it."

Tess smiled weakly. She somehow doubted that. She knew that whenever Ollie Andrews or Helene Harper was giving her grief she would think back to this moment and be sorry she'd agreed to backtrack on her life. But it would give her a chance to save some money and plan what she was going to do next.

As she watched Jack turn to leave, she knew a large part of her decision was because going back to Atlantic meant she would see more of him. There was something about him that made her want to be near him, in his orbit, absorbing his almost ridiculous sense of enthusiasm for life.

She stayed to finish her wine, sitting at the pretty mosaic table, thinking about the evening. She was disappointed that she wouldn't be moving to Dublin after all, but there were parts of working at Atlantic that she missed – the buzz of the daily deadline, Sara's unique take on life, the camaraderie she'd shared with Andrea.

Thinking about Andrea made her realise that she hadn't spoken to her friend for nearly a week now. She pulled out her mobile and scrolled down to her number, looking forward to telling her about everything that had happened since. How she had somehow become enrolled in the Chris Conroy Crack Academy for Career Advancement at the same time as resuming her relationship with him. The ill-fated elevator speech! And, of course, about Jack asking her out to dinner, and the fact she was coming back to the station.

When she heard Andrea's voicemail click on, Tess finished her wine and stood up. If she hurried, she'd make the last train back to Killty and she could arrange to meet Andrea for lunch tomorrow. She didn't want to go back to Chris's apartment tonight anyway. She needed time to figure out how she felt about him now and besides, she couldn't face him quizzing her about why Jack McCabe wouldn't give her a second chance at the agony-aunt slot, and what exactly he'd said at dinner. She wanted to be at home in her own cluttered apartment. She needed time – to organise getting back to work, to figure out how she would make a better go of it this time, to *think*. Dammit, Tess smiled to herself, she needed *Me Time*. Maybe Andrea's husband, Paul, had a point about that after all.

She walked back into the restaurant to leave and stopped dead. Because, almost as if her thoughts had conjured him up, Paul McAdams was sitting at the other end of the restaurant, his side profile in clear view. Tess automatically looked around for Andrea. It was so unusual they should both be in Dublin on a weeknight.

She started to walk over to say hello when she stopped short again. A woman was slipping into the chair opposite Paul. She had short dark hair cut in an elfin style. She was dressed in a maxi floral dress and pink cardigan. And she most definitely was not Andrea. Tess watched Paul lean over and interlink his hand casually through hers. There was something wrong about the gesture – something unnervingly intimate and Tess sidestepped out of sight, desperate suddenly for Paul not to see her.

She was vaguely aware of the waitress looking at her quizzically.

"Are you all right? You look as if you've seen a ghost."

But Tess barely heard her. She was too busy trying to work out who the woman sitting with her best friend's husband was.

CHAPTER FIFTEEN

Two days later, Tess was sitting at her old desk. She was fiddling forlornly with the settings on her computer. Someone had changed all the passwords since she was here last and she had spent the last hour trying to sort them out. And they weren't the only things to have changed in Atlantic 1FM. The atmosphere was even tenser than before. An hour ago Tess had spotted Paulina Fox swanning into Helene's office, and now they were both lurking in the corridor, their heads bent together conspiratorially, as if they knew some top secret everybody else was excluded from.

And where was Ollie, Tess wondered? *This Morning* was due to start in just under an hour and she needed to run through the show with him. She was not looking forward to it. Ollie would *not* like the content of the programme today. Tess looked dubiously at her running order. Helene was coming on to talk about her *Ten Years Younger* project. And Grandma Rosa was booked in for a *Psychic Granny* slot – a pilot Helene wanted to try. The content of the show had changed so much since Tess was here last that Sara was already calling it *Ollie Lite*.

Tess cast her mind back to her first visit to the fortune teller and smiled. If anyone had told her then that the old woman would have a slot in Atlantic 1FM she wouldn't have believed it. What was it that Grandma Rosa had said to her back then? *"There are big changes on the horizon for you. There's a big romance showing here."*

She'd been right after all, although she doubted she'd use the world 'big' or indeed 'romance' to describe her relationship with Chris which had that functional quality about it which bothered her. She had texted him on the train home to Killty and said she wasn't feeling well and had to go home. It wasn't a lie either. On the train home, her stomach lurched each time she replayed the scene in the restaurant over in her mind. When Andrea had returned her call, Tess had pretended there was no coverage and hung up on her friend. Then she'd switched her phone to silent, rammed her headphones over her ears, and listened to loud pop music, trying to forget the evening had ever happened. But of course it had, and she was dreading having to face Andrea later that day.

She looked up and saw Ollie marching down to his desk. Tess tried to hide her surprise at the sight of him. He was pale and dishevelled – his shirt crumpled and his trousers baggy, as if they were too big for him. He was clutching a gigantic take-out coffee to his chest and Tess could see a light sheen of sweat glistening on his bald spot.

A stab of sympathy for him took Tess by surprise. The takeover was hard on all of them, but probably it was most difficult for Ollie. If, or when, he got axed, it was going to be a very visible humiliation. And since her agony-aunt debacle, Tess knew what that felt like.

"Morning, Ollie!" Tess said cheerfully, determined to start over on a new, more positive footing.

"What's good about it?" Ollie pushed a lank lock of hair out of one eye. "You're back."

Tess felt her positivity evaporating, to be replaced by a cold fury at Ollie's dismissive attitude. She felt like shouting: *It's not as if people were queuing up to work with you! Jack McCabe had to take me out to dinner and practically beg me!*

"So, what have you got for me this morning, then?" Ollie sat down, took a deep slurp of his drink and turned on his computer.

"We have Helene at the top of the programme – she'll be talking about her efforts to look ten years younger – remember she talked about going to that top spa?" Too late, Tess remembered that that had been the meeting where Ollie and Helene had their big bust-up.

"Who cares whether that old bat looks ten years younger or not?" Ollie didn't bother looking up from his screen. "It's not as if she's a celebrity!"

"Well, she's coming on the show, nonetheless." Tess tried to make her voice sound steely. She was determined not to be subservient this time around. Chris had given her express instructions to avoid what he called 'status-lowering signals'. These included hand-wringing and self-grooming gestures, apparently. Tess looked down at her fingers and saw they were locked together so tightly her knuckles were glistening bone-white. She prised them apart and laid them flat on the desk to prevent herself from committing the next cardinal sin of touching her hair.

She opened her mouth to tell Ollie about the second item on the morning's show – the *Psychic Granny* slot. But no words came out. Tess swallowed. She guessed Ollie would be bitter about the *Ollie Lite* tag and how Jack McCabe was driving down the content of the station to reach a more popular audience. He would *not* appreciate a fortune teller coming on his show. Still, what could she do? Helene had

201

booked Rosa – when Tess had arrived this morning it was a fait accompli.

Suddenly she remembered one of Chris's techniques for getting on at work. The mirroring technique, he'd called it. Tess tried to recall what he'd said. *Subtly mirror a difficult person's body language and they will instantly warm to you.* That was it! Tess stole a glance at Ollie. He was still staring at his computer, his eyes bulging slightly, his mouth turned down in a disappointed slope, one shaky hand on his coffee container and the other God knows where. Tess suppressed a sigh. She was supposed to mirror that?

Still, she'd have to try. Tess stared hard at her own computer, pretending to study something on the screen, watching Ollie's every move surreptitiously from under her lashes. Each time Ollie took a sip of coffee, Tess obediently took a swig from her own mug. Every time he sighed – which was every twenty seconds – Tess too let out a long-suffering sigh. When he blew his nose on a none-too-clean-looking hankie, Tess fished a paper tissue out of her own handbag.

Ollie finally looked up.

"Is there something wrong with you?" he snapped.

"What?" Tess asked innocently, the tissue halfway to her nose.

"What? You're sighing every twenty seconds." Ollie sighed heavily again.

Tess wondered fleetingly if Ollie had become clinically depressed since she'd seen him last. She took another deep, mirroring sigh. "We have the Psychic Granny for our second item. She's the … um … fortune teller."

Ollie's eyebrows met in a belligerent frown on his forehead. "That nutcase who rang you on your fiasco of an agony-aunt slot?"

She took a deep breath. *Flatter them into submission* – that was another of the techniques. "Yes. Her. But if there's anyone in the world who can make this item interesting – it's *you*, Ollie."

Tess stopped. She hadn't intended to sound quite so saccharine. He would hear how insincere she sounded and turn on her! But then, as if by magic, his whole body seemed to change in front of her eyes. His sat up straighter and his features lost their look of perpetual defensiveness.

"D'you really think so?"

He sounded so hopeful that Tess felt a stab of guilt for wilfully misleading him. She nodded dumbly.

"And what makes you think that, exactly?" Ollie peered across the desk at her.

Tess bit her lip. "Because ... of the depth of your experience? And the fact that you're er ... naturally good with people? And ..." She racked her brain for more improbable compliments.

Then she realised she didn't have to. Ollie was on his feet and making his way around to her desk.

"Let me see what you have on the old charlatan!" He sounded positively jovial now. He stood behind her, one hand brushing her neck as he peered over her shoulder.

Tess tried not to flinch.

"Right, er ... let's see ... here it is." She passed him the two-page brief she had written earlier for the *Psychic Granny* slot and watched nervously while he read it through impassively.

"You'll be able to handle her better than I could. I mean, as I said, you have so much more *experience*, Ollie." She sounded a bit desperate now.

But Ollie looked up, his eyes shining with something unfathomable. "You're absolutely right! Of course. This fortune-telling lark is a load of old codswallop but, you know, I *do* have the experience and the talent to make anything interesting. I'll see you in studio shortly." He walked off, calling over his shoulder, "Watch and learn, Tess! Watch and learn!"

Tess sank her head into her hands as soon as Ollie left. It had been that *easy*? She remembered the months of turmoil when she'd tried to manage Ollie with logic and rationale and failed miserably. And all she'd had to do all along was to *flatter* him? She felt a fleeting sense of resentment for all the effort she'd wasted but she shrugged it off. If this was what she had to do to keep Ollie Andrews sweet, so be it.

"*If there's anyone in the world who can make this item interesting – it's you, Ollie!*"

Tess looked up in surprise at the sound of Andrea's voice mimicking her.

"*I'm sure you'll be better able to handle her than I could, Ollie,*" Andrea continued, a nasty note in her voice. "*You have so much experience.*"

Tess flushed. "It's this mirroring technique that I talked to Chris about," she tried to explain. "It ... er ... really works."

"Apparently so." Andrea gave a wintry smile and turned her back on her.

Tess stared after her in panic. Had she found out something about Paul? Or that Tess had been in the same restaurant that night and hadn't told her she'd bumped into him? A quick glance at the clock determined that she didn't have time to find out. *This Morning* was about to go to air and she had no choice but to turn around and follow Ollie.

He was sitting in the soundproofed part of the studio, bent over a newspaper, and he didn't look up when she arrived. Helene was nowhere to be seen. And neither was Grandma Rosa. Tess took her seat on the other side of the glass window and glanced down at the running order, trying to figure out what she could open with if neither of them turned up on time.

She was reaching for her contacts book when Sara arrived, a breathless Rosa in tow. "Helene's been delayed in a meeting so we'll have to start with *Psychic Granny*," she explained, already leading Rosa in and settling her down opposite Ollie.

Tess exhaled quietly. She had been expecting Sara to be in a major sulk today because her own arrival back at work meant that Sara's promotion had been short-lived, but here she was, being completely professional about it, making sure the guest felt comfortable.

She had to smile at the sight of Rosa. She was wearing a black-and-white dotted gypsy-style scarf tied jauntily around her neck, and her huge hooped earrings dangled almost to her shoulders. She had replaced the purple hair with a violent shade of red and she was expertly shuffling and cutting her deck of tarot cards.

Ollie darted a nervous look out to the control room at Tess.

"Helene is a bit late," she explained on the talkback system. "So we're going to start the show today with *Psychic Granny*."

Ollie looked mutinous, so Tess added, a bit jadedly at this stage, "But *you'll* know how best to handle it, Ollie." This flattery was becoming exhausting, she thought, pressing her cheeks into her hands. She held her breath for the final few seconds before the show began. And then, just as the familiar signature tune for *This Morning* started up, Tess heard a rustling behind her.

She turned around to see Helene had arrived. Without stopping to explain or apologise or even to greet Tess, Helene barged breathlessly through the studio door, plonked herself down on the chair beside Rosa, and clapped the headphones over her ears.

"I'm here," she announced needlessly.

Tess flipped the talkback switch again.

"Ollie! Go back to Plan A. Start with Helene now that she's here!"

Ollie sighed peevishly, but nodded in agreement.

Tess breathed a final sigh of relief and sat back in her chair. They were On. Ollie was happy – or as happy as Ollie could be given that he was Ollie. Helene's *Ten Years Younger* would be a hoot. And the *Psychic Granny* was bound to get lots of reaction.

Not a bad start for her first show since she'd come back. This time around, Tess decided, she would cultivate a healthier attitude towards her job. Today, instead of being hyper-vigilant for things going wrong, she was going to trust that everything would go really, really well for a change. And that was the last Zen-like moment she had all morning.

It all started so well. Helene began by explaining the background to how she had started on what she called her *Ten Years Younger* journey, how she had researched lots of treatments – Botox, non-surgical facelifts, anti-ageing creams with almost miraculous properties – all claiming to stem the tide of time. She would, she promised, be explaining to the listeners how all of these treatments worked in reality. She was breathless from her late arrival and, as usual, she was speaking much too fast. But at least, Tess acknowledged, she wasn't stuttering over quite ordinary words like she normally did on air. And she was genuinely enthusiastic about this topic, which was always a plus.

But then, halfway through Helene's recitation of the scientific ingredients in one of her treatments, Ollie got bored. Tess knew it the moment he began to run his fingers through his hair, followed by fiddling with his pen, clicking the top of it on and off noisily.

Helene ignored him until he finally interjected: "And tell me, Helene – what's so important about looking ten years younger in the first place?"

"Well, it's more important for women to look young because they are judged as much on their looks as their ability," she replied confidently.

"Really?" Ollie sounded sceptical.

Tess shifted in her chair, her antennae up.

"Really! In fact, women have to do better than men in all areas of life simply to get the same results. As someone said about Ginger Rogers, she had to do everything Fred Astaire did, except she did it backwards in high heels." Helene smiled flirtatiously at Ollie, delighted with this opportunity to portray her sense of humour on air.

"And what does that mean?" Ollie asked irritably.

"What does it mean?" A note of defensiveness crept into Helene's voice. "It's a *metaphor* – for how much more difficult things still are for women in the workplace."

"I don't know if I agree with that, actually." Ollie folded his arms and stared at her.

"You don't have to agree with it." She leaned forward in her chair, enunciating her words very carefully, as if she were talking to a two-year-old. "Which part of it do you not understand, Ollie?"

Tess pushed the talkback switch. "Go back to talking about the treatments, Ollie."

But Ollie's earlier acquiescence had vanished. "Let's see what someone else thinks, shall we? Our Psychic Granny is here with us in studio too and she'll be telling us about her psychic abilities in just a moment. But what do you think of all this, Grandma Rosa?"

Rosa, who had been studying her tarot cards, looked up when she heard her name. "Er ... about what?" she asked.

"Helene has just said women have to do everything men do to succeed – except they have to do it backwards and in high heels." Ollie didn't bother to keep the sneer out of his voice.

Rosa considered his words silently, her neck to one side, like a little bird. Say something, Tess implored via mental telepathy, as several seconds of dead air ticked away.

"I think Helene probably has something there," Rosa said finally. "Things are harder because women have to have their babies at the same time as they are building up their careers. Whereas *men* can put off that lark until they're in their dotage, so it's not exactly a level playing field, is it?"

"Thank you, Rosa." Helene turned back to Ollie. "So. To get back to my *Ten Years Younger* journey ..."

"But what I'd like to know is how to *feel* ten years younger!" Rosa said suddenly. "Have you any tips on that, Helene?"

"No, I don't," Helene said shortly. "That's not what my journey was about."

"It's just that when you get to my age – and I don't mind telling the listeners," Rosa leaned into her microphone, "that I'm over seventy – feeling ten years younger is a lot more attractive than simply looking it. Do you *feel* better since you had all these treatments and therapies?"

"No, actually."

Tess, who had glanced down at her notes, and was wondering how soon she could pull the *Ten Years Younger* item, jerked her head up at the strange note in Helene's voice.

"In fact, I feel … very peculiar …" And then her voice trailed away altogether and she slumped sideways in her chair.

Grandma Rosa and Tess were on their feet at the same time. But by the time Tess had pushed through the door, Rosa, displaying remarkable strength for her age, had caught Helene, stopping her from hitting the floor.

"Play some music!" Tess hissed at Ollie. She hunkered down beside Helene. "Is she okay?" She looked fearfully at Rosa, who had two fingers on Helene's wrist. She turned back to Sara who was hovering in the doorway. "Ring for an ambulance!"

"She's okay," Rosa said soothingly. "She's just fainted."

Tess looked at Helene. Her bright-red lipstick was like a gash against her pale, translucent complexion. Beads of moisture gathered on her forehead and she looked clammy and sick.

"I'm not taking any chances," Tess decided. "Sara! Dial the emergency services."

"Honestly, there's no need," Rosa said calmly. "I was a nurse in a former life and I know what I'm talking about. Look – she's coming around already."

Tess looked down as Helene's eyelashes fluttered like spiders on her cheeks. She opened her eyes, and looked about her, dazed.

"We need to get her out of here, it's too hot. She needs something to drink." Rosa gently helped Helene to sit up. "Are you okay, love?"

Helene blinked, looking as if she didn't know where she was.

Rosa and Tess helped her to her feet. Then Tess left Sara in charge and followed Rosa, who was guiding Helene towards her office.

"I'm fine," Helene insisted. "You can go back to the programme, Tess."

"Yes, you can," Rosa interjected. "But only after you get her a cup of hot sweet tea." She turned to Helene. "You look very shaken, love."

"I'm just a bit – maybe I will have something to drink then." Helene's voice was fading again.

Tess rushed to the kitchen and rooted in the cupboards for something sweet. She returned with a tray of tea, as Rosa had instructed, and a packet of chocolate biscuits. She stopped outside the office, balancing the tray on her hip and angling herself so she could push open the door without having to disturb Rosa.

She could hear Helene's voice, explaining plaintively, "When you asked me if I felt ten years younger I remember thinking 'I've never felt worse in my life, actually'. And then I must have fainted. But it's true. I feel fat and fed up and exhausted all the time lately. This morning I felt so tired I actually threw up. I knew I was on air first thing so I didn't bother with breakfast. That's obviously why I fainted, because nothing like this has ever happened to me before. But I'm fine now. I'm going to tell Tess I'm okay to go back on air and finish the slot."

"Tired? Fat? Morning sickness?" said Rosa. "The Stork card appearing in the Tarot? What does all that say to you, Helene?"

"What?" Helene said in a strange, high voice.

Tess froze at the door. Helene was *pregnant*?

Then she heard Rosa again, asking urgently, "Helene! Helene – are you okay?"

Tess barged into the office and plonked the tray down on the desk. Rosa was holding Helene's head in the crook of her arm and fanning her face with the script Helene had prepared for her *Ten Years Younger* slot. A slot which she definitely wouldn't be resuming any time soon.

Because Helene had fainted again.

CHAPTER SIXTEEN

Helene lay on her sofa, Grandma Rosa's words echoing in her head. *"Tired? Fat? Morning sickness? The Stork card appearing in the Tarot? What does all that say to you, Helene?"* That's when she'd fainted for a second time, when she'd heard those words, words that were both bizarre and terrifying. But words that Helene knew she couldn't ignore nonetheless. Not when she remembered how she'd almost been sick on the side of the road on the way back from the spa, and how bone-tired she was lately. And how her boobs were really sore.

Of course, there were perfectly reasonable explanations for all those symptoms, other than pregnancy, she reasoned. Food poisoning from that wretched spa, for one. And who wouldn't be extra tired with all the additional pressure at work? As for sore boobs, they were a normal symptom of PMT – everyone knew that. Helene had never had that particular symptom herself, but she was nearly forty, her body was changing.

The most relevant symptom – an overdue period – was difficult for her to work out because her monthly cycle had never been regular. And the real test – a pregnancy test kit – was not something Helene wanted to think about right now.

She had enough to worry about. Like how much of the conversation with Rosa had Tess Morgan overhead? By the time Helene had recovered from her second fainting fit, Tess had a taxi waiting outside to take her home. She had insisted on escorting Helene to the cab, making her promise to see a doctor as soon as possible.

Helene had no intention of doing so, at least not today. Richard was on his way over. He'd been listening to the radio when she'd fainted and had phoned her when she was in the taxi, wondering what had happened. She had successfully sidestepped his questions, but she was going to have to tell him *something* when he arrived.

It was typical, she mused. All the nights she'd wanted him here and he hadn't been available, because he'd been busy with work or his kids or the eternal "family stuff" he had to attend to with his wife. Now tonight, when all Helene wanted was to be on her own, to gather her wits and to think, Richard had brushed aside her protestations and insisted he'd be over just as soon as he finished work.

Helene hadn't the strength to argue. As soon as she got home, she switched her phone off and crawled into bed, literally pulling the duvet over her head. When she woke up, three hours had passed. Her head still felt muzzy but that was probably because she still hadn't eaten. Richard was bringing food later so she'd wait for that.

She spent the rest of the afternoon pampering herself. She switched on some music and relaxed in a warm bath, mulling over what to tell Richard about what had happened earlier. She didn't want him to get even a hint that she might be pregnant. What was the point in frightening him when it might not even be true? They had only barely made up after their row at the press conference. Richard had apologised for his behaviour, explaining how he had completely freaked out when he realised Jack McCabe had cottoned on to the fact that he was having an affair.

"I overreacted and took it out on you. It wasn't fair," he'd said tenderly, taking her hand in his and kissing her slender fingers.

No, it wasn't, Helene thought, hauling herself out of the bath. But that didn't mean it wouldn't happen again, if the going got tough.

She stretched out to paint her toenails, clearing her mind by concentrating only on each brushstroke of black varnish. By the time the doorbell announced Richard's arrival she had decided she would ask all about his plans for her fortieth birthday party, as a way of distracting him.

She opened the door to find him half-hidden by an enormous bouquet of flowers – extravagant white lilies and blowsy red roses nestled in a sea of artfully arranged greenery. He held a brown-paper carrier bag.

"Food!" He thrust the flowers at Helene and strode past her, straight through to the kitchen. "I've got your favourite."

Helene hovered in the doorway to the kitchen, trying not to gag at the distinctive scent of the lilies and watching Richard as he produced a smoked-salmon salad from the bag and a container of handmade ice cream for dessert.

As she watched him bustle about her tiny kitchen, looking for cutlery and crockery, she thought how handsome and virile he looked. The silver streaks in his dark-blond hair made him look sexier, not older. He had his contact lenses in and his eyes were vividly blue. She still found them mesmerising. Smiling, she found a vase for the flowers and sat down at the table.

As they settled down to eat, he looked at her keenly.

"So? What happened this morning?"

"I fainted," she shrugged. "It must have been a bug. I've slept it off, I think."

He watched her push her food around her plate. "Aren't you hungry?"

"I am." She forced herself to eat a forkful of salmon. "So – what about my birthday bash? Where's it going to be?"

Helene had originally thought of asking him to throw the party in a public place, simply because she knew it would be so difficult for him – a foolhardy test for him to prove his commitment to her. Now, with a secret of her own to keep, she didn't have the appetite for that sort of game-playing.

"I thought we could have it here." Richard looked around the cramped apartment. "I mean, you don't have that many friends, do you?"

Helene's features darkened, and Richard quickly changed the subject. "Look, we can talk about that later. I have some news. The party for the relaunch of Atlantic has been brought forward so we need to have your party before that, so they don't clash."

Helene stared at Richard in dismay. "But that means we'll need to have our pitches for *It's My Show* in earlier! People have barely had a chance to develop their plans."

"I'm not sure that's true, actually." He stroked his chin thoughtfully. "My desk is piled up with proposals already."

"Really? You've seen the proposals?" Her eyes widened. "What are they like?"

"I didn't play a blind bit of attention to them." Richard shrugged. "I opened them – just to show willing – but I didn't bother reading them. It's not going to be my call, after all. That PR woman, Paulina Whatshername ...?"

"Fox. Paulina Fox." Helene was still thinking of the

proposals on Richard's desk.

"She's going through them." He leaned back in his chair and linked his hands behind his head. "Once the launch party is over I'm hoping I'll be out of there for good. And it won't be a moment too soon." He smiled secretively. "It will be a whole new chapter for me."

Helene felt a surge of panic. A whole new chapter for *me*? Surely he'd meant to say *us*? Even though Richard had been behaving oddly lately, she had no intention of giving up her dream of a future with him without a fight.

But then he stood up, walked around and pulled her up into his arms and she thought how lucky she was to have such a dynamic man in her life.

For once, there appeared to be no dramas chez Armstrong and Richard didn't seem to be in a hurry anywhere. They spent the rest of the night chatting, drinking wine and making love and Helene completely forgot about her pregnancy scare.

He stayed much later than normal. She noticed the time glowing in red neon on the clock as he slipped out of her bed to go home. Four o'clock. She smiled drowsily in the dark. He'd never stayed so late before. Unless they were away for work, he would always be tucked up in his own bed by now. It was a start.

At breakfast, she felt absolutely fine, with no queasiness whatsoever. She made herself eat a breakfast of tea, toast and a boiled egg, and by the time she got to work, she was chiding herself for giving any credence at all to Rosa's prediction.

She swapped her high heels for the pair of flats she kept under the desk, switched off her phone and spent the next two hours working on her pitch for *It's My Show*. She thought Jack McCabe was proceeding with unseemly haste but, then, wasn't that what he was famous for – being a human dynamo who forged ahead with his plans and expected everyone else to keep up or drop out? Well, he wouldn't find Helene wanting on that score.

In fact, she could feel the adrenaline surging through her now that the deadline had been shortened. She decided she would continue with her *Ten Years Younger* series and air it each day over the coming weeks, giving herself maximum on-air presence. She could also take credit for Grandma Rosa's slot, which, judging by the amount of calls Sara had taken from listeners wanting to know more about *Psychic Granny*, was destined to be a huge success.

She would weave *Psychic Granny* into her new show proposal, which would be called ... Helene's brow furrowed as she tried to think of a name. Finally, she scribbled down 'The Silver Surf Hour'. She held up her A4 pad to consider it. The name wasn't strong enough – too clichéd – and it was a risk not going after the youth market, but then everyone else would be pitching for that. She was going to go with her hunch that there was something in this grey-power trend Rosa had mentioned. If Helene could convince Jack McCabe that she could capture a sizeable chunk of older listeners with disposable income she would illustrate that she knew something about the business side of radio as well as having an obvious creative streak.

She smiled to herself. All those hours listening to Richard droning on about the pressures of his work had come in useful after all. And, she thought happily, at forty she would practically seem like a teenager to her target audience. Helene put her memo pad down on the desk, allowing herself to bask in the familiar fuzzy, warm feeling of knowing she was on to something. This was why she did it, she realised. This was why she put up with all the long hours and the dramas and the histrionics.

She reached into her bag for a mint and a business card fell out. She picked it up and turned it over. It was for the Travel Café. Of course! She could get Matt to come in and do a *Gap Year for Grown-ups* slot, keeping the positive-ageing motif going. Genius! She picked up the phone, twirling a strand of hair around her fingers as she waited for someone to pick up.

"Travel Café! How can I help you?"

"Hi, Matt. It's Helene Harper here. From Atlantic 1FM."

"Helene! It's great to hear from you again. How *are* you?"

She looked at the telephone receiver, slightly taken aback at how pleased he sounded. She was used to people being defensive, or wary or even sycophantic when she spoke to them. But not genuinely happy to hear from her.

"I'm fine," she said cautiously. She started to explain about her idea but she only got so far before Matt interrupted her.

"Oh my God! I've just been sitting here thinking that what I need right now is a bit of publicity to really get the café out there, you know? And then *you* ring. Talk about serendipity!"

He sounded so enthusiastic that Helene felt a pang of guilt. She had been thinking of using Matt for her own ends, not about what it might mean for him. Still, she thought, if it was mutually beneficial all the better. Helene outlined her idea a bit more and waited for his reaction.

"It's a fantastic opportunity, Helene. Thank you so much for thinking of me. So, when would you like me to do it?"

She hesitated. She wanted to keep it under wraps for the competition.

"I'll get back to you with all the details soon, yeah? Oh,

and Matt? I'm having a birthday party shortly ... and I was ... er, wondering if you c-c-could come?" She found herself stammering. She had been brooding about Richard saying she only had a few friends. Her older sister, Zoey, lived in New Zealand with her grown-up family and Helene only ever saw her now on Skype. And she had allowed her circle of friends to gradually wither away while she was focussing all of her attention on Richard and Atlantic 1FM.

"I'd love to come – thanks so much for asking me." Matt was positively ebullient now. "Is it a special birthday?"

"The big Four-O, I'm afraid," she said, a bit shyly.

"*What?* I can't believe you're forty!"

"Flattery will get you everywhere!" she said, but she couldn't stop smiling and, when she hung up the phone, she was alarmed to hear herself *humming*.

The next phone call interrupted her good mood, however. It was from Paulina explaining how everyone needed to have their *It's My Show* proposals in by the end of the week.

"It's very short notice," Helene pointed out. "I'm not sure if anyone will have their pitches perfected by then."

"Well, Tess Morgan has been working hard on hers," Paulina sniffed.

And then she relayed a bizarre story about Tess stalking Jack McCabe at a hotel where Paulina and Jack had been meeting with Ollie. Something about Tess pitching an elevator speech at Jack, in a bid to get her agony-aunt gig back.

Frankly, Helene found it difficult to believe that a mouse like Tess Morgan would have the imagination or the gumption to do any such thing. But then, why would Paulina make it up? When she hung up from the call, she squeezed her feet into her stilettos and went to find out more.

Sara saw her coming and covered her notebook with both hands. Helene smiled. She knew Sara was calling her pilot 'Sundays with Sara' and that Ollie, with an ego the size of a small planet, had hired an outside consultant to devise his proposal. And now Tess Morgan had used an elevator pitch. She wondered what Andrea was planning. She was out of the office today, supposedly researching a story, but Helene was sure she was using the time to work on her entry for It's My Show. It was unbelievable the lengths people were willing to go to. Helene didn't mind. She liked the competition.

"Listen up, everyone," she announced. "The launch party for the new look Atlantic 1FM takes place in two weeks."

Sara whipped her head around. "Really? That soon?"

"That soon – which means the deadline for your proposals is the end of this week. The winner will be announced at the relaunch party, apparently." Helene waited for the cries of dismay to die down before adding, "So, good luck with them. May the best man – or woman – win!"

"It's mine, Helene," Ollie warned.

Helene's mobile rang and she fished it out of her pocket. It was Paulina again.

"Hi, I forgot to say. We want to provide coaching for current staff who are pitching for It's My Show – so can you set up a rota so I can see all of you as soon as possible?"

Helene frowned. "Why do you want to do that?"

"It's standard management strategy. We want the people who don't win the contest to still feel valued by the station.

After all, they're going to be working crazy hours to make the eventual winner into a household name. People are going to lots of trouble with their submissions, so it's important they feel they are getting a fair crack of the whip. Especially if the gig eventually goes to an outsider."

Helene's antennae shot up. "Is an outsider in the frame to get it?"

"Not necessarily." Paulina's voice was soothing. "But I have to say it – we do have some pretty good external candidates."

"Really?" Helene's voice came out in a squeak.

"Really. So let the others know about the coaching, will you?"

"Okay." Helene clicked off her mobile and suppressed a sigh. She wondered why Paulina, who had never worked in a radio station in her life, thought she could offer the rest of them coaching advice.

"What was that about?" Ollie asked.

"Er … Paulina is setting up coaching sessions for all the contest entrants working here." Helene was still trying to figure out if there was some ulterior motive behind it.

"Coaching? What will that involve?" Sara asked.

"I've no idea. I presume Paulina will go over your proposal with you, give you a chance to enhance it in some way. Would you like me to look over it with you first, Sara?"

"No thanks, I'd rather keep it private."

"What about you, Tess? Would you like me to go over your proposal before Paulina arrives? Apparently it's mandatory that we all attend."

"No thanks." Tess didn't look up from her computer screen.

"What are you working on – another elevator speech?"

Joan Brady

Helene looked over Tess's shoulder.

"A what?" Ollie's head jerked up.

"Haven't you heard? Apparently, Tess here stalked Jack and Paulina to pitch them her idea that she should have a second chance at the agony-aunt slot. In some hotel in Dublin."

Ollie's eyes narrowed. "I met Jack and Paulina at a hotel in Dublin. Was it there?"

"I don't want to talk about it," Tess muttered.

But Helene had already seen a crimson rash creeping up her throat.

"Oh, you can't leave us in the dark like that!" she taunted.

"I can, actually!" Tess suddenly blazed. "I've said I don't want to talk about it, so just leave it at that. And, while I'm at it, will everyone please shut up about this stupid contest! It's all anyone has talked about since I've come back and I am completely sick of it. I'm trying to get some work done here."

"Okay, no need to bite my head off!" Helene backed off, suddenly remembering how kind Tess had been yesterday after she'd fainted. She didn't think she would have been so magnanimous herself in the circumstances.

She walked towards Richard's office, hoping he could tell her more about the coaching. But even though the door was ajar, his chair was empty. She turned to leave but then remembered what he'd said about the proposals for *It's My Show* piling up on his desk. Cautiously, she stepped into the office and, sure enough, there they were – stacks of submissions scattered about carelessly where Richard had thrown them.

Helene didn't hesitate. She had taught herself years ago to speed-read – a skill she had found extremely useful

222

during her career, enabling her to read other people's private information with ease. She leaned over now, intent on scanning through as many of the rival proposals as she could. But the sudden movement made her dizzy and she stood back up sharply. She put her hand to her mouth, aware of the by-now-familiar sensation of retching rising up from her stomach. She turned and ran from the office, barely making it to the Ladies' before throwing up.

Afterwards, she leaned against the white bathroom sink, staring at her ashen complexion and the uncertainty in her eyes. She couldn't go on like this. She was scared stiff but she knew now she had to find out whether she was pregnant or not. As soon as possible.

CHAPTER SEVENTEEN

She stood in front of the mirror, her head to one side as she considered her reflection. She was wearing an eye-wateringly expensive set of lingerie, but it wasn't the oyster silk bra and panties that Helene's eyes were trained on. She folded her hands across her belly, hardly able to believe it. She was actually pregnant.

She had finally worked up the courage to use the pregnancy test, just two days ago, and the result had changed everything. The idea of travelling the world with Richard was ridiculous now they were expecting a baby. There were other considerations to ponder – moving to a bigger place maybe, somewhere with a garden.

She'd felt as if she were inhabiting a surreal, parallel universe, but as soon as she knew she was positively, definitely pregnant, the panic had been replaced by the sure, calm knowledge that this was where she was meant to be in her life right now. Sometimes, the strange sensation of living in a twilight zone would return. Today, while one part of her was rushing around, getting ready for her party, another, deeper part was pondering how her whole world was about to change.

When she was clearing out her fridge to make room for the caterers she'd been shocked at the contents – a bottle of white wine, a black banana and a half-empty carton of milk. And the urgent necessity to upgrade her diet was only the start of it. How would she manage her long working days with a baby in tow – especially now that Richard wouldn't be there to smooth the way for her? How was she going to find the words to tell him, without him freaking out?

But at other odd times, sheer elation stole over her. Like now, as she stood in her underwear, her mouth curved upwards in a smile. Long ago she had accepted that she had probably forfeited her chance to become a mother – another unfortunate consequence of falling for a married man. And then out of the blue, it had happened. Helene had given up trying to figure out how it had occurred. Even Richard must realise there was no foolproof birth control. What was it her grandmother used to say about unplanned pregnancies? *"Sometimes nature makes fools of us all."*

Her eyes strayed to the clock. She had better get a move on. Her guests were due to arrive and she wanted to look her best. She fingered the red silk dress she had bought for the occasion. It was a knockout, folding cleverly over her stomach – she hadn't a clue about when she might start to show – and clinging to her curves. Her boobs were definitely fuller, she thought, leaning forward to inspect her cleavage. And her complexion had a new, luminous quality to it that made her look different. Softer, maybe?

Helene smiled a secret smile, pulled the dress over her head and slipped on her heels. She gave herself a last spritz of scent, tossed her hair over her shoulders and wandered into the living room. The party planners Richard had hired had arrived earlier to create what they had called "an atmosphere of discreet luxury". Expensive flower arrangements of red roses and white gypsophila were dotted around the room and a couple of silver champagne buckets held the celebratory fizz. There was just one balloon with the figure 40 on it floating in a corner, almost hidden behind her silver standard lamp. Lauren, the boss of the party-planning company, had explained they would be back tonight to serve the food and drink.

"If you give me a key we can clear up tomorrow while you're in work," she offered. "By the time you get back it will be as if you'd never had a party at all."

Helene found it a little bit sad that all the evidence of her big night would be cleared away so soon. But then, she consoled herself, she could have all the big parties she wanted in the future. Big, showy parties. She and Richard couldn't be discreet about their affair when she was as big as a house, after all, or when they had a little baby to rear together.

But would Richard still be around when she was big as a house? One part of her, the logical, rational part she was most familiar with, had to concede that there was a distinct possibility that he would not. Look at how he had reacted when she'd suggested they go travelling together – something about how he couldn't leave his "children".

But since she discovered she was pregnant, Helene had discovered a different part of herself, a part she didn't recognise and was slightly alarmed by, a part that was ridiculously optimistic and vulnerable all at the same time. And it was this part that whispered to her now that Richard loved her, as he'd told her often enough. And the one thing she could never fault him on was his role as a father. His devotion to David and Anna had been a source of constant conflict between them, but now, in this new situation, Helene thought that it wasn't such a bad flaw in a man after all. Because this new baby of hers was his baby too. That in itself was bound to change his level of commitment to her.

A movement behind her made her look up. Richard had arrived. She caught her breath at the sight of him. He was wearing a navy work suit but he'd pulled off his tie and his white shirt was unbuttoned. The tiredness which had dogged him for the past few months had vanished.

"Happy birthday, baby!" he called out, positively carefree.

Helene slipped easily into his embrace. "Thank you. I'm glad you're the first to arrive – it's nice to have some time alone."

"You look wonderful!"

He pulled her closer to him and, as she buried her face in his chest, she felt all the stress of the past few weeks leave her. Everything was going to be all right, she thought, breathing in the Richard smell – a mix of aftershave and masculinity – that made her feel safe.

"So, what will you have to drink? Champagne, I presume?" He gently released her and went over to pick up a bottle.

"I'm okay for now." Helene gestured vaguely to the glass of sparkling water on the coffee table. "You have some, though."

"Water?" Richard frowned slightly. "You're not feeling ill again, are you? Maybe you should get the doc to check you out?"

"Maybe I will."

He poured himself a glass of bubbly and placed it on the coffee table. Then he slouched onto the sofa, interlacing his hands behind his head, a reminiscent smile on his face. "The only time Louisa didn't want champagne was when she was pregnant," he joked.

Helene turned away. She'd go into the kitchen, or the bedroom, somewhere she could escape from this conversation. But she wasn't quick enough.

"Helene?"

She looked back at him and saw he was now sitting bolt upright.

He stared at her. "Is there something you're not telling me?"

She thought briefly about lying. But now that Richard's suspicions were aroused she knew she couldn't placate him with some flimsy story, even if she could think up one in the next few seconds. Besides, he had to know sometime.

She dropped onto the sofa beside him. He moved away a fraction, perched gingerly on the very edge now, bouncing on the balls of his feet, as if he was getting ready to literally run.

Helene felt her stomach give a small, warning flip. But she forced herself to answer.

"There is something actually." She glanced at him fearfully.

His eyes widened. "No! You're not – ?"

He left the question hanging between them and in the split-second silence Helene knew everything was about to change.

She swallowed. "I am. I'm – *we're* – expecting a baby, Richard!"

She scanned his features anxiously, trying to gauge his reaction but now his face was a mask of inscrutability. She forced herself to take deep, calming breaths. She wasn't going to say another thing until he responded. She didn't want to put words in his mouth. She had to hear his first, gut reaction. She watched as he tried to digest the information.

"I don't understand." He stared at her. "I thought you were on the pill?"

"I was, but ... well, sometimes nature makes fools of us all," she said, quoting her late grandmother's words of wisdom solemnly.

"What the hell does that mean?" Richard snapped.

"I don't know! It just sounds … comforting." She felt like an idiot now for saying it.

"Comforting?" He looked at her incredulously. "This is not something we ever planned for, Helene."

"No, we didn't," she acknowledged. "But is it so bad? I mean – you love kids! Look at how you always put Anna and David first."

"That's just it. I did. Still do. But I'm tired, Helene." He said the word *tired* as if he were halfway up a mountain and had no idea how he was going to get to either the top or the bottom of it.

"We're all tired, Richard," she reminded him. "I've been working ten-hour days trying to win that ridiculous contest, as well as coping with morning sickness and fainting fits."

"Helene, I have just finished rearing my family." He stared into space. "I have been looking forward to having time for *myself* for *so* long. This is my chance!"

"Your chance to do what?" she asked, puzzled.

"I'm not sure." He looked around her living room as if he might find the answer there. "Smell the roses?"

"It's nappies you'll be smelling, Richard, not roses," Helene said bluntly. Then she noticed the horror on his face and added more gently, "It's a baby, Richard – not a prison sentence." She gave him a playful slap on the shoulder. "It will help to keep you young."

He shot her a disbelieving look. "With all due respect, I think I know more about the effects children have on your life than you do, Helene. And keeping you young is not one of them!"

"Well, we'll deal with it together." Helene was implacable. "This is not something I can do by myself."

A tic pulsed at the side of his mouth. "And, eh … are you sure it's mine?"

"*Excuse me?*" Helene's voice cracked like a whip into the air. In all the scenarios she had envisaged, when doubts had jostled with hope every time she had tried to predict his reaction, not even the most negative had come close to this.

"It's just … eh … well, I didn't think … I mean, I was thinking of having a vasectomy," he stammered.

"I see," she said slowly. "And just *thinking* about a vasectomy is a reliable form of birth control now, is it? The scientific and medical world will be thrilled with that breakthrough."

His eyelids flickered. "Look, I wasn't going to tell you this until later because I wanted you to enjoy your party. But I think we need to break up for a bit. Until things have settled down …"

Helene felt a peculiar buzzing sensation in her head. "I don't understand." She was genuinely puzzled. "How can we break up when I'm pregnant?"

He rubbed his eyes with the heels of his hands. "There're still a few weeks before everything at Atlantic is legally binding – before I get my money, essentially. But I suspect Jack knows about us. And I can't risk confirming that for him. He could make things really, really difficult for me. This *baby* thing," he said this as if he didn't quite believe it was real, "well, it's unfortunate timing, I'm afraid."

"Unfortunate timing? Are you mad? It's a *baby*!" She searched his face, and saw something unfathomable in his eyes. She felt panic grip her. "I thought you loved me?"

"I did. Do." He gave a tiny sigh. "But things change, Helene. Circumstances change."

His eyes were full of misery, but Helene caught the hint of steel in his voice. The buzzing sensation in her head was back. She gripped the edge of the sofa, her fingernails leaving indentations in the soft leather. How did he think he could just waltz away from everything, when the baby they were expecting was already affecting every aspect of her life? She opened her mouth to say as much, but he held up both his hands to stop her.

"I don't want to do this." His mouth tightened. "But I don't see that I have any choice. If you say the baby is mine, I'll deny it, Helene."

Helene felt cold. Freezing.

"I think you'd better go." The words came out of her mouth but they sounded as if someone else had spoken them.

Richard, however, didn't need to be told twice. He strode towards the hall door.

Then her mood switched again, frightening her with its unpredictability.

"You can't leave me, Richard!" she wailed after him. "Not tonight. It's my birthday! People are about to arrive for the party!"

Richard half-turned to look back at her. "It's not as if anyone ever knew about us," he pointed out. "So they won't think it's odd that I'm not here."

"They'll think it's odd when I have a huge bump in another couple of months and no father for my baby!"

He took a few steps back towards her. "Why don't we think about this? I mean – you don't have to have it, do you? I mean, it must be only a few weeks ..."

"*It* is a baby, Richard." Her voice was icy and this time actually felt like her own as another bewildering mood change came over her. "It's a gift. I actually thought you might have been happy about it. But that was before I realised what a lily-livered wimp you are. So you want to check out as soon as the going gets tough? So go. Do it. Get out now if you're going."

She turned away. She wasn't going to think any more about what he had just suggested. She would just block it out, pretend that he hadn't. She put her face in her hands and bit hard on her top lip to stop it trembling. She heard the soft click of the hall door.

He's gone, she thought dully. On the night she told him she was expecting their baby Richard had left her. On the night of her fortieth birthday when people were due to arrive any moment for the celebrations, Richard had come to tell her he wanted a *break*? The tears, which had been threatening all evening, finally started – great shuddering sobs that made her feel as if she might choke. This cannot be happening to me, she told herself. This weeping and babbling was not her! She was a strong person. She struggled to regain control of her emotions but it was useless. Big wails of fear and grief shook her body and she covered her face with her hands, trying to stem the tears. Hormones! It must be the hormones.

She stiffened at the creaking sound of her hall door opening again. She sat up straight, pure relief flooding through her. He was back! Of *course* he was back. She tried to compose herself, wiping her tears, patting her hair. She would find it difficult to forgive him for his initial reaction, of course she would. But, she rationalised, maybe it had been unfair to spring it on him out of the blue like that in the first place. After all, she'd had time to get used to the idea. They would get over this, she promised herself, and their relationship would be the stronger for it in the end. She lifted her tear-stained face to the door, ready to welcome him back into her life.

"I'm a bit early, I'm afraid. The hall door was ajar."

Matt from the Travel Café was standing awkwardly in the hallway, almost invisible behind the giant bouquet of sunflowers he was carrying.

The flowers, with their yellow and black faces reminded Helene of sunshine and hope and optimism and she couldn't bear it. She burst into a fresh, uncontrollable flood of tears.

To his credit, Matt didn't waste time asking awkward questions. He took one look at her red-eyed face, her make-up destroyed with tears, and marched into the kitchen where he put his flowers in the sink.

"I've obviously come at a bad time," he said when he came back. "But tell me what I can do to help?"

"Nothing," she snivelled. "Nothing can help."

He kneeled down beside her, handing her a paper tissue to wipe her tears.

"I met a guy on the way out – he was practically running down the stairs so he was hard to miss. So is this crisis to do with him? Did you have a row? Or is it worse than that?"

She lifted her head to look at him. "There's a worse feeling than this?"

"I don't know what you're feeling," he admitted. "I hardly know you. But –" He stopped, suddenly awkward, as if he wasn't sure if he should go on – but then he continued, "It *will* get better. It always does."

Helene was about to launch into a tirade about how exactly he could know that when she stopped. Something about the expression on his face, the guarded look in his eyes made her realise. *He's been here too.* So Matt hadn't landed back in Killty just because he'd got fed up with travelling the world or because he missed his folk. Something else had made him run for home. Something hard and heart-breaking.

Her anger subsided and she looked about her helplessly. "I could do with some help," she admitted. "There are people due to arrive any minute, and and ..."

He took charge before she could break into a fresh outbreak of sobbing. "So here's what you can do. You can stick a note on the door cancelling the party, citing an outbreak of a disease so contagious that nobody will bother to knock on the door to ask any questions."

Despite her grief, her mouth curved upwards. "Or?"

"Or you can put on a psychological mask when you're repairing your make-up. Psych yourself up to get through tonight and deal with everything else tomorrow." He glanced towards the hallway. "The choice is yours, but you're going to have to make your mind up quickly. The invite said for eight sharp."

Helene breathed in deeply. It would be difficult to explain away the contagious disease story, tempting as it was. And if she were going to survive as a single mother, faking happiness at a birthday party would probably be the least of the challenges ahead of her.

"I'll go for the mask," she said, sitting up straight. "Most of the people coming are from work and –"

"No need to explain. Decision made." Matt offered his hand and helped her to her feet. "Now go and repair the damage." He traced a finger along the side of her face where her mascara was mingled with tears.

Helene could hear her guests arriving as she scrubbed her face clean and started over with the face-painting. She brushed her hair, sprayed on more scent and gave herself a good talking-to in the mirror while she worked. *You can do this. Just put Richard out of your mind. Pretend none of it happened. You can sort it all out tomorrow.*

By the time she arrived back out to the living room, nobody would have guessed what a snivelling wreck she had been reduced to earlier on. She played her part like a pro and, with the help of Matt, the near stranger with a kind heart who had come into her life just when she needed him, her party went ahead.

Matt took on his self-appointed role of host for the evening with panache, filling people's glasses, dealing with the caterers when they arrived, even arranging an impromptu karaoke competition when everyone had a few drinks on them.

Everyone came from work. Even Ollie turned up for an hour. Helene watched the celebrations as if she were behind a glass screen. A deep sense of shock enveloped her in a protective shield and she was surprised to find it was quite easy to get through the evening. She watched vaguely as Sara and Andrea sang completely out of tune, and wondered in a detached sort of way how the hell her life had arrived at this point with so little warning?

The one concession she allowed herself was that the party should finish early. Again, Matt rose to the occasion and managed to get the last person out of the apartment just after midnight.

"Will you be okay?" he asked when there were just the two of them left.

"Absolutely," Helene reassured him.

He seemed reluctant to leave but she was adamant she wanted to be alone.

As soon as she closed the hall-door on him she walked into her bedroom and stuffed a change of clothes into her overnight bag. Earlier in the evening, she had slipped away from the celebrations and quietly booked herself into a nearby hotel. She couldn't bear to stay here on her own tonight.

When she was leaving, she noticed a white envelope lying on the hall table, wrapped-up with a thin silver ribbon tied in a bow. She picked it up and looked at Richard's familiar handwriting. *To Helene, Happy Birthday.* She smiled sadly. He would have written this earlier, before she told him about the baby, before he'd told her he'd come to break up with her. Another lifetime ago, before her world had tilted on its axis. She slid it unopened into her bag.

She looked back at the debris of the party – the empty bottles and uneaten cake and the fortieth birthday balloon already deflating in the corner. She stood there for a few seconds, trying to fix the image of her guests enjoying themselves in her head. But all she could see was the earlier ugly scene between her and Richard.

She gave a tiny sigh and opened the hall door. The party planners were coming in the morning to clear up. By the time she arrived home from work tomorrow, all evidence of tonight would be erased from her home. Which was now exactly the way Helene wanted it.

CHAPTER EIGHTEEN

"I have hired my own, independent counsellor on this matter. One with a law degree," Ollie Andrews was muttering darkly from behind his computer screen.

"You're right, Ollie," Sara said. "And here, what do think about this coaching thing that Paulina Fox is setting up? Like, can you *coach* someone into having the X-factor?"

"No, you can't," Ollie said. "You either have it or you don't. And I have, so what is the *point*?"

Tess sighed. It was the morning after Helene's fortieth birthday party, which had been pretty tense for a celebration. She had gone because she wanted to make an effort to get on with everyone at work better this time around. But Helene had acted strangely out of character – she had hardly spoken to anyone all evening. Tess had been unable to look Andrea in the eye because she still hadn't worked out whether to tell her about seeing Paul in the restaurant. Consequently, she had drunk too much wine, had slept in late this morning and was now nursing a giant hangover. And all this talk about the contest was getting on her nerves.

"It's just another stunt dreamed up by Paulina," she muttered. "They probably already have their winner picked if you ask me."

"*If* we asked you!" Ollie glowered.

Sara looked at her curiously. "Are you going in for the contest, Tess?"

"Of course she is," said Ollie. "Haven't you heard about her elevator speech?"

"What's this about an elevator speech?" Andrea strolled by, looking at Ollie curiously.

"It's nothing, I'll tell you about it later," Tess said quickly. Thankfully, Andrea had been out of the office when Helene had announced to all and sundry that Tess had been stalking Jack McCabe. She wanted to explain what had happened without the nasty spin Helene had put on it.

"Tell her now, why don't you, Tess?" Ollie challenged. "Why keep your best friend in the dark? Let me save you the bother, actually." He turned to Andrea. "What do you think of this? Tess has been *stalking* Jack McCabe. She trapped him in a lift so she could pitch her ideas to him in private." He raised his eyebrows meaningfully. "Hence the term 'elevator speech'."

Andrea stared at Tess. "So when did you decide to enter the contest?"

Tess sighed. "I wasn't talking to Jack about the contest – I was trying to get the agony-aunt slot back!"

"Yeah ... because that was such a success the first time around!" Ollie chortled, snapping the lid of his coffee container open and taking a long slug.

"So that explains how Paul saw you having dinner with Jack," Andrea said slowly. "He said you pretended not to see him, but he was pretty sure you had."

"She was having *dinner* with Jack?" Ollie almost choked on his coffee.

"But that's so cool!" Sara was full of curiosity. "So tell us, Tess, what's he *really* like? Is he ruthless? Is he going to sack everyone over thirty? Is he as *hot* as he looks?"

"I wouldn't know," Tess muttered, her mind racing in another direction altogether. If Paul had told Andrea he saw Tess at the restaurant, there must be an innocent explanation for him being with that woman. Thank God.

She turned to Andrea now. "Listen Andrea, I've loads to tell you. How about lunch?"

"I've a pretty busy day. Sorry." Andrea switched on her computer and stared at the screen.

Tess bit her lip, wondering how to get back their old, easy friendship.

The phone rang.

"Hello, Atlantic 1FM. Oh! Okay, I'll tell her. Tess!" Sara covered the receiver with one hand. "It's Paulina." She made a jabbing gesture with her finger towards the telephone. "She'd like you to pop along to see her. She's starting the coaching sessions immediately."

Tess was still trying to figure out how to approach Andrea. "I'm a bit busy at the moment," she said absentmindedly. "Why don't you go along for the first session yourself?"

Sara spoke into the phone again before replacing the receiver and raising her eyebrows at Tess. "The coaching schedule is non-negotiable apparently. She wants you for the first session."

"For heaven's sake!" Tess snatched up her notebook and marched up the corridor to the small office Paulina had commandeered for the day. It just wasn't good enough that she could order people to her at a moment's notice, she thought crossly. She had absolutely no preparation done for this meeting. In fact, she wasn't even sure what a coaching session *was*. She knocked on the door sharply.

"Come!" Paulina commanded.

Tess pushed open the door, not bothering to hide her displeasure at being summoned so abruptly.

"Tough start to the day?" Paulina smiled, showing tiny, even white teeth.

"It's been fine so far," Tess said shortly.

"It must be difficult having to deal with Ollie again, though?" Paulina pressed.

Tess shrugged. "I can handle him."

"Well, I can't get him to listen to my ideas, at all," Paulina said plaintively. "He seems to be on the defensive all the time."

Tess hid a smile. It was gratifying to see how the ultra-capable Paulina Fox felt flummoxed by Ollie – it made Tess feel less inadequate. But she wasn't here to exchange stories about Ollie. She looked at Paulina levelly. "So – this coaching – can we get on with it?"

"Ah yes – the coaching." Paulina scribbled something on the A4 pad in front of her before looking up. "What do you need to know to help you to win the contest?"

"Well, we've already put in our submissions so is all of this not a bit late?"

"The submissions were only one part of the process." Paulina leaned forward in her chair. "We shall be carefully monitoring people between now and the relaunch day next week."

Tess racked her brain. "So what is it exactly you're looking for in the winner?"

Paulina sighed heavily as if she'd just been asked for the Third Secret of Fatima.

"Everybody is asking that," she said. "But it's sort of intangible, you know?"

"Right," Tess said uncertainly.

"What I *can* tell you," Paulina said, "is that we want the winner to portray a certain image. For instance, if we choose a female presenter then we'll be looking for a woman who is sexy, but with a girl-next-door approachability at the same time. Do you know what I mean?"

Tess very much doubted if even Paulina knew what she meant. "Not really," she admitted.

Paulina narrowed her eyes. "Look, each contestant will need something different to get them up to the standard we're looking for. *You* for instance," she looked Tess up and down appraisingly, "should consult a stylist."

"Really?" Tess looked down with surprise at her outfit. She had given up dressing down for work since she'd met Chris again and had chosen today's outfit with care – dark suede jacket, tailored grey dress, much higher heels than she was accustomed to.

"I'm not saying there is anything particularly *wrong* with your image," Paulina clarified. "But I have worked with the stylist Mai Mooney extensively in the past and she will know instinctively what we're looking for. I know Andrea McAdams has already been to see her twice. I can give you Mai's address if you like." She began to rummage through a brown leather wallet for a business card.

Tess watched her with rising indignation, remembering Mr Cheung and his astronomical haircare prices. How many more bloody makeovers was she going to have to endure for this job? Then her heart skipped a beat as her mind played catch-up on what Paulina had just said.

Andrea had seen Mai Mooney twice already? So how come she hadn't told her? She and Andrea told each other everything. Or used to, she thought uncomfortably, as the image of Paul and his female companion flashed into her mind.

243

Of course, she'd jumped to the wrong conclusion about that night. Maybe that's what she was doing again now. Andrea probably hadn't had a chance to tell her. Tess had been busy avoiding her after all. And she had a lot going on with the children and the pressures at work. Seeing a stylist was probably just another task on her to-do list.

"Tess?"

Tess snapped back to the present. Paulina had evidently asked her a question and was expecting an answer. She forced herself to focus and for the next twenty minutes tried to concentrate on the conversation. But Paulina remained as irritatingly vague as ever and at the end of her allotted session Tess felt the whole thing had been a waste of time.

She needed to find some way of establishing herself as a serious candidate, she thought, as she left the office. She needed to prove to Jack McCabe that she was more than the flitter-head who had walked out of studio during her debut on-air slot and then trapped him in a lift to persuade him to give it back to her again.

She had heard nothing from him since the night in the restaurant. Not even an email to welcome her back. But then what had she expected? Jack had been upfront about his interest in her from the start – she was a temporary solution to an annoying problem, namely to keep Ollie Andrews sweet while Jack and Paulina got on with the task of relaunching Atlantic 1FM. Any spark of attraction had clearly been in Tess's own imagination, even if it felt at the time that there was enough electricity between them to power up a small city.

"Tess!"

She turned to see Jack coming down the corridor.

"I was just coming to see you, to welcome you back!"

He stopped, pushing one hand through his hair. "So, how have you been getting on?"

Tess thought of the useless coaching session she had just sat through with Paulina, of Ollie and his constant hectoring of everything she said and did, and of her on-going misery because of the misunderstanding between herself and Andrea.

"Fine." Her voice came out in a high-pitched squeak.

"Why do I find that hard to believe?"

He sounded amused and Tess flushed with annoyance.

"It's not funny," she said shortly. To her horror, she felt her eyes filling with tears. "It's hard trying to fit back in," she confessed. "And I'm not at all sure that I've done the right thing in coming back."

"It's that bad? Look, let me buy you lunch and we can talk it through, see if there's any way we can improve things. I feel a bit guilty because I'm only getting around to checking in with you now. It's been crazy trying to get everything done in time for the relaunch night."

She hesitated. The thought of spending her lunch break with a friendly face was almost too tempting to turn down. But what would Andrea have to say if she found out she was having lunch with the boss? Not to mention Ollie and Helene.

"I'm sorry but I really have a lot of work I need to be getting on with," she said reluctantly.

"Coffee then. Please?" He was hard to resist. "I like to iron out difficulties as they occur – it's not good to leave them to fester."

"Coffee would be nice," she conceded.

She made sure they only went as far as the local greasy spoon, Zelda's, so that if anyone spotted them, they would know the meeting was work-related. And she kept up a professional stance the whole time they were there. She told him how Helene had fainted and how Ollie was on tenterhooks all the time, and how that was making her role even more difficult than it had been first time round.

"It's just teething problems. It always happens in a transition period. Everything will settle down soon enough and, when it does, I promise you the radio station will be a much better place to work in than it was before I came along."

She looked at him and wondered if she could believe him. She wanted to. And he was so full of energy and optimism it was hard not to be affected by it.

Even after they had said goodbye and she was making her way back to the radio station, Tess still felt her spirits buoyed up by their meeting.

She was stopped at the traffic lights, waiting for a green light, when she felt a sharp poke on her shoulder. She swirled around to face Paulina Fox. She was dressed in a black suit with a tight skirt and fitted jacket, and was carrying a soft leather cream briefcase. Tess caught the scent she was wearing, something strong and expensive, adding to the overall picture she projected of someone who was in total control of her life

"So what have you been whining to Jack about this time?" Paulina narrowed her eyes. "You're not still trying to get your agony-aunt slot back, I hope?"

Tess looked at the other woman in astonishment. "With all due respect, I don't see what that has to do with you."

"Everything that happens with Jack concerns me," Paulina snapped. "You do know we're seeing each other?"

So Andrea had been right. Tess wasn't surprised. The sophisticated Paulina Fox was exactly the sort of woman she could imagine Jack being interested in. "I don't see how that's my business," she told the other woman.

"Your Little Miss Scatterbrain act doesn't fool me for one minute. I haven't quite worked out yet just what game you're playing, Tess Morgan, but just because Jack doesn't see through you doesn't mean that I don't."

Tess took a small, involuntary step backwards. Maybe Helene had been bad-mouthing her to Paulina? But the other woman's animosity felt more personal than that.

"I don't know what you're talking about," Tess said finally. "But I need to get back to work. And you're barring my way."

Paulina blinked, but didn't move for several seconds.

Then abruptly, she turned without saying another word and walked off. Tess stared after her, her good mood already vanished.

By the time she got back to work, she was still feeling shaky from the bizarre encounter. She stepped into the Ladies' to gather her wits and saw Andrea was there. She was touching up her make-up, peering into a small compact mirror, pressing her lips together to set her lipstick.

"Hi!" Tess looked at her cautiously. This was her chance to break the ice. "I've just bumped into Paulina Fox. She is seriously strange!" She turned on the cold tap and bent to splash water on her face.

Andrea didn't reply. Tess straightened up and pulled off a sheet of scratchy paper towel. She looked at Andrea carefully, remembering what Paulina had said about her consulting the stylist Mai Mooney for advice on her image. Andrea was such a stunner it was hard to see what Mai Mooney could have offered by way of improvement but, now that she was looking closely, Tess thought maybe Andrea's appearance *had* changed, albeit in a very subtle way. She looked *glossier* somehow.

"Are you changing your image?" she asked casually.

Andrea closed her mirror compact with a snap. "Not especially. Are you?"

"Well, yes! Trying to anyway." Tess hesitated. "I have been through two makeovers already, if you count my efforts to do myself over for the reunion. But Paulina has just suggested now that I should see a stylist – a Mai Mooney?"

"I wouldn't bother with what Paulina says. Not when you have the ear of Jack McCabe."

"I don't have his ear!" Tess protested.

"Come on! Going out to dinner with him must have been pretty productive!"

"Not really." Tess wasn't sure she liked the tone in Andrea's voice.

"Why not? Didn't he buy your elevator speech?"

"What is *wrong* with you, Andrea? There was a time when you would have found the elevator speech *hilarious*."

"Hah, bloody hah!" Andrea turned to the mirror over the sink and began working on her hair, shaking her head to settle it back into shape.

"Oh, get down off the cross, Andrea!" Tess suddenly snapped. "You're doing stuff to win the contest! Seeing Mai Mooney, for instance. Twice, according to Paulina."

Andrea looked at her coolly. "I'm ambitious. It's not against the law. But I've always been upfront about it. You, on the other hand, were so good at playing Little Miss Scatty, promising me how you'd help *me* to win, while all the time you were planning your own secret strategy to bag it for yourself."

"I said I'd help you because I'd been sacked!" Tess exclaimed. "I didn't think I would be coming back to work here. But ... look, it's tough out there, Andrea. It's not as if jobs are growing on trees. And I've already explained, my so-called elevator speech was just an attempt to get another shot at the agony-aunt gig, like you've been advising me to do from day one. Okay, so my method was a bit unorthodox – I got carried away with Chris Conroy's bizarre methods of career coaching." She shook her head in disbelief at what Chris had talked her into. "Don't ask me how."

"So how did the dinner date come about?" Andrea persisted. She was looking at Tess as if she didn't know whether she should believe her or not.

"Jack turned me down for the agony-aunt slot. Or should I say Paulina turned me down."

"Paulina was there?" Andrea's eyes widened.

"In the lift, yes. But not at dinner. Jack wanted me to come back to produce Ollie until the relaunch. I didn't want to at first. Producing Ollie feels like going around in circles. Unpleasant circles. Anyhow, Jack asked me to dinner to talk about it." She shrugged. "What can I say? He's very persuasive."

Andrea still looked suspicious. "Paul said you and Jack looked very cosy together. It didn't look very business-like to him."

"Well, Paul's dinner didn't look very business-like either, Andrea!" Tess pointed out. "But clearly it was. *I* jumped to all the wrong conclusions – thinking that just because Paul was having dinner with a woman, he must be having an affair or something. That's why I've been avoiding you, Andrea. Because I didn't know how to handle it. But Paul wasn't doing anything wrong at all! So just accept that it's possible that *you* could be doing the same thing right now. Jumping to the wrong conclusion about myself and Jack."

Tess stopped, alarm bells ringing far too late.

"What woman?" The blood had drained out of Andrea's

face, leaving it waxy white.

"The woman he was with at the dinner ... I thought you said he told you ..."

Andreas's nostrils flared slightly. "He told me he was having dinner with a former colleague of his called Terry – said he might have a tip-off about a new job. Well, I presumed it was a he – and Paul didn't say anything to make me think any differently."

"Well, what does it matter if Terry was a man or a woman?" Tess's voice was too bright. "It was a business colleague. That's all that matters, right?"

"Right," Andrea said grimly. She dropped the compact mirror and lipstick into her handbag and walked away without a backward glance.

Damn, Tess thought, putting her face in her hands. *Damn, damn, damn.*

CHAPTER NINETEEN

Finally, the day of the relaunch party rolled around. Tess took a deep breath, turned sideways and sucked in her stomach. She was spray-tanned and squeezed into a black dress that pushed up her cleavage and gave her lots of *va-va-voom*. Her hair was a credit to Mr Cheung and her kohl-rimmed eyes and Purple Passion lipstick made her look like a vamp. But inside she felt like a wreck.

Nerves were now so frayed at work that no matter what happened tonight, Tess felt things could only get better once the wretched contest was over. Ollie was still treating her like an outcast. Helene had taken to wandering around the office like a ghost, looking so preoccupied and downright lost that Tess almost found herself wishing for the old, snappy, dynamic Helene back. And as for Andrea – Tess's stomach lurched when she remembered the look on her friend's face when she'd revealed that Paul's work colleague was a woman. They had been avoiding each other since and Tess had never felt so miserable in her life.

She sat down to wait for her taxi, pleating the sofa cushion-covers absentmindedly between her fingers. She was meeting Chris later, at the party, and she felt as confused as ever about him. She still hadn't collected her clothes from his apartment. She had told him she was too busy putting the final touches to her pitch for *It's My Show* and Chris had empathised only too well. It was partly true anyway, she reflected. Things had been manic for everyone as they tried to perfect their entries for the contest. A last-minute stipulation obliged each entrant to submit a six-minute recording, illustrating why they felt they had the elusive X-factor.

Tess had been glad to have something to focus on, because it meant she had neither the time nor the energy to think about Chris, Andrea or Jack. Tonight, though, she was going to have to face all her demons together. The sound of the taxi honked outside and Tess stood up reluctantly. She did a last quick check in the mirror, forcing her shoulders down from around her ears. Showtime, she thought automatically. Then she clattered down the stairs to the waiting taxi.

Traffic was unusually heavy and they inched their way towards the hotel. Tess had eaten very little all day but, by all accounts, tonight was going to be a lavish affair, so there'd be plenty of food at the party. Sara had said there would be a red carpet at the hotel entrance and that lots of national media were expected, hoping to report on Atlantic 1FM's national licence award.

As the taxi slid to a halt, Tess saw that Sara was right as usual. There was the red carpet laid up the steps to the hotel door. There were the burly bouncers dressed in black and white, standing guard against gate-crashers and a posse of photographers lined up on either side of the two ropes, which formed a pathway for guests. A knot of local people stood by curiously. They were probably wondering whether any real celebs would show up, Tess thought, as she passed by with her head down. She showed her invitation to one of the bouncers, feeling like an idiot as he scrutinised it, and then her, closely, before finally waving her in.

Paulina Fox, looking immaculate in a white silk, sari-style dress, was handing out press packs to the arriving media in the lobby. Helene stood beside her, scanning the crowds anxiously. Tess ducked out of their sight and made her way to the function room where tall, lanky models looking beautiful and bored posed for the press, while a coterie of media and business types leafed idly through Paulina's handouts. She spotted Sara perched on a high stool by the bar, nursing a very colourful cocktail. Tess weaved her way across to her.

"Who *are* all these people?" she asked, looking back at the crowded room.

"VIPs," Sara murmured, sucking her drink through a straw and watching the action from under long, spidery false eyelashes.

Tess looked admiringly at the skinny strip of fuchsia pink chiffon that was masquerading as a dress on Sara's skinny frame. "You look fantastic!" She gave her a nudge.

"Thanks!" Sara grinned and looked down at her outfit. "It's my slut dress – in case there's any talent here. Or Jack McCabe is looking."

Tess nodded at the bartender. "I'll have whatever she's having."

"Hey up!" Sara nodded towards the door. "Look who's arrived."

Tess looked up to see Richard Armstrong enter the room, one arm draped around a dark-haired, plump woman who, even from this distance, looked uncomfortable.

"She must be his wife," Sara said thoughtfully.

Louisa. Jack's sister. Tess craned her neck, to see her better. She felt a stab of sympathy for her. If Rosa was right, and Helene was pregnant, it was going to be a nightmare for everyone involved. But Tess had made enough mistakes herself to know that people often found themselves in situations they had never envisaged. The truth was, she wouldn't like to be in Helene's position tonight.

The barman returned with her cocktail and Tess clinked her glass against Sara's.

"Good luck for tonight. When are they announcing the result anyway?"

"I'm not sure," Sara said through her straw. "Are you nervous?"

"Not at all. I'm not going to get the gig anyway." Tess sipped the pink sugary cocktail, the strong alcoholic kick on an empty stomach making her feel slightly giddy.

"None of us are going to get this gig," Sara said gloomily. "Daddy says it's definite now that the winner is an outsider. And after all that work we did with those bloody recordings! Honestly, we are so not appreciated. I'm going to look for another career after tonight."

"Mmmm ... well, good luck with that," Tess said through her straw, thinking of her own recent brush with unemployment.

The two women scanned the crowds to see if they could read any small gesture of triumph in the body language of any of the guests.

"Hey – there's Ollie!" Sara poked Tess in the ribs and nodded towards the other end of the bar.

Tess followed her gaze to see Ollie balefully surveying the pint of lager and shot of whiskey lined up in front of him. Ollie drinking whiskey chasers at this hour of the evening didn't bode well for later on, especially if, as Sara had predicted, the gig was going to an outsider. That particular rumour had been circulating around Atlantic for the last couple of days, ratcheting the tension levels in the office to near hysteria, and Ollie was clearly brooding about it now.

"Excuse me, ladies, can I take your picture?" Tess turned to see a photographer with his camera trained on them. He was a young guy with dirty-fair hair and slightly protruding eyes. He was wearing jeans, runners and a long trench coat.

"Who's it for?" Tess asked.

"I'm a freelance so I'm not sure yet. But photos of beautiful women always sell!"

Tess smiled at his cheek and moved closer to Sara so he could get his shot. He spent the next few minutes barking orders at them, directing them to first look cheerful, then sultry, and finally, moody.

"Thanks, ladies!" He fished in his pocket and pulled out a grubby-looking business card.

Sara took it and giggled. "Gai Gordan Ryder? Seriously?" She raised incredulous eyebrows at him.

"What? That's my real name," he said, surveying the room for more photo opportunities.

"Yeah, right!" Sara laughed.

"Food!" Tess spotted several large silver trays of canapés being carried around by waitresses dressed in short black skirts, opaque black tights and white frilly blouses.

Sara nodded towards the entrance. "See Andrea's just arrived with the hubby."

Even from a distance, Tess could see the stiff set to Andrea's shoulders and the grim expression on her face. When Paul quickened his step to close the gap between them, she shrugged him away angrily. Tess winced. Clearly they were still having trouble.

"I'll go and see if they want to join us – you go and get some food." Tess placed her drink on the bar and started across the floor before she could change her mind. If she didn't face Andrea now, she would spend the rest of the night fretting about it.

Andrea had her back to her, trying to attract the barman's attention.

"Hi!" Tess smiled at Paul who responded by giving her a warning shake of his head: *Don't make matters worse.* But Tess was already tapping her friend on the shoulder.

Andrea stared at Tess. "Did you want something?"

Tess was horrified to feel tears welling up. "I was just going to ask if you and Paul wanted to join myself and Sara."

"We'll stay on own for the time being. Thanks."

"Oh! Okay then." Tess turned away abruptly, trying to hide her discomfort, and bumped into someone standing directly behind her. "Sorry! Sorry," she muttered automatically, and looked into the face of Jack McCabe.

"Tess!" He looked at her curiously. "Are you okay?"

He was wearing black tie, looking ridiculously handsome.

"I'm fine." Tess blinked away the tears and pasted on a smile. She stared into the crowd to distract herself from both the effect he was having on her and the upset she felt over Andrea's reaction. "Amazing party. It must have taken some organising?" she said brightly.

Jack shrugged. "It's just work. But you're right. It did take some work – all Paulina's of course."

Of course, Tess thought.

He followed her gaze into the crowd. "I can't help wondering if the woman Richard is having an affair with would have the nerve to show up here." He scanned the crowd hungrily, as if he could figure out who it was just by staring into it for long enough.

"Right." Tess felt a wave of discomfort. She didn't want

Jack asking her more questions about Richard's love life.

She was relieved when Paulina pitched up, enveloped in a cloud of her Power Woman perfume. Even in a room full of beautiful people, Paulina still managed to look standout stunning. She leaned in and kissed Jack on both cheeks.

"Everything is going marvellously, isn't it?" she said softly, her voice full of muted excitement.

"So far it certainly is." Jack air-kissed her back.

Paulina's eyes swept over Tess. "So – are you here alone?"

"Er ... I'm meeting someone later, actually."

"Really? Anyone we know?" Paulina leaned forward in a conspiratorial fashion.

Tess bit her lip. "You might know him. Chris Conroy?"

Paulina's eyebrows arched. "The journalist? Oh, we know him all right. Is he your boyfriend?"

"Er ... yes," Tess said, wondering why she felt so defensive.

"Really?" Jack seemed astonished and his eyes flickered towards Paulina.

Tess wondered what she was missing. Paulina had a secretive smile hovering on her lips, as if she was enjoying some private joke.

"Look, I'd better be getting back – Sara's ordered food," Tess said lamely.

"Indeed. I got top caterers in so it should be delicious. Enjoy ..." Paulina turned back to Jack.

Tess pushed her way through the crowds to Sara. She had a tray of canapés set up at the bar and had ordered more cocktails. Grandma Rosa was with her, wearing a very exotic hat and sipping something yellow and lethal-looking.

"I was just telling Rosa how the switchboard was lit up

with callers looking for more from Psychic Granny! Isn't that right, Tess?"

"It was pretty popular all right," Tess said absently. She was looking over at Jack and Paulina, still deep in conversation, and wondering about their reaction when she said she was meeting Chris later.

"So, do you think the slot will continue once the pilot period is over, then?" Rosa asked eagerly.

Tess shrugged. "With all the changes going on it's difficult to predict what's going to happen for any of us any more. But surely I can't be the only one who is sick of talking about work? We're at a *party*!" She took the straw out of her drink and swigged back a very large mouthful. "So c'mon! Tell us some of your predictions, Rosa. You're the expert. What's in store for Sara and me?"

"Well, a tall, handsome man is about to walk into *your* life, Tess!" Rosa said.

"Yeah, right!" Tess laughed.

"He really is."

Rosa nodded over Tess's shoulder and Tess turned to see Chris had arrived. At last. He looked flushed and harried and, as he got nearer, Tess did a double take. He was wearing *combats*?

"Didn't you have time to go home and change?" She looked down at his khaki trousers.

"I'm coming straight from work – I was doing an insert into a TV programme about what it means to cover a war," he said vaguely. "So, has the winner been announced yet?"

"Not yet. Rumour has it that it's gone to an outsider." Tess held up her glass. "I can recommend one of these while you're waiting."

Chris ignored her offer and grabbed the top of her arm. "Here – isn't that Jack McCabe over there?"

"*Ow!* You're hurting me!" she protested as the drink spilled down her dress.

"Sorry," he said half-heartedly. "Is that him?"

Tess rubbed her arm and followed his gaze. "Yes, it is – with Paulina Fox, the public relations woman handling the relaunch. I think she and Jack are a couple," she added, a bit forlornly.

Chris was staring across the room with an intensity that was unsettling – like a hunter stalking his prey.

Tess turned back to the bar. "I'll just get another drink for myself so. How about you, Sara? Rosa? The same again?"

But before they could answer Chris slid his arm around Tess's waist and swivelled her around to face him again. "Let's go over and say hello, shall we?" He caught her hand and moved forward, trying to pull her after him.

"Er … I don't think so." Tess twisted her hand out of his grip.

"Come *on*, Tess!" Chris said impatiently. He grabbed her hand again but he was stopped by a very inebriated Ollie Andrews, who was barring his way.

"Chris Conroy. We meet at last. The boy who's out to take my job!"

"I don't know what you're talking about." Chris tried to sidestep him, but Ollie moved with him, and put a restraining hand on his chest.

"That's not true, Ollie." Tess tried to mollify him. "Chris has been helping me with my submission, that's all."

Ollie swayed on his feet. "Helping *you*, Tess?" He started to laugh. "Helping himself, more like!"

"Take it easy, man." Chris put one hand on Ollie's shoulder to move him out of his way and reached back with his other to clutch Tess's hand again. "C'mon, Tess – let's go."

But Ollie squared up to him, pushing him back hard. In normal circumstances there was no way Ollie could take on Chris, who was younger and fitter, and who wasn't under the influence of six pints ... and the rest. But Ollie seemed to think he was Superman tonight.

"Ollie," Tess intervened again. "Don't do this."

He turned, pushing his face so close to Tess she could smell the whiskey fumes on his breath. "What sort of an idiot are you? Haven't you heard your *boyfriend* is the main contender to win this ridiculous contest we're all hanging around here waiting to hear the results of?"

Tess looked at him, startled. Chris was in for *It's My Show*? But that couldn't be true. At some time during the last few weeks, he would have told her. Wouldn't he?

She glanced across at Chris and was surprised to see a secretive, stubborn look on his face. What was going on? She'd thought it was odd that he'd hardly been in touch with her since the night she'd had dinner with Jack. They'd been texting of course, but they hadn't seen each other. Chris had said he was super busy at work and that had suited her as she was still confused about her feelings for him. She'd assumed he might be feeling the same way. But now she asked herself if Chris had had a different motive for staying away?

"The penny's finally dropping, is it?" Ollie sneered.

Tess struggled to find her voice. "Chris. Is Ollie telling the truth?"

But Chris barely seemed to be listening to either of them now. He still had his eyes trained on Jack. He turned and tried to propel her across the room again.

"Stop it!" Tess jerked away.

But Chris merely tightened his grip on her arm.

Suddenly Grandma Rosa slid down off her stool, pulled

a dangerous-looking pin out of her hat and jabbed it into Chris's wrist.

"Step away, big man!"

"*Yeow!*" Chris jerked his hand away and swirled around to see what had happened. As he did so, he banged into Ollie who stumbled and lost his balance, toppling over into the crowd before landing with a thud on the floor.

"Ollie!" Tess went to help him to his feet. Out of the corner of her eye she saw the photographer who had snapped her and Sara earlier jostle his way through the crowd, beaming. He looked at Ollie spread-eagled on the ground and immediately adjusted his camera.

"There's no need for that!" Tess snapped at him. She leaned over to help Ollie up.

"Ah here, I can't afford this sort of publicity – I'm out of here!" Chris suddenly announced.

In his haste to escape he jostled against Tess, who was already slightly off balance as she tried to help Ollie to his feet. She grabbed at Chris's arm to stop herself from falling but he pushed her off impatiently. She swayed and fell, landing awkwardly on top of Ollie. She could feel his whole body convulse beneath her and realised he was shaking with drunken laughter. While he seemed to find the situation hilarious, Tess was grimly aware that her dress was riding up around her thighs and her legs were tangled up in his like a contortionist's. She moved to wrench her dress down, but the movement provoked Ollie into a fresh fit of mirth and, as his body rocked again beneath her, Tess fell off him onto the floor, her legs splayed open and her hands clutching at his shirt.

She squeezed her eyes shut, but as she heard the ominous sound of a camera shutter she opened them again and looked into the cold, ruthless eyes of Gai Gordan Ryder.

Snap! Snap! Snap! He was angling his camera a dozen different ways, trying to get the best shot he could.

"Sorry about this, love," he said with not a shred of remorse. "One of these will *definitely* make the papers tomorrow!"

As he turned to leave he bumped into a television cameraman who had rushed over to find out what all the commotion was about.

Gai Gordon turned back to Tess, some sympathy in his voice, "And it looks like you might make the television news, too!"

CHAPTER TWENTY

In the event, Gai Gordan Ryder was wrong. The photos of Tess and Ollie didn't make the television news. But that was scant consolation for Tess as she sat at her desk next morning, staring at the headline 'Duel to the Death for It's My Show!' Underneath there was a large picture of Tess, spread-eagled on top of Ollie Andrews, her black knickers clearly on view. Ollie was looking down her cleavage, a stupid smile on his drunken, red face.

Fuck Chris Conroy, Tess thought, with unexpected rage. If it hadn't been for him, she wouldn't have been wearing such a short low-cut dress in the first place. What kind of an idiot was she anyway, she wondered, taking style advice from someone who arrived at a party in combats?

She rubbed her eyes. She needed coffee. She had been awake most of the night, the debacle of the night before buzzing about in her head, making sleep impossible. By six she was in the shower and, knowing the papers would be delivered to the office first thing, she had come straight in to work, not even stopping for a takeaway coffee. Two hours later and she had read and re-read the newspaper report so many times she felt she could recite it off by heart.

The sound of high heels clicking down the corridor interrupted her reading and she looked up to see Sara arriving with two takeaway coffees.

"Is it in it? What's it like? Let me see!" She dumped the coffees on Tess's desk and looked over her shoulder at the front page of the *Killty Times*. "Omigod! What are you *like*?" She turned startled eyes towards Tess. "Jack is going to be so, like, *furious*!"

"Thanks," Tess said drily.

"It's true!" Sara shrugged. "I did try to distract that idiot photographer. And Rosa jostled his camera equipment and everything but none of it fazed him at all. He just kept on snapping." She looked at the photo again and repeated in awestruck tones, "*Oh! My! God!*"

Tess took a grateful slug of the hot, strong coffee. "Oh My God, indeed. What happened after I left?"

"Ollie was poured into a taxi by Paulina. And your boyfriend – what's his name, Chris? – he disappeared like a magician. He was making sure he wasn't going to be associated with any trouble. Rosa said that's not a good sign in a man."

Tess sighed. She didn't have to be Einstein to work out that Chris Conroy wasn't going to be walking over hot coals for her any time soon. Maybe she'd had a lucky escape when Chris had dumped her all those years ago. She opened up her computer.

"Well, I guess we'd better do some work," she said half-heartedly.

"Yeah," Sara agreed, picking up her pen and doodling in her notebook.

But for the next hour neither of the women did a tap. Andrea had phoned in sick and there was no sign of Ollie. Eventually Sara went off for more coffees and muffins and on her return she engaged Tess in a detailed post-mortem of the night before. Had Tess seen Helene's reaction when

Richard arrived with his wife? Did she know that Richard's wife was Jack's sister? Was that why Richard hadn't turned up at Helene's birthday party?

Meanwhile Tess had a big question of her own. "So," she asked finally, "who got the gig in the end?"

Sara laughed. "It wasn't announced, after all that. As soon as Paulina Whatshername found out about *that*," she gestured towards the picture of Tess and Ollie, "she whisked Jack out of there. Probably spent the night talking about damage limitation with him."

"Hmm – I'd say she had more on her mind than damage limitation." Tess pursed her lips.

Sara looked eager to pursue this line of conversation but they were interrupted by the arrival of Helene, looking pale but resolute.

"Jack is on his way in," she announced, "and he is not a happy man. Last night's announcement was ruined by the melée." Her eyes flicked towards Tess.

"So, who won the contest?" Sara asked eagerly.

"No idea," Helene responded, "but apparently it's to be announced 'imminently'. Whatever that means."

She disappeared down the corridor and Tess tried again to concentrate on work. But her heart wasn't in it. Her eyes kept on flicking back to the photograph, and her mind kept re-playing last night's debacle.

She was snapped back to the present when Sara hissed, "They're coming!"

Jack was striding down the corridor, pulling at his tie, his face tense. Paulina walked alongside him, clutching a clipboard, while Helene was left to scurry along behind, trying to keep up. Jack turned in to where they were sitting and sat down in Ollie's chair.

"As you know the winner of *It's My Show* was supposed

to be announced last night," he said without preamble. "I had also planned to confirm that Atlantic 1FM has just been awarded a national licence." He paused while there was a collective intake of breath. "However," he raised one hand to stem any questions, "all of that was ruined by what you will have seen reported in this morning's newspapers." His mouth tightened. "The competition was designed to drum up publicity for the station. Well, we got publicity all right – the worse kind possible. Key personnel getting drunk and disorderly was *not* the image we were going for."

Tess stared at her notebook.

"A lot of people are depending on the success of this station," Jack continued. "As it happens I am not one of them. I have other irons in the fire and this was always going to be a gamble for me – a personal project that I have always had reservations about. If I haven't made a success of Atlantic 1FM within six months – with or without your help," he stopped to look around the room, staring out anyone who had the nerve not to look away, "I will close the place down. Have I made myself clear?"

"Crystal!" a sneering voice came from behind them.

Tess looked back to see Ollie had arrived. He looked dishevelled, hung-over and in the mood for a fight.

"Not now, Ollie!" Jack snapped and turned to go.

"Er ... excuse me?" Sara said.

"*Yes?*" He turned back impatiently.

"So who's got *It's My Show*?" Sara beamed.

Jack glanced at Paulina who shook her head almost imperceptibly at him before announcing tersely. "Everyone will know by close of business today."

Tess continued staring at her notebook. She didn't want to look at Ollie who, from the sound of it, seemed to be throwing things around his desk. And she certainly didn't want to look at Jack McCabe.

"Tess? Can I see you in Helene's office, please? *Now.*" Jack's voice cracked through the air.

Something inside Tess shifted at that. She was fed up being treated like a doormat. It was bad enough that there were embarrassing pictures of her splashed across the newspaper. If Jack McCabe thought she was going to meekly take a tongue-lashing from him and his lapdog, Paulina, over it then he was very much mistaken.

"Sure," she said. "Lead the way." It wasn't as if anyone had *died*, she thought resentfully, snatching her notebook and biro off her desk.

Inside Helene's office she sat opposite a stony-faced Jack.

His eyes flickered towards Paulina. "I can handle this myself," he said.

"Oh?" For a moment, Paulina looked as if she was about to argue, but then she thought the better of it. As she swept past Tess, she threw her a look of intense dislike.

Tess heard the door close with a tiny click. It was the signal she needed.

"Before you say anything," she held Jack's gaze across the desk, "I don't appreciate being spoken to out there as if I were a two-year-old. What happened last night was an *accident*. You know – an incident that is outside of our control? Even you must have had at least one in your life."

Jack drummed his fingers on the desk. "Were you drunk last night?"

"No, I wasn't." Tess folded her hands in her lap. "But if I was, what about it? It was a party."

"It was a work function! You ended up on the floor on top of our most well-known presenter, for fuck's sake! Which is now splashed across the newspapers. How do you

267

think that looks for Atlantic 1FM?"

"You'll have to ask Paulina the answer to that one. She's the PR Goddess. I could tell you how it *feels*, though. Not that you'd be interested in anything that's not directly related to your precious business. But it was a bit of a nightmare, actually."

Jack sighed. "What happened?"

"What happened – which you would know already if you'd bothered to ask anyone who actually saw it – was that I was trying to help Ollie to get to his feet when an accidental push from Chris made me fall over. Olly and Chris had had an altercation and I was trying to contain the situation. More fool me!"

"Ah yes. Chris Conroy." Jack shifted in his chair. "How long have you two been an item?"

Tess raised her eyebrows. "I thought this was a business meeting?"

"It's a business question. It must have been difficult competing with him for *It's My Show*."

Tess flinched. So it was confirmed then. Chris had been in for the contest all along. How had she not spotted it? "I didn't know he was in for the contest until last night," she said slowly.

"Come on!" Jack raised his eyebrows. "Next you'll be telling me you didn't know he has a fiancée either!"

A fiancée? Tess looked at him stupidly. She searched his face, convinced he was making it up, that it was another of his weird mind games. Another test, this time to see how employees react under pressure, maybe? But the look in his eyes told her otherwise. What sort of idiot would she look like now if she admitted that she didn't know that either?

She took a deep breath. "Actually, I did know."

"Really?" Jack sounded surprised. "Well, I have to say

I'm disappointed, Tess. I didn't think you were the type who would try to steal someone else's boyfriend."

"Chris is not a possession. Somebody doesn't *own* him." Tess was trying hard to cover up her shock, desperate to preserve the tiny bit of pride she had left.

Jack laughed. "The same old justifications. Richard Armstrong's mistress undoubtedly trots that one out as well." He stared into space for a few seconds. "Louisa has stood by that bastard and still he breaks her heart." He looked at Tess with ill-disguised disgust. "If people would only think about others before they go all out for what they want."

"Like buying a radio station as a toy for yourself and pitting all the staff there against each other in a stupid contest?" Tess countered. "It's been nothing but back-stabbing since you showed up. I've lost the only friend I had here in the process." Thinking about Andrea fuelled her anger further.

"Ah, the contest," Jack said heavily. "That does seem to have caused more trouble than it was worth. What can I say? It seemed like a good idea at the time."

His phone bleeped. He picked it up, squinting at the screen. His face darkened as he read the new text message. He placed the phone down again, his fingers tapping impatiently on the table, his mouth set in a grim line.

"Louisa thinks she's just discovered who Richard's mistress might be. Helene Harper." He looked at Tess. "Is it?"

Tess bit her lip.

"I asked you in the restaurant and you said then you didn't know," he said.

"I didn't know! And I don't know now either. Not for sure." He stared at her so hard that she felt obliged to offer him more. "Helene was – is – my boss, not my friend. She never confided in me."

"So, who does she confide in?" He was drumming his fingertips again, his voice ominously low.

"I don't know!" Tess felt uncomfortable as she thought of Rosa suggesting to Helene that she might be pregnant. "I don't think it's any of my business," she said finally.

His face twisted. "You know, you're right. And what you do in your personal life is none of mine."

Tess offered an olive branch. "Look, I am sorry the station got the wrong sort of publicity. But as I've tried to explain, it was accidental."

Jack clicked and unclicked his pen into the silence.

Tess felt unnerved in the distinctly chilly atmosphere. "So, if there's nothing else?"

He looked at her appraisingly, as if he was trying to make up his mind about something. "No, that's it," he said finally.

Tess scraped back her chair, stood up and left without a backward glance.

She felt shaky after the altercation and badly wanted to go and have a cup of tea to calm herself down. Then her mobile started to ring. She fished it out of her pocket and stared at the name flashing in the glass panel. *Chris.* She felt sick when she thought of what she had just learned about him.

"Chris. How are you?" She forced herself to sound pleased to hear from him.

"Tess! Have you seen the *Killty Times*?"

"Not yet," Tess lied. "Er … how bad is it?"

"There's a picture of you and Ollie Andrews and … well, it's pretty bad, actually. How come you haven't seen it yet?"

"Oh, I heard about it, but I can't bear to look at it. Maybe," Tess had a brainwave, "we could meet up and we can look at it together?"

"Oh! Okay so." Chris sounded reluctant. "Look, I'm near Killty today on a bit of business. I can meet you now if you like? I have ... er ... something to tell you."

Don't bother, Tess felt like screaming at him, *I already know*. But some masochistic part of her wanted to see how he would handle the situation.

"I can meet you later, after the show," she said. "Say the Travel Café at lunch?"

"Em ..." Chris began but Tess closed down her mobile. For the rest of the morning she forced herself to concentrate on work but, as soon as she left the radio-station building, she could feel the fury rising up in her.

She broke into a power-walk down the coast road, each stride bringing her closer to the showdown.

She could still hardly believe Chris was engaged. There had been no trace of a woman in his ultra-masculine apartment. Come to think of it, her own bits and pieces were still there, actually – that hideous business suit he'd talked her into buying. Business-like but sexy, indeed! And her to-die-for reunion dress. How had he explained those to his fiancée?

On the other hand, it made sense of some of the things she'd found so confusing. How Chris knew so much about women's fashion, for instance. How he was on first-name terms with celebrity hairdresser Mr Cheung when he had so little hair himself.

By the time Tess arrived at the café, she had worked herself into such a state that she had to stand outside for a few minutes, taking deep, slow breaths to try and calm herself down. It had started to rain and the café window was fogged with condensation. She rubbed out a patch of visibility with the sleeve of her jacket and spotted Chris, nursing a coffee and reading the newspaper. Reluctantly, Tess pushed open the door.

"Hi." She slipped into the chair opposite him and nodded towards the photograph of her and Ollie that he was scrutinising. "On a scale of one to ten, how bad would you say it is?"

Chris slid the newspaper across the table to her. "Nine?"

Tess pretended to study it for a few seconds. "You know, I've never seen Ollie so drunk. I suppose the news that the gig was going to an outsider made him feel threatened."

"Right." Chris coughed and gestured for the waiter to take Tess's order.

"Just coffee, please." Tess smiled before turning her attention back to Chris. She reached out and grasped his hand. "You seem a bit edgy this morning. Anything wrong? Apart from the fact that your girlfriend made a show of herself last night, of course."

He snatched away his hand and ran it through his hair. "No – there's nothing wrong. It's just I feel sorry for you with this splashed all over the newspapers, that's all."

"So what did you want to tell me?"

"Em … it's true that I went in for the *It's My Show* contest myself. And before you say anything – I would have told you if you'd ever asked me!"

Tess laughed out loud at his cheek. "But why would I? It never occurred to me – or to anyone else at the station. So why were you so keen on coaching me to get the gig?"

"I was coaching you to get the agony-aunt slot back," Chris corrected her. "I always said your own show would be a bit of a stretch for you."

That was true enough, Tess had to admit. He had. "*You*

can't go from hero to zero overnight, Tess." Another of his patronising mottos.

"You used me," Tess said quietly. "You wanted me to get my job back so I could get you inside information about Atlantic 1FM."

"Yeah, well, that didn't work very well, did it?" Chris grumbled. "I found out more myself in the end."

"Quite the intrepid investigator, aren't we?"

"Look, I heard a rumour months back that Jack McCabe might be taking over Atlantic 1FM. Everyone knows how he's made a success of everything he's turned his hand to, so I figured he would definitely get a national licence. I started to listen to the station day and night, trying to figure out how to get a gig for myself." He looked hard at Tess. "That's how I found out that you worked there. I heard your name credit as a producer on *This Morning with Ollie Andrews*. Er ..." he looked a bit shamefaced, "that's why I organised the reunion. So I could meet you again."

Tess exhaled. "That's a very elaborate plan."

"Don't make it sound as if it's the crime of the century." Chris went on the attack. "It's the business we're in. You have to do stuff to thrive in it. But then you wouldn't know that – traipsing around the world for the last ten years like some hippy. Some of us have to work *hard* for a living!"

Tess sipped her coffee in silence.

"And was what I did really so bad, if you really think about it? It was of benefit to both of us. Look at you now. Your hair, your make-up. You look like a different person to that dowdy girl I met at the reunion!"

"*Woman*, Chris, not girl," Tess hissed. "And as it happens, I don't think there was so much wrong with me in the first place that I had to be transformed into a completely new person!"

"Well, that's debatable," Chris said huffily. "Anyhow, I'm surprised you're taking all of this so personally. You need to toughen up. If I was to tell you all the things I've done to further my career over the last few years ..."

"Oh, I can guess. Like portraying yourself as free and single when you're actually engaged," Tess said quietly.

Chris's nostrils flared. "Who told you about Penelope?"

"Jack McCabe told me, earlier today. So then I knew it had to be true." Tess gave a short laugh.

"You were talking to Jack today? Did he say who got the gig?" Chris asked quickly.

Tess looked at him in astonishment. "What sort of person cheats on their fiancée to get inside information about a *job*, Chris?" she exploded. But she knew there was no satisfactory answer to that. Chris was a cheater, end of. He'd cheated on her ten years ago, he'd cheated on his fiancé with her, and he'd probably cheated on every other woman he'd been with in between. It was in his DNA.

"Penelope lives in Spain part of the year and we don't get to see each other often enough. So when you came on to me in the hotel room that night you were hard to resist."

Tess flushed at the memory and his face softened.

"Look, I should have told you – I'm sorry. I intended to – but then Penelope flew back unexpectedly for a week and I got caught up with that. I had to get rid of your stuff by the way. Sorry."

He didn't look in the least bit contrite. Tess pulled out her purse and placed some money on the table to cover her coffee.

"Goodbye, Chris," she said quietly.

But he seemed to have forgotten that Tess was in the same room, let alone at the same table. He was staring at his phone, a strange expression on his face. She stood up and walked towards the door.

"Tess! Come back!"

"What is it now?" She turned around wearily.

"*I did it, Tess!* I got the gig! *It's My Show* is mine ... *I won the contest!*" Chris punched the air with his fist. "Ollie Andrews was bloody right to be so worried last night! And I bet he had one hell of a hangover this morning!"

Tess stared at him. *Chris* was going to be the new star of Atlantic? Chris, with his devious behaviour and questionable morals had swooped in and stolen the prize from right under their noses? Suddenly she was outraged at the injustice of it all.

"But we worked so *hard,*" she wailed. "All of us. And it was all for nothing."

He stared at her. "Have you been listening to anything I've been telling you these past few weeks? Working hard at your job keeps you in that job. You're supposed to be working on getting your next position." He gave her a pitying look. "Keeping your head down and expecting someone to come and reward you is the classic good-girl mistake, I'm afraid."

Tess supposed he must be right, because there he was, the victor, sitting with that smug, self-satisfied smile on his face, and here she was, whining about life being unfair and sounding like a victim again. But somehow she didn't care any more. All the office politics was making her head hurt.

"Well," he was looking at her expectantly, "say something!"

"I don't know what to say," Tess said honestly. '*Fuck off*!' 'crossed her mind but she honestly felt too drained to get the words out.

"Try congratulations," Chris suggested. "Because it's important we get on together. I may as well tell you now – I've asked for you to be my producer."

Tess looked at him with incredulity for several seconds.

"You're joking?"

"No. Why would I be? You know what works and what doesn't work on that show. I'd be mad not to look for you."

"And I'd be mad to allow myself to come within ten feet of you ever again, Chris Conroy."

"I'm sorry you feel like that," he said innocently.

She didn't bother answering. Instead, she walked away, finally letting the door slam shut on another chapter of her life.

CHAPTER TWENTY-ONE

Helene stared balefully at the radio. The weird wallpaper music reminded her of her visit to the spa, before Richard had fired a torpedo into her life. The music was a temporary replacement for the *This Morning* show, because Ollie hadn't been seen since he'd been summoned to a meeting with Jack McCabe the morning after the launch party. It was a sign of the new, meaner atmosphere at Atlantic 1FM. Richard may have given Ollie a warning shot for getting drunk at the party but that would have been the end of it. This time, there had been a brief announcement that Ollie was gone on an "extended break" and that Chris Conroy, the rank outsider who had scooped the *It's My Show* contest from underneath all their noses, would soon be hosting his own, "hot new show".

According to Sara, Tess Morgan hadn't even realised Conroy was in for the gig. Helene shook her head in disbelief at Tess's naivety. But then, was she in any position to judge other people's gullibility, considering how her own life was going? She gripped the yellow pencil she was holding more firmly and tried to concentrate. All her life she had worked out her dilemmas in this fashion, on a plain sheet of paper. She would list pros on one side, cons on the other. Then she weighed the lists up, added on what her gut instinct was telling her to do and – there it was – a decision she trusted, and one that she rarely veered from once she'd made it.

But now her tried and trusted method wasn't working. Helene shrugged her shoulders, trying to unknot the tension in her muscles. The night of her birthday had been the strangest of her life. She had checked into the hotel and sat in her single room in dazed silence, trying to piece together how her life had started to unravel. But she was still too shocked to work it out and she went through the motions of her well-practised bedtime routine like a zombie: taking off her make-up, doing her stretches, brushing her hair one hundred times like her grandmother had instructed her when she was a little girl and which she had carried out every night of her life since.

It was when she finally lay down on the strange hotel bed and tried in vain to go to sleep that she remembered the envelope Richard had left for her. She stared into the dark, wondering whether she should open it. She switched on the bedside lamp and pulled it out of her overnight bag which was next to the bed.

She stared at the oblong shape for ages. When she finally looked inside she found a birthday card with *To the One I Love* emblazoned across it. Inside, she found an around-the-world-ticket, with her name on it and a cheque. She scanned the accompanying note.

Sweetheart, he had written in expensive, black-inked pen, *I know you always wanted to travel, and I thought this would be a good time for you to get your wish.*

Helene stopped reading, her brow crinkled up with confusion. Why had Richard still left this for her, even after she had told him she was pregnant? How, exactly, did he expect her to use an around-the-world ticket now? The answer came to her in a flash of unwanted insight. It was because he was determined that nothing would interfere with his pay-off money from Jack McCabe. Not even her. Especially not her! He probably figured she would have an abortion and use the ticket to get over it. The hurt hit Helene with such force that she had to squeeze her eyes shut against the pain.

She leaned her head back against the headboard, wondering how she was ever going to get over this. She had to force herself to finish reading Richard's note.

I am enclosing enough money to cover your hotel and living expenses and I'll try to arrange for your job to be kept open for you. When you come back in six months' time, I will have severed all ties with Atlantic 1FM and I'm sure we will resume our romance then. All my love always, Richard x

Helene let the letter flutter out her hands. Richard wouldn't have known when he was writing this that in six months' time she would have a belly like a whale. The thought of him coming around to resume their romance when she was in that condition started her giggling. But it was a high-pitched, nervous snigger that turned rapidly to tears and the more she thought about the situation the more hysterical she became. The best-laid plans, she thought wearily, finally drying her cheeks with a corner of the duvet. Too exhausted to worry any more she pulled up the crisp hotel covers, turned off the unfamiliar lamp and breathed into the black darkness, in and out, in and out, until miraculously she managed to block everything out and fall into a deep, dreamless sleep.

When she woke up she found she'd slept a straight six hours and a curious sense of calm had descended upon her. Over breakfast, she phoned to arrange to have the locks on her apartment changed. Not that she expected Richard to bother coming back any time soon. But it was the only thing she could think of to wrestle some small piece of control back into her life. Since then she had gone through each day on automatic pilot, and it was only when she saw Richard arriving at the relaunch party with Louisa that she had been jolted back to the painful reality that she really was on her own now.

A sharp, breaking sound jolted Helene back into the present. She looked down, startled at the sight of her yellow pencil, snapped into two halves. She had been holding it so tightly she had broken it. Disgusted, she threw the pieces onto her desk and stood up. Nothing in her life was working. She walked out into the open-plan office, trying to distract herself from her troubles.

Andrea was busy at her computer and, as Helene drew alongside her desk, she could see she was browsing through a website called *New Nannies*.

"Looking for a Mary Poppins?"

Andrea jumped guiltily and swirled her chair around to face Helene. "Sorry – I know I shouldn't be doing personal stuff on company time but I need to arrange childcare urgently." She broke off and looked at Helene keenly. "Are you okay? You look a bit pale."

Helene looked at Andrea absently. "Oh yeah ... I'm fine." She was staring at the computer screen. "Em ... how difficult is it – to get good childcare?"

Andrea laughed hollowly. "How long have you got? Possibly easier to get the proverbial camel through the eye of a needle." She went back to scrolling down the pages.

"Oh," Helene said in a small voice.

Andrea looked up sharply. "Are you sure you're okay, Helene?"

Helene turned away before Andrea could see the panic in her eyes. "I'm just a bit hot. I think I'll just go out for a breath of air, actually."

Helene turned and practically ran out of the building. She stood on the pavement, fighting off a fresh wave of nausea. She was having morning, noon and night sickness now. She pulled out a tissue, held it over her mouth and forced herself to take slow, deep breaths. Until now, she had been too distraught over Richard to give much thought to the practical nuts-and-bolts problems of her pregnancy. Like childcare.

She thought back to all the times she had been annoyed with Andrea's childminding crises. The time she couldn't cover an assignment because one of the children – Helene couldn't remember which one – had a bit part as a sheep in the school Nativity play. And the morning Andrea had missed the planning meeting altogether because the toddler was having night terrors. Why couldn't her bloody husband take up the slack once in a while, Helene had often fumed, and not always silently. She had always felt that if women wanted equality in the workplace then they shouldn't be looking for special privileges all the time.

"How hard can it be to organise your life so you're not lurching from one childcare crisis to another?" she'd actually asked Andrea once.

Well, she would find out the answer to that one soon enough. If she'd won *It's My Show*, she might have managed. She wouldn't be working such long hours. There would be back-room people like Tess to organise the programme for her. She wouldn't have to make fifty decisions a day, a feat that had once filled her with a sense of her own power but now simply made her feel faint. In fact, she could barely make up her mind what shoes to wear these days. And now she was expected to cope with having a baby on her own?

Was there something she could have done to keep Richard? Perhaps if she hadn't been so preoccupied with winning the contest she would have been more attuned to his mood. She might have sensed his decision to leave her and somehow found a way to pre-empt it.

But Helene knew she couldn't afford to spend too much time in the land of what-might-have-been. The reality was that Richard was gone and she was going to have to cope on her own. Get used to it, Harper, she told herself sternly.

A taxi pulled up by the kerbside and Paulina Fox stepped onto the pavement. She was dressed in a lemon linen suit, teamed with high black wedges and her ash-blonde hair was tied back in a neat chignon. She looked calm and carefree, as if the chaos that was reigning inside Atlantic 1FM had nothing to do with her.

"Paulina!" Helene called. Ever since the news had broken that Chris had won the contest, she had been trying to get an explanation, but all her phone calls had gone unanswered.

"Hi …" Paulina looked at her warily.

"I need to talk to you." Helene pushed herself away from the wall.

"About what?" Paulina kept on walking and for a fraction of a second Helene thought she was going to ignore her completely.

"About why some outsider won the contest!" Helene hissed.

"Let's take it inside, so."

Paulina pushed open the doors to the radio station and strode along the corridor so swiftly Helene had to practically run to catch up with her. By the time they reached her office, she was having trouble breathing.

She sat down heavily and stared at Paulina.

"So?" she challenged.

"I'm sorry, Helene." Paulina didn't bother to sit. She loomed over Helene, fiddling with the catches on her briefcase. "I know how much it meant to you."

"I doubt that!" Helene snorted. "So: what has this Chris Conroy got then?"

"Let's see. He's on the radio and TV every other week as a commentator. He's a former foreign affairs correspondent."

Helene frowned. "What I meant was – what has he got that qualifies him for his own show?"

Paulina arched her eyebrows. "I don't think it's constructive to go down that path."

"Well, d'you know something? It's not all about what *you* think, Paulina." Helene slammed both her hands onto the desk. "I want to know. I *deserve* to know."

Paulina's eyebrows went even higher. "Fine! So, let's see. As I was saying, Chris Conroy is confident, outgoing, with a brilliant CV. He's coming in from the outside so there is a sense that we're getting something new and fresh. And he's very, very hungry for success."

"But I am confident and outgoing and ..." Helene tried to remember the list of winning qualities Paulina had just recited, "... and hungry! Actually," she looked at Paulina meaningfully, "you wouldn't believe just how hungry I am right now."

"Of course you are. Lots of people are. Ultimately, I suppose it's what I said we were looking for from the beginning. Chris Conroy has the X-factor."

"Oh, come on!" Helene shook her head in disgust. "What a red herring that is!"

"If you take my advice, Helene, you won't waste too

much of your time analysing why he got it and you didn't. Move on."

"That's easy for you to say," Helene snapped.

"I suppose it is," Paulina said it easily. "So I'll say it again, just so you understand. Chris Conroy is the winner. It's over. Look for the opportunity here."

"Yeah yeah, every cloud has a silver lining, look on the bright side, dah de dah de da," Helene said bitterly. "So what's happened to Ollie?"

"Ollie is toast." Paulina pulled a pile of press releases out of her briefcase and dumped them on Helene's desk. "But on the bright side? You get to keep your job. Barely."

"Barely?" Helene's breath caught at the back of her throat. "What the hell does that mean?"

Paulina gave her an odd look. "It means that Jack knows you are having an affair with his sister's husband, and it was all I could do to persuade him to keep his personal feelings out of his business decisions."

"*Was* having an affair," Helene tried to keep the tremble out of her voice. "It's over."

"Really?" Paulina looked at her appraisingly. "Well, that's something, I suppose."

"Well, sort of over. I don't know if I should be telling you this but ... well, the thing is ..." Helene took a deep breath, "I'm pregnant." She waited nervously for Paulina's reaction.

"Seriously? Is it Richard's?" Paulina couldn't keep the surprise out of her voice.

"Of course it's Richard's!" Helene was outraged. Was everyone she told going to ask her that question?

"I was just wondering." Paulina looked at her coolly. "Being pregnant will make it harder for Jack to sack you. A lot harder."

"Is that actually meant to make me feel better?"

"Look, Helene, I like you. And you once asked me for career advice, which is why I am going to give you some now. Jack will be relying on someone to hold Chris Conroy's hand over the coming months – to make sure he fulfils his potential. We need him to become a household name – a star – and pretty sharpish for the whole relaunch of Atlantic 1FM to work. So make sure that that someone is you. Copper-fasten your position here," Paulina's eyes flickered to Helene's waist, "and do it before your pregnancy becomes obvious."

A phone rang and Paulina fished hers out of her pocket and squinted at the screen.

"Sorry I can't stay longer, but I have a rake of stuff to do." She winked at Helene. "But call me if I can be of any further help."

Helene watched her go in disbelief. She had actually *winked* after hearing about Helene's life-changing dilemma? She stared after her as Paulina strode unconcernedly past a huddle of staff watching her fearfully from their desks, head bobbing until she'd disappeared from sight.

Helene picked up one of the press releases and scanned it lethargically.

Chris Conroy will soon be the name on everyone's lips. The broadcaster and journalist won a nationwide contest to host his own show on new national station Atlantic 1FM and is now facing a meteoric rise in his fortunes. What was once a low-key local station will soon be transformed into a ...

Blah blah blah. Helene let the sheet of paper slip out of her hand and watched it waft down to the floor. Could the day get any worse? But after a few minutes she realised that sitting holed up in her office wasn't going to make it any better. Listlessly, she took up the pile of press releases. She might as well hand them out to people, put them out of their misery by confirming the rumour about Chris and *It's My Show*.

"This has been a long time coming," Helene announced as she passed by each desk. "And it is certainly a pity that it isn't one of us who is getting the chance to host our own show, especially now that the station is finally going national."

She started off on the pep talk automatically, and was about to continue with a host of platitudes about how everyone should now put their shoulder to the wheel and get behind the new presenter, and how a rising tide would lift all boats. But suddenly she couldn't stand the fearful, subdued atmosphere a moment longer. And so, for the first time her life, she pulled a sickie.

She was home within an hour and, as she turned her key in the new lock, she tried not to think about the fact that she would never again hear Richard opening her hall door, surprising her with flowers or food or an unexpected night off from his family. She opened her wardrobe, looking for something more comfortable to wear. The skirt of her business suit was already starting to pinch at the waist. All her designer clothes and shoes looked pretty useless now, she thought ruefully, inspecting some of her dresses, wondering half-heartedly if any of them could be altered to accommodate her bump once it started to grow.

The dress she'd worn to her fortieth birthday party slipped off its hanger as she rummaged and, as she watched it float to the floor, everything that had happened came rushing back to her. What the hell was she going to do, she asked herself for the thousandth time? It was all very well for Paulina to fork out advice about Jack needing someone like her to make Chris a star. Helene knew that even if Jack went against his instincts and kept her on – and legally he would probably have to, now that she was pregnant – he could still undermine every decision she made.

And even if he didn't, did she have it in her to make Chris Conroy into a star? Helene knew more than anyone the kind of dedication, energy and sheer bloody-mindedness that particular task would require. To expect her to do it for the rival who had come from nowhere and scooped her dream job from under her nose was a big ask. Too big, Helene realised. And there it was. The answer she had been waiting for, ever since she had started her pros and cons list early that morning. She didn't want to make anyone a star, ever again. Unless it was herself.

She would have to leave the station. But what then? It might be a welcome escape right now, but would it mean a slow spiral into single-parenthood poverty over time? She thought again about Richard's cheque. It had seemed sizeable when she had a salary going into her bank account every month. But it wouldn't last long by itself.

Still, it could buy her some time. Time to find out who she really was, or who she could become when she was no longer Helene Harper, executive editor at Atlantic 1FM, or Richard Armstrong's lover. She had dismissed Richard's idea that she should take time out to travel, because of her pregnancy. But maybe she could go somewhere once the baby was born? Somewhere she could recover from her broken romance and learn how to be a mother?

She thought of Zoey, living on the other side of the world in New Zealand. She and her sister had never been close, but Helene knew she would welcome her, especially once she knew she was pregnant. They were family. She could visit her, for a start.

Helene felt a great surge of energy course through her body. She could face the future after all, she realised. She would do it by taking each day as it came with her head held high and a smile on her face no matter what. Already she could feel the ghost of a grin pulling at the corners of her mouth.

The one thing she hadn't been able to cope with over these past few weeks was not having a Plan. Because planning was Helene's forte.

CHAPTER TWENTY-TWO

She noticed him immediately. He was at a corner table, deep in conversation with a young couple who had a map spread out in front of them.

"Helene!" Matt's face lit up when he saw her. He finished up his conversation with his customers quickly and came over to greet her. "It's so good to see you. I was a bit worried about you after the party night and ... ah, but never mind all that now. How are you?"

"I've had better birthdays." She gave him a rueful smile. "And better days than today, to be honest."

It was true. She'd been shocked by her appearance this morning. No amount of make-up could disguise the purple shadows which were like bruises under her eyes. Her complexion was chalk white and she had an acne breakout on her chin. Halfway through trying to camouflage it all she'd stopped. What was the point? She needed a new life, not more make-up. And to think her main concern had, not so long ago, been how to look ten years younger!

"Carrot cake sometimes helps?" Matt offered.

"It certainly wouldn't do any harm," Helene conceded. "And I'll have a full-fat cappuccino to go with it." Being pregnant had some compensations after all.

"Coming up." He flung his blue-and-white check

teacloth over his shoulder and walked towards the kitchen, stopping to share a joke with a customer on the way.

It was the first thing she'd noticed about Matt, she reflected. How good-humoured he was. Even when he had been struggling to get the café opened, he'd had a smile and a chat for everyone. Even for her that day she'd arrived after the big row with Ollie, when she'd been so off-hand with him.

Helene wondered when, exactly, she had become such a bitch? Maybe it wasn't one moment, she reflected. Maybe it was a series of incremental steps – instances when she'd decided that her perspective was more important than someone else's, that her needs came first, every time, until she somehow got used to that and started to think that her viewpoint was the only valid one. And Richard had turned out to be every bit as selfish as she was.

Matt, on the other hand, seemed to go out of his way to help other people at a moment's notice.

"I never got a chance to thank you for being so kind the night of my birthday party," she said when he came back with a giant chunk of cake and a mugful of steaming coffee.

"It wasn't a problem. Did you er … sort everything out, after?"

"Not really. Actually, I've come to ask you for another favour. I need to pick your brains about flights and stuff."

"Oh? Going on holidays?" His eyes crinkled at the corners and Helene noticed for the first time that he had odd-coloured eyes, one sea-green, the other hazel, flecked with dark speckles.

"A bit more than that." Her stomach lurched when she thought about her plans.

"Sure." Matt looked about the café. It was almost closing time, and there were only a few stragglers left, finishing their food or flicking through brochures. "Look, if you can wait for a bit I'll close up and I can give you my full attention then."

"Great."

Helene spent the time thinking about her plans. Going to see her sister in New Zealand seemed to be the most logical first step. But should she wait until she had the baby? She couldn't make up her mind. She seemed to have developed brain fog when it came to decisions and she kept falling asleep! She guessed it was the pregnancy hormones, but that was alarming when she had so much to figure out.

"Do you mind if we have our chat upstairs in my apartment?" Matt was finished work. "It's been a long day and I could do with a break from the café."

"I'd love to." Helene drained her coffee and stood up. It would make a change from sitting in her own silent apartment night after night. She followed him through a door at the back of the café and up two rickety flights of stairs, where he stopped outside a purple door.

"Here we are."

Helene stepped into the apartment and blinked in surprise. Floor-to-ceiling windows flooded the open-plan living space with light and the last of the evening sunlight sparkled across blond wooden floors. The walls were crammed with colourful abstract artwork and framed photographs of Matt's travels. A pot of purple and white orchids formed an exotic arrangement on the coffee table.

"Make yourself comfortable, I'll only be a few minutes." Matt disappeared into his bedroom.

Helene sank onto the floral sofa, and looked about her curiously. It didn't actually look like a man's apartment. Her eyes fell on a small, framed photo sitting on a side table and she picked it up to examine it more closely. Matt beamed out at her, one arm around a waifish-looking woman who was wearing an oversized cowboy hat and a wide smile. They both looked tanned and happy. Sydney Harbour Bridge soared in the background.

The sun had enveloped the living room in a warm golden glow and it wasn't long before Helene's imagination had transported her to the other side of the world. She felt her eyelids drooping and when they fluttered open again Matt was sitting on the other end of the sofa, his feet on the coffee table. He had changed into casual jeans and a T-shirt and was nursing a large glass of red wine.

"How long was I out for?" Helene rubbed her eyes.

"Half an hour." Matt glanced at the photograph that had slipped onto Helene's lap.

She followed his gaze. "Is she the person responsible for your beautiful decor?"

"No, that was me!" Matt grinned. "Clearly I'm in touch with my feminine side."

Helene tapped the glass frame with her fingertips. "She's very pretty. Is she your girlfriend?"

"Ex-girlfriend. Roseanne." He waved his glass in the air. "Broken romances. Don't you just hate 'em?"

His words were light but Helene knew this was the woman who had broken his heart. She leaned over and propped the photo back on the table and saw a letter there addressed to Matt. *Matt Carver.* So that was his name.

He looked at her curiously. "Did you break up with the guy I met leaving your birthday party, then?"

"I did." Helene looked at the photograph again. "And you? How long ago was your break-up?"

"A year ago now. She met someone else." He sounded wistful. "What happened with your guy?"

"Girl meets boy. Boy dumps girl. Same old story."

Helene pushed her hair out of her eyes.

Matt pointed to the wine bottle on the coffee table.

"A drink to drown our sorrows?"

"Hah!" Helene laughed. "That's where the complication comes in, actually. Not only is boy who dumps girl married in this case, but also dumped girl is pregnant at the time! So I'll pass on the alcohol, thanks. But I'd murder a cup of tea, if it's not too much trouble."

"Seriously?" Matt looked shocked. "So what are you going to do?"

"Be a great mother, I hope!" Helene laughed at his troubled expression. "Now that I've got over the shock I'm sort of looking forward to it. I thought that ship had sailed for me. And now that it hasn't ... well, it's beginning to feel like a brand new adventure."

Matt smiled. "Well, that's a very positive attitude to take, I must say." He put down his wine and loped off to the kitchen, returning with a tray of tea and an array of colourful cupcakes on an ornate stand.

Helene's eyes widened. "You're a demon baker?"

He laughed. "I run a café!"

Helene poured out her tea and helped herself to a cupcake. She may as well start eating for two now, she decided, biting into the pink-and-white icing. She wasn't going to have to worry about her figure for a while. Maybe never. Maybe she'd just grow fat and stay that way – it would be one less thing to worry about.

"So. You wanted to pick my brain," Matt reminded her.

"Yes, I did," Helene sighed. "It's hard to know where to begin, actually."

"Pick a place – any place," Matt suggested. He folded his arms and waited.

And so she did. And once she'd started talking, she

found she couldn't stop. The whole story came bubbling out, about how for so many years she had deluded herself into believing that Richard was going to leave his wife for her; how some outsider had swiped *It's My Show* from under her nose; how Jack McCabe had taken over Atlantic 1FM; and how Richard hadn't bothered to tell her that Jack was actually his *brother-in-law*. How for a while she had been terrified about how she was going to cope with a baby on her own. The only bit she left out was Richard's suggestion that she have a termination because, almost as soon as he had the words out, Helene had pushed them to the back of her mind and refused to think about them again.

"Paulina's advice is that I concentrate on making Chris Conroy – he's the one who won the contest – into a star." Helene finished the last crumbs of her cake.

"And what do you think?" Matt enquired.

Helene rummaged in her bag and pulled out the travel ticket and Richard's cheque and handed them to Matt.

His eyes widened. "Generous guy!"

"Rich guy. Rich, guilty guy. It was his birthday present to me. His brilliant idea was that I could go travelling – alone – until he'd got his settlement out of Atlantic 1FM. But of course I went and got pregnant and ruined his big plan. Anyone would think I had done it on my own."

"So what are you going to do?" Matt asked.

"At the time I dismissed the idea of travelling out of hand because of the baby. But then I got to thinking – well, you must meet lots of people who travel with babies, right?"

"All the time," Matt confirmed. "You just need to take your circumstances into account when you're deciding where to go."

"I have a sister in New Zealand. She settled there with her family years ago. I've never been."

"Well, you'll *love* New Zealand!" Enthusiasm made him sound like a small boy. "And you won't have any problem at all travelling there with a baby. When do you want to go?"

"I'm not sure. I don't know if I should wait and have the baby first – I don't know what to do about anything really."

"Sure, there's no rush. I can give you all the advice you need over the next couple of weeks. Are you going to stay on at work in the meantime?"

"Don't know about that either," Helene mumbled. "My future isn't there any more. But I'm dreading drafting my resignation letter at the same time." She shivered just thinking about it.

Matt looked at her speculatively. "I could do with a hand in the café. On a strictly casual basis. It might be something you'd consider."

"Like . . . wait tables?" Helene couldn't hide her astonishment.

Matt laughed at her expression. "It's not like being down the mines! It can be quite pleasant waiting on people. You get to meet the most interesting characters." His eyes met hers. "Like you, for instance."

Helene blushed. Was Matt hitting on her? Even after she'd just told him she was pregnant? But before she could think of a reply, he was back talking about work again.

"I was thinking more about someone to work on strategies to get more out of the café. That's your forte, isn't it – new ideas?"

"Broadcasting is all about new ideas," she conceded. "Or old ideas presented in a new way." In fact, she could think of lots of ways to improve the Travel Café now, right off the top of her head. Matt could run a competition for the most interesting itinerary, and right away you'd get lots of fascinating stories about people's journeys and why they were doing them. Rachel Joy from *Killty Times* would snap it up. With the right sort of publicity, she could really put the Travel Café on the map.

"It's just an idea. Think about it," Matt said easily.

"I will … and thanks." Helene stuffed the cheque back in her bag thoughtfully. Matt made her feel as if her life might not be in so much of a cul-de-sac after all. "I'd better be getting back."

"Keep in touch now." Matt stood up and reached to help her off the sofa. She felt the heat of his hand on her arm and there it was, a sharp flash of attraction, unmistakeable.

But of course it was her treacherous hormones, making mischief again. Tricking her into finding any man attractive, a biological urge to find someone to share the rearing of her offspring with.

But then Matt wasn't pregnant and he seemed to be feeling it too. When she stood up he kept his hand on her arm and looked as if he'd like to kiss her.

It made Helene feel confused and defensive. "You did hear me when I told you I was pregnant, didn't you?"

"I did." He drew back. "And I probably have no business asking you this – but are you still in love with your baby's father?"

Helene looked away. Was she? She didn't think so. But how could she trust her feelings when she was having such alarming mood swings? She nodded at the photo of Rosanne. "That night at the party. You told me it would get better. Did it for you?"

"Eventually it did. At the time, you can't see how it will.

You can't imagine meeting someone you're interested in ever again. But then – you do."

He looked at her meaningfully. He meant her. Helene was surprised at how pleased she felt about that.

"Don't you love her any more?"

He looked at the photo. "I think I'll always love her. But in a different away. I moved on some time ago. Long enough now to know the good stuff doesn't come around so often that you can afford to dismiss it just because the timing isn't perfect."

He reached out and took one of her hands in his. She left it there, enjoying the feel of his skin on hers. Maybe he was right. Maybe love could feel like this – strong and supportive and *easy*. A million miles from the complexities of her affair with Richard.

"We could take it slowly," he pushed a little.

She smiled. "Slow enough to let me have a baby?"

He shrugged. "To have a baby, go to New Zealand for a bit. I'm not in any rush."

She laughed out loud at that. She couldn't imagine Matt Carver being in a rush about anything. She looked at him speculatively. "So how about I take you up on your job offer and we'll see what happens?"

"Really?"

He looked so delighted with himself that Helene felt tears pricking at the back of her eyes. So this is what it felt like to be with someone who really wanted to be with you.

As Helene drove home, after promising she'd phone within a couple of days, she knew she'd a made a true friend in Matt Carver. One who would stick around, regardless of how tough the terrain got. Someone who would still be her friend even if he didn't get what he wanted and their tentative romance didn't flourish into something deeper. She thought of Rosanne, his ex-girlfriend, and wondered what sort of fool she must have been to let him go.

By the time she pulled up outside her apartment block she felt more at peace with herself than she'd been in a long time. Tonight, she decided, she would finally draft her letter of resignation.

She was turning her key in the lock when someone pushed out of the shadows and put his hand on her shoulder. She swung around to face the intruder, her pulse racing.

"My key wouldn't work!" Richard shot her an accusing look.

"You've just put the heart crossways in me!" Helene snapped, on edge again. "And your key doesn't work because I changed the locks." She opened the door and turned back to face him, intending to keep him at the door, but he was too quick for her. He stepped in after her, standing so close to her in the tiny hallway that for a moment she found herself transported back to a time when she and Richard had been lovers and the best of friends.

Or so she'd thought. She turned away from him and went into the kitchen.

"These are for you." He handed a bouquet of flowers to her. "I'm sorry," he added.

"Why? Because I changed the locks?" She took the flowers and dumped them on the table.

"You need to put them in water, to keep them fresh," he advised.

Helene laughed mirthlessly. "So now you're concerned about the well-being of a bunch of flowers but you haven't asked about your unborn baby?"

"Don't be like that." He shifted uneasily from one foot to the other.

Helene snatched up an empty vase and half-filled it. She shoved the flowers, cellophane wrapping and all, into it and turned back to Richard, flattening the small of her back against the wall to create a distance between them.

"Ollie is sacked, apparently," she said.

"I heard. But in fairness, he had it coming." Richard looked at her gravely. "What about you?"

"I am about to write my resignation letter."

He frowned. "I thought you'd want to keep your job at all costs now. With the er ... pregnancy."

"Well, I don't." Helene thought she saw a look of relief pass over his features.

"But are you sure you're doing the right thing? In resigning?"

"No, I'm not sure. But my job at Atlantic would take way too much energy when I'm a single mother," she said pointedly.

"You'd get maternity leave," he reminded her.

"Yes, I would. If I spend the next six months of my life faking an interest in the fame and fortunes of Chris Conroy. And trying to forget that Jack McCabe knows I was the third person in his sister's marriage. I don't have the stomach for it frankly. I couldn't care less what happens at Atlantic now." She reached out and began to absentmindedly shred one of the flowers in the bouquet, peeling away the delicate pink rose petals one by one. "Richard, why are you here?"

"I wanted to explain things to you. I'd bought the plane ticket for you before I knew you were pregnant. And I know I shouldn't have left it there, the night of your birthday. Not once I knew about the baby. But I was shell-shocked. I didn't know what I was doing."

Helene stayed silent, for once resisting the urge to tell him not to worry, that everything would be all right.

"Of course you must have been pretty shocked too," he continued after a while. "What with the pregnancy and the pressures at work ..."

"And getting dumped by you." She raised her eyes to his.

Richard looked away. "Yes. And that. And not winning the contest. I'm sorry about that. I know how much you wanted it."

"There're lot of things I wanted that I didn't get," Helene said flatly. "But now that I am going to be a single mother, I need a job that's a little less challenging than trying to tune in to the psyche of the nation, or whatever rubbish Paulina had on the press release."

"What sort of a job?" he asked.

"Working in a coffee shop, apparently." She smiled at the thought of it.

"A coffee shop? Are you mad?" He was looking at her with astonishment. "You're an executive editor! Look, you know I'll support you and the baby financially. In fact, that's why I'm here. I've got my financial settlement from the station! It all went through a lot earlier than I expected. "

"Well, that's great for you. And of course you can support the baby," she agreed readily. God knows the child would need all the help it could get, with only her as a parent. "But you don't owe me anything. I knew the score when we got involved."

"I've told you," Richard said peevishly, "I wasn't thinking straight when you told me you were pregnant. There was the stress of the takeover and Louisa being extra-needy and –"

"It's in the past, Richard," she interrupted him.

"But how can it be in the past when you're expecting my baby?"

"Oh, it's *your baby* now. The baby you wanted

terminated?" There, she'd finally said the words. Her stomach churned at the sound of them.

"Don't," he begged. "I've had time to think things over. And, well – I still want us to be together."

"You do?" Treacherous hope flared in Helene. She looked at him seriously. "Have you brought your suitcase?"

"*No*. I mean, obviously, I can't leave Louisa at this precise moment because ... well, I'm sure you don't care why at this stage. But by the time the baby is born ..."

"You'll get around to it then," she finished his sentence for him. "Or maybe it will be by the time the first birthday rolls around? Or the first day at school, perhaps? Or maybe university?"

"You don't seem like yourself, Helene," he said huffily.

"Things have changed, Richard," she said wearily. "I've changed. Going back to the way we were, with you pitching up whenever you feel like it is not enough any more. Not when I have a baby to consider. And to be honest, it never was enough. You already have a family, Richard – something I should have considered much, much earlier."

"But having me around part-time has to be better than nothing, surely? It won't be easy on your own," he warned.

She looked at him. He hadn't been there for her when she was in trouble, and something had changed in her then, something fundamental. No matter what he said now, she knew she would never trust him again.

"I think the term 'too little, too late' may have been invented for situations like this," she said sadly.

"But how will you cope?" he demanded. "It's not as if you have family close by to help. Please, Helene. Think about it."

"I have thought about it. As soon as the baby is born, I'm going abroad – to New Zealand. To my sister." There. Another decision made. She'd have the baby here, at home. And then, as soon as it was old enough, she'd set off on her travels.

"New Zealand?" He couldn't disguise his shock. "But it's so far away!"

She shrugged. "I need to find out what I want to do with the rest of my life, and I think it would be easier for me to do that if I wasn't around here. Around you. The further away the better really."

"How long will you stay?"

"I'm not sure. Long enough."

"I could come and visit you, you and the baby?" His eyes were bright with hope.

And if Helene had ever wanted revenge on Richard, she had it right then – as she saw the hope fading when she explained she wouldn't be leaving him a forwarding address.

"I'll give you details of a bank account where you can deposit money for the baby. But that's all. I don't want any more contact with you. Not for a long time."

He looked baffled then and so utterly defeated that for a few mad seconds Helene almost changed her mind. Because whatever had happened between them, she knew that part of her would always love him. But she needed her energy for other things now, she reminded herself. She folded her hands protectively over her stomach. For someone else. She walked over to Richard, leaned up and kissed him softly on the mouth.

"Goodbye, Richard."

CHAPTER TWENTY-THREE

The sound of the phone jangling cut through Tess's thoughts. She looked up warily. After her showdown with Chris in the Travel Café, she had simply emailed Helene to let her know she was resigning her position and that she would take her remaining holiday entitlement in lieu of notice. Then Chris had taken to phoning her daily, wondering when she was coming back to work. Even after she'd convinced him that she was definitely finished with Atlantic, he would still ring at all hours of the day and night, looking for advice about his new role.

In desperation she had switched her phone off and spent a week staring at the walls, feeling nine kinds of stupid for getting herself into such a mess in the first place. She felt mortified when she thought back to all the mad stuff Chris had talked her into. Delivering an elevator speech to Jack McCabe. Thinking of herself as Cinema Tess. It had all seemed a bit zany at the time, a bit brave, actually. But in retrospect it just seemed as if an alien had taken over her body, forcing her to do things she would never normally do. And she couldn't blame all of it on Chris. When she thought about how she had come on to him the night of the reunion, she felt faint with embarrassment.

But, in the end, there was only so much self-incrimination

Tess could endure. This morning she had switched her phone back on, grabbed a notebook and sat down to work through her options. But before she'd had time to commit one thought to paper, the phone calls had started up again. She snatched up her mobile.

"Chris!" she snapped.

"Tess?"

"Verity?"

"Where the hell have you been? I've been ringing you for the past two days." Her sister sounded worried.

"Er … it's a long story. What's up?" Tess's heart started to hammer. What if something awful had happened to someone in her family while she'd had her phone switched off, moping about just because she was going to have to start over yet again?

"Are you okay? I was starting to think something awful had happened to you. I phoned your job and they said you didn't work there any more."

"I don't. But I'm fine. Really. As I said, it's a long story. So what's so urgent?"

"It's not urgent. I was just wondering when you're coming over to see us? I could visit you, but I'm not sure if there're flying restrictions for very early pregnancy?"

"That's late pregnancy," Tess said absent-mindedly. Then as her brain did catch-up, she shouted, "Oh my God, Verity, you're not?"

"I am!" Verity's laughter rang down the phone. "You'll be an aunt and a godmother. And I need help to go through baby name books and look at nursery furniture, and oh, a million things."

"I'll be on the next flight," Tess said immediately. She hadn't seen anyone in a week and she was going stir crazy in this apartment. In this town. In this *country*. She was so anxious to get going, in fact, that she cut Verity off after another few minutes, saying they could catch up on all the news when she got to London.

As she bustled about the apartment, booking her flight online and packing her bag, Tess felt the sense of excitement she always got when she was about to go on a journey. She had been in Killty for less than a year but she was already feeling stifled and stressed and vaguely victimised by her circumstances. Maybe she wasn't meant to settle down? Maybe she could just keep on travelling. Forever. Where was the law anyway, she argued with herself, that stipulated you had to be on a corporate career ladder just because you were thirty?

In less than twenty-four hours she was sitting in Verity's stylish Kensington home, enjoying a glass of chilled white wine. Verity worked as a self-employed interior designer and, looking around her elegant living room, with its white sash windows and Scandinavian furniture, Tess felt a sharp pang of envy. It had always been that way, ever since they were little girls. No matter how hard Tess tried, Verity had always achieved more. She effortlessly took the gold medal, while Tess had to work like crazy for the bronze. In fact, Verity was the reason Tess had chosen to study journalism in the first place, over her first choice of going to art college. She knew she would only be setting herself up to forever trail in Verity's ultra-successful footsteps if she had gone into the same area.

Listening to Verity now, enthusing about her shiny new future was lovely, but it was also dredging up that old, uneasy feeling Tess had – that she would always be an also-ran compared to her sister.

But when she started to fill Verity in on her own news,

Tess began to relax. Her sister found the details of Chris Conroy's career-coaching hilarious – the way she'd imagined Andrea should have – and by the time she got around to explaining about her elevator speech, tears of mirth were pouring down both their faces.

"God, I've missed you," Verity said finally, drying her eyes.

"To new beginnings!" Tess raised her glass in a toast.

"New beginnings!" Verity raised her glass of sparkling water. "But come on! You must have known that Chris was an idiot?"

"But that's just it. I didn't!" Tess exclaimed. "I *still* can't believe he was using me to get insider information about Atlantic."

"Well, I can," Verity said bluntly. "Nobody ever knew what you saw in him." She looked at her sister shrewdly. "Did he break your heart again?"

"More like dented my pride this time. Getting back with him was nothing like I'd dreamed it would be. It was like I was seeing him without the rose-coloured specs this time around. But when he dumped me that first time around? I lost all my confidence and I swore then I would never let that happen to me again. And yet somehow I did – with the same *guy*! Did I tell you he has a fiancée?"

"Three times." Verity raised her eyebrows. "Look, it's not you, it's him. He's a philanderer and a user."

"But how come I didn't see that?" Tess persisted. "How come I was – am – such a bad judge of character?"

"Love is blind, I suppose," Verity said matter-of-factly. "We've all been there."

"Except I don't know now if I ever loved him." Tess straightened up. "Staying hung up on him for all that time – cyber-stalking him and checking out his career – it all meant I didn't have to commit to another relationship, and risk getting hurt all over again." She looked away. "I've been such a coward about life, Verity."

"And here was me envying you all this time," her sister said calmly. "The way you took off on your own like that, travelling wherever the wind took you. I would never have the courage to do that. I need everything in my life to be planned and predictable or else I become stressed and cranky."

"Really?" Tess was shocked. She had never for a moment thought that her sister might envy *her*.

Verity smiled ruefully. "And now that I'm pregnant, backpacking around the world is a ship that has definitely sailed for me. Shopping for the baby is my biggest thrill these days."

It was Tess's biggest thrill now too, and her days in London fell into a pattern of preparing for the new arrival. When Verity had time off they shopped for baby paraphernalia and when she had to visit clients or disappear into her office on the top floor of the house, Tess went out to enjoy the city by herself.

One sunny afternoon she was strolling along Kensington High Street and saw a man coming towards her with a long, loping gait, pushing dark hair off his forehead in a familiar, impatient gesture. Her pulse quickened. Was it Jack McCabe? But as he drew closer, Tess found herself staring into the face of a perfect stranger. She stopped walking, taken aback by the sheer force of the disappointment which swamped her.

She had refused to think about Jack at all these past few weeks. The only way she could deal with her feelings about him was to banish them to the furthest recesses of her mind. She had been so hurt when he'd laid the blame for the debacle of the relaunch party at her feet, automatically assuming she had been drunk, when she had been trying to save Ollie from himself.

But then, wasn't that what she had spent the majority of her time doing since she had taken the job? Trying to manage Ollie, figuring out what mood he was in, how she could make him happy so he might become bearable to work with? She had been so focussed on him that she'd stopped taking her own feelings into consideration. Even if she'd won the contest, it would have meant months, maybe even years, of trying to shoehorn herself into a position that didn't suit her. At least she'd faced up to that much.

Then Verity threw a dinner party. She and her husband had built up a good social life in London and were eager to introduce Tess to some of their friends.

Tess was sitting beside a woman called Sally, a tall, skinny redhead who worked as an editor with one of the top monthly magazines.

After dinner, everyone brought their drinks out to the conservatory. Tess tilted back her head to look at the stars through the domed glass roof and wondered what the future held for her.

"By the way, there's a maternity-leave vacancy at the magazine for a sub-editor right now. Would you be interested?"

"Me?" Tess turned to Sally, astonished. She had been telling her over dinner about some of the freelance work she'd done over the last few years as a way of financing her travels. But she had no experience of working for one of the top glossies.

"Yes – you're a trained journalist, aren't you? And there might be some writing opportunities for you too, if you come up with suitable ideas. Your extended gap year would make a great feature for our readers, for a start."

"Thanks. I'll certainly think about it." Tess was thrilled with the tip-off.

Later on, Verity explained that she'd recommended her to Sally earlier in the week. "I bigged up all your freelance work, and your journalism degree, and told her you were a producer on a top national radio station in Ireland."

"*Seriously?*"

"Well, it's all true, isn't it?" Verity frowned.

"Er … *no*. Atlantic 1FM was a small local station when I was there."

"But it's a national station now," Verity pointed out. "Anyway, it's only to cover someone's maternity leave. Of course, you'll have to go through an interview and impress the hell out of her bosses, but Sally seems to think you'll walk it. What do you think?"

Tess thought it sounded like an opportunity offered to her on a silver platter. It would be a chance to reinvent herself at a stroke, an opportunity to redeem herself – in her own eyes at least. But then she remembered the last time she thought she was getting a dream job – it had been at Atlantic, and look where that had got her.

"I don't want you to go for the interview unless you're serious about the job. It will reflect badly on Sally if you do," Verity warned, noticing Tess's hesitation.

"I understand. When does she need to know?"

"Her boss is out of the country at the moment apparently, so the interview won't be for another couple of weeks at least."

It was the breathing space Tess needed. She could think about whether this was the right move for her and, while she was weighing that up, she could go back to Killty. She needed to tie up loose ends.

She needed to go back and give up the apartment, pack her stuff, say her goodbyes. She had been in London almost a month now and the time and distance had allowed her to put her troubles at Killty into perspective. Except for the feud with Andrea. That was her biggest regret. The most important thing she needed to do was to try to fix things between them. Before she left Killty for good.

CHAPTER TWENTY-FOUR

As it turned out, Andrea couldn't have been more delighted to hear from her.

"I thought I was never going to see you again," she said softly.

They were sitting in the Travel Café. Tess was dressed in her oldest faded jeans while Andrea was dressed for success – navy business suit, white shirt, dotted scarf and a big briefcase by her feet. "I did try to contact you the day after those pictures were in the *Killty Times*, but your phone was switched off. The paper made it look like Ollie was fighting you on the floor for *It's My Show*!"

Tess laughed. "Of course it did. Gai Gordan Ryder actually said something to that effect in his report, if I remember correctly."

Andrea sighed. "Jack and Paulina set us all up to compete with each other and we went for it like obedient nodding dogs, didn't we?"

"I suppose we did."

"I convinced myself that winning the contest was the most important thing in my life. I focussed on it so hard I couldn't see anything, or anyone, else. When I heard you were getting coaching from the hotshot Chris Conroy *and* going to dinner with the boss – hands up – I was jealous and resentful."

Tess gave a rueful smile. "And you had so little to be jealous of as it turned out. By the way – did you ever find out who Terry was?"

Andrea's face closed over. "Paul still insists she was just a work colleague. But to be honest, I don't know if I believe him. I mean, why did he let me think *she* was a he if it was all so innocent?"

Tess stayed silent, thinking of the intimate connection she had witnessed between Paul and the woman that night in the restaurant.

"For a while there I thought we were over – I was even looking up new day care for the children. But," Andrea shrugged awkwardly, "it's a marriage, you know what I mean? And we've two small children to consider. So we're trying to work it out."

"I'm sorry we fell out over it," Tess said quietly.

"And are you sorry for going to dinner with Jack without telling me first?" Andrea attempted to lighten the mood.

"Of course. And are you sorry for getting secret sessions with a stylist?" Tess countered.

"Desperately!"

Tess laughed. "So how have things been apart from all of that?"

"Good! There have been lots of changes ..." Andrea broke off as the waitress arrived to take their order, "and ... er ... here's one of them."

"I'll just have coffee," Tess looked up and did a double take. "*Helene?*"

"Don't look so surprised!" Helene smiled. "Or judgemental."

"I'm not. I mean, of course I'm *surprised*." Tess stared at her former boss.

312

Helene was wearing a loose-cut, floral dress with flat, open sandals and her glossy dark hair was pushed back into a ponytail.

"Well, you shouldn't be. Being a waitress means you get to meet all sorts of interesting people." Helene's mouth curved in a secret smile.

Tess shook her head, trying to make the connection between this barefaced, smiling, *hippy* and the sharp-suited woman who had made her life a misery for months.

"Of course, I only actually waitress the odd time," Helene continued. "When it's very busy or staff haven't turned in. I do it as a favour to Matt but I get ideas from the customers for my real job here – to put the Travel Café on the map. I'm doing the PR for him."

"Er … sounds great."

"So – what have you been doing with yourself?"

"I've been in London for the last few weeks." Tess was about to explain about her potential new job on the magazine. But the germ of an idea which had been bubbling just under her consciousness for ages, rose spontaneously to the surface. *If Helene Harper can work as a waitress, why can't I go to art college?* Tess blinked. Where the hell had that come from? It was a ridiculous idea anyway – she couldn't start all over again. She wanted to move forward in her life, not go backwards.

"London must have been interesting," Helene said. "I'm actually thinking of moving away myself. To New Zealand – after the baby is born." She looked down at her as yet non-existent bump proudly.

"Congratulations!" Tess smiled.

"My foot she's moving to New Zealand," Andrea snorted as soon as Helene wafted out of earshot. "Remember that guy who rescued her fortieth birthday

313

party and stopped it from turning into a complete disaster?"

"Yeah, Matt. The guy who owns this place."

"Well, I think they're an item now." Andrea's eyes were glinting with amusement.

"*Seriously?* What about Richard and the baby?" Tess stared after Helene.

"They're finished. And you saw how Helene lights up when she mentions Matt. She's different since she met him. Softer. And when you see them together – well ..."

Tess shook her head in disbelief. "Typical of Helene to land on her feet no matter what happens. And if that sounds as if I'm jealous, it's because I am."

But then Tess thought maybe things had worked out for Helene because she was brave. Brave enough to leave a situation that was making her unhappy and to take a risk with someone new. Maybe, instead of begrudging her old boss her happiness, she needed to concentrate on developing her own courage muscles.

She pulled her attention back to Andrea. "So, how have things been at work for you?"

"Really good, actually. As soon as I realised Chris had won the contest, I knew I had to change tack immediately. And guess what – I pitched for Helene's job and got it!" Andrea clapped her hands in anticipation of Tess's reaction.

Tess's eyes widened. "Wow! Congratulations! Is it ... er ... as stressful as Helene seemed to find it?"

"Not at all. You were right from the beginning. Helene and Ollie did make out that their jobs were a lot more difficult than they actually were."

"Ollie's was a lot harder as I remember." Tess shuddered at the memory of her Agony Aunt of the Airways experience.

"I suppose it depends on whether the position suits you," Andrea conceded. "But I love my new role, and so does Chris Conroy – for now at least. And Sara is having no trouble at all keeping him under control – she keeps telling him he's cute, apparently!"

Tess smiled. "He'd like that. So what happened to Ollie?"

"Ollie," Andrea smothered a laugh, "has gone to New Zealand! Helene has no idea about it yet but, when she finds out, I bet she'll use it as an excuse to stay put."

"Tea, wasn't it?" Helene arrived back at their table and plonked Tess's mug down so hard that the hot liquid slopped all over the table.

"It was coffee, actually," Tess said apologetically.

"Damn!" Helene looked irritable.

Tess took up a napkin and started mopping up the mess. No matter how lyrical Helene was waxing now about working as a waitress, Tess somehow didn't see this phase of her life lasting too long. Helene Harper would be bossing someone around somewhere, before too much longer. Probably Matt, if Andrea was right.

"Thanks. I'll get you coffee so," Helene said half-heartedly. "Unless you don't mind drinking tea?"

"Tea is fine." Tess hid a smile.

Helene gave her a speculative look. "Hey, have you heard about Jack and Paulina yet?"

"No?" Tess stiffened.

"Paulina's hoping he's going to put a ring on it soon."

"Good for her."

"And apparently Richard and Louisa have finally split up," Andrea whispered as Helene moved away. "The story is that as soon as she heard Helene was pregnant, that was it – it was curtains for Richard."

Joan Brady

Tess was only half listening. She was already mentally making arrangements for her return to London. The very last thing she wanted was to be in Killty if Jack and Paulina were planning their nuptials.

Andrea reached for her briefcase. "Listen, I need to go over some urgent work stuff with Jack because he's got a plane to catch first thing in the morning. But we can meet again tomorrow and have a proper catch-up if you're free?"

The door to the café swung open and Andrea stood up.

"Here he is now, actually. Jack? Jack, we're over here."

Tess followed her gaze and found herself looking up into the solemn brown eyes of Jack McCabe.

CHAPTER TWENTY-FIVE

She couldn't stop staring. Seeing Jack so unexpectedly like this had thrown her completely. He was wearing a light summer suit and plain white shirt and he looked indecently sexy.

Tess's eyes darted suspiciously to Andrea – was it really a coincidence that Jack should pitch up at the Travel Café just when she was here? But Andrea was studiously leafing through a sheaf of documents.

"Tess." He seemed to be as surprised as she was that they should meet like this. "You're back."

"I was just going, actually. I'll let you get on with your meeting." She stood up abruptly.

Jack put his hand on her shoulder. "Please. We need to talk – or at least I do. I don't want us to part on bad terms."

"We're not on bad terms." She forced a smile. "But I really do have to be going. I'll call you tomorrow, Andrea." She made a beeline for the door and stepped gratefully out into the cool air of the early evening. She couldn't understand how flustered she got every time she met him.

"What's the hurry?"

She looked back to see that Jack had followed her out. "Honestly, I do have a lot on – I'm moving to London."

"Oh! When?" He looked disappointed.

"Soon. And Andrea says you need to go over some urgent work stuff with her."

"She does?" He looked towards the café where Andrea was now in a window seat, peering out at them. He smiled. "I wondered why she was so insistent about meeting here. Obviously she's figured out how much I wanted to see you again."

The sun slipped out from behind a cloud and Jack squinted in the unexpected light. "Look," he pressed on, "I'm flying to New York tomorrow for a business trip. But I'm staying at a hotel just outside here tonight. Would you come and have a drink with me? I'd really like to clear the air."

Tess hesitated. What was the point? Clearing the air sounded a lot like getting closure, didn't it? That was what she had told herself when she was going to meet up with Chris again. And look how that had turned out. On the other hand if she was going to live in London, she'd never meet Jack McCabe again after tonight. And she could still feel the full force of that charisma thing he had going on. It was as if the world was a more colourful, fun place to be when she was with him.

"Just the one then."

"Brilliant," Jack beamed.

He ushered her towards his car and Tess slipped into the passenger seat. Jack switched on a classical station and Tess sank into the soft, leather upholstery and allowed the music to waft away any misgivings she might be having. As the car rounded a bend, she took a surreptitious look at him from beneath her lashes. He was staring straight ahead, his brow furrowed as if he was trying to work out a puzzle. She was conscious of how close they were – that if she reached out her hand she'd be touching him and how the thought of that was making all her senses sing in a way they never had before. Not with Chris, not even the first time around. Not with anyone.

How was that for lousy timing? Finding out how much Jack meant to her just when she was about to say goodbye to him for good? By the time they pulled into the hotel's grand, cobblestoned driveway, all of Tess's doubts had resurfaced and she had convinced herself she'd made a monumental mistake in coming.

As they entered the reception, Tess gravitated towards the fire burning in an ornate fireplace while Jack checked himself in. What good was having one drink with him going to do, she thought as she stared into the flames. It was like torturing herself.

"I have a suite because I need to get some work done." Jack returned with his key card. "So I've ordered drinks for the room – if that's okay?"

"Sure." Tess couldn't help wondering how Paulina would react if she knew Jack was inviting her up to his hotel suite. It was clear now why she had been so hostile towards her. Paulina's intuition had told her there was *something* between her and Jack – the same something Tess herself had felt that night when they had gone for dinner.

The only one who hadn't felt it, unfortunately, was Jack. He was marching across towards the lift now, oblivious of any tension between them at all. As they travelled up to the penthouse, Tess wondered if he was remembering the last time they'd been in a lift together and her ridiculous elevator speech.

They came to a stop and the doors slid open silently, leading them directly into the suite. Tess blinked at the opulence of the surroundings. The sitting room was furnished with an enormous yellow sofa, stuffed with matching cushions. There was an expensive, red-leather writing desk slotted into an alcove. A small dining table was dressed with an enormous bouquet of roses arranged in a cut-glass vase and a bottle of champagne was chilling in a silver bucket.

Jack threw his jacket across the back of the sofa and reached for the champagne. Tess walked over to the window and stared at the storybook scene outside – a patchwork of green fields and an actual babbling brook flowing alongside the walls of the hotel, the water glistening hypnotically as it skimmed over the smooth pebbles of the riverbed.

"Cheers!" Jack came up behind her and handed her a glass of champagne.

"Cheers!" She hoped she wasn't about to find out that Helene was right, and that Jack had plans to propose to Paulina. She wanted to enjoy this last, fantasy evening with him first.

"So where did you go that awful day after the launch party?" he asked. "I tried to find you but there appeared to be an *omertà* about it at Atlantic 1FM."

"That's because nobody there knew. Not even Andrea. I met Chris. Then I switched off my mobile. And then I went to London, to visit my sister. I needed to get away from everything and everyone."

"I'm not surprised. It all went a bit pear-shaped," he said ruefully. "Look, I want to apologise for my behaviour. I'm afraid I overreacted on several fronts."

Tess shrugged. "It's in the past."

"But I blamed you for that debacle with Ollie – without even checking if I had read the situation correctly. And I blurted out that Chris had a fiancée – it was cruel."

"Yeah. That was a shock. I pretended I knew already but

you probably guessed that was just to save face. Nobody likes to be taken for a fool."

Jack's face darkened. "I know what you mean. One of the reasons I was so angry with you was because you told me you didn't know who Richard was having the affair with. And all the while it was common knowledge."

Tess bit her lip. "Jack, I was never one-hundred-per-cent sure about Helene and Richard. There was talk but I wasn't going to help ruin a marriage without having first-hand evidence."

He stood beside her, staring out at the countryside, twirling the stem of his glass around. "There was a silver lining, I suppose, because when Louisa found out that Helene was pregnant, she finally threw Richard out. She's broken-hearted now but, with Tricky Dickey out of the picture, I'm hoping she'll have a chance to recover."

Tess raised her glass again. "To new futures, so! For everyone. I have a new job in London." She swallowed. "And Paulina and you have plans for the future too."

There. That had sounded friendly and mature, just as she had wanted it to.

He frowned. "You mean for the station?"

"No." She mustn't back down now. "I'm talking about your – your personal lives."

"What do you mean?"

"Something Helene Harper said," she murmured, blushing. "I met her earlier at the Travel Café. Did you know she's waitressing there now?"

He grinned. "I heard. And part of me is not surprised. But for a journalist she can sure get her facts wrong. I don't have any 'personal' plans with Paulina, if that's what she told you."

"Oh?" Was he going to try to lie to her? That would be

unbearable. "Well, maybe she had some of the details wrong but she seemed quite sure you were practically engaged. Anyhow, it's none of my business."

"We had a thing in the past but it was over. When I rang her to come on board for the relaunch of Atlantic she seemed to think it was for more than just business – that it was my way of getting back with her." He frowned. "But it wasn't."

Tess wondered whether she could believe him. She remembered Paulina's words when they'd met at the traffic lights that day, when she was returning to work after having coffee with Jack: *"You know we're seeing each other."* And then Helene's: *"Paulina's hoping he's going to put a ring on it soon."*

Had Helene got her facts wrong, like Jack was suggesting? Was Paulina spinning the story the way she wanted it to be? Spinning stories was how she made her living after all.

Or – and she had to face this – was Jack another lying cheat like Chris Conroy?

He caught the look in her eyes. "Maybe I need to have a conversation with Paulina, to make sure there's no crossed wires. Just in case. But look, I didn't ask you here to talk about her. The thing is . . . " He paused, took a deep breath. "I can't stop thinking about you, Tess. And if you and Chris have split up for good – which I assume you have because, and forgive me if you haven't heard this yet, he announced the date of his wedding the other day – do you think there might be a chance for us to get to know each other better?"

Tess thought of her conversation with Verity – about how she'd clung on to a fantasy about Chris because it meant she didn't have to get involved with anyone else, didn't have to risk getting her heart broken again. About how she'd wished then she'd lived a braver life.

Maybe now was the time to start. It was true she had been taken in by Chris not once, but twice. But she'd allowed herself to suffer for it for far too long, at least the first time around.

Her instincts were telling her to believe Jack but maybe that was just because she wanted to believe him? The fact was that she could be proven wrong about him too.

But she knew if she wanted her life to be different she was going to have to start taking risks. Hearts got broken all the time. But she knew now they also mended, when they were given the chance.

"There's this job in London," she said. "Sub-editing at a top glossy. And the chance of writing too. I'm not sure if I want to take it."

"What's stopping you?"

"I thought I might go back to college – to art college. Or do both, you know? The magazine is only a temporary gig."

"Sounds exciting."

"It is. But it's not that simple."

"Actually, it is," Jack said firmly. "I'm just glad you're not thinking of going to work in New Zealand, which is where all the ex-Atlantic 1FM staff appear to be heading. London is only an hour away. So can I get back to my original question? If you're really over Chris, I suggest we leave all the boring career stuff for another time and make the most of this lovely hotel."

"I thought you said you got a suite because you had work to do," Tess reminded him with a smile.

"I have a five-hour flight ahead of me. Plenty of working time there if you want to do something else tonight?"

Something else was *exactly* what Tess wanted. And she

was done with putting obstacles in her own way. Whatever she decided to do in the future, right now, in front of her, was a delicious chance of happy ever after. Or, at the very least, a wonderful night of unbridled lust with Jack McCabe. Who wouldn't want it?

She closed the distance between them and from there it was only a short step to the bedroom. Tess gave up thinking about anything but being in the here and now, feeling Jack's skin on hers, the taste of his mouth, the way he spun magic into the night with his whispered endearments.

Just like she'd imagined, everything was different with him. It wasn't just the way he looked – the dark hair curling around the nape of his neck, his tanned, athletic body, the girlishly long eyelashes she loved. You'd have to be blind not to have noticed already that Jack McCabe was drop-dead gorgeous. She'd experienced his distinctive scent before too, that expensive aftershave mingled with his own, unique essence. But the feel of him was new. The heat of his skin; the strength in his muscled arms as he folded her into him; his touch, sure on her body. It felt as if he was one-hundred-per-cent present with her. All of his senses seemed to be so acutely tuned to hers that, at one time, it felt like they were breathing as one person.

"Do you believe in soul-mates?" he asked her at one point. He was propped up on one elbow, looking at her quizzically.

"I didn't," she said. And it was true. She'd had plenty of romances, apart from the torch she'd carried for Chris for all that time. But she'd never felt this magnetic pull to a man before. "Do you?" she turned the question back on him. "Believe in soul-mates?"

"Never gave it much thought before now to be honest." He raised his eyebrows. "Maybe we should get a joint reading done with Rosa and see if she can explain this connection between us?"

"I'm not sure I want it explained." She shifted beside him.

"Me neither." He pulled her closer.

They stayed awake all night, until five in the morning when Jack had to leave for the airport. She heard the soft click of the door behind him and sometime after that she must have fallen asleep.

When she woke, it was to the unmistakeable voice of Chris Conroy filling the room. Tess jerked up into a sitting position, adrenaline flooding her system. Her eyes darted to where the radio had come on automatically.

"*And now it's time for your very own Agony Aunt of the Airwaves on Atlantic 1FM. On this morning's programme we're relaunching a slot that was very popular with listeners earlier on in the year. So here to answer all the problems of you lovelorn listeners we have our own Psychic Granny! Rosa is ready and waiting to solve all your dilemmas. Good morning, Rosa!*"

Tess looked around her, disorientated by the strange surroundings. She noticed the enormous yellow sofa, the pink roses, still resplendent in their vase, the empty bottle of champagne. But Chris and Rosa were prattling on, spoiling everything. Tess felt herself catapulted out of the room and into the past. She thought about all the hoops she'd forced herself to jump through as she tried to fit in at work. How she had become so fixated on playing catch-up with her peers that she had almost lost sight of the great adventure she had been on – travelling the world, seeing unforgettable places, making lifelong friends along the way.

That's who Cinema Tess is, she realised. Not the person

Chris had tried to convince her to become – someone who would change herself over and over again to suit external circumstances. But then, if she hadn't met up with Chris again she might never have learned that lesson. To listen to her own inner voice, the voice that would always tell what the next best thing for her was.

And if she hadn't worked at Atlantic 1FM she wouldn't have met Jack, who was hopefully scheduled to have a starring role in her next Big Adventure. She reached over and switched the radio to 'off'. She nestled back under the duvet, savouring the silence. Jack would be halfway to New York by now, but delicious fragments of the night before teased the corners of her mind. She closed her eyes and allowed herself to replay their magical night together over and over in her head. Eventually, only when she knew she couldn't delay her checkout time any longer, she packed away the memories for some other time.

Then she swung her legs out of bed, eager to begin the next phase of her life.

Showtime, she thought excitedly.

THE END

If you enjoyed
The Cinderella Reflex by Joan Brady
why not try an exclusive first chapter of
Reinventing Susannah before its release in 2017?

REINVENTING
SUSANNAH

JOAN BRADY

CHAPTER 1

Reinventing Susannah

When the phone rang, Susannah deliberately rejected the idea that it might be more bad news. It was nine months now since her mother had died, nine months since every time the phone rang she leapt up from whatever she was doing, her heart hammering as she snatched up the receiver.

"Susannah – can you get away?"

"Rob?"

Susannah was surprised to hear her husband's voice. According to him, he rarely had time to do *anything* apart from the mountains of work which had built up since the bank let half their staff go under a redundancy scheme, meaning the remaining "lucky" ones got to do two jobs instead of one.

"Is there anything wrong?" she asked.

"Wrong? Why should there be something wrong?"

"No reason." Susannah put her hand on her chest, aware that her breathing had speeded up and her muscles had tensed at the sound of the phone.

"Are you busy?" he asked.

She glanced out at the black plastic bags lined up like sentries along one wall of the conservatory, destined for the dump or the charity shop. She had just finished a marathon clear-out, with the twins' permission and certain strictures, ruthlessly culling anything to do with the past.

"Not especially. Why?"

"I wondered if you could come into town – meet me for lunch?"

"*Lunch?*"

"Yes – what's so strange about that?" Rob's voice had a definite edge.

Apart from the fact that you haven't asked me for lunch since the girls were about twelve? Susannah wondered silently. Plus, she remembered Rob making his sandwiches last night, slapping on the butter with a lot more force than was necessary. Or had that been the night before? All the days seemed to run into each other nowadays.

"How come you have time for lunch?"

"It's Dress-down Friday," Rob said aggrievedly.

"Oh right … I forgot."

Dress-down Friday was a new policy the bank had initiated for staff who weren't working directly with the public – a misguided attempt to soothe the simmering outrage among them as their terms and conditions were quietly eroded. They got to leave their career suits at home and got an extra half-hour for lunch in the hope that morale might improve.

"So I'll see you at one," Rob said brusquely. "In that restaurant near the office – you know the one. It does pasta and pizza."

"Oh yes." Susannah felt a flicker of optimism. "I like it there. I haven't been in years. I can walk down the canal from the train station."

Silence.

"Rob?"

Susannah stared at the phone. He'd hung up on her.

She shrugged. At least it meant a reprieve now from getting rid of the bags.

She couldn't look at them without an ache in her heart. They contained over twenty years of twin paraphernalia. Susannah tried to appreciate the benefits of a household that looked as if nobody lived in it. No cups scattered in every room, no mascara and make-up caked into every available surface, no trying to unplug Good Hair Day instruments from the most awkward places.

She had what she'd said she wanted for years – a house that stayed that way when she cleaned it – but she'd have given up the neatness in a heartbeat to have them back.

But no matter how long or how little a time Jess and Orlaith stayed in New York, even if they moved back home for a time, Susannah knew things would never be the same again.

They had moved on, and she had to find a way to move on too. But how? Before Rob had phoned unexpectedly, her day had been empty, apart from the run to the charity shop.

Now, though, her husband wanted to have an impromptu lunch with her, so she pushed down the thought that she was in an almighty rut and got ready for the trip into the city.

She swapped her jeans and sweatshirt for a brown skirt and sparkly top she'd bought for Christmas, pulled on her winter boots and coat and started off for the train station.

The wind was icy and she pulled up her collar. All the festive decorations had been taken down but the village still had a lovely, bustling feel to it. It was a seaside, middle-class suburb with lots of shops, bars and restaurants. A big proportion of the young people had moved abroad, for work or for adventure, and sometimes because they married someone from another country, or even continent, a fear that haunted Susannah whenever she thought about her daughters living in New York.

Orlaith and Jess were only twenty-one, on an internship at an international fashion-and-style magazine in Manhattan, and were due back within a year. But a year was a long time when anything could happen.

Or nothing, if you were living her life, Susannah admitted. She thought back to the tense exchange between her and Rob earlier and felt a flutter of anxiety. They hadn't adapted well to being empty-nesters, but it was nice of him to try and cheer her up, to share his Dress-down Friday with her.

She pressed her forehead against the train window, watching the green fields give way to a more urban landscape. Soon enough the train was crossing the Liffey, the river that divided Dublin's north and south sides. Susannah watched the tugboats and cargo transporters on the water, a sight that never failed to cheer her up. When she saw that a huge cruise shop was docked today, an unexpected spark of optimism flashed through her. Maybe she would suggest to Rob that they should go on a cruise. They could visit the girls in New York and then fly down to Fort Lauderdale and board a ship bound for the Caribbean. That's what they needed now. New adventures for just the two of them.

Out of nowhere, a memory came to her. The twins had been tiny, and first one of them had caught a bug and then the other. She was working as a newspaper reporter on a big High Court case while Rob was struggling with his long hours at the bank.

They had spent the evening changing puke-filled clothes, sponging down hot little foreheads and calling in favours from friends so they could both go to work the next day. At one o'clock they were still awake, lying on top of the bedclothes, wondering if it was safe to finally go to sleep or if one of the girls was going to be sick again, when Rob had suddenly leapt out of bed.

"Hang on, I've just thought of something." He hurried out of the room.

Ten minutes later he arrived back with steaming mugs of hot chocolate. He placed them on the bedside locker and went away again, this time returning with a big notebook, an atlas and some coloured pens which he spread out across the bed.

"One day we'll look back on this night with fondness," he told her.

"Why's that?" Susannah asked half-heartedly. She was desperate for sleep, but she still had one ear cocked in case one of the children stirred. She sipped the hot chocolate, trying not to think about how overwhelmed she felt lately, caring for two toddlers and trying to keep on top of her career.

"Because we'll remember it was the day we planned our Big Adventure," he said happily.

And he had sat there with his map and his foolscap pages and fancy pens and brought her all around the world with his imagination. They would travel in a camper van, he explained, sketching it out on a page. They would stay in each place until they tired of it, and then they'd set off for somewhere new.

"The girls will love it!" She was sitting up now, and wide awake, carried away by his enthusiasm.

"All my girls will love it!" He reached over and kissed her.

"The twins might be little nerds who won't want to take

the time off school," she warned him.

"It will be educational," he said airily. "And it will be so *exciting*. Who could resist it?"

The girls, as it turned out.

Susannah smiled ruefully as she thought about how they had turned out to be two lovable social butterflies who enjoyed getting a suntan and shopping in the Mediterranean resorts where they spent their summer holidays.

The idea of touring remote Eastern European caravan sites had been greeted with horror each and every year, and gradually Rob had stopped mentioning it. Susannah spent the holidays reading on a sun-lounger while the girls amused themselves, and Rob exercised his itchy feet by heading off on his own to visit an ancient ruin or the next village or whatever, really, was around the next corner. She used to tease him that he was like the bear in the song who always wanted to see what was on the other side of the mountain.

And now there was nothing to stop them going on their Big Adventure. They could do more than just seeing the girls and a cruise. Rob could probably swing an extra couple of weeks' unpaid holidays. That would give him almost two months. They could plan it all out together, and while they were away maybe she'd even figure out what it was she wanted to do with the rest of her life.

The small fantasy made her so happy she was smiling to herself by the time she reached the restaurant.

She looked around curiously. It was already filling up with people on their lunch-breaks and Susannah knew a lot of Rob's colleagues dined here.

The Dress-down Friday girls were wearing short skirts and high heels, glittering jewellery and sexy, fitted jackets.

It hadn't been like that in her day. With women's equality in the workplace still in its infancy you walked a fine political line between looking too much like a ball-breaker (shoulder-pads) or being accused of using your feminine charms to get ahead (low necklines).

She smiled at the memory as a waiter led her to a table near the back of the restaurant.

She chose the seat facing the door, so she could watch for Rob arriving, absorbing the buzz of conversation rising and falling around her. This is what her life would be like now if she hadn't given up work to look after the girls, she reckoned. Her days would be filled with colleagues and conversation and getting things done, instead of the empty suburban existence she had now.

She'd have been promoted by now, for sure, she decided. Probably several times. She'd loved her job and had been very good at it.

But the decision to quit had been made for her, not long after the Big Adventure night when another child-care crisis had finally finished her and Rob off as a working couple.

They couldn't go on the way they were, feeling exhausted all the time. Susannah felt she was doing neither job properly, so she'd left without giving it too much thought, assuming she could pick her career back up again after a few years, after the hard bit of the child-rearing was over.

But she hadn't predicted how much she would love spending time with two chubby-cheeked little girls who had grown up to be her constant companions. Except when they were teenagers and they didn't want to know her for – oh, about ten minutes.

She'd discussed going back to work with Rob then and a few more times since, but he always pointed out how work had changed since she'd been at the coal-front. Now it was all backstabbing and cut-throaty apparently and he told her she'd be mad to even consider it.

But, she noticed, the Dress-down Friday girls didn't look like they were backstabbing each other. They were all on that high of a week's work well done, a feeling Susannah still remembered and hadn't ever got during all her years of housekeeping.

The waiter arrived with the menus and a basket of warm bread. Susannah ordered a bottle of white wine and took out her reading glasses to peruse the menu.

But then she saw Rob pushing open the restaurant door. He hadn't spotted her and for a few seconds she watched him as if he were a stranger. His Dress-down Friday clothes consisted of neatly pressed blue jeans, a flannel checked shirt and polished, brown boots. His hair needed a cut – it was curling over the top of his shirt-collar – and he looked more like a cowboy than a stressed-out banker.

He caught sight of her and gave a small wave, weaving his way through the crowded tables to slide onto the chair opposite her.

"I'm loving the dress-down policy." Susannah leaned over to brush his hair out of his eyes but he pulled his head back a fraction, out of her reach. "You okay?" She raised her eyebrows.

"Sorry. Stressful morning." He opened the menu and studied it intently.

Susannah's spirits dipped. This was starting to feel less like an impromptu lunch to cheer her up and more like an opportunity for Rob to tell her something bad had happened.

"Is there talk of more redundancies?" She knew this was one of his recurring nightmares. A lot of his colleagues had lost their jobs in the last few years as the banks shed staff in an effort to absorb some of the losses of the economic crash.

"There's always talk of more redundancies."

The waiter arrived with the wine and Rob nodded at him tersely to fill his glass. He'd knocked back half of it before the waiter had even filled hers.

"Well, you know what they say," she quipped. "The beatings will continue until morale improves."

"Is that supposed to be funny?" His head jerked up to look at her.

"No. Well, yes, actually, it was." She dropped her bread roll back onto the plate. "Look, Rob. I don't want to have to keep on asking you. So just tell me. What is going on with you?"

He coughed, his brown eyes blinking nervously behind his glasses.

"It's not you," he said finally. "It's me."

"I know that. That's what I'm asking you – what's going on with *you*?"

"I've done something – significant. Without discussing it with you." He lifted his chin in a gesture of defiance.

Susanna pushed her plate away.

"What? What have you done?"

"I … I've applied for a career break. It's for one year. I didn't tell you because I didn't think they'd let me go. But … er …" Rob faltered a bit at this point and took another gulp of wine. "But … they did. I got the email this morning."

His features darkened and Susannah knew he was mortified that he hadn't been as indispensable to the bank as he'd thought.

"I've been accepted for it, Susannah. I'm free."

Susannah swallowed. Questions shot through her mind.

Why didn't you tell me you were going to do this? What are you planning to do with the time? Can we afford it? Why are you talking to me as if I'm a work colleague?

But when she went to speak she felt like something was stuck in her throat. Maybe a piece of that crusty bread had gone down the wrong way. She poured herself some water from the pitcher and sipped it cautiously. No crust in her throat. Just an uneasy feeling there was more to come.

"So ... what's the plan? For this career break?" she finally managed to ask.

"I'm going away for the year. In a camper van."

Susannah laughed out loud. "Really?"

"Well, that's what I'm thinking." He sounded vaguely defensive.

"I must be psychic!" Susannah felt relief surge through her. It was their Big Adventure! Rob had remembered.

"What?" He sounded irritated.

"I was just thinking of that night on the train over here," she said excitedly. "The night both the girls were sick and you said we'd look back on it fondly one day because we'd be having such adventures. How we'd get a camper van and go travelling. We'd stay in each place until we got tired of it ..." Her voice trailed off as she noticed how puzzled Rob looked.

"I don't remember any of that," he said flatly.

"You said it would be the dream that would keep us going through the hard times," she prompted him again.

But he just shook his head and picked up his wineglass. "I don't. And, Susannah, this has nothing to do with your dream."

"It was *your* dream, not mine," she reminded him stubbornly. "And I know it won't be the same without the girls. I suppose we should have done it years ago while we still had the chance to have them come with us. But we can still have fun, just the two of us."

"I'm going on my own."

"*Hah!*" Susannah choked on her wine, grabbed her napkin and pressed it to her mouth.

"Are you okay?" He was watching her cautiously.

She didn't answer him. She wanted the lunch to stop now, for neither of them to say anything they would regret later.

"So," he queried, "what do you think?"

Susannah chose her words carefully. "I think all the stress of work is getting to you. I think you should go back to work and explain you made a mistake about the career break and that what you really want is a few weeks of unpaid leave."

"But that's *not* what I want!" He was suddenly belligerent.

"But you can't actually be considering going away for a year on your own. In a camper van? Really?"

"I want to find my smile." He bit his lip.

Susannah laughed out loud. "That's out of that Billy Crystal movie – about men going off to be cowboys!"

"Actually, the line came from the female character telling her husband to go and do what he had to do to find his smile," Rob challenged her.

Susannah blinked. "Why are you quoting from that film now? It's ancient."

"I watched it again recently."

"So you think I should be encouraging you to leave me?"

"I'm not leaving you. Not forever." He paused. "And not for a twenty-five-year-old intern," he added meaningfully.

The waiter arrived to refill their glasses, overheard Rob's side of the conversation and walked straight past their table.

Susannah raised her eyebrows. Rob was referring to his

ex-colleague Kevin who had done exactly that – left his wife and three teenage children for some young one who had come to work at the bank under a government scheme to give graduates experience of the working world. But it was Kevin who got an experience nobody had been banking on.

And now here was Rob comparing himself to Kevin – as if it was inevitable that all the middle-aged men at the bank were going to do something crazy and it was just a question of degree and timing.

"Rob. Listen to me." Susannah addressed him kindly. "You're not Kevin. And you're not someone in a movie. You're just … a guy who works in a bank. You're probably suffering from work-related stress – and missing the girls as much as I do but not admitting it."

"I do miss them." He looked relieved. "Do you think that's what it is? This awful miserable feeling I wake up with every day?"

"Of course it is." She reached over and took his hand in hers. "You just need a break. It's *normal* to be feeling the pressures of mid-life at our age."

Rob snatched his hand back. "Thanks for the analysis. But you can't treat me like I'm a child you can coax out of a tantrum." He sniffed. "I have *dreams*, Susannah."

"We all have dreams," she said softly. "Don't you think I have things I want to do too?"

"Well, the difference between you and me is that I'm doing something about mine!" His voice rose. "Whereas all you do is walk around the house like a ghost."

She flinched, aware of the curious stares of other diners. She offered him the wicker basket of bread. "Here, eat something."

He pushed his glasses back from where they'd slipped down his nose and glared at her. "You're doing it again.

Treating me like a child. Well, do you know what – I'm not very hungry any more."

He stood up, bristling with anger, nearly toppling over his chair in his haste to get away.

Susannah stared after him as he stomped off in his boots, swinging through the restaurant doors like he was John Wayne in a western instead of a banker in an upmarket bistro in Dublin.

The waiter reappeared out of nowhere and refilled Susannah's glass.

"Thank you." Susannah was mortified. She sat there, paralysed, trying to figure out what the hell had just happened while the Dress-down Friday girls threw pitying glances her way.

Her husband had just told her he was leaving her. Not in the catastrophic way of having a terminal illness. Or even, as he'd put it himself, for a twenty-five-year-old intern. But he was leaving her nevertheless.

For a *camper van*.

She drummed her fingers on the tablecloth, wondering how the hell she hadn't seen this coming. How many times in the years gone by had she wished her husband would do something to surprise her? Something out of the ordinary to lift them both out of the humdrum routine of rearing a family? Or to take her out of the depths she'd fallen into after her mother died last year?

Something to make her remember the man she'd fallen in love with, the man who'd beaten off the exhaustion and stress all those years ago to keep her enthralled with tales of the Big Adventure they would have one day.

Well, he'd surprised her today, she thought, the irony not lost on her. Because he'd just told he was going on their Big Adventure without her.

If you enjoyed this book from
Poolbeg why not visit our website:

poolbeg.com

**and get another book delivered straight
to your home or to a friend's home.**

All books despatched within 24 hours.

Why not join our mailing list
at www.poolbeg.com and get some fantastic
offers, competitions, author interviews,
book launches and much more?

CHECK US OUT ON TWITTER AND FACEBOOK

FOR OFFERS, UPDATES, NEW RELEASES AND EVENTS!